I0672055

KILL RONNIE CAMPBEL
Outlaw Vendetta

Ron Bell

THE RONNIE CAMPBELL SERIES BOOK 3

ISBN # 978-0-578-75063-7

Acknowledgements

When you start on a project like writing your third book you think you know how things are going to move forward in the writing process. But things change when you get started, I have my wife Susie Bell who is and has been the principal editor for my last two books. She does a good job getting my jumble of words pushed into a form that does look like a book. So, thank you Susie for your hard work to make my work look like a book.

This book I also have a second helper Connie Stanton. Connie had read my first two books (THE PONY EXPRESS RIDER AND RUBY GOLD) we started talked at church about this third book and she said that she would like to help with the pre-read of this book. Later we talked about helping with the pre-read and the editing process. Oh my, Connie has been so much help with getting this book in order and corrections made. So, to my loyal helpers I offer a heartfelt thanks for all their hard work.

Thanks,

Ron Bell

Book Review:

All volumes have interesting and informative stories with the mid-to late 1800s era and the Pony Express mail service as their theme.

Reading about the westers based tales is exciting for your "inner pioneer. "

True facts, mixed with intriguing fiction makes Ron Bell's books a Must Read

Book Review

from

Pat Kennedy who lives in Texas.

Ron Bell's background with "The Pony Express", his passion for the land and his persona makes him unique among writers of the old west. Many have expressed the opinion that Ron was born 150 years too late. His colorful depiction of characters puts you in the saddle with the wind in your hair and his detail in describing settings lets you know that he has been there. His main character, Ronnie Campbell, his family, friends and enemies are pictured in words that will fill and inspire your imagination. His books are filled with emotion, action, love, hate, remorse and happiness. If you like the old west, you will love Ron Bell's books, they are easy to read and hard to put down.

PHOTO CREDITS

Front Cover was shot by Nick McCabe.

Back Cover picture was taken by Dennis Doyle.

2 Photos in the book on page 44 were taken by Ron Bell.

MY FRIEND ROBIN TRAVIS

Contact: robintravis.com

Robin Travis is a local photographer in Carson City Nevada who I feel has a nice eye for framing her pictures, Robin shoots a lot of black and white photos all around Nevada. I felt that showing some of her work in this book would make for a better end result. I asked Robin to pick some of her favorite pictures from around Nevada to use to fill the blank pages inside of this book. To land the new chapters on the right side of the book you are forced to deal with some blank pages, or you can choose to offer this space to a local photographer to fill the open page with an interesting photo they have taken over the years of recording the history of our great state of Nevada. Thank you, Robin, for allowing me to have some of your quality work gracing the pages of this book.

Page 12 Poem by Ron Bell, Jon Dugan's Ride into Hell

Page 44 Two pictures I like. I think they both depict the time period and feeling that I hope this book brings to my readers.

Robin Travis Professional Photographer

FORWARD

Ronnie was sitting on Diamond with his right leg curled around the saddle horn. He had ridden up onto a small ridge that looked out over his ranch, with cattle grazing by the river along the flats. He could see what was going on around the ranch and he could hear the hammer blows ringing from the forge's anvil telling Ronnie that Andy Sams was at work. All was quite with no major problems with any outlaw gangs in the area for a change. Abby, Ronnie's wife, was pregnant, Maggie, his partner's wife, was also pregnant, the ranch family was growing.

The past year had been full of events with some losses that are still hard to take. His second family who helped raise him, Sam and Betty Applegate, were killed by a gang who came into the valley to steal cattle and horses. Little John found a wife after the loss of both of his parents. Jane's parents were killed by the same gang just days later. Marty and Rose are building a house on a piece of ground that overlooks the stream the mine is located on; their cabin is started and should be finished in another month. Rose is hunting for the meat for the mining crew's, she rides into the back country every three to four days to kill an elk or deer. Marty and Rose are cooking for the mining crew, they catch trout every few days to make a change to the food.

Andy Sams was still working the forge when Ronnie came back to the ranch and stopped by to talk over some projects, he wanted Andy to work on over the next few weeks. Ronnie wanted Andy to think about making some harvesting tools for the alfalfa Ronnie planted when he returned from Salt Lake City after racing Buster and Lightening.

Andy was thinking about building a system so they could stack the cut hay in the fields in a way that the weather would not damage the alfalfa. This will be the winter feed for his cattle and horses. Andy had worked on a tool to dig the irrigation ditches that will supply the water to the alfalfa fields along the river by the ranch. His Indian wife's two young boys are helping Andy in the forge most every day. They like to watch the sparks flying from the steel as Andy shapes it into tools and horseshoes. Ronnie and Andy decided that by putting in a series of ditches they can grow other crops like corn and even some wheat. By being able to use the horses to dig the ditches, they are making changes to the existing Fresno dirt mover, the Fresno dirt tool is a one-horse dump bucket for moving dirt. It is good for leveling but not so good at making ditches. Ronnie thinks that they can put wheels or a skid on each side of the bucket and make the bucket deeper so they could move more dirt using 4 horses instead of one. The goal is to be able to move dirt down to about two foot and have the dirt move up and out of the ditch.

As Ronnie and Andy were talking, they heard a rider entering the ranch yard, they walked out from the forge to see who was paying them a visit. U. S Deputy Marshal Larry McPherson was coming in with his pack horse and leading his extra saddle horse. Ronnie said, "step down, let's get a cup of coffee". Gray Eagle came and gathered up the horses and led them to the corral and stored the packs and saddles in the barn. Ronnie and Larry walked up to the porch to have a seat, Abby was walking out to deliver the two cups of coffee, Maggie also came along to say hi to Larry.

Ronnie asked Larry what he was doing in Nevada. "Don't you have enough bad guys in California to keep you busy"?

"Well", Larry said. "We have a problem".

Ronnie asked, "what is the problem and are we part of it"?

"When we killed the Baster Gang they were heading into California with the cattle and horses. You remember I suggested that we just go to the ranch that is owned by his brother Jarvis and finish off the whole family. Well, the brother Jarvis Baster has now, from what I can gather recruited about ten men to come after you and Little John to finish what his brother should have done the first time.

Ronnie asked. "How long do you think we have to get a reception party ready for his gang".

CHAPTER 1 START OF A BAD PLAN.

Tray Davis had just finished the count with the cattle buyer on the 600 head of cattle he had driven to the stock yards in Manteca from Jarvis Baster's ranch on the edge of Nevada and California. Jarvis had been stocking this ranch with stolen cattle for a few years. Jarvis told Tray to sell 600 head of cattle because he needed some extra cash. He is getting ready to make a raid over into the Ruby Mountains in Nevada. He also needed to free up some grass because he was getting ready for some new cattle he was going to steal, and he needed the grass for this new herd. After a few days on the trail Tray had delivered the cattle to the stockyards in Manteca. Tray had the bank draft in his pocket from the buyer and headed to the bank to turn it into cash. This would give him enough money to pay off the boys after the drive and send them home after a night on the town. The temporary riders were not Jarvis's regular ranch hands, so with the cattle in the stock pens their part was done. After Tray had paid them off, they all rode down the street to the local saloon to blow off some steam before heading home. Jarvis needed this cash to pay some gun hands for the next job he had been planning.

Tray had seen a restaurant called the Gold Star Café as he had moved the cattle through town to the stock pins at the far edge of town. He was more than ready for a good meal after a few days of trail food without a real cook. This drive each man had to cook for themselves from supplies carried by the two pack horses Tray had brought along. Tray turned Blaze down the street to the restaurant leading his two packhorses, dropping Blaze's reins over the hitch rail. Stepping up onto the boardwalk, he opened the restaurant's door and walked in. He found a seat and the waitress came over and introduced herself saying,

"Hi, I am Bridget". "The special is real good today, it's steak, potatoes and apple pie".

"I will take the special, but can you make it a big steak and plenty of potatoes with a pot of black coffee if that will work for you"? After giving his order to the cook Bridget came back with a cup of coffee and a big smile. She asked his name and if he lived around Manteca.

"No", "I am Tray Davis". I live a few days ride east over along the Nevada border. I work on a ranch owned by Jarvis Baster. I am a horse trainer and ranch hand, Jarvis sent me over to sell some cattle". After a bit Tray's dinner came, delivered with another big smile, as she turned saying. "I will be back to check on you and bring more coffee in a few minutes".

Tray was a great horse trainer and was also one of the best cowboys on Jarvis Baster's ranch, but he had a bit of the wild side in him just like his brother Sid. Sid was killed by Ronnie Campbell, along with Jarvis Baster's brother, Jules, after the Baster gang had killed Sam and Beth Applegate, a longtime friend of Ronnie Campbell. Tray reached into his pocket for money to leave on the table for his meal along with a big tip for Bridget, Tray stood up and re-settled the colt 45 back in place as he started to the door. He stopped and turned to Bridget to thank her for the meal.

Bridget said, "I would like to see you again so come back. I will be working in the morning so please come in to see me before you head back to the ranch". Tray walked out with a bit of a lighter step as he walked to his big stud horse Blaze.

Tray walked over to his horse and untied him; Blaze stuck out his nose to get a rub. (Blaze was 17 hands and could walk most horses into the ground). After a bit of a nose rub, he led him to the livery stable for the night along with his two packhorses. With the supplies from the pack horses in a safe storage area and after giving a good rubdown to his horses, Tray added some oats and hay in their manger's, walking out of the stable he decided he needed a drink. Two doors down was the saloon. He wanted a drink to top off his meal. Pushing the batwing doors open he stepped in and took a step to the left side letting his eyes adjust to the light in the room. After looking the place over he walked up to the bar and he ordered a shot of rye.

With his drink in hand, he turned to check out a card game in progress, Tray walked over and asked if he could join the poker game.

The dealer said, "I am Larry and what do you go by".

"Tray Davis", he replied. After a few hands two of the others at the table got up and cashed in and headed for the door. One new man came and asked to join the game saying he was Alan Bell, a whisky salesman from back east in Chicago. Larry and Tray both said, "you are a long way from home, friend".

Tray was staying about even with his money, but after a few more drinks he started to talk about his dead brother, Sid Davis. Tray was telling that his brother was not much good but had been his only kin. Later, he said he had been killed by Ronnie Campbell and he would be getting even soon. US Deputy Marshal Larry McPherson just kept on dealing the cards. His badge was in his pocket and would stay there until the poker game was finished. Larry and Tray talked about cattle and horses. During the game Tray gave Larry additional information as to when this raid was going to happen over the next few hours. Larry made sure that Tray kept a bit ahead so he would just keep talking. Larry could have cleaned him out, but it was better to get an idea of the size and timing or this raid. It was getting late, the game had lasted a few hours when the whisky salesman Alan, cashed in his chips and headed to his room. Larry and Tray joined Alan, also heading for their rooms for the night.

Tray staggered out of the saloon and headed down to the livery stable to check on his three horses before heading to his bed. Tray like many men living on the edge needed a horse that was much better than horses most western men owned. This was the horse that Tray was going to start his own ranch with after this last raid to repay Ronnie Campbell for the death of his brother. Tray had never got along with Sid even as young kids, but he had been his only brother and living relative.

Tray looked down the street and could see the café. He started to think about Bridget-she seemed to like him. This was new to Tray. He had never talked to any girl before. This was new and he for sure was going to eat there in the morning to see if what he felt was real. The next morning Tray was up and washed after sleeping late for a change. All he had to do was start back to the ranch whenever he was ready. Walking down the boardwalk he was feeling like he had never felt before. When he opened the door to the cafe, he felt flushed and could hardly speak. Bridget came over showing him a table, it was next to the kitchen. Bridget came out with hot coffee and a big smile he felt was just for him.

With the coffee on the table, the last customer was walking out the door. Bridget came over and sat down at his table. She used his name. "Tray Davis, what do you want for breakfast"?

Tray finally got out, "anything would be great, eggs, ham, potatoes would also be good". She got up and put in his order, then came back with a cup of coffee for herself.

"Tray, are you a solid man? I like you and would like to get to know you better, but I am alone and don't want to spend time with anyone who is not an honest man, and I couldn't have a future with". Bridget got up and went to the kitchen to get Tray's food. After putting it on the table she sat back down to talk some more.

Tray looked over at Bridget saying "I have never talked to any girls. I may need some help along the way. I like you and would like to get to know you better, I have a trip I am committed to. It will take at least two to three weeks. When I get back would it be ok for me to come back to town and spend some time with you"?

Bridget said, "yes", then she leaned over and kissed him, turned and went back into the kitchen. Tray dropped his money for the meal on the table and walked out the door, a thought crossed his mind, do I really have an obligation to Sid?

*

Tray had returned with the cash from the sale of Jarvis's cattle. During Tray's time on the drive Jarvis had been making his plans and gathering some gun hands. With Tray back now, Jarvis had seven good gun hands and with himself it was eight men who had a debt to repay. Jarvis Baster had his gang ready to head to the Ruby Mountains in Nevada to kill Ronnie Campbell and Little John Applegate for killing his brother, Jules Baster and all of his gang. Jules had been robbing banks and anything else that he could either sell or spend. Jarvis had received hundreds if not thousands of cattle and horses for many years from his brother's outlaw ways.

Jarvis had his eight men gathered with two pack horses and ten extra horses in the remuda, they were ready for a two-to-three-week raid into the Ruby Mountains, Jarvis was on a mission an outlaw vendetta to kill Ronnie Campbell. Jarvis closed the door on his ranch house telling his cook and housekeeper to expect them back in about two or three weeks. Jarvis had been planning this raid for months, after selling the six hundred head of cattle he had the money to pay the gun hands a nice bonus when the job was done. Jarvis was making sure of the details just like his brother who always had extra horses on each raid, so he would do the same. He would also have plenty of extra horses from the two ranches. Jarvis planned to move all the cattle and horses from both ranches in Nevada to his ranch. The plan was to skirt Jim Brown's store and come up the backside of the Ruby Mountains and make the raid from the east side of the mountain so neither ranch would know that anyone was even in their area. Jarvis had found a hot spring with a great camping location having plenty of feed for the horses and game for food on a scouting trip a few months earlier. He was going to drop over the mountains and pick up all the cattle and horses, then drive them into the ranch headquarters as the gang kills everyone, then move on to finish with Little John Applegate. Jarvis then would take his time to move the cattle and horses back to California to his ranch, this is a great plan.

As the small army moved out from the California ranch heading east, Jarvis sent out two scouts, Jim Rutherford and Willie Hightower, to take up a position about two miles ahead of the main force, he didn't want any surprises on this raid. Jarvis had recruited extra gun hands, six men total; then with Tray Davis and his gun he had a good size crew. Jarvis had planned to only ride about fifty miles per day to save the horses, with the ten extra horses he could drop off any horse that became lame during the ride east toward the Ruby Mountains. Any horse they left would just return home within a few days. Jarvis was not in any hurry, he had plenty of time to get into position to kill everyone on those two ranches.

At the first noon stop they made some coffee and had a bit of meat and cold biscuits. After giving the horses a one-hour rest, Jarvis sent out two new outriders, Matt Olam and Frank Burks, telling them to stop at some water if they could find it for the night stop. The dust was bad, so the men fanned out so not to eat as much dust, Tray was

moving the horses along, keeping just a bit behind and up wind of the
main body of men. Late in the afternoon the outriders found some
water with grass for the horses. Trip and Jordan had just stayed with the
gang during the day, so Jarvis told them to get two fires started and have
coffee on when the others joined them, Jordan and Trip had the two
cook fires started for dinner and after eating they were assigned the
guards for the first night watch. Some of the men felt it was dumb to
post guards this far away from the ranches. Jarvis called a meeting and
told anyone who did not want to follow orders could walk back now or
he could plant them right here and now.

*

Gray Eagle, the younger brother of White Bird, and White Bird's
cousin Raven were over on the east side of the Ruby's hunting antelope.
They had a camp set up in one of the small canyons leading up into the
high country. The hunting had been good, they had killed and dried
meat from four big bucks, they would only kill a doe when times were
hard. Late in the afternoon Gray Eagle and Raven could see a large dust
cloud to the southwest heading their way. Gray Eagle and Raven
watched the two scouts pass by and ride east only a bit further, then
turning back to the camp that was being set up a mile or so to the west
of their camp. The Indians followed the scouts back to the camp.
Everyone was looking into the fire and starting to fix their dinner, each
of the men had to cook his own food. The men all had their horses tied
to a high line by the campfire between two trees. After eating, the men
would be taking their horses out and turn them in with the extra mounts
in the remuda for the night.

When the sun was getting low Gray Eagle and Raven started to
move closer, but they could see one man that was making a trip around
the horses to get them settled in for the night. When this rider rode into
camp with the other men, they moved closer to the camp, they could see
that they all were cooking some food around two campfires. While Jarvis
was telling the gang how this raid was going to work.

Gray Eagle asked, Raven why don't we just move those horses east, they have not even put out any guards. As they moved around the camp real slow, they could hear Ronnie Campbell's name, cattle and kill them all. They mounted their horses when away from the camp. The horses had been moved by one rider for a few days so when Gray Eagle and Raven started to get close, they just started to move along ahead of the two Indians. After a mile or so of heading east they came across a dry riverbed with about all sand, so they turned the horses back to the mountains and their camp thinking they would not leave any tracks to follow in this soft sand.

With the horses moving so easy, Gray Eagle rode over to Raven saying, "I am going back to camp and pack everything, and we will just start taking the horses back to the ranch in the morning". Gray Eagle was finished packing all the meat on the two extra horses when he rode out to meet Raven. They turned the horses along the foothills heading northeast. They knew of a good spot only a few miles further with good water and grass, this would make a good campsite for the night, the horses would not move much with good grass and water within reach. The two Indians took turns keeping watch during the night just in case they had company. They figured that the tracks could not be followed in the night, and they would be hard to follow during the day in deep sand, but it is good to be ready.

With light just starting to show they started northeast heading for the pass with the old camp site they had used many times. This ride would take them all day. It will be dark when they made it into the canyon and up to the campground by the hot springs. Gray Eagle moved into the lead with the two pack horses with the antelope meat, the ten horses following along with Raven keeping them moving along from behind. The sun was down when they reached the camping spot. Raven moved the ten horses across the river onto a little island with a lot of grass with the stream was flowing at its edge. Gray Eagle unloaded the two pack horses and turned them out with the others for the night. They put their two war horses on a picket line by their bed after being fed and watered, these horses would blow if anyone came close to them.

The fire was going, and they cooked up some of the fresh antelope for dinner, this was the first time they had time to talk other than make a plan to remove the extra horses that were not guarded from the strange men and to see if they could find out what these men were doing in this area. Gray Eagle asked Raven what he had heard, "Ronnie Campbell, kill them, cattle and horses". Gray Eagle had heard the same thing. Both Indians had been learning to speak white man talk after moving into the Indian camp at the Campbell Ranch with their extended family.

"We'd better get these horses over the mountain and tell Tee; he will know what to do".

*

Jarvis had a cup of coffee in his hands when one of the men said I don't see the horses, they were just out beyond the fire a few minutes ago. Jarvis told everyone to look away from the firelight so your eyes can see better in the dark. Tray was the horse wrangler; he had just come in from making a trip around the horses and making sure they were settled in for the night. When Jarvis started yelling, he also moved out so he could see better, he could not see any horses anywhere around. Jarvis started yelling for all the men to get mounted and find them horses and do it now. Tray was on his horse looking for tracks. He could not see any tracks; the horses were just gone. The gang rode around for an hour but found nothing.

Returning to camp, Jarvis was fit to be tied. How could ten horses just disappear with no trace of them? Tray said we will get on the trail at first light. During the night Tray dreamed he could see Bridget and recalled what she had said. "What am I doing riding with this bunch of horse thieves and murders? This is just how my brother got himself killed". Jarvis had two guards out all night, one on each side of the camp, each taking a two-hour shift. Jarvis was having a hard time figuring out what or who had moved all the horses and why. No one knew about this raid other than the men with him, the only thing that came to him was Indians must have come in and stolen the ten horses. This is not good, but they would not know about the raid on Campbell and Applegate ranches. They would look for tracks during the day as they headed for the next campsite Jarvis had picked out to use as a staging ground for this raid.

At first light and breakfast finished the men were in their saddles looking for the tracks of the lost horses. They found tracks heading east, so they followed them for a mile or so and then after reaching a dry stream bed, they could not find any tracks going up or down it is like the horses just vanished. Jarvis was thinking that was what got his brother Jules killed by not having fresh horses when he needed them. Jarvis figured that they better just move forward and hope to find tracks of the stolen horses.

Jake was riding ahead as a scout on the left side of the gang and about one mile out ahead when he found the horses tracks. It looks like he found where they were heading. There tracks led into the canyon that they were going to hole up for a few days getting ready for the raid. He turned back to the main body of riders to talk to Jarvis about what he found. When he rode in, Jarvis met him asking what is up. Jake told him about the tracks, he was sure that it is their horses being moved by two riders and with two pack horses. "I think they are Indians and only six to eight hours ahead of us". Jarvis was thinking about sending some men to go after those ten extra mounts. But if he pushed his horses hard and did not catch up and recover his stolen ones, he would just have used his up with no gain. Then he would need to rest those horses at least one or two days extra, delaying the raid. This is a problem with trying to not be seen by any of the ranch hands.

The horses his men rode are big and fast, he felt that no ranch would have any horses that could keep up with his or his men. If by chance things went wrong, he wanted rested horses that he could get some hard fast miles on if they had to make a run for their lives. Jarvis told Jake to just keep following, we will see where they go, we may just get lucky if they find a spot to rest up for a day or two feeling they were not being followed. Jake was waiting for Jarvis with the other scout Jeff when Jarvis rode up. Well, the tracks are going up the canyon along the stream. Jarvis had three of the men move forward to see if they could catch the horse thieves taking a nap and recover his horses. As the men started up the mountain, they found the trail narrow and filled with trees, each time they came to what looked like an opening in the trees they spread out to make it harder for anyone to get a shot at them. When the three men rode into the camp site the horses were nowhere to be seen, but they could see where they had grazed along the river on a small island by the campsite. It looked like they had been gone most of the day.

Later in the day the rest of the gang rode into the camping area and started to get the camp site setup. "Tray set up a rope corral so the horses could eat and get to water without needing anyone to keep watch during the night". The horses were just over the stream from the camp on a small grassy flat, Tray would keep watch from the camp and make a ride over and check on them every few hours. Tray pulled out his fishing line to see if he could catch some trout for his dinner, on raids like this each man took care of his own food. Most of the men kept a two-day supply of food in their saddle bags and each man could pull other needed supplies from the pack horse before each meal. Tray went up the stream a bit to get to some calm water and see if he would have any luck catching some trout. With only a few casts he had three fish, plenty for him and some left over for his morning breakfast.

Jarvis was talking to Jake about the tracks and asked if he thought the Indians could have a camp in the mountains this close to the Campbell Ranch. Jake said that he figured that the Indians would hit the pass and then move off to one of the higher meadows to their own camp.

*

With Gray Eagle in the lead and from behind Raven pushing the ten horses, they rode into the ranch yard in a cloud of dust. White Bird and Tee opened the corral gate by the blacksmith shop to hold the horses and see what was going on. After a short talk, Tee and White Bird went to get Ronnie and tell him what they had found out from Gray Eagle and Raven. Ronnie asked if Tee could go and get the men so they all could talk this over in the ranch kitchen. Deputy US Marshal Larry McPherson who had talked to Tray during a poker game in Manteca had ridden to the Campbell ranch to talk with Ronnie about what he had discovered a few weeks earlier and he wanted to also hear this new information. Tony, Ronnie, and Andy Sams all came in to take a seat. White Bird had taken a seat along with all the girls. Tee came back with Gray Eagle and Raven. Tee had a hard time getting the

Indians to take a seat, they had never talked to Ronnie or any of the other people at the table. Tee asked the questions so the two Indians could talk in Paiute to get better details. After a bit it was plain to all that they were going to have a war, Abby got up and gave the two Indians some cookies to take back to the Indian camp for the kids, they were happy to get back to the village and out of the ranch house kitchen.

Ronnie asked Tee to set up a watch over the gang's camp, so he would have some warning if the gang started toward the ranch before they could get ready for a proper greeting. Larry told Ronnie that he had been sent a wire a week ago that the ranch was going to be attacked but Ronnie had never received the telegram with his warning. Ronnie said, "Well, men, let's set up a nice reception for them or do we want to hit them in their camp with a surprise raid". Ronnie thought it would be the best to catch them after they dropped over the pass, their horses would be tired from the climb, and it would be safer to fight from cover. By stopping them away from the ranch the girls would be safer, everyone agreed with him. Ronnie mentioned he would like to keep bullet holes out of his house and save the windows, they take a long time to get them to the ranch.

This poem is kind of a fun bar type poem, but it just came to me after writing a story of Jon Dugan in my second book RUBY GOLD.

Jon Dugan's

Ride into Hell

In Manteca the robbery
planned so well
Now my gang is shot to hell
With the posse left behind
My horse is done, so many days on
the run
Jon Dugan is a bad man
Riding out of the trees
I spot a man riding my new horse
coming down the road
When he gets close, I draw my gun
kill him for fun
I take his horse, money and leave
him bleeding on the ground
Jon Dugan is a bad man
Riding east into the hills
Over the mountain into Nevada on
the run
With his gold in my pocket I head
to town
Riding up to the Saloon
Jon Dugan is a bad man
One drink and a game of cards
Hours later my gold is gone
Waiting outside behind the door
To kill the man who took my gold
Jon Dugan is a bad man
Out the door he came, I shot
him down
Reaching for his money, I see the
gun just in time

The shot rang out, I shot back
I am again on the run, heading east into
the sun
Jon Dugan is a bad man
A trading post I rob, I need the
money for my ride
The owner is down, his life leaking on
the ground
I have his money and his gun
I have my luck again. I ride east into the
sun
Jon Dugan is a bad man
I cross the river late at night
Salt Lake City is my goal, another
holdup to be done
I see some dust up ahead, I ride into the
brush
When the boys ride past, many horses I
will have
Jon Dugan is a bad man
My luck is good
I will kill the boys before the dawn
I sneak up the trail unheard by them
Easing back the hammer I shoot to kill
Jon Dugan is a bad man
Two shots rang out
I step forward to view the dead
I hear a noise, I turn to shoot again
I feel the bullet hit my chest
Jon Dugan is a bad man
My hands feel weak
I sink to my knees
The light is going dim
Damn them boys, Damn my luck

Jon Dugan is a dead man

Author & Cowboy Poet Ron Bell

CHAPTER 2 **RANCH UNDER FIRE**

Tee came riding in to report that the men had killed an elk so this should give them food for at least three days. Ronnie was going to send for Little John and Jane. He wanted Jane to be with Abby and Maggie so Little John could join in on the gun battle that was coming in a few days. Ronnie asked Tee how many Indians he had that would join with him to fight. Tee said he would have six men to support Ronnie. Gray Eagle and Raven are watching the men now, White Bird will move the women and children up to another camp until this fight is over and he will be back to the ranch in the morning.

Ronnie sent Tee over the short cut to get the message to Little John and Jane. Little John and Jane should be at the ranch in the morning of the second day. Ronnie, Tony and Larry rode into the mountains to see how they would defend the ranch. Andy Sams started to move wagons and other equipment into defensive positions around the ranch headquarters. Ronnie was sure that the gang would take the easy way over the mountain. Lazy men like this always take the easy way. Ronnie said, "let's take a look at that little meadow just before the top, the trail leads through the middle of the meadow and we have good cover on both sides, what do you think"?

"Let's ride."

*

When Tee rode into the Applebee ranch, Little John was just getting ready to saddle a horse to check the cattle in one of the back canyons. The two Indians that had started to work for Little John came over to talk to Tee. He told them about the coming fight with some very bad men. Tee told Little John about the eight men that were camped at the hot spring. Ronnie needed his help to stop a raid on their ranches and check if that Elk Man and his wife's brother Running Deer would also come to fight. Little John asked them to harness the team and hitch it to the light wagon, so he could get Jane and pack for a few days stay at the Campbell Ranch. Jane was ready in a few minutes. Little John pulled two extra saddle horses and tied them on the back of the wagon, and they were ready.

Little John slapped the reins on the horse's rumps. They left the yard at a stiff trot. He wanted to save the horses so he would pull them back into a walk a few times so they would not need to rest them as long at the lunch break. After a solid five hours Little John made a stop to give the horses a thirty-minute rest, grain and water. Jane had packed a bit to eat so they started to work on some of the food that she had packed. Jane asked, "who do you think is going to attack the ranches"?

Little John said he figured it must be someone left from the Baster Gang that killed both of our mothers and fathers.

After the short rest they started back on the road to the Campbell Ranch. Little John would not use the normal campground today but make a camp after dark further up the trail. He wanted to get to the ranch early the next morning. Little John would stop at a spring just off the trail. It would only hold enough water for the horses if they were lucky. Two hours after dark the moon was just coming up when they reached the spring. Little John removed the saddles and harness from the team, then Jane took the horses to water. When the team had been watered Jane had the fire going with dinner started, Little John came to the fire saying, "you are a wonder Jane".

Jane asked, "Where did the Indians go"?

"They took the shortcut back to Ronnie's ranch with Tee".

"Great", Jane said "I can have you all to myself tonight". Little John just smiled and was ready for dinner to be finished. With the fire just coals, Jane was doing her best to take all the tension out of Little John. With the first round done Little John said you are sure good to have around camp. The next thing they knew the light was starting to show.

With the light just showing they were on the road. "When will we get to Ronnie's ranch Jane asked"?

"It should be just before noon I think, I sure hope we are in time to be of some help in this fight",

Little John said. "This could be a real problem depending on how many members the gang has and just who we are dealing with. I hope Ronnie has some idea by the time we get at the ranch".

*

Ronnie, Tony and Deputy McPherson reached the meadow. Ronnie went on up the trail for a bit to see if the gang could get around them if they set up an ambush at the junction of the tree line just as they reach the meadow. Tony took one side and Larry rode to the other side to check out cover and field of fire so they would not hit any of the ranch crew.

They met at where the trail joined the meadow to go over what they had seen at each location. Ronnie said, "by dropping two trees one on each side of the trail it would make it hard for the gang to get behind us on either side".

Tony said he had two deadfalls ready for protection on his side,

Larry felt that they would need to cut down at least one tree for cover, and that on his side the hill drops off fast so they could not be approached from behind.

Ronnie, after getting the reports, said, "let's go back to the ranch and get the two-man buck saw so no one could hear an ax being used to cut trees". With a plan in place for defense away from the ranch, Ronnie felt they could stop the gang in this spot without exposing any of his men to very much danger of being shot. When they reached the ranch, Little John was just pulling into the yard, Ronnie went over the plan. He joined the crew and headed back to the meadow to set the trap. After two hours the saw was cutting down trees to make their defensive positions. By late that afternoon everything was ready at the ambush location. After the defensive positions were set and extra limbs cleared, so everyone could move around if needed during the gun fight. On the way back to the ranch Larry told them this is much like the trap we set for James Barton's gang; this should end about the same way.

While the men set up for the gunfight, Abby, Jane and Maggie were sitting at the table talking about getting ready for the gun fight. Abby felt that the best thing was to get everything ready to doctor anyone who got hurt, so they started getting things ready for when and if needed.

White Bird had returned from getting the Indian camp moved. Now with Eagle Feather and Badger, Tee had returned with Running Deer and Elk Man, joining them. They started talking about watching the gang. Tee found Ronnie and asked him what he wanted them to do. Ronnie laid out the plan for what he wanted. First the most important thing is to keep watch on the men at the camp. When they start to get ready to move, get a message back to the ranch. It would take the gang two hours of hard riding to get to the top of the ridge before heading down the mountain leading to the meadow. From the ridge it should take another half hour to reach the meadow. Ronnie timed the ride going to the ambush site, taking only one hour without pushing the horses. Things were coming together with the Campbell Ranch reception party.

*

Jarvis had Tray check all the horses and make sure they were ready to ride. Jarvis was going to ride right after breakfast, he wanted to hit the ranch just before lunch the next day. The elk they had killed was just about finished so his men would now be eating the food they carried. Tray had checked the horses and had brought his stallion Blaze back into camp, he had pushed all the gangs' horses over the river into the camp so the men would not get their feet wet going after their own mounts. Tray wanted his horse ready to go at any time if anything started to go wrong.

Tray was having some very bad feelings that this may not be a good raid to be involved in. Ronnie Campbell had wiped out Jarvis Baster's gang with little problem. This girl Bridget just keeps coming back into his mind, the more he thought the less he liked the idea of this raid. Now he was riding into a gun fight. No one had looked into how this ranch could be defended or how many men were at the ranch. He knew his brother and he was a planner but somehow, they got caught without any extra horses. This sounds like the same type of raid, now they didn't have any extra horses either. Jarvis was planning to steal horses from the Campbell ranch and then hit the Applegate ranch the next day, then take all the horses and cattle with them back to his California ranch along the Nevada border. That plan may just not work out very well he was thinking, these mountains only have a few trails to move around on in case trouble. With this lack of options, it is not too good for your health.

*

Back at the ranch Sean, Marty, Randy and Rose along with the Jenkins brother were armed and ready to go. This was a strong group of fighters. Rose was not going to be left back at the ranch. If Marty was going, she was also going. As she put it, I can outshoot most of you anyway. Ronnie just shook his head and gave her a hug saying, "it would be great to have you along Rose". Ronnie had shut down the mine and had everyone come into the ranch. Andy Sams had finished up the second line of defense at the ranch. If the fight went wrong, he had everything ready with extra ammunition and loaded rifles placed all around the barn, forge, wagons and other outbuildings. At each corner of the buildings Andy had a water barrel full and buckets ready.

Tee came back late telling Ronnie that it looks like the gang will move at first light, they started to move horses back into the main camp early today. Ronnie gathered everyone at the kitchen table to go over the plans for the ambush and how to handle anyone who may get past them up on the mountain. Abby, Maggie and Jane told everyone that if any of you get hurt to grab a horse and get to the ranch, we have everything ready to patch you up.

As light started to show the horses were saddled and food was on the table. After eating breakfast, Ronnie and Tony went to spend a few minutes alone with Abby and Maggie. Little John and Jane had moved out to their wagon to talk until they were getting ready to ride to the ambush site. As Ronnie stepped into the stirrups he turned back and told the girls to stay inside and have your rifles ready.

Ronnie led off, heading back into the mountains. He was followed by the whole crew, the mining crew along with all the men on the ranch. The Indians were already in place, they had spent the night in the mountains keeping watch just in case the gang started to move in the night.

*

Tray was finishing up breakfast and was cleaning up his kit. With his saddle bags packed, he took his stud for a little ride back down the trail. Riding up to Jarvis, he told him that he was going to check the back trail just to make sure no one was coming up from behind. Jarvis said, "Great idea, we sure don't want any surprises at this time". Tray had that feeling deep down that this was not a good spot to be in when they attacked the ranch. Tray was talking to himself; I don't have any reason to feel this way, but horses were stolen and moved in the direction of the ranch they were about to raid. Turning in the saddle he could see the pack horses still on the picket line. They would be picked up after the raid and as the last rider was just going up the trail and out of sight, he made his decision. I need some extra supplies and they are already on the two packhorses just waiting for me to pick them up and get out of this fight now.

Tray rode up and picked up the two pack horses loaded with supplies and headed back down the trail leading back to California. Tray was thinking what if Jarvis just didn't make it back to the ranch. Jarvis did not have any other kin so it may just work out that he could just move in and take over that ranch. He could move the stolen cattle to market and purchase some legal young stock and a few horses to start a real ranch. Money is going to be hard to find but he hoped he could make it work.

How will I know if everyone was killed in this raid? Tray thought he would just need to keep watch for anyone heading for the ranch over the next few weeks. If Jarvis were able to come back to the ranch, he would just tell him that his horse pulled a tendon and could not get back in time to get into the fight. So, he just walked back and stayed with the packhorses. After no one came back after four hours he just picked up the pack horses and headed back to where he had left his horse. He eased back to the ranch to wait for the men, without any extra horses he had to go slow.

*

Jarvis was in the lead and just reached the pass. He waited for the other six men to reach him. "Let's just rest the horses for a bit and let them eat before we head down to the ranch and get this show started. Look, men when we get the ranch in sight we will want to spread out and start firing, use your rifles and then your short guns. Remember no one is going to live, so kill everyone you see we cannot have anyone left to figure out who did this. Remember all of the cattle and horses we get you all get an equal share, so don't leave anyone alive to talk". After about 30 minutes they all followed Jarvis down the mountain trail to take revenge on his brother's killers.

As he started down the trail it was quite narrow so they could ride only single file. After he had come down about a mile, he could see a meadow peeking through the trees. Jarvis turned back to the next man telling him to spread out when we reach the clearing below. We will all cross together.

*

Tee and White Bird and the other Indians had been shadowing the gang from when they rode out of their campground. Tee had waited for a bit watching the campground and the pack horses when the one man started back down the mountain. After a bit he came back and picked up the two pack horses and rode back down out of sight. Tee then moved out onto the trail to catch up with the gang and the other Indians to be in place when the fight started. Their job was to make sure no one was able to ride back up the trail and over the mountain pass. As the gang started to move closer to the meadow, the Indians started to close in from behind. The escape over the mountain was closed and they just had to wait until the shooting started. Tee gave the bird call to Ronnie.

*

Abby and Maggie were working with Jane to get towels and tape along with hot water ready to treat anyone who got hurt in this fight. All the girls were good shots and would not think twice about shooting any of the gang who might get by the men. Each window was open and had a rifle with extra ammunition ready to fire at anyone who threatened the ranch house. Also, each of the women had a pistol in their dress pocket with the knowledge to use the weapon. Ronnie, Tony, and Little John had spent many hours showing the girls how to shoot during their time together. They all felt that at this time in history every person needed to know how to protect themselves and their families under any circumstance.

*

Ronnie was waiting on the signal from White Bird that all the gang had reached the meadow and the Indians were set to stop anyone from retreating up the trail. Ronnie was set up on the left side of the meadow with Tony, Andy, and the two Jenkins Brothers. US Marshal McPherson had the mining crew. Sean, Marty, Randy and Rose were ready to open fire on his first shot. Jarvis had reached the meadow and moved to the right and the others filed in moving left. Just as the last rider cleared the trees White Bird gave the call. Jarvis heard the call and levered a round into the chamber and spun his horse to escape, when all hell turned loose, he felt the first slug hit him in the chest as he turned. The second slug hit him as he was turning, followed by a third one hitting him in the back just as he reached the tree line. Jarvis knew he was hit hard but felt he had a chance. With the clearing behind him he was now in the trees and could see the trail heading back up the mountain. As his eyes adjusted to the low light, he could see two Indians in the trail. When he got a good look, he could see they had just released two arrows at him, he then knew he should have just left Ronnie Campbell alone. Tee and White Bird along with the other Indians could see the rider entering the timber and they all released their arrows. Ronnie had hit Jarvis with his first shot in his chest and the second one in his side. As he turned his horse the third bullet hit him just as he reached the trees. Larry's crew emptied all the saddles on their side and Tony and the others emptied the saddles on this side, not any of the seven got a shot off. The gunfight lasted only about 30 seconds. As the smoke cleared everyone came out into the meadow and started to check to see if any of the gang had lived through the hail of bullets, only one horse had been cut with a bullet on the shoulder. Two other horses were injured but would heal fast, but none of the gang had lived. Life is hard in the Ruby's.

Ronnie asked Larry about checking the saddle bags and pockets to see if he can identify any or all the men, Ronnie walked up into the timber to take a look at the first man he shot. When he reached him, he could tell this man was dead for sure, he had three bullets in him, and he also looked like a pin cushion with all of the arrows in him. After checking his pockets, he found $1,200.00 and a letter from Jules Baster addressed to Jarvis Baster. Ronnie asked, "Tee, when he came out of the trees what happened to the other man? There had been eight and we only have seven on the ground".

Tee told Ronnie about the man who started down the mountain as the other men started over the mountain pass, and he was only gone for a bit and then came back and picked up the two pack horses and rode back down the trail. Ronnie was checking with Larry if the man that he had talked to in the poker game was among the dead.

Larry said. "He was not in this bunch".

"Larry what do you think about this other man"? Ronnie asked.

"Well,", Larry said, "I think he was a bit smarter than this bunch".

"We can talk about him later today Ronnie said".

Marty, Randy and Rose had gathered up the horses that were unhurt, they had them tied head to tail so when they were ready to head back to the ranch, they would be ready to go. Rose had picked up one horse and when she checked the boot it had a Sharp's 50 caliber rifle and in the saddle bags there was plenty of ammunition. This is a great long-range rifle for hunting she was thinking. When she got the horse back with the others, she asked Ronnie if she could keep the Sharps for hunting.

"Rose, you keep any of the equipment you need or want, these horses are also good so pick out any of the riding stock and keep it for your own". "If it is ok, Marty and I will keep this horse and Sharp's rifle then, it looks like a real good horse".

The Jenkins Brothers each picked out a riding horse and a rifle of their own, they thought it was a good day for a gun fight in the Ruby's. They both moved up in the world. Jack and Billy had been dirt poor without much going on until they got the job as helpers working for Ronnie Campbell. The boys were starting to turn into men and able to do a man's job around the mine and on Ronnie's ranch.

As the cleanup was about done, each of the men had been identified by US Deputy Marshal McPherson.

Larry said to Ronnie. "I can say that you have just earned over seven thousand dollars this morning, all of these men have paper on them".

"Larry, when you get the money let me know and I will divide it among all of the crew".

Ronnie called over Little John and Tony. "Let's get our horses, we better get back to the ranch and tell the girls we are all ok. Larry, can you help clean up this mess? We will meet you at the ranch later". Larry asked Tony if there was a location that they could just drag the dead men to without having to dig seven graves. Tony talked to Tee and they figured out a good spot they could just dump them over a cliff, Tee said just a short ride there was a big drop off that would work. (After getting Larry to handle the dead men they were his problem now). Ronnie, Tony and Little John started back to the ranch. On the trail back they were talking about telling the girls how scared they were so maybe they could get a bit of extra attention tonight. They all agreed that would be a great plan and hoped for some positive results. Riding into the yard, all the girls ran out to greet them asking questions about who this gang was. Abby said, "girls let's get some food and coffee on the table for the men and Rose when they get back to the ranch".

Ronnie thanked them and said. "Great idea, that way we can all talk over what went on and why they came after us".

CHAPTER 3 **RIDE BACK TO BRIDGET**

When Tray started back to check the trail leading back down the mountain leading to California and the Jarvis Ranch, he felt the hair standing up on the back of his neck. Someone was watching him; he could just feel it. Every little bit he would stop and check around to see if he could see anyone. This was the final thing that made him decide it was for sure time for Tray to ride back into camp and untied the two pack horses, then head home with all the extra supplies. After he tied one to the other's tail and stepped up on Blaze, he started down the mountain for California. When he had ridden about a mile, he thought he heard gunfire but could not be sure. As it looked now, he either had a chance to own a ranch or get shot if Jarvis lived to come and find him. He was feeling much better every mile he covered getting away from the Ruby Mountains. Riding late, he reached one of the campsites they had used on the way, so he got a fire going and unloaded the pack horses and settled in for the night. He was not going to be in any hurry to get back to the ranch, he was keeping a look over his back trail to make sure that no one was coming up from behind.

Coffee was on and meat cooking in his frying pan for dinner. He was feeling good about his future, meeting Bridget may have just saved his life. Tray was thinking that he would have been killed in that raid if he had stayed with the gang. When Bridget kissed him, his life had made a change. Tray had been on the edge of becoming an outlaw during the time he had spent with his brother Sid. Twice Sid had asked him to go on a job, but both times he was moving cattle and was not around. Tray had been working for different ranches breaking horses or leading small cattle drives for them over the past five years. His ability to gentle horses was his best asset and many ranchers had been using him over the past years for just that specific talent.

*

Tray was thinking back on how Blaze had come to him during one of his riding jobs about two years ago over in Arizona. An offer had come from one of the foreman's he had worked for when he was just getting started breaking horses at a local ranch close to the Jarvis ranch. It had been a long ride over to Prescott, Arizona. He had hoped it would be worth his time but when the offer came it had a fifty-dollar bill attached. Out of work at the time and fifty bucks in his pocket for travel money, he put new shoes on his horse and started to Prescott. When he reached the ranch, he found they had hundreds of horses out on the range. Three years earlier the ranch owner, Jason Smith, had killed two mustang band stallions and turned loose two big young stallions that were over sixteen hands to take over his two herds with all mustang mares.

The owner needed faster and larger horses than the mustang stallions could produce, so after two full years Mr. Smith wanted a trainer who could provide him solid horses that could last a full day of hard riding in the desert. Bridge Thomas, who had come from California about that time and is now Jason Smith's foreman, he recommended Tray Davis for this job. Bridge had ridden horses that Tray had started and found them to be calm and willing partners when working cattle. When Tray reached the trading post in Prescott Valley, he asked directions to Jason Smith's Ranch. The owner told Tray to just follow the road southwest about ten miles and just keep heading toward the Bradshaw Mountain. The ranch will set just this side of the foothills along a small creek. Cross the creek. When you are on the far bank you will see the ranch yard just ahead set in among some trees.

The sun was dropping behind the hill to the west when Tray reached the ranch yard. Stopping back about twenty feet, he called to the house. The door opened, Jason Smith the ranch owner, filled the doorway as he stepped out onto the porch asking Tray what he needed.

Tray said, "I am Tray Davis. Mr. Bridge Thomas sent for me to tame and train some horses".

"Step down son and come in, my stable man will take care of your horse". Jason opened the door and Tray followed him into a sitting room. "Would you like some coffee now or wait until dinner is served? That should be in a half hour or so", Jason said.

"No, I am fine for now Mr. Smith. Bridge told me in the letter you had horses to gather and start gentling for ranch work".

"Bridge told me he had ridden some horses that you have trained and that you have a soft hand and can get the best out of each horse, is that correct Tray"?

"Yes, sir I do my best". "In the letter he offered to pay me $50.00 per month and I get to pick any horse I want for my own from the gather, is that correct Mr. Smith"?

"Yes, that is correct, and I will tell you I have some great looking horses on my range".

"Mr. Smith how much help will I have making the gather and how large of an area are your horses running in"?

"Tray, you got a look at the big mountain behind us that is Bradshaw Mountain and from that to the Northeast is Sedona. They have free range covering all of that total area. I will have all of the ranch hands help and we will gather one herd at a time, separating the breeding stock from the two- and three-year old's".

"Tray, you will have about fifteen horses or so to work with from each of the two herds, how long do you think it will take to have them saddle ready and able to do ranch work with them"?

"Mr. Smith, I think I should be able to have them all ready for ranch work, but if you want to offer some for sale it could take a bit over four months. This length of time is dependent on the disposition of your horses, you said that they have not had any handling, but the stallions are of good quality. Much of the disposition of young horses is dependent on the stallion".

The next day Tray rode out in search of the two horse herds so he could get a look at what he had to work with. With three days of food along he would stay out with the horse herds for a few days, then Tray would start the gather after looking both herds over. He found the first herd just after noon on the first day out, the stallion was not too happy with a visitor, so he moved the herd back further into the hills. Tray followed and then after two more moves the stallion came over closer to take a look at Tray, Tray was just sitting with a leg over the saddle horn looking and talking low to the stallion. Jason Smith was correct. He did have about 10 to 12 good prospects in this herd.

After two hours of watching, he rode by at an angle to get a better look. As he was riding by a two-year-old stallion walked out to look at the horse and rider. He was large for his age and had a big blaze on his forehead. Tray said to himself this is one to keep in mind. After about five miles he found a nice camping spot, good grass with a seep coming from the rocks feeding into a nice pool. After he had his horse on a picket line and had built a small rock fire pit, he was cutting some bacon into his frying pan and with a few cold biscuits he was set for the night.

Early in the morning he found fresh tracks leading east. When he rode over a small cut in the hills the herd was just below him at a water hole. Tray pulled out his field glasses and had plenty of time to see what he had to work with in this bunch-he had a couple of three-to-four-year old's along with ten strong two-year old's. Without any of the horses knowing he was around he eased back over the cut and returned to his previous campground for the night.

Back at the ranch late the next day he told Mr. Smith about what he had seen during the past three days. Jason asked Tray, "How do you want to handle the gather"?

"I think we could use the box canyon in the foothills over on the east side of Bradshaw Mountain it has water and good grass. The grass should last until I can get the horses, we want to work with separated from the two herds, some of the young stallions are going to be pushed out of the herd soon by the band stallion anyway. I saw the band stallion get a bit pushy with a couple of those young guys, we may be doing this at just the right time. They need a new friend and a job to do.

"Mr. Smith, I need a couple of pack horses and supplies for three weeks, I will go and build a fence to close off the box canyon and clean out the spring so we will have better water. Have your men at my camp in one week, we will do one gather that day". I will have a fence to hold the horses from the first gather for separating. Mr. Smith, I found a small opening in the rocks that I can close off to use as a round pen". Leaving the ranch with the supplies he needs; his pack horses were loaded. With two axes with four coils of rope, wire and food I was ready to build the holding pens. Tray had only just seven days to get ready for the ranch hands to show up and make the drive into the holding pen.

"Well, Mr. Smith, I will be looking for your men in one week, I should be ready by then. If your men see the herd, have them take note but ride wide so not to scare them". Tray picked the most direct trail to the box canyon so he could get started with his first project. It will be a round pen for training. Reaching his campsite early in the day he had some time to look over the box canyon without being in a hurry. When he was investigating the canyon, he found an opening between two large boulders. Tray tied off the two pack horses so he could check out what he had found. Riding in between the boulders he found another nice spring and a small meadow with plenty of grass. It was the game trail leading between the rocks that had alerted him to this hidden water and grass. He had found the perfect location for his base camp.

Tray went back and picked up the two pack horses and unloaded them under a rock overhang, this will protect his supplies and it offered Tray some protection from the elements. After camp was set up, he only had to cut one pole to put across the opening, the overhang was back enough to allow game to use the water hole without being bothered by his presence. He had some time before dark so he started following the deer and elk trail to see if it would lead out of the canyon, sure enough it did lead out of the canyon to a plateau after about a half mile. Returning, he fixed dinner and got his equipment ready for building the large corral with a brush fence to lead the horses into the trap. Over the next few days Tray cut brush and using rope he had the opening to the box canyon closed and the gate at the edge of the brush fence leading out into a dry wash for about 100 yards. The ranch crew should be arriving in early afternoon the next day. Tray still had a few hours left to scout the first herd he was going to trap. Saddling up, he headed back along Bradshaw Mountain to see if the horses were in the same area. He found them midway back to the ranch so he would ride out to meet the crew in the morning.

After getting the gate covered with brush Tray headed off to meet the ranch crew so they can make the roundup. Tray will try to move the horses slowly this way. After they get them moving, he could ride around to the front and act as a leader. The stallion had been trained to ride before being turned loose with the mares a few years ago, so he may just follow along. Tray had told the ranch crew to push the herd faster when they see him move out at a canter ahead of the horses, this would mean that the trap is only a short distance ahead. Tray wanted the horses to be running when he led them into the corral, with the dust it would be harder for the horses to see the brush fence.

Tray met the ranch crew early so they could just ease the horses with only a little bit of pressure from the ranch hands. Tray could see things were working out, so he told the men he was going to get around in front of the herd. With about a half mile from the box canyon Tray moved out ahead of the herd and the stallion followed. With the pressure from behind, the herd followed Tray into the corral. Tray circled the large holding pen back to the gate. After he got it closed Tray came back to meet with the ranch hands. Tray asked the ranch crew to cut out the two- and three-year old's that he was going to start breaking. With that done they could turn the rest of the herd back on to the open range. After about one hour, the separation was finished. Tray had eleven horses to work with including the young colt he called Blaze. Blaze was roped and moved into the round pen by camp. He would start by having Blaze alone and the other ten were allowed to move around in the larger corral until time to start working with them.

Blaze was not that keen to have Tray move in and start working with him, it only took about one hour to get a hand on him by rubbing his neck. Tray had some oats with him, so the next move was to rub his neck and give him a taste of a new treat. Before Blaze knew what was going on he was standing with a saddle on him. After four hours of Tray talking and handling him, he was returned to the larger holding pen to get the feel of the saddle overnight. Tray had three saddles with him, he was able to gentle two others enough to put the saddle on them and leave it for a full day. When each horse received the saddle, they also had a halter with a twenty-foot lead rope trailing, this allowed Tray to just get close and get hold of the rope to lead them back into the round pen for further training. After two weeks he had halters on all the eleven horses from the first herd, Tray had spent time leading them from his horse, so now he was ready to tie the horses head to tail with Blaze being led by Tray heading for the ranch.

Mr. Smith and Bridge Thomas were surprised when Tray rode into the yard with all the horses, with halters and three had saddles on them.

Jason said, "Well, Tray it looks like you had a fun three weeks of horse training".

Tray said that all had good dispositions, so they were easy to get them to accept their new job.

"Mr. Smith you see this first horse is the one I want to keep, so I am not going to spend any of your money working with him, I will do that later back home in California".

The next roundup went about like the first one had. Tray led the horses into the corral in the box canyon at a full gallop, none had seen the brush fence until it was too late. After the ranch hands separated the two- and three-year olds from the others, they released the mares back to be with their stallion running free over thousands of acres. Tray went to work training the horses for Mr. Smith. Three months later Tray is on his way back to California with Blaze and a pack horse Jason had given him for a job well done. His friend Bridge Thomas was very happy with the new crop of ranch horses for his crew to finish training working cattle on the Smith Ranch.

*

Riding west back to the ranch with the two pack horses from the Ruby Mountains, Tray had starting to feel that a dark shadow of death had passed over him when he was in the campsite getting ready to go on the raid to kill Ronnie Campbell. Tray was still feeling that he just had been given a second chance on life the day he started back down the mountain and the others started over to kill everyone on the two ranches.

He would be back to the Baster Ranch in another few days if he kept up this pace, Tray was wondering if anyone made it out alive, he felt sure that Ronnie Campbell was not an easy person to ambush let alone kill on his own ranch. When he had looked back on Jarvis Baster, even his brother Sid Davis all being hunted down and killed without any problem. He was getting a feeling that everyone who rode over that mountain would never make it to the ranch alive. Tray started to think that if he just rode on over to Manteca and see if he could get another kiss from Bridget. He was already on the trail so what would be an extra few days' matter? Turning just a bit north he was going to do just that.

*

Ronnie, Tony and Little John were sitting around the table talking to the girls about how the gang got killed. Abby asked, "why would they make a dumb try to kill everyone on the ranch with only seven men"? Ronnie started to tell about how US Deputy Marshal Larry McPherson had played cards with one of ranch hands that worked for Jarvis Baster. So, the best we can figure is this Tray Davis was the brother of Sid Davis who was also killed by us. The funny thing is this Tray was with the gang until he rode off leading the pack horses just as the others started over to raid the ranch.

When Larry gets back down off the mountain, we will figure just what action we want to do about this Tray Davis, it just maybe he was the only one who had any smarts. The conversation was still going on when Larry came in and sat down after pouring a cup of hot coffee.

Ronnie asked Larry what do you think about this guy Tray Davis. "Ronnie, I think I am going to swing over that way and have a talk with him to see if he needs to visit my jail or if he just picked up some smarts and headed back home. My guess is he had enough time to think this raid over and made a decision to get out while the getting was good, you see that he picked up the pack horses just after the gang left the campsite just like Tee said. You know how sometimes you get a bad feeling about what is going on and I think he had one of them moments and just pulled out and headed home".

Ronnie said, "this is what I am going to do. I will ride along with you Larry, to check this Tray out. We will just make a house call on the Baster Ranch and have a little talk with this Tray Davis. I am not going to have him thinking about heading this way unless he is just passing through".

"When do we leave"?

"In the morning I will ride Diamond and take Dandy as my pack horse".

The girls said, "get away from the table and do something else. We are fixing dinner". The men went out to talk with everyone, only to find Sean, Marty and Rose along with the Jenkins Brothers had headed back to the mine to pick up where they left off. Rose was delighted with her new Sharps 50/90. This could now kill an elk at 400 yards and further if needed. Rose and Marty and the Jenkins Brothers kept horses, saddles, and Henry rifles the prior owners would not need any longer. For Jack and Billy Jenkins this was the first real thing they had ever owned, neither had ever figured they would have a horse, rifle, pistol and even a saddle. Life is good in the Ruby's.

After an early dinner Little John and Jane hitched up the wagon and started for home, Little John felt he could reach the spring they stayed at coming to the ranch. This spot had enough water and some shelter. They would be getting there about dark. When Little John had the horses taken care of Jane had the fire going with coffee and dinner heating. Jane asked him "how was his appetite after the shoot-out". He asked for what food or other? Jane said and smiled saying I think "I can take care of both dinner first then we have all night". In the morning Jane said, "Were both of your appetite's taken care of last night Little John"?

"Jane, you do have a real talent of making a campsite feel just like home, yes they were taken care of, thank you".

With food that had been cooked at the Campbell ranch they just had coffee and ate some cold meat and bread then loaded up and got on the road, they would be home late tonight.

Jane was asking, "why do you think those men felt that they had to come after us for killing those killers, even with one being a brother of one of the worst killers in the west"?

"I just don't know why but evil people just do exist in the world, we will always need to be on alert for such people Jane", replied Little John. With the sun behind the mountains Little John drove into the yard and was met by his two Indians, Elk Man and Running Deer. They told Little John that they would take care of the team and wagon.

"Jane, having ranch hands like this is sure great. I feel that they also know who is around our ranch more than we do".

*

Ronnie came out of the house after eating breakfast with everyone and laid out what he and Deputy McPherson were going to do about Tray Davis. Ronnie felt that he had to find out why he rode west instead of following the gang over the pass to raid the ranch. Abby came out onto the porch following Ronnie out of the house to get mounted and he was ready to have this talk with Tray Davis. Abby came over to Ronnie telling him to be safe and giving him a nice warm kiss saying to get home soon if you want more. Tee had Diamond and Dandy ready to travel and Larry's horses Rob and Steal that he had picked up from some past gang members were also packed and ready to go.

Ronnie checked his guns and ammo before stepping up on Diamond. Turning and giving a wave they rode out of the ranch yard heading toward the pass and over the mountain leading to a little talk in California. Deputy McPherson asked Ronnie how hard shall we push these horses on this ride to the Baster Ranch? "I think at this pace we will be able to make good time", Ronnie said, "I think we can make it to the ranch in about three days, but I want to ride over to Manteca to see what I can find out about this Tray Davis before going to the ranch. What do you think"? Larry said that he was ok with that, and they have a good place to eat and a real cute girl waiting tables. Well, that is enough reason to slide a bit north then.

CHAPTER 4 **A SOLID MAN**

Tray reached a seep at the base of the mountains that looked like it had been used in the recent past. As he unpacked one of the two pack horses that carried the food he found a set of saddle bags under the food in that pannier, they had a J/B burned into each side of them. They must be Jarvis Baster's. When Tray opened them, he found a stack of money. Thinking this must be money from some of his prior cattle sales or who knows what it was from. Finishing unloading, he figured he would count it later after he fixed dinner. After getting the three horses on some good grass and a fire going, he pulled out some canned meat and some pan heated biscuits for dinner. With the fire started in the small circle of rocks he placed his cooking grate over the fire. As the last light faded away, he was eating his meal and drinking some coffee.

After getting a good count on the money over twenty thousand dollars, Tray had to start thinking over just where this money came from, could it be some of Jarvis's money from robberies? How could that be Jules? He never made it to the ranch before his gang was killed by Ronnie Campbell. No, this had to be money from the sale of cattle. He would need to think about this. Blaze was ready to cover ground at first light. Tray had saved a couple of biscuits and some meat from last night's meal. Pack saddles on and packed, he was getting excited to see Bridget in Manteca. It would take a few more days to reach Manteca so he was pushing along at a good speed. He had to use the water from his four canteens to water his horses at mid-day, he had not found any water. Late in the day he could see some trees ahead. He was hoping to find some water for the horses and some to cook his meal. When he was getting close to the trees, he was relieved to find a stream flowing behind a line of cottonwood trees. Willows lined the waterway. Riding upstream he found a break in the willows, and it looked like a path used by wild horses and other animals.

Tray followed the trail down to the water and all three horses moved up to take a drink. After letting all three drink a little, he rode across the stream to the base of a bank that had some bushes growing along the bank to hide the horses so he could get a good look at the area. He tied off the three horses. Tray walked around his horse and pulled his rifle out of the scabbard. He walked up the bank to have a look see, he wanted to make sure he was alone. This is an area that he had never ridden over before, so he felt he had better be safe and take his time to make sure he was alone. Tray waited for a while and found nothing he felt was out of place, now to find a sheltered location to make a camp. He still had a good hour before dark to set up his camp.

With the horses watered again, he had them picketed on some grass along the stream, he let them eat for a couple of hours. He would bring them in and give all some oats to give them a bit of punch for the next day. He felt that he could make Manteca late tomorrow afternoon. He had been thinking about Bridget more and more each day, he now had to figure out what to do with the money, was it his or just what should he do with it? After dark he had pulled the horses back in close to his camp, Blaze is like having a dog, he stomped a front foot if anything came around. With the horses close he went back up on the bank to get the feel of the night, sound would carry a long way and if anyone had a fire close, he could see its location. It would be hard to find a location like this unless someone just stumbled onto his camp as he had. His camp is well hidden in the trees so the smoke from his fire will disperse among the tree branches making him hard to find.

Starting early, his mood was high. Hoping to get into Manteca and see Bridget, he hoped she was also thinking about him. He knew that his past ways were done, he had the shadow of death pass him by and he would not take any more chances on the wild side. Late that night he rode into Manteca and stopped at the restaurant to see if Bridget was working. Tying off his horses, he heard the door open, and Bridget said "Hi Tray. Come on in and I will get you fed". The last of the customers were coming out of the door when he walked in to find a seat. Bridget walked up and gave him a kiss and he did his best to do his part. Finding a seat, Tray sat down, and Bridget did the same and asked him what he wanted to eat. Anything would be fine. She went back into the kitchen and returned with the special for the day along with his coffee. Bridget sat down with him and asked if he had made his trip and was back for good.

Tray said that he was glad to be back and yes, he was back to stay. Bridget asked him what his trip was about, and she would like to know. "I know you are the brother of an outlaw named Sid Davis".

"Yes, Sid was my brother, but I am not an outlaw. Bridget how soon do you close up the restaurant? I want you to walk with me over to the livery to stable my horses and we can talk after I get Blaze and my two pack horses taken care of. I am going to be staying in town for a few days depending on how we get along. I really do like you and would like to work on our kissing, if you don't have any objections".

"No" she said. "No objections on my part. I was the one who started it if you remember".

Tray was the last one to eat before the restaurant was closed. Bridget and Tray walked the horses down to the livery for stabling. Jeff Watts came out when they approached the door of the stable, Jeff said "well, you are back. How long do you want your horses put up"?

"Let's start with three days and then we will see", Tray said.

"That will be three dollars for all three". Tray asked if he could store his supplies in a locked-up space. Jeff said you sure can, no one had the key but me, your things will be safe.

"Do I need to pay extra to get some oats for the boys"?

"No, Tray, it's included". Bridget helped Tray unload the pack horses and store the supplies, Bridget walked into the tack room with Tray following. After putting down the supplies, Bridget turned only to be met by Tray doing his own brand of kissing. After a bit they were both a bit warmed up and doing a bit of touching. They heard Jeff coming so they kind of moved apart to clear the air a bit. Jeff had the panniers with the money in it so Tray asked him to put it in the corner and he would move his other supplies over around it to save some room. Jeff said that that would be ok and not to worry about taking up too much room, he had plenty.

Tray asked Bridget if he could walk her home, she said that she lived in a boarding house just down the street. She said why don't you stay there, we can talk in the sitting room, there are only two other people staying at this time so we should be able to talk as late as we want. Tray asked if she had any time off or did she need to work every day. "I do have tomorrow off; it is my only free day but if you stay at the boarding house, we can see each other after breakfast and after lunch. I have time between each meal. We can spend time getting to know each other better".

Tray and Bridget started down the boardwalk to the boarding house to meet Doris Watson, the owner. Doris had been a mail order bride taking a chance on marrying an older man. Her husband had been killed some years ago during a roundup. Without knowing anything about ranching she sold her ranch and purchased this rooming house. When Bridget opened the door, Doris was seated in the sitting room. She got up when they walked in to greet them.

Doris, this is Tray Davis. He needs a room for a few days. He just got back from a trip, he came into the restaurant to eat, and I told him about your rooming house".

Doris said, "the cost is one dollar a night with meals. Is that ok"? Tray pulled out five dollars and said let's start with three and then we will see. Doris asked Tray to follow her, and they would get him a key and sign the register. With Doris leading, Tray and Bridget followed to look at his room. At the top of the stairs Bridget pointed to her room and stopped to open her door and said I will meet you in the sitting room in a few minutes. Tray said OK and followed Doris to the last door on the left. She opened the door and stepped back to let him in to look at the room. Doris said the bathroom was just across the hall. "Well, Tray if all is ok, if so, this is your key. Will I see you downstairs later"? Tray said that he was to meet Bridget in the sitting room later so I may just see you there also.

Tray checked out the room and put the saddle bags under the bed and locked the door. He looked left and could see a door leading to a stairway leading to the ground. He headed downstairs to the sitting room to meet Bridget. Bridget was sitting with Doris when he entered the room. He took a seat across from the two women. They looked like they could have been sisters, Doris looked to only be a few years older than Bridget. Doris asked Tray what he did for a living and Tray said he was a horse trainer and helped run a cattle ranch, a two-day ride southeast from here. After some other questions, Doris got up and said she was going to her quarters for the evening, asking Bridget to turn off the oil lights when she went to her room, "ok" she said. Tray and Bridget looked at each other for a bit. "Tray, I know that your brother is Sid Davis". Then Bridget moved over a bit and Tray moved over beside her to hold her hand. Bridget turned to Tray and asked if he would tell her everything about his trip, she had to know before she would move forward with their relationship. She spoke to him in a soft voice, "I need to know the good and bad, tell it all please".

Tray felt the color coming up from his toes. He knew this was a defining moment in time and he had to get it correct or he would ride away without any chance with Bridget. "Let me start with I have never broken the law that I know of, now that does not say that I have not been on the edge, just by working for Jarvis and selling his cattle I could be in some trouble with the law. I did not steal the cattle, but I did know that the brands had been worked over to read the Baster ranch brand. I did not do any of the brand rework nor was it done at the ranch. Jarvis had a bill of sale made out to Jarvis Baster with the reworked brands, I sold them to a cattle buyer who inspected the paperwork so I should be ok. Yes, I should have not done that, but I did it and can't undo that either".

"You know about Sid Davis my brother. He was killed by Ronnie Campbell and his ranch hands after Jules Baster stole cattle and killed Ronnie's longtime friends, Sam and Beth Applegate. Sid was in on that killing and stealing of the cattle and horses from them. Ronnie and his crew ran their gang to the ground and killed every one of them. Jarvis has gathered six new gun hands and with me we were going to get revenge on Ronnie Campbell and what was left of the Applegate family". Bridget had tears running down her face but was still holding Tray's hand. Tray said, "Bridget you saved my life".

"How could I have done that"?

"Well, when you kissed me when I was here selling the cattle it changed my life. I had never been on any raid with any gang, but Sid had asked me to and just by luck I was never around at the right time. Yes, I went with them, each day and night I could see you and feel that kiss and by the time we had reached the campsite close to the ranch I was having second thoughts. So, the morning of the raid I told Jarvis that I was going to check the back trail and then meet them up the mountain. Well, I started to get a feeling that I was being watched, my hair on the back of my neck was standing up, I even pulled my rifle when I rode back to the two pack horses and tied them off to Blaze and headed home or should say back to you to see if we could have any future. I still have a problem, first I don't know if anyone lived that day. If so when will Jarvis come looking for me? Another problem is I found a lot of money in some saddle bags on one of the pack horses, there is over twenty thousand dollars in Jeff's tack room. I will have to figure out what to do with that money, it's not mine".

Bridget wiped her eyes and asked if he would kiss her, Tray touched her lips with his and he could taste the salt from her tears. For a long time, they just set looking at each other.

"Bridget, can you forgive me, and can we still be friends? I am not a bad man".

Bridget pulled him close and said "I need to go to my room. We will talk tomorrow". Tray felt like his whole world was caving in around him. After some time, he turned off the oil lights and went up to his room. The bed was great, but he could not find sleep until just before dawn. Getting up and washing around nine, he could not think of a time he had slept that late. The morning meal was finished when he got around and downstairs, Doris said she could fix him a bite if he wanted. "No, I am good".

Stepping out onto the porch, he turned to the livery to check on his horses and then he would go over and see if Bridget would talk to him. He finished with the horses and walked to the restaurant to see Bridget. When he walked in, he could see Bridget was not there. Then he remembered that she was off today. Walking back over to the livery he asked Jeff if he had a buggy for rent, and if he could get it ready in an hour. Tray walked back to the boarding house and walked in and found the sitting room empty so he went up the stairs and knocked at Bridget's door. She opened it and he could tell that she had been crying during the night. He asked if she would go for a ride with him, he had a buggy ready in an hour. After a bit she said that she would meet him in an hour on the front porch.

"Will you bring a blanket, and I will get some food for a picnic lunch out by the river". Tray walked away feeling that he may still have a chance if he could get her to believe he was what she said was a solid person. It was evident that he had really been on the edge, he could have been an outlaw if things had not worked out that he was either on a ranch training horses or moving cattle for another rancher.

Picking up the buggy, he pulled up to the front of the boarding house and Bridget was just stepping out onto the porch, Tray jumped down and helped her into the buggy and stored the blanket behind the seat with the basket of food. Tray turned and asked if she had any location, she liked or do they just take the drive out to the river on the road. Bridget said that there was a nice location a few miles south of town, just follow the road. Just before the river Tray could see a road along the river in the trees so he turned and followed until he found a nice spot under some big cottonwood trees and a nice carpet of grass. Helping Bridget down from the buggy seat and laying out the blanket, he then unhitched the horse and put him on a picket line after taking him to water for a drink.

Bridget was sitting on the blanket. When he finished walking back, he stopped and reached out for her hand and asked if she would walk with him. With a little smile she reached for his hand, and he pulled her up. The day was just perfect for a walk, with the trees giving cover the sun was not too hot. Tray started by asking her if she had always lived in Manteca. "Oh no", she said. "I ended up there because my parents had both been killed by a runaway team and wagon just two years ago. I was lucky that my father had left me a small amount of money, so I was able to find a place to live and find a small job to help with my living expenses. I was able to purchase part of the restaurant when the owner's other partner died. I am so lucky that my father had given me the money so I could live without turning to being a crib girl and selling my body to make a living".

Tray was shocked by what she had told him, he had figured that she was just working in the restaurant for something to do. "Bridget, do you think you can forgive me for almost being part of a killing. I will say it again, you saved my life. When I was riding down the mountain, I felt the shadow of death pass over me. I know I have been given a second chance. Can you also give me one? I like you so much and want to get to know you and you really know me". Bridget stopped and turned and raised up on her toes and gave Tray a kiss that lifted his spirit back to the living. "Bridget, do you want to go back and get a bite to eat and talk some more? I want to listen to your life story, and I would like to talk to you about what I want to do".

When they reached the blanket neither wanted to eat, they just needed to explore what they were both feeling. The afternoon was about done, so they each grabbed a piece of chicken and a piece of pie, then Tray hitched up the buggy and they headed home feeling that they do have a chance to make a life together with a friend. Bridget was waiting in the sitting area when Tray came in from taking care of the buggy and horse at the stable. Doris Watson was waiting for Bridget when she came in from the picnic with Tray. "Well, I see you have a new friend. Do I need to know anything"?

"No", said Bridget. "We are just getting to know each other. We have both had a bit of a less than perfect life up to now, but I think he is a keeper".

"Bridget, I am going to retire to my living quarters for the evening so you two can get better aquatinted, if I would stay it might be a bit awkward don't you think"?

Tray came in and joined Bridget on the couch in the sitting area. They had just started talking when one of the other male boarders, Bill Davis, came in from one of the local saloons and was feeling no pain. It took him three tries to make it up the stairs to his room. His room is beside Bridget's. Tray ask if they would have time to meet between meals at the restaurant, Bridget told him to just come on over and they would talk over coffee. It was getting late, so they turned off the oil lamps and went up the stairs. At her room they stopped and started kissing and doing a bit of exploring. After a bit, Tray said that they better stop, or he was going to ask to join her in her room. Bridget opened the door and went in for the night. Tray had a bit of a stiff trip to his room.

*

Ronnie and Deputy McPherson are camped on a bit of water for the night and looking forward to a long day's ride to reach Manteca late.

They were up early loaded and on the trail as the light had just starting to show in the east. "Larry, do you think we should get a drink first or a good meal, if it's the meal I sure hope the young girl is working", Ronnie said. "We will see in not too many hours if we keep up this pace, Larry you did a good job picking up those two horses, they are the only two that can keep up with Diamond and Dandy. Dandy looks slow but he is always on my right boot all day every day, how old do you think Rob and Steal are"?

"I would think about five or six". Larry felt that was about the correct age for the two. After a short noon stop to give the horses a bit of rest and some grain, they were indeed seeing the lights just as the sun was going down. Larry said, "I think I want to get a meal in me before trying out the whiskey".

*

Tray was eating a late supper with Bridget; all the other diners had left the restaurant, so they were alone. Tray reached over and took Bridget's hand and said, "look at me". When she was looking into his eyes, he asked her if she would marry him.

Bridget said "yes, when do you want to make it official"?

"How about tomorrow is that too soon? We can go see the judge after the lunch crowd is gone". Both looked up when the door opened, and two men walked in. Tray jumped up when he saw Larry, they had played cards a few weeks ago.

"Larry what are you doing back in Manteca? Come in to eat".

"Tray, this is Ronnie he is one of my best friends". Bridget told them to take a seat and she could only serve them the special. Larry said that would be fine and asked Tray to come over and sit with them. With coffee all around Larry asked Tray about the revenge mission he was planning on over to Nevada.

Tray said, "I had ridden over with the gang and the morning they were planning to make the raid I had a feeling of death and a black shadow fell over me. When the extra horses were stolen, I started to get a feeling I need to get away from Jarvis and his gang. So, when they all got loaded, I had made up my mind that I was not going any further. So, I told Jarvis that I was going to check the back trail and after they went up the hill, I picked up the pack horses and came back to Manteca. You know after we talked at that poker game, I came into this restaurant and Bridget kissed me and told me to come back to her".

"I feel that I was given a new life. I am now worried about Jarvis because I just rode away, he will come looking for me and it will come to gun business when that happens". Larry reached into his pocket and dropped his US Deputy Marshal Badge on the table. Tray said. "Oh no, am I going to jail"? Bridget came over to see what was going on with Tray and the two men.

"Tray I would like to introduce you to Ronnie Campbell". Tray was about ready to cry when Larry said. "Tray you are the only smart one of that whole bunch". "We came over to talk to you and see if you had any hard feelings with either of us for killing your brother Sid Davis and his gang". Ronnie looked at Tray. "I want you to know that we came here to either kill you or be friends, your choice. I will also tell you we killed every one of the gang, so you will not need to be looking for Jarvis Baster, he and his gang were left in the bottom of a canyon for the wild animals".

Tray looked at Ronnie and said, "I am starting a new life. Bridget and I are going to be married tomorrow and start our new life together". Tray asked Bridget to come over and meet Ronnie and Larry.

'Bridget, so you two are going to start a new life together from what Tray has just said".

"Yes, we are, we decided this just before you two came in the door to eat".

"Deputy McPherson I have a question", "Tray asked, When I unpacked one of the pack horses I found a large stash of money, what should I do with it? I do not know who it came from and if it could be mine or what and the other question is, what can I do with the Jarvis ranch? With him dead, Bridget and I want to start training horses and run some cattle. Could we get title to that ranch"?

"Tray, I am a US Deputy Marshal and from what I have seen in cases like this, Ronnie and I may just need to write a paper saying that Jarvis named you in his last words as the owner of all of his assets. What do you think Ronnie? Was that how you remembered his last words"?

"Well, I think that is just what I heard him say just before he died. Tray when you get settled you may want to make a real visit to my ranch, because I have some very good young fillies you may want to look at and Little John also has some very good young stock also". With coffee all around Larry and Ronnie finished their meal and were heading to the bar for that shot of whiskey.

When you get to travel around the different states you find pictures of the historic past, I hope you can find your own story in this picture. (photo by Ron Bell)

This old log cabin housed a young man and his new wife, the husband had homesteaded the land and for two years he lived in a dugout in the side of a small stream just behind this cabin. After proving up the land he built this home for his bride, and they moved in and raised their family. (photo by Ron Bell)

CHAPTER 5 **NEW WIFE NEW RANCH**

Tray and Bridget were excited beyond belief with the news from Ronnie Campbell and Deputy McPherson, they even have a paper signed by them saying that they are the owner of the Baster Ranch and all the cattle and even the money Tray found. After closing up the restaurant Bridget and Tray walked back down to the boarding house. The lamps were turned down low, so they knew Doris was in her room for the night. Tray turned off the oil lamps and they made their way up the stairs, at Bridget's door they stopped. They could hear the two men boarders snoring. Tray asked if she would like to start out married life one day early, Tray said "let's go to my room". With the door closed they looked at each other and asked if the other had ever had sex before. Bridget said no never, "but what I do know is we can't start if we have our clothes on, let's see who can get naked first". The race was on, Tray had one boot that gave him a problem, so he lost. Bridget pulled back the covers and jumped in pulling the covers up to her neck, Tray was just a few seconds behind.

Bridget asked, "can we turn out the light"? Tray said, "no. I want to see you, all of you". He slid under the covers and with his right hand he pulled down the covers real slow, Bridget had her hands covering her breasts. Tray gently removed them and replaced them with his. With a few kisses she was asking for more. They spent the night in each other's arms. With the first light Bridget grabbed her clothes and headed for her room to get dressed so she could open the restaurant. Tray laid back and looked at what his new life was giving him. After getting cleaned up he headed over to check on his horses and see if he could buy the buggy for the trip home to the ranch, the buggy would make picking up supplies much easier than using the pack horses or the large wagon.

Tray walked into the restaurant and got a smile that about stopped his heart. He found a seat. Bridget came over and took a seat. She took his order and returned with coffee and, taking a seat again, "Tray, I just told my partner that I would not be working after breakfast today, I found a young girl who is also in a bad spot and needed a job, she came in this morning early looking for work, so I just gave her my part of the restaurant. She will be coming in any minute to start waiting tables. I will help her for a while to get the feel of how to serve customers". Bridget came back with the new owner delivering his food. "Tray, this is Wanda Smart she is starting a new life". Wanda said, "I am sure glad you two are getting married because I was down to my last few dollars with no hope. I walked into get some breakfast and walked out a part owner. My life has made a turn for the better. Bridget how do I repay you the money for my half of this restaurant"? "Don't worry about that. It is yours, just remember to help someone else", Tray reached into his pocket and gave her a one-hundred-dollar bill, saying this should hold you over until you get money coming in.

Bridget helped Wanda for another hour with Tray sitting and enjoying watching Bridget offer suggestions and introducing her to the customers. Bridget pulled off her apron and gave it to Wanda saying, "Good luck". As they walked out onto the boardwalk Tray said. "Bridget, we need to go and get some new clothes, rings and then find a judge. I am ready to be married". Just a short walk to the general store they found everything they needed.

James Witherspoon was the owner and helpful in getting then ready for their wedding. Tray told James that he was the new owner of the Baster Ranch. "I am Tray, and this is to be my new wife Bridget, we will be back later to place an order for the ranch before we start home. We have a date with the judge in about one-half hour, we just have time to get changed and head to the courthouse". James said, "pay me when you pick up the other order so you can get on your way to get married".

"Ok, James you can start setting out the normal order and we will add some when we get back".

Tray and Bridget headed to their rooms to wash up and get dressed to meet the judge. Tray was ready first, so he walked down to Bridget's room and walked in to find her just getting dressed, "so you came to have a bit of a show".

" Yes, I did, and this is quite a show I must admit, plus I am looking forward to many more. I only hope this show has a happy ending".

Bridget said, "Tray I asked Doris to be our witness today".

"Great, "he said. Show over and they walked out of her room to meet Doris downstairs and then go over to the courthouse. When the three walked into the court room they found Ronnie and Deputy McPherson waiting and talking with the judge.

"Well, Tray who do we have here"?

"Larry this is Doris. She is the owner of the boarding house. Doris, meet US Deputy Marshal Larry McPherson".

"Nice to meet you Larry. If you need a room, please come over to my boardinghouse and I will fix you up".

Larry turned to Tray and Bridget. "I want you to read this before you two get married", "This is an official paper giving you clear title to the ranch signed by Judge Barfield". "After you get married both of you need to have the title recorded down the hall at the recorder's office, you also need to register your new brand".

Judge William Barfield told Troy and Bridget to step forward and we will make this marriage official. After the paperwork was signed Tray asked if everyone would go have lunch with them to make this feel more like a family wedding. "We are so happy with our new life starting today". Everyone went over to eat so they could give Wanda a bad time as she was trying to learn her new job. Miles Weber came out from the kitchen to offer his best wishes. He is half owner of the restaurant. Just by chance Larry found a seat beside Doris and they started to have a very good conversation during the meal, Larry always had an eye for a pretty girl.

Tray thanked everyone and started to pay the bill, Ronnie said, "this is on me and make sure you two come over and look at some of my horses. Did I say I also have some real fast racehorses you may want to look at? I have a jockey and trainer by the name of Jingles. He has won some real money for me in Salt Lake City last year". Tray asked Ronnie if he would like to give Blaze a little run in a few months if he and Bridget came over to the ranch. "You are on, replied Ronnie".

Bridget gave Tray a bit of a tug and looked at the boarding house. "Tray we had better get packed and go finish that order at the general store". "Yes, we better get started, Tray said". Doris said, "I have had an errand to take care of so I will see you two later, if I don't get back, please stop by on your way out of town".

The boarding house front door was open in a flash and the two newlyweds flew up the stairs and tested out Bridget's bed this time. Later in the afternoon they made their way over to the general store. James had the order about ready when they walked in. After the congratulations they looked at what was on the counter, Tray found some additional items he wanted and told Bridget to get her some new riding clothes and dresses-just get anything you need. "James we are going to stay in town another night so if I bring over my four panniers for the pack horses could you fill them"? Tray asked. "The heavy stuff we will put in the back of the buggy, oh yes we will also need some rope to tie the supplies down. Thanks James, see you in the morning".

"Let's go over to take a look at the buggy and pick out a horse to pull it". Reaching the livery Jeff Watts came out to meet them, "Jeff I need to pay for another night, and we need to look at a horse to pull our new buggy".

"I think I have just the horse for you, this gilding came to me just last week and he is a real looker. I had him hitched once so I know he will pull, he has a real fast trot. We can go to the back corral and take a good look at him; I want to see if you can pick out the one, I am thinking about for you". Bridget and Tray reached the back corral and Bridget pointed to a blood bay with three white stockings. Bridget asked Jeff if that is the one in the back I am looking at"? "Sure is" Jeff replied, "Lets walk back and see if he will stand or come to you, Bridget, I think he will".

Bridget walked right up to him, and he stuck out his nose for a rub. She said, "I want this one". Jeff said, "that is the one I felt would be the best for you". Tray picked up each foot without any problem, "Jeff can you have new shoes on him in the morning before we leave"? "Yes, I can, and I had to reset two shoes on the one packhorse they were coming lose". "Thanks Jeff now how much do you want for this horse"? "Well, I need sixty for the horse and another twenty for the harness". "Jeff why don't we just say seventy for the horse and harness, I am also going to be purchasing that buggy". "Seventy it is", Jeff said.

"Come on Bridget, let's look at the buggy, and see how much Jeff is going to take from a poor newly married couple with no money".

Jeff said, "I am not going to fall for that one Tray. I think you may want to look at one other buggy I have, it is a bit better and has stronger wheels with a larger storage area and it is only one hundred dollars. It is used, but the past judge ordered it and only used it a few times before he died last year. This rig has been setting for a long time, but it is covered up. The judge paid over two hundred and fifty dollars and only used it two times if I remember, it is just like new". Reaching the back of his livery barn they could see a buggy covered with a tarp, the tarp was covered with hay and dust. Jeff and Tray eased off the tarp and there sat a brand-new buggy with leather seats with black wheels with red striping. Tray said "sold. Jeff, can you have the wheels hubs greased by tomorrow morning so we can be on the road by say nine"?

"Yes, I can", Jeff said. "Let's go back to the office and I will write up a bill of sale for the total".

Tray turned to Bridget, "why don't we get two travel trunks from James Witherspoon to pack all of our new stuff, we now have room to take everything home with us and ride in style".

*

Ronnie and Larry entered the saloon after the wedding to have a drink. Larry still had his badge on as he entered the double doors and stepped to the left just inside of the door to look over the room, letting his eyes adjust to the low light. Ronnie walked up to the bar and ordered two drinks. Turning, he could see a man at one of the card tables push back and start to draw his pistol. Deputy McPherson had also seen the man start to draw and stepped left behind a post as he drew his colt 44 and let her bang. The man was spinning to his right when Larry's bullet hit him in the chest just after Ronnie's bullet took him in the left shirt pocket. The card player got off one round, shooting into the wall to the left of Larry.

Larry yelled, "I am US Marshal McPherson, everyone put their hands on top of the table. Now Ronnie, tell that barkeep to move out in front of the bar, and will you remove every gun in the room and put them on the table to my left". With all the guns on a table Larry walked over to the dead man to see if he had a wanted poster on him. Emptying his pockets, Larry found two hundred and fifty dollars in bills. "Ronnie take a look at what I found this guy is one bad actor, he is Willis Beal's, he is wanted for murder and robbery all over California and beyond. Ronnie, you just made over one thousand dollars for bringing this guy to justice plus the two hundred and fifty he had in his pockets". Larry had each man in the room tell him who he was and see if he remembered if any of them had a wanted poster with a reward. "Any of you with this man"? No one spoke. "Ok barkeep what do you know about this man"? Larry asked,

"Barkeep what is your name, and do you own this place, and have you ever seen this man before"?

"I am Jerry Walker; I just work here".

"Take note Jerry. If I find out, you told me a lie you will not live to tell another".

"His brother is worse than this guy, they come through here every few months. It has been a while so the gang could be on their way into town the next few days".

"How many does he travel with? You said his brother, what is his name"?

"Dan Beal's, I think".

"Is that big black his at the hitch rail?

"yes".

"Ronnie, could you go out and pull his saddle bags? I want to go through them to see if I can find out any kind of news as to the location of this gang".

Larry told the barkeep to resume business and you men go get your guns, latch them down and don't make any fast moves and get this dead man over to the undertaker. Ronnie came back in with the saddle bags and laid them on one of the tables in the corner just inside of the door.

"Well, why don't we see what we have. Dang, Ronnie take that roll of money, and see what else we have, two boxes of 44-40's some food, oh look at this a telegram to Willis Beal's from none other than Dan Beal's telling Willis to meet him in Manteca for a job so no trouble. Ronnie, I am going to find the local sheriff and see if they have a large amount of money in either of the two banks in town. We need to go and see if this town has any real lawman, I haven't seen any badges during my time here, have you Ronnie"?

"No, not a one Ronnie answered".

Larry asked the barkeep for the directions to the sheriff's office. "It is just one block further down the street". Reaching the office, they opened the door to find a man with his feet up on the desk reading a dime novel. Dropping his feet to the floor he asked what can I do for you two, Larry pointed to his badge and ask who are you and what is your job.

"I am Jake Sanders this is my town, what do you two want"?

"Well, Mr. Jake Sanders, you may have a bank robbery about to happen, what do you think about that Mr. Jake"? Jake started to tell Larry he had no authority in his town as he started to get out of his chair. Larry pulled his 44 sticking it into Jake's Sanders chest. "Now, how much authority do you think I have now? Ronnie grabbed the keys and open a cell door, I will relieve Mr. Jake's gun and let him sit in a cell until he figures to be of a more helpful nature". Jake was yelling you cannot do that to me, I am in charge of this town. "As a US Marshal, I have the authority to remove any local law that is not helpful to me or any other marshal".

"Ronnie, grab the keys and we'll go get some dinner and then we will see just how much better this Jake gets in helping us and his town. We should go back to the restaurant and see if the new owner is learning how to wait tables and get some dinner. I think Wanda Smart could use some more of our business; I am hungry enough to eat about anything".

Walking into the restaurant, Wanda came over to see if they wanted coffee and to take their order for dinner. Ronnie ordered steak and potatoes with pie, Larry said he would take the same. "Well, Ronnie how long do you think before Jake will start to get the point"?

The door opened with a bang and a little fat man came running in yelling "I am the Mayor, why is the sheriff locked up in his own jail"?

"Well, you see as a US Deputy Marshal, I have the legal right to remove any officer of the law that is not willing to work with our officers. He was just not helpful, so we can see how he acts when we get back. Mayor, you may need to be ready to get yourself a new law man. I and only I will make that decision as to his future. You, mayor, do not have anything to say in the matter. Now if you want to buy our meal that would be fine with us, join us and we will inform you what is going on or about to go on in your fine city'.

"I am Mayor Dicks. I own the hardware store down the street and am part owner in one of the two banks in town".

"Well Mr. Dicks, what is your first name"?

"William", he said.

"Sit down and we will tell you what is about to happen in your town, we just shot Willis Beal's, a noted bank robber. He is part of a gang that is in the bank robbing business and are very good at it. Mayor, you need to read this". Larry showed him the telegram stating that Willis was to meet his brother in Manteca, and he is not to start any trouble. "Well, as we said Willis is dead and we expect to see the Dan Beal's gang in town starting tonight and they will most likely try to rob the bank when it opens in the morning at nine. Are you going to eat with us and go over some ideas or are you just going to waste our time"?

William Dicks sat back and asked, "what could he do"?

"It is only about three hours before closing time, do you have a safe in the hardware store"?

"Yes, I do".

"Does the general store have a safe in their store"?

"Yes, they do".

"Now this is what you can do after we eat, we will go and talk to James Witherspoon about taking some of the money and put it in his safe and you take the other banks money and put it into your safe. Now no one can know about this, we will help the two banks move the money after closing hours so not even the employees know. You cannot talk to anyone about this. Now, shall we go see if Jake wants to help or stay in jail"?

At the jail, Jake was getting madder every minute and when he heard the front door open, he started yelling up a storm. Mr. William Dicks walked into the jail cells and told Jake to shut up or he was going to have Larry, hall his ass back to Sacramento and lock him up. With things settled down Larry went back and unlocked the cell door, telling Jake to keep his mouth shut or he would close it for a good long time. Jake decided to be of more help as the time went on, he found out he was in a pile of shit and would have probably been killed when the robberies got under way in the morning. With the time getting close to closing for the two banks, William Dicks along with Larry headed for the first bank. Jake and Ronnie had a covered freight wagon on the move down a back street to meet Dicks and the bank president to move the money. When the last employee closed the door the bank president locked it and went to the safe to help move all the cash into bags, it was all now in large bank bags, so it was easy to get loaded. Mayor Dicks signed the release for the money from the bank. Dicks and Larry got into the wagon and moved to the back of the Dicks Hardware Store. Dicks opened the back door and transferred the bank bags to his safe. Larry had him sign the receipt for the money that was now in his safe. Larry and Mayor Dicks went to the back door and checked that no one was around to see the transfer being made. First one done and on to the general store to meet James Witherspoon, James opened the door, and they moved the bank money into his safe for the night.

"Mayor Dicks, I am going to spend the night with the money, I will sleep in the office with my shotgun".

"James we will talk tomorrow". Larry asked all the players if they were set until tomorrow around seven. We will all meet at the restaurant for some breakfast. "All ok"

This is the true spirit of the Battle Born State, the wild horses on the run bring joy to most who venture back in time like you will with my Ronnie Campbell series western books. (Photo by Robin Travis).

"RUN WITH THE WIND"

CHAPTER 6 **IN TOWN TO MEET WILLIS**

Just outside of town about two miles Dan Beal's and his gang had found a camping spot just off the main trail. They will wait for Willis to show up today or in the morning then they would split up so they would have three members of the gang per bank. Dan Beale liked to hit the bank just as they open for customers at nine. We all need to get some sleep so we will be ready for action in the morning. Dan was up and ready to move at five, Willis should be showing any time he was thinking. The other four men were drinking coffee and eating a cold biscuit, normal breakfast food for outlaws. "Everyone check your guns so we will be ready, do you all have an extra pistol-fill all of the holes, we don't want to take any chances". By eight Dan was having a fit trying to figure what was up with Willis, I told him to not go drinking, just look over the town so we would know in what direction the law would come from. He was telling the other men the last time he and Willis were in town the sheriff was not much of a law man, this sheriff liked his office way too much and his chair fit his ass just perfect.

"Ok. We need to go. Willis must be in jail; we will slip in the back way and check the jail cells from our horses we can see in without any trouble. If he is not there, we will go ahead and pull off the job and worry about him later, he may have just got drunk and never made it to Manteca. His loss, this should be a big haul, there is supposed to be thousands in each bank. The Hide Plant payroll is a lot of money just for that". "Let's ride. Dan rode around to the back side of town and entered behind the jail to check on Willis. Looking in, he could not see anyone. "Spud, you go with me, you three take the other bank and make it fast. We will need to ride hard to where we left the other horses. Dan and Spud worked around to the back side of the bank; they would need to tie off the horses just outside of the side door of the bank.

*

Smiley Thompson was on time just as planned, he walked up to the bank doors and pulled his key, opening the double doors and walking in. As he came in, he could see two figures through the shades on the other side of the bank building, so he moved to the side door. When the front door opened, he went out the side door and locked the door and left the key in the lock so it could not be opened from the inside. Then he ran like hell to the sheriff's office.

Sam Weaver had just opened his bank's doors as three men rode up to the hitch rail in front and two stepped down. As the two men started for the door, he was opening the side door and left as fast as he could. When clear of the bank he circled around to the sheriff's office to meet Smiley and wait to see what was going to happen.

*

Ronnie Campbell, Jake Sanders, Mayor Dicks and US Deputy Marshal McPherson were all heading to their assigned location to greet the Beale Gang. Ronnie and Jake could cover both the front door and the side door of Smiley's bank and Larry, and Mayor Dicks had the other bank covered. When Smiley and Sam were both in the sheriff's office it was time to see who wanted to die.

Dan ran into the bank with his pistol cocked and ready. He yelled on the floor everyone, no one was there, he ran to the vault, and it was open and empty. Dan hollered to Spud "let's get the hell out of here", they ran to the side door and tried to open it, it was jammed. "Out the front and be ready to shoot, get both guns out we may need them".

Down the street the other gang members busted through the front doors and found the bank vault empty. Checking the vault, they knew they are in major trouble. Grab your guns and get our horses.

*

Tray and Bridget had arrived at the livery stable to make sure everything was ready to go, the new horse and buggy hitched and ready. They thanked Jeff. Tray helped Bridget up to the buggy's seat, just getting a little butt squeeze and a smile from her. Tray walked around to the other side to get into the driver's side, he stopped and went back to Blaze and pulled his Henry rifle and came back and laid it under the seat. Stepping up, he clicked up his new horse and started for the general store to pick up his supplies James should have ready. The two pack horses both were ready for the two panniers each. Tray had Blaze and two pack horses tied behind the buggy ready to head home. Just as Tray turned the corner to head to the general store, he could see two men enter the bank with guns drawn, "Bridget, get down, I am turning between these two buildings, the bank is being robbed". Slapping the reins to his horse he jumped into a fast trot going in between the building. Reaching the back, Tray tied off his horse and grabbed the Henry and headed back to the main street.

Tray could see that the robbers were on the way out the front door, he heard Larry tell them to drop their guns. Spud and Dan both opened fire at Larry. Tray could see another man run back behind one of the buildings. It looked like Mayor Dicks left Larry on his own to handle the two shooting at him. Tray called over to Larry, telling him that he was covering this side. Larry got a bullet into one of the men's legs, but he was still moving trying to get his horse. Tray popped up and got two rounds into him and he went down. The other man snapped off a shot at Larry as he was moving to another location trying to get a better angle. Just before Larry reached the cover he went down with a bullet in his shoulder. He was now in the open. The second man was getting ready to start shooting at Larry again. Tray levered a new round into the Henry and fired three quick shots at the last man. Tray could see the puff of dust as the bullets hit him and he went down to stay. Tray ran forward to check if the robbers were both down for good and they were both dead. Moving over to Larry he was able to help him up and get a hanky out to plug the bullet hole and stop the bleeding. Larry looked at Tray asking how did you get into this little gun fight anyway? "I was just going to the hardware store to get loaded so I could go home. When I saw those men running into the bank with guns cocked, I decided to join in to see if I could help stop the bank robbery".

Ronnie and Jake watched the three men enter the bank, then they came rushing out the front shooting at anything that moved. Ronnie hit the first man out in the right shirt pocket. As he was falling Jake got a second bullet into his chest as his gun was falling onto the boardwalk. The second and third robber came out at the same time. Jake was ducking as a bullet took out a chunk of wood just inches from his head. Ronnie got a 44 bullet into each of the other two in two quick shots, they were going down. As the smoke started to clear they could see all three men were down and not moving.

"What the hell", Tray said, "there were two bank robberies going on at the same time".

"Tray, can you help me down to the other bank to see if I can help them stop the robbery"?

"Larry, I think you just need to sit down, and I will go check. Who is down there? Ronnie and Jake Sanders, the question is will Jake be much help in a real gunfight". Tray ran down the street until he could see that three men were down by the bank and Ronnie and Jake were walking over to check on them. Tray called out to Ronnie telling him that Larry was wounded but not too bad. Ronnie came running over and they headed to check on Larry, Tray said he was going to get the doctor he is upstairs two doors further down. Tray ran up the steps to get Doc Bittle's. He was just coming out of his door. "Follow me, we have a gunshot wound for you to take care of out in the street. US Deputy Marshal was shot by one of the bank robbers. Larry was sitting up when Ronnie reached him". "How are you doing Larry"?

"Other than being shot I think just fine". The Doc showed up and took over. With the bleeding stopped, Doc could tell the bullet went just under his collar bone, so it is just one side in and out the other.

"Larry what do you want me to do"?

"Ronnie, get the money back into the banks, and get both sets of paperwork signed by both bankers and the store owners who held the money overnight".

"Larry did you say Tray kept you from being killed"?

"I sure did, he saved my bacon today. Tray killed both men I had hit one in the leg, but he finished him off and killed the other one after I got hit, he did a great job. The second one had me for sure, I was down and without any cover, Ya, he saved me today, that kid is ok".

Doc Bittles took over and told some men to move Larry up to his office and be careful with him. Doris heard the shooting and could see Larry get hit and was falling down. As she ran off the boardwalk, Tray jumped up and shot the man that was getting ready to shoot Larry. By the time she got to Larry he was being moved up to Doc Bittles office. The Doc had Larry's shirt off and was looking at the hole to see if any cloth could be still inside of the wound. It looked like the cloth had parted so the wound would probably not get infected. Larry looked up and asked, "Doris what are you doing up here"?

"Well,", she said, "I saw you get shot from my window so I came to see if I could help".

*

Tray went back to pick up Bridget and his buggy so he could get started home to the ranch. When he reached the buggy, Bridget asked what happened, I heard a lot of shooting. "Well, the bank was being robbed, Larry was trying to get the robbers to give up their guns, they just started shooting, you should have seen the mayor run, I think he messed his pants. Larry got hit in the shoulder, so I shot one man two times and the other three times with my Henry. I think their robbing days are done, let's get over to the general store so we can get started for home. If this stuff keeps going on we will be a week getting home to our new ranch". Tray pulled out a box of 44's then he reloaded his Henry and put it back under the seat and clicked up his horse. "Bridget, we do need to name this horse, I can't just keep saying go or stop. Got any ideas"?

James was just opening when they stopped at the general store. "Tray, do you know about the bank robbery? You know that Larry and

Ronnie talked the two banks to move all of the money to my safe and the other to Mayor Dicks hardware store's safe".

"Shit James, I bet when they ran into an empty bank, they knew trouble was coming and coming fast".

"Tray, the panniers are ready to load I can help you with them". After a few minutes, the two pack horses were loaded and tied down for the trip.

"Say, I like this buggy-it has a lot of room in the boot. I think all of the heavy stuff should fit. James, we want to buy two travel trunks, they will hold all of the new clothes and other loose items".

"Great idea, I have three or four back in the corner on the left, we can take a look. Bridget why don't you come and help pick out the trunks that way you can get just what you want". After checking them out she picked two. "Let's check and see how they fit before we finish the sale". Great idea. "James and Tray each took one out to the buggy to check the fit". Both worked great, "let's just open them up and bring the items out to them to save some time and lifting". Buggy packed, horses tied on the back rail, Bridget in the seat, Tray was getting ready to load up and head home.

When he heard his name being called. Larry and Ronnie were coming up to the buggy a bit slow due to Larry's shoulder wound and his arm in a sling. Larry said, "Tray, what do you want to do with the five horses"? Ronnie said "you forgot one Larry, remember the Big Black that got all of this shit started, six horses then. Also, you have just added about seven thousand dollars to your bank account, all of them have rewards on them with two over fifteen hundred dollars. None of us can claim it, so it all is filed in your name. Bridget, you and Tray need to stop over to either bank and open an account".

"Oh yes, I did forget the money in the gang's saddle bags also goes to you, that was over twenty-five hundred dollars on top of that. I think you just had a new life started but you just got a bunch of cash to go with it. Tray, thanks for saving my life, he had a live one aimed at me when you killed him, thanks again".

Well, Bridget you name the bank, "I think it will be with Smiley Thompson when he came in, he always gave me a big tip". Off to the bank, Tray figured he may just as well deposit a major part of the money he found in the saddle bags of Jarvis Baster. Turning to Bridget, "I don't think we would ever need to work with all of the money we have now".

"Tray, we have a ranch to build and start a horse ranch with lots of fast horses".

With the banking done and buggy loaded, Tray and Bridget started for home, it was quite a sight to see, horse and buggy, Blaze and two pack horses then 6 saddle horses from the dead gang tied head to tail heading out of town. "Tray I have it". "What do you have"? "Shooter is the horse's new name". "Yes Bridget, I think that is a fitting name".

*

Back in Manteca, Ronnie and Jake Sanders had just finished returning all of the money to each bank and watched the signing of the release papers by Smiley and Sam. Mayor Dicks had just showed up as they were finishing and was thanking everyone for a great job saving their money. When outside, the mayor said, "Jake, why don't we go over to your office. I think US Marshal McPherson is waiting there to talk to the two of us". Doris was talking to Larry about coming over to the boarding house so she could take care of him during his recovery time. Ronnie had cleaned all the guns and was listening to Larry put a line of smooth talk on Doris and he was thinking that she was liken every bit of the message.

Mayor Diggs and Jake Sanders walked in with Larry sitting in Jake's chair, Larry wanted to see if Jake reacted in any way. Jake walked in and sat on the corner of his desk when the mayor started talking about the day's events. Mayor was talking to Ronnie and Larry, he was saying that the whole town is in debt to you two, the insight into the problem and by having the money moved to other locations saved our town. If we had lost all of that cash, I don't think we could ever be able to continue being a town. Larry looked at Sheriff Sanders. "What do you think as of now"?

"Deputy McPherson I feel like I have a better idea of just what my job should be. I know that it is my job to protect this town and try to be ahead of trouble. In fact, I need to start thinking and acting like a law man". Larry got up and told Jake to take his chair and that he was going to get some rest and see if Doris could get him well fast. As they were heading out of the door Mayor Dicks said the city will pay all of your expenses during your stay in our town. "Doris, just bring your bill to my office and you will be reimbursed for any food or rooms".

"Thanks Mayor".

Ronnie, Larry and Doris headed to the boarding house. Larry asked Ronnie what his plans were. "I think we have had about enough fun for one trip don't you think? I will stay tonight and head home in the morning. I do have one question can you stay out of trouble if I don't stay with you so I can keep you safe? Larry, I am going down to the telegraph office and send a message to Abby to let them know I am going to be heading home soon".

*

Tray and Bridget had been traveling for four hours and were just reaching a stream with some trees. This looks like a good spot to rest the horses and get a bite to eat. Tray pulled under a large cottonwood and pulled Shooter to a stop. "Bridget, I will get a fire going. Can you get some food going? I will see if I can get this herd of horses watered and, on some grass,". Tray reached up and helped Bridget down from the wagon and let her just slide down his chest, when her feet hit the ground, they greeted each other with a very long kiss. "Bridget, I do feel we are going to have a great life together", He reached around and found a nice place for his hands to rest as he pulled her to him. He could feel her nipples harden on his chest as she moved into him.

"Tray, let me get started with our lunch and you get the horses taken care of. I think we just may need to let the horses graze a bit longer today, I have so many feelings that are going to need to be taken care of and you are the one man who can do that for me".

Tray eased away so he could gather some wood to put in the fire ring, this spot had been used many times before. Wood gathered, fire started, he led each group of horses to water, not bothering to un-tie them. They would stay close with all the good grass along the river. When he finished, he walked over to Bridget to check on lunch, the coffee was on, and some cold meat and bread was ready to eat. Tray could see she had a blanket on the ground. As he reached her the dress kind of fell off of her shoulders and laid on the ground. She asked what menu he wanted first, an hour later they were laying by each other still kind of intertwined talking and watching the horses as they ate. Tray said I sure hope you enjoy this as much as I do. By the way, you are great, I am still trying to get my breath back. Tray got up and went and got two cups of coffee and each a sandwich for their second lunch. Later they got up and reloaded the buggy, gathered the horses, and started on their way to the ranch. Bridget had been asking everything about the ranch and what they should do to make it a home. Tray was talking about ideas of what they could do with the cattle and said we should take Ronnie up on his offer to visit his ranch in Nevada. He told me that he has Indians working for him and are all from the tribe that killed his dad a few years ago. "Bridget, keep an eye on the horses and see if any of them you would like to have as your own to ride".

"Do I need to name all of those six new horses"?

"You can if you want to. Shooter was a great horse that could cover a lot of ground. The only horses that were having a problem keeping up were the two packhorses, Bridget I think I am going to change the packs to two of the new horses, they are all longer legged and can keep up with Shooter easier, I may just turn them loose, they can either follow or stay. That way we can keep up a faster pace".

Early the next morning Tray placed the packsaddles on the new horses and adjusted them to fit, this may just work out better. After a good breakfast, they saddled the other horses and put the extra saddles on top of the supplies in the boot of the buggy. Tray clicked up Shooter into a stiff trot. Looking back, he could see the two new packhorses were able to keep up just fine. Tray had not tied off the two old packhorses, they were coming along behind. I guess they did not want to be alone. Shooter even had a fast walk so during a resting time walking they still were making good time. "Bridget, we should make it home around noon tomorrow at this speed".

The sun was getting high when they came over a tree lined pass. Tray stopped so Bridget could see the ranch layout. "Tray, this is beautiful, and we really own all of this"?

"Yes, we do. Now we need to go and see what condition the ranch and house are in without anyone looking out for this operations". Just under an hour they pulled into the ranch. Tray could see smoke coming out of the chimney for the kitchen, Tray came around to help Bridget down from the buggy seat. As he just got her down, Max the cook came out the front door with a shotgun. Tray said, "Max, put that gun away, go put some coffee on and fix some lunch. This is Bridget, I am going to show her around then I am putting up the horses and buggy". Max helped move all the supplies into the kitchen and got the coffee started. About a half hour later Tray came in to find Bridget and Max talking and making some lunch. "Max, I want you to know that Jarvis is not coming back. He was killed a few weeks ago over in Nevada. Bridget and I are now the owners of this ranch. You need to tell me if you want to stay and still be the cook or move on to someplace else".

"No, Tray I want to stay, Jarvis was always going to either kill me or fire me over nothing. He was crazy I like this ranch and I like you".

"Max, how many of the hands are still working on the ranch"?

"I am cooking for three, one left a few days ago. I think he was not much good-the other men were pushing him hard to do his work, so I think he just rode away to someplace else".

Tray could hear some horses walking into the ranch yard. He got up and walked to the front door to look. "Bridget, come here and take a look at this". The two packhorses were walking over to the corral and waiting to get let in to be with the others, I would never have figured those two would follow along for two days. "Max, what time are the men coming in from the range each day"?

"Just about dark give or take a bit".

Well, it looks like the three who want a job and are doing it without being told. "Who has taken on the job of telling them what job is next and how to do it"?

"That would be Wally Stewart. Pete Tuttle and Bill Franklin just want to work and be told what to do".

"Bridget what did you find? and what do you want to change"? This is your house so do with it just what you feel like.

"I have a few ideas, but I think we need to live here for a week or two then I will have a chance to figure things out". Tray went into the ranch office and looked at the safe, he had no idea what the combination would be. Bridget came in to find Tray looking in the desk draws, looking for that combination. Bridget pulled a picture off the wall and taped to the back was the numbers. "Oh, are you not the smart one".

"I don't know why but it just seemed the right thing to do". Turning the dial he heard the click, turning the lever the door came open. Inside they found the deed to the ranch, some other papers, old letters and a stack of money. This must be the ranch operating money. It was all twenties and ten's, there was just over one thousand dollars in the two stacks. Tray would find out who needed to be paid. After counting the money Tray pulled out the ledger with the ranch records and head count on the cattle. He and Wally would go out in the morning to get an accurate count on the cattle and see if they were still in good condition. He would see if he needed to ship others, he had told Jarvis that they should move more cattle than they did on the last drive he had taken to Manteca and found his wife Bridget.

This combination of color is so Nevada, through this book the Campbell's lived with this as their inspiration for holding the land. (Photo by Robin Travis).

The Tree

CHAPTER 7 **WILLSONS GONE BAD**

Jessie Wilson and his three sons rode out of Carson City just ahead of the posse after robbing the Carson City National Bank and killing two tellers and one customer who was making a deposit. Jessie had been getting more violent with each robbery, this is surprising because he had been a small-time rancher. After his wife died of consumption, things for Jessie Wilson had went downhill over the past two years. He had been a harsh man with a bad temper for years causing many problems in and around the little town of Chico, north of Sacramento. Over the past years Jessie had kept track of the James Barton Gang thinking that just may be the way to make a living for him and his five boys. After hearing that James Barton and his gang are all dead. It may just be the time to replace them with the Wilson Gang. Every town could use a bank robbery to keep them on their toes.

The corn they planted was not growing anything but weeds. Neither he nor his boys except Ellis ever wanted to go out and hoe them or even open the ditch to water their fields. Everything around the ranch needed to be fixed. Jessie had just returned from town with bad news, none of the stores would sell him any more supplies on credit, he had tapped out. Walking in, he found all but one of his boys were just setting at the kitchen table drinking coffee. Ellis came in from the corn field after spending the day weeding with a hoe, his father had just ridden in and tied off his horse and went inside of the house. Ellis led his horse to the barn and unsaddled him then he took time to feed and water his father's and all of his brother's horses. All the boys were just over one year apart. Homer had just turned twenty-six just a few days ago, Simon was twenty-five, Sandy was twenty-three, Raymond was twenty-one and the last of the litter was Ellis at the tender age of eighteen.

"Well boys, we got to get some money now we have no food, no money, no credit. What ya say we go to town and rob all the stores and finish off with the bank.

Ellis piped up and said, "we can't do that, they are friends and neighbors".

Homer turned to Ellis, "shut the hell up. You will do just what we say and like it, that is final. Do not say another word. I am tired of you thinking you are better than the rest of us. We sure have not any friends around here. Pa, that is a good idea. I don't like to work on this farm anyway".

"Anyone other than Ellis's no vote, that don't want to go and pick up some money to live on say so".

Sandy asked can we use some money on whores and beer"?

"Yes, we can", his father replied", "we will get more money in one day than we have seen in over three years".

Homer asked, "just when do we want to get this plan started"?

Now Jessie said, "Listen to this, we will go into town and rob the hardware store and the general store. They should have some cash laying around, Homer, you and I will hit the hardware store at the same time Sandy and Simon will hit the general store, Ellis you hold the horses. Raymond, you go down to the bank to keep an eye out for the law, we put the money in my saddle bags and Ellis you walk the horses down between the hardware building and the bank. Ellis, you will have your rifle ready if anyone comes out to cause us a problem".

"Remember, when we leave this shack, we will never come back so take what you want, the rest will stay here". Ellis walked out to think, he was not going along with this plan. Now how can I get out of this mess my family will be getting me involved with. Ellis came back into the house and picked up a few items then went out and saddled his horse, loaded his saddlebags, bedroll and slicker along with his Henry rifle having only part of a box of cartridges. Ellis just stepped up and rode off into the forest behind the barn. "What am I going to do now? No money, food, job or any idea of how I can make a living". Ellis remembered hearing about a horse trainer who had had one of the Barton gang working for him before they got all killed. I have an idea where he has his ranch so why not ride over there and tell him I need a job.

Jessie came out of the house with his other four sons to see that Ellis's horse was gone with all of his kit. "Well, I guess Ellis the softie ran off, he will never make a man. Load up we need to go to town and get some money. Raymond you are going to hold the horses and we will go get some traveling money, we should be in town just before closing time. Lock the owners in their storerooms, we cannot afford to have any shooting before we hit the bank. Let's ride".

Reaching town, they walked their horses up in front of the hardware store. Jessie and Homer stepped down handing the reins to Raymond, walking down two buildings. Sandy and Simon stepped down and entered the general store. Raymond went around the corner with the horses. He stepped down and pulled his rifle while holding the other four horses. He could see in the bank window; he could tell that they were about ready to close for the day. Jessie and Sandy walked to Jessie's horse and dumped the money from the two other robberies into the saddlebags. Tuning back to the bank all four walked in. They all pulled their guns, and they all rushed the counter. Jessie walked around to the offices and had the bank president and two others come out and get on the floor. "Simon, go over and pull down the shades and put the closed sign in the window".

"Homer, grab all of the teller's money, Sandy, get into the vault, Simon you also get into the vault and help Sandy, I am keeping watch". Just up the street a man came running out of the hardware store with a rifle and started shooting at Raymond holding the horses. Raymond fired back and hit the post above the man's head, he stumbled back into the store, the town was waking up and Jessie hollered "let's get the hell out of here and now". The three men ran out the door with the money sacks and shooting at anything that moved. As they were turning back behind the bank, Simon was hit by the sheriff in the center of his chest, Jessie turned back but could see that he was dead. Simon's horse followed the others out of town with a money bag hooked on the saddle horn.

Down the road after two miles Jessie slowed down to a slow trot to rest the horses. Homer said "we are going to have a problem when it gets light in the morning. Our horses are way too soft. We either need to steal others or we need to lose our tracks. That damn sheriff has a horse that can go all day and night". "OK. Jessie said, "we need to find a camping spot and think this out it will be dark in about two hours. Sandy said, "there is a spring just off to the left of this trail about one hour ride from here, Raymond you ride on ahead and see if you can kill a deer so we will have something to eat". Handing the reins of Simon's horse over to Sandy, he loped forward to get some distance between his father and brothers that were left. Reaching the turnoff to the spring he stepped down pulling his rifle and leading his horse, he eased back into the forest hoping to catch a deer drinking at the spring. It was just the right time, so he felt he had a good chance to make a score. Rifle ready, he could see some movement ahead, oh ya just another few feet he could get a clear shot. Easing his rifle to his shoulder he pulled the trigger. The small buck was down, we will have dinner tonight. Pulling the deer out of the campsite about one hundred yards he cut it up to cool out and ready to cook. Raymond returned to the spring with the meat cut up and wrapped in the deerskin. Jessie rode in so Raymond asked him if anyone had a cooking grate or any other food to go with the deer meat. Jessie said, "I think we moved a bit too quick on this robbing business. We have the money now how do we keep it without getting hanged or shot is the question"?

Homer had a suggestion on how to lose the sheriff and posse. First, we each take a hundred dollars then we swim the river, and we sack our horse's feet and ride right back to Chico. The livery man just brought in eight or ten real nice sixteen hands to seventeen hand horses for a man who is starting to do some racing, he has not picked them up yet. "Great idea let's cook some meat and swim over and head back in the morning".

*

Ellis thinks he found the horse ranch and started up the lane and was greeted by some rather large workhorses. They walked along with him until he reached the ranch yard. As he rode up, he could see a man walking out of the barn. Ellis rode over to him saying, "hi I am Ellis Wilson",

"Step down I am Garry Gee. This is my stable what can I do for you".

"I am looking for a job. I just left home to start my life on my own".

"Why did you leave home"?

"Well, I would not go with my dad and brothers, they are going to start robbing banks, they think they are going to be the next Barton Gang".

"From what I read that line of work didn't work out so good for them in the end". Garry asked, "do you know when they are starting down that outlaw trail"?

"I think they were going to start in Chico today. I would not go with them; I just rode off and I am here if you don't need anyone or not want me because of who my family may end up as robbers that is ok".

"Step down Ellis", we need to get you another horse and we need to ride into Chico and talk to the sheriff now. Ellis, have you had anything to eat today"?

"No sir".

"Get down and we will go fill the hole then we will ride back into town. Is that ok with you"?

"Yes, I will not rob anyone, and I will talk to the sheriff". With a glass of milk and two beef sandwiches down, they went out and saddled two horses and headed into town. When they reached town, Garry went directly to the sheriff's office to tell him Ellis's story.

When they walked in, Sheriff Duward Buford was just getting up to head out of the door. "What do you need Garry"?

"Well, you may want to talk to this young man, he came looking for a job and told me that his father and brothers were going to rob the bank today or tomorrow".

"One thing wrong with that, they also hit the hardware store and the general store about one hour ago. Ellis what is your story, why are you not on the run with them"?

"I won't rob anyone, they called me a sissy and a sorry brother and other things, all I want to do is work and have a good life. After our mother died two years ago, no one would do any work around the farm, my father owed everyone in town money. When he came home without any supplies, he made up his mind to start robbing banks. So, he came home yesterday and told all of us we were going to live like the Barton Gang. I just want to work and have a job".

Sheriff asked, "Ellis do you have any idea what direction they were going in after the bank robbery"?

"They said, they were going to head to the big city for drink and women. Sounds like Sacramento to me but, none of their horses would make it fifty miles. "They all need new shoes and have not been ridden hard for years. My horse is the best and Garry will tell you he is not much of a horse".

"Garry what do you think? He has a good idea of their lack of planning and not having any good horse flesh under them. Garry if you needed some good horses where would you go? You know about everyone around with good horses"?

"Sheriff, are you going to take out a posse tonight Garry said"?

"No, it is too late, we could never follow the tracks in the dark".
"So, we have about three locations that may have some good horses, one is at our livery owner. Wilbur Jefferies just got in eight or ten really good long-legged horses that can run. Over east about thirty miles there is a horse ranch with good stock and southwest about fifty miles there is another horse ranch with racing stock".

"Garry, I think they will never come back to Chico so I think I will send the posse down to that ranch that is fifty miles in the direction they are going in and I will ride over to the ranch you told me about thirty miles from here. Can you write down the directions so I can give it to the deputies, and I will need the other one for me to use".

Garry asked the sheriff if he needed to talk to Ellis '. "No and thanks for the information",

"I do need to tell you, Ellis, that one of your brothers was killed before getting out of town after the bank robbery. I also need you to come with me over to the undertaker to make an identification of the body, someone has to do a positive identification. You are here and he is your brother".

Ellis said, "I will go with you, that is not a thing I want to do but let's go and get it over with". Ellis said that is his brother and what a waste to be killed because he did not want to work for his money.

"Ellis let's go and get a bite to eat and we will go back to the ranch".

"Garry, after this could I still have a job"? "I was not part of any of this, I hope you know that".

When reaching the ranch Garry showed him to the bunk house by the barn.

"Pick a bunk and come up to the house when you get up in the morning and we can talk about work. Ellis was not ready to go to sleep, so he went out to the corral to look at the giant horses Garry had on this ranch.

As the sun was coming up Ellis was up and looked to the house to see if any smoke was coming from the kitchen's smokestack. There was, so he walked up and knocked on the door, he heard come on in, the coffee is on. The big table was empty, but the cook handed him a cup of coffee and said that he would have breakfast soon. Garry walked in about that time saying well I see you are up before breakfast. "Yes, I am up with the sun every day. I had no choice if any work around the farm was to get done, I had to do it".

"Did you take a look around after I came up to the house",

"Yes, I did. You have a great place. Those are some very large horses, but they all wanted to have a rub, so I think they are very gentle but strong".

"Yes, they are. Did you get a hand on the two big studs? They can sometimes be a bit of a challenge for some people".

"Oh Yes, they laid their ears back, but I just turned by back and waited to see what they would do if they were not challenged. In only a few minutes they came over to get a bit of a rub".

"Well, Ellis that information just got you a job, starting pay is thirty dollars a month, can you work for that amount"?

"Garry thanks, "that is more money than I have ever seen in my life.

*

Sheriff Buford had his men on the road at daylight and would ride over to the other ranch after coffee and breakfast, in fact he would go eat now then saddle up and head out. After eating, he went to the livery to pick up his horses. He was saddling his horse Pete, when Wilber walked over asking what was going on with the three robberies in one day. Did he have any leads as to who the gang was. "Yes, I do, and they came from around Chico. It is Jessie Wilson. They have a farm just out of town, but this is interesting. One of the brothers, a kid by the name of Ellis, rode off and would not be involved. He seems like a great kid. By the way keep an eye on those new horses the kid told me that none of the family had a decent horse, so be careful for the next few days". Willis assured him that he would keep a tight watch on his stock.

*

Jessie and his boys swam the river and put bags on the horse's feet and rode back north taking their time, not wanting to get back into Chico until well after dark. They found a spot to watch the Sheriff's office and the livery stable. Around nine that night, they could see Wilber lock up and go back inside by the side door to his room inside the stable. "Do you see that he didn't take all of his new horses inside for the night? I see five of the ten still in the corral just waiting for us".

"Homer, we need to wait another two hours to make sure that Wilber is sound asleep".

They were about to start down to the corral when Wilber walked back out to the corral and made a second walk around. Jessie told his boys after another hour it was time. "Ok, we can ease down to get ready to ease them out of the corral".

"I want each of you to use your rope and we will ride in real slow so not to make any noise, drop the loop over one of the horses and just walk back out slow. We will meet back here and change out your saddles and equipment to the new horse". After another hour they all rode down to the corral and opened the gate letting themselves in, each eased up to the new horses real slow and got their rope over the horse's neck without any noise. After sliding the gates latch back in place, they all headed back. At the exchange point they made fast work changing tack and were on the road leaving their old horses standing as they rode back south heading for Sacramento.

Jessie said "we will ride back to the spring, cook some more of the meat and rest the horses. Then we will hit the trail hard". Later, with the horses having time to eat and get a drink, the Wilson Gang headed south with their dead brother a distant memory. "We need some supplies and soon the deer will be gone, and we will have nothing to eat. We should find a small store along this trail soon; we need to pay and only one of us should go in to make the purchase. We also need a packhorse and a good one when we get into Sacramento or sooner if we can find one", Jessie said. "With five of us eating we will need to pack a bunch of food; we only want to hit a town if we are going to rob the bank until we get some miles away from Chico". "I think Homer should call the shots; I am getting too old. He seems to have a better idea of how we should keep alive. Homer you are the leader from now on, you tell us what to do and we will do it".

"Ok, when we get supplies, we are going to split up then we will meet at a location where we are going to do a robbery. That way we will be harder to follow if the law gets on our trail, is that ok with all of you"?

Jessie asked Homer who was riding with him into purchase supplies when we find a trading post, "no one". You all pick a riding partner. Just before dark Homer could see what looked like a trading post about a mile ahead. "You all circle around to the left and I will meet you on the other side of the trading post down the road about a mile, find a spot and stay there".

Homer rode in at a slow walk seemingly in no hurry. As he reached the hitch rail two men were sitting on a bench by the door. Homer said hello then walked inside. He stepped to the right and let his eyes adjust to the low light in the building. Great, this was a small but well stocked trading post. The owner came up to the counter and asked if he could help him.

"Yes, I do need some supplies for the road, I have a small crew moving a few head of cattle down to Sacramento and we are running short of supplies. Can you help me out"?

"Do you have a list"? Homer asked for a pencil and paper to make his list,

"I will have that on the counter in a few minutes". "Do you have a packhorse for sale? I lost mine in a river crossing yesterday, we lost everything".

"Yes, I do and the packsaddle and panniers that go with him".

"Can I see the horse and gear"?

"Yes, you sure can mister. Come with me I will show you everything. A man was killed a few days ago and I now have both his horse and packhorse for sale".

As he walked out the door, he watched the two men walking around his horse, one started to pull his rifle from the scabbard. "Just what the hell are you doing? Get away from my horse".

The short one of the two men that had been sitting on the bench when Homer rode in was walking from behind Homer's horse, saying "I like your horse. I think he is mine now, you won't need him anymore". He started to pull his pistol when Homer drew and dropped the hammer on two rounds, he divided the two rounds between the two men, both bullets found their right shirt pockets. Homer asked the trading post owner what that was about.

"These two just came in about an hour ago looking for a horse, they didn't have any money so I told them when they get sixty dollars, they could have the other horse but not the packhorse".

"Did they have any horses"?

"Yes, they do, but only one, it's the bay tied out front he said".

"Well, you just became an owner of whatever those two men had. I will still pay you for the packhorse and gear".

"Great I will only charge for the packhorse if that is ok".

"Fine with me, you need to make money and I need a packhorse ready to go". Deal done; Homer was on the road with extra ammunition along with food for the trip. Riding down the road he met the others riding to the trading post to see what the shooting was about.

"Look guys, when I say stay you stay, I don't want you to be seen together. At the trading post a man who had lost his horse yesterday wanted mine so when all is said and done, he is dead, and I have a packhorse and supplies. Now we need to split up some of the supplies so we each have two days' worth of food in each of our saddlebags". After dividing up some of the food the packhorse had a lighter load. Everyone ready, we need to make some miles today. As they rode south Homer dropped back to talk to Jessie about splitting up and then meeting in Sacramento later in a few days. "Dad you take Sandy with you and take the packhorse, ride to just outside of Sacramento, pick a spot along the trail as it joins the river. Raymond and I will delay for the rest of the day before we head your way, I don't want us to be seen riding together".

This is a great landscape showing the rugged features we who live in Nevada have the pleasure of looking at most if not all days. (Photo by Robin Travis).

TWIN PEAKS

CHAPTER 8 **THREAT FROM THE NORTH**

Ronnie had Diamond and Dandy ready to start back to his ranch in Nevada. This trip had been quite eventful after becoming friends with Tray Davis, whose brother he killed only a few months back. Tray had helped eliminate a gang trying to rob the local bank and saved his friend US Deputy Marshal McPherson. Yes, quite a trip. Just before he was ready to ride out of town, he went to the telegraph office to check if he had any new news from home. Ronnie asked the operator if he had any replies for him.

"No, you are with Marshal McPherson aren't you"?

"Yes, I am". "I have two telegrams for him, can you deliver them to him for me"?

"Yes, I can do that I am heading that way now", Ronnie walked back down to the boarding house only to find Larry and Doris talking in the sitting room, kind of close, kind of side by each as they would say. "Larry, you have to get better soon, looks like you have some trouble heading your way", handing him the telegrams for him to read.

US Marshal Johnson Sacramento to Deputy US Marshal Larry McPherson

New gang heading south from Chico toward Sacramento.

Farmers turned to bank robbers. I think they killed one man at a trading post south of Chico.

Update your condition. How soon can you travel?

US Marshal Johnson Sacramento.

Second telegram

US Marshal Johnson Sacramento to Deputy US Marshal Larry McPherson

I was on a two-day trip, Sacramento National Bank, bank president wounded, one teller killed, and one local deputy sheriff killed.

Sheriff Buford from Chico following they have a two-day lead.

US Marshal Johnson Sacramento

"Ronnie, I think I should be ready to travel in another two days, but I will check with Doc Bittles later today. What is your idea on which way do you think this new gang will go"?

"With Sheriff Buford following them you should get updates every few days. I think your boss will also join in the pursuit. Most gangs are lazy and want to spend some of the money at the first town they come to. I think they will land in Carson City in about one week to blow off some steam".

"Ronnie, I need to ask you about waiting two days and then ride to Carson City with me, I would also like to make you a Deputy Marshal, I am going to need some help on this as you can see".

"Well Larry, I just may do that. Let me go back down to the telegraph office and get everyone informed as to our plans".

"Ronnie, raise your right hand and say I will" Larry said. "When you go to the telegraph office stop by the stable and get a badge from my saddlebags, pin it on. You are now a real-live, US Deputy Marshal Ronnie Campbell".

Telegram sent, Ronnie went over to the stables, found the badge and pined it on, then went to check on Rob, Steal and Larry's pack horse Cash, along with Diamond and Dandy. After going over all five horses he found that Cash needed new shoes, he asked if the blacksmith could have them ready to travel in two days. Ronnie found a worktable at the stable and started cleaning all the guns before they headed for Carson City.

Larry and Doris were enjoying their time alone, now the talk turned to Larry having to head to Carson City. Doris suggested that she could doctor him better in bed, if he felt it could help his recovery. So, the afternoon was spent with Doris taking care of Larry and they both seemed to get some benefit. Late in the afternoon Larry and Doris walked over to Doc Bittles to see how he was doing with his recovery. "Doc, do you think I could ride in two days? I have some real bad men heading to Carson City and I need to be there when they arrive".

"Yes, I think you can, it looks like Doris has been a great help in your healing, I would like to see you before you ride out just to make sure everything is ok". As they walked from Bittles office

Doris said, "I know everything is working just fine". "Let's go find Ronnie and get some food".

"I need the energy for my recovery don't you think Doris"?

Ronnie had finished cleaning and checking all the guns, then asking Jeff if he would re-lock the tack room, with all the guns back in storage. Ronnie was just going to find Larry to see if he was ready to eat. Walking out of the stable he could see Larry with Doris on his arm heading his way.

Larry said, "Let's eat". They all turned to cross the street and walked into the restaurant, Wanda greeted them, "grab any seat". Larry walked to the back wall and sat down with Doris and Ronnie. Wanda asked, "Coffee all around"? "That will be fine, and what is the special today"? "We got in some pork chops today with mashed potatoes, carrots and cake". Larry looked around and they all would take the special.

"Well Larry, I checked all of the horses and guns, we only had one small problem and had to re-shoe Cash, he will be ready late today. Now it is all up to you and the Doc to tell us when we can head for Carson City".

"Ronnie, I got in some exercise today just to check out the shoulder, in two days we can get on the trail". Doris was feeling some heat rise so she had her head down trying to keep the color from showing. "If I sleep late and take a nap in the afternoon, I should be rested up enough for the trip". Doris was not saying anything, just drinking her coffee.

Dinner was served in short order. Wanda came back and took a seat, she wanted to get to know Doris better. They started talking about Manteca and other girl things. Wanda was new to town she wanted to get to know everything and everybody. The door opened and two young men came in taking seats by the window. Wanda went over to take their order. She could tell that they both had been drinking. When she reached the table, she asked if they would like some coffee to start. One of the men reached out and pulled Wanda into his lap saying "how about I just take you. I think you would do just fine". Wanda was trying to get up, but she was being held tight. She felt the man release her and then there was a large crash and a solid thud, as she is turning around after being released by the drunk, she could see the man on the floor and was starting to pull his pistol. Ronnie had already pulled his pistol and it was pointing right between his eyes. "Go ahead and finish your draw you dumb ass". The man let the pistol drop back into his holster, Ronnie told him to ease the gun out with two fingers and do it slowly.

"Now roll over and get on your hands and knees". After doing that Ronnie instructed him to crawl out the door and do not get up. As he cleared the door, Ronnie kicked him in the ass, sending him out into the street on his face. Larry had his gun on the second man, he had his hands on top of the table looking into Larry's 44 pistol. Larry indicated with his pistol to get down on the floor with his partner and crawl out of the restaurant. Ronnie gathered the guns and the two men on their hands and knees in the middle of the street. Larry said, "Ronnie, mister new US Marshal why don't you take them down and see if Jake can figure out what to do with them".

Jake looked out his door and could see Ronnie walking behind two men crawling toward the jail, this should be interesting. "Need any help Marshal Campbell"?

"No, we are moving along just fine, you may want to unlock a cell for these two". With the two men in jail, Jake and Ronnie went over the charges facing the two men.

Jake asked, "who are they Ronnie"?

"I have no idea, but they came close to getting dead. The one in the checkered shirt grabbed Wanda Smart and told her that she was on his menu, so I went over and persuaded him to let her get off his lap. He can be charged with trying to kill a Deputy US Marshal with the name of Ronnie Campbell".

"When did you get a badge"?

"About fifteen minutes ago, I am protecting Larry. We are going after a new outlaw gang we think are heading for Carson City, seeing Larry is kind of laid up, he asked me to come along for the ride".

"Protecting me hell, I asked you only because you do seem to like shooting people and are quite good at it, I would say, from riding with you a few times".

Jake asked. What do you want me to do with the two in my cell"?

"If it were me, I would look for any reward posters then talk to Wanda and see if she wants to press charges. I feel that you may also have a real man to man talk with them boys, if they check out ok to not having any record. They do need to change their ways; it is a good time for them to take a good look at how close they came to being dead. Ronnie added if that one who tried to pull iron on me had gotten his gun about another inch out of his holster he was going to die. You need to explain that to him".

"Larry let's go back over to check on Wanda, she may still be some upset by all of the ruckus those two dumb ass kids caused". Walking in, they could see Wanda, she was working hard to get all the people's orders and deliver others their food. She looked over and mouthed I am ok, so they walked out and headed to the telegraph office. Larry was telling Ronnie that after checking for any messages he was going to head back to the boarding house and take a nap. Ronnie looked over to Larry with a smile, "so you say". "I have just been shot and need extra sleep". Ronnie came back with, "so you say". "Go and get your nap over, I am going to take Diamond out for a little ride to take a bit of edge off him and check on some of the local farms to see what they are growing in their fields; I may get some ideas for my ranch".

Ronnie walked over to the livery stable to pick up Diamond. He was greeted by Jeff, "what can I do for you today Mr. Campbell"?

"I am going out for a ride and will need some of my equipment out of the storage room".

"No problem, I will unlock the door for you, when done I will relock the storage room". Great, Ronnie walked with Jeff and pulled out his saddle with his rifle and shotgun in the scabbards. When he got close, Diamond nickered a greeting. Undoing his halter Ronnie walked out to an open place to brush him before saddling up for his ride. Diamond followed him out and stopped, waiting for Ronnie to saddle him. Dandy tried to follow but was tied with a lead rope and halter. He let it be known that he wanted to go also. Ronnie walked back and untied the lead rope throwing it over his back, Dandy followed him back to be with Diamond. With both horses brushed and Diamond saddled, they headed out of town heading to the river a few miles south of town. Just south of town Diamond kept pulling on the bit, he wanted to run. Pulling Diamond up to a stop, Dandy walked up beside them, Ronnie undid the lead rope so Dandy could run free. After putting the lead rope in one of his saddlebags he let Diamond have his head. With both horses running hard, they made the river in short order. Ronnie was surprised to see Dandy with his nose even with his right leg. Ronnie had never let Dandy have his head for a flat-out gallop, this horse must be faster than he thinks. Dandy did run down the outlaw Joe Harding with little problem, he knew this horse can run longer than Diamond, but he had never raced him.

Ronnie reached the river and turned downstream letting the horses catch their wind, it had been about a two-mile run, the river has cottonwoods providing a great cover, so he had a cool ride. After about a mile Ronnie could see what was left from a campsite. Looking around, this must have been the site Don Beal's and his gang had used while waiting on Willis to show up with his scouting report on the banks. Willis won the race into hell but by only ten or so hours. It was a pleasure to have helped them along, better place to live with them removed. Turning back, the sun was getting low when he rode back into the livery, taking another hour brushing both horses. He went to see if he could find Larry and see if he got a restful nap. Ronnie felt that he may have had a bit of medical attention provided by Doris, having your bandages changed by a pretty woman is not all that bad.

Ronnie was up early getting Dandy and Cash packed. With Diamond, Robb and Steal saddled, he paid the balance to Jeff and walked over to the restaurant to meet Larry and Doris for breakfast. Wanda Smart delivered his coffee with a smile and Ronnie asked her if she was ok after the problem with the two young men. "Yes, I am ok.

Jake marched them over to tell me they were sorry and would not ever do that again. Did you get any story on where they worked or were they just passing through"?

"Yes, I did, they work on a ranch north of here, having just went to work for this ranch and having been paid, they came into town to have a good time. I think they will be two changed up young men, the one you about shot was ready to cry as he was making his apology. You scared him about to death. Jake let them go this morning with the assurance they would never do that again. Jake said if he ever had a problem like this again, he would shoot them himself".

The door opened, Doris and Larry came in taking a seat with Ronnie, "Well Doris, do you think this sorry excuse of a US Marshal is ok for a little ride to Carson City"?

"Yes, I do. The bullet holes are both looking really good. He will need to have the stitches removed when you get to Carson City". Giving Wanda their order, she went back to give it to the cook and brought three cups of coffee back with her. Larry asked Wanda how she liked being a part owner of a restaurant. "You know that Bridget just gave me her half ownership, she saved my life. I was out of money when I walked in to ask her for a job, my next option was going to be working in a saloon. I do not know how to ever repay her, but I hope to be able to help someone else later on. Let me go and pick up your food so you two can get on the trail".

Larry walked Doris back to her boarding house and picked up his bedroll and rifle from his room. Doris was sad to see Larry leave, she was quite fond of him. He came down with his stuff and with a kiss he opened the door and walked down to the waiting horses.

"Well, Larry. I do feel that you will be missed by Doris". Larry stepped up and they turned northeast to pick up a trail over the mountains to Carson City. "Larry how is your shoulder? Do you have much pain? You pick the speed we travel I am good with whatever you want to ride at". They pushed their horses hard till about noon before stopping at a stream with trees for shade and plenty of grass for the horses. They pulled up, loosened the cinches on the horses, and led them to water for a short drink. After half an hour Ronnie took the horses back down to water, they had cooled down enough so they could drink without hurting them".

"Larry are you about ready to get on the trail".

"Yes".

"Ok let's do it, we have a long way to go yet today". Ronnie cinched up all the horses and with Larry back aboard they headed northeast to meet the trail over the mountains, this trail is twenty-five miles south of the Pony Express Trail that Ronnie and Larry had ridden only a few years ago. Ronnie asked if they should stop short of the small village of Jackson or hole up at the river just up the trail about five miles.

"Ronnie, I think I could use an early campsite today, I am about done".

"OK, we need to just let the horses walk along for a while, we won't need to hurry, we have plenty of light. I feel like a decent meal today, you just come along slow, and I am going to see if I can find a couple of rabbits for dinner. There is a shallow crossing ahead so just cross over and we can set up camp on the other side, I will see you there in an hour or so, no hurry".

Ronnie had cantered to the river and after crossing, he started to look for dinner. He killed two rabbits just after he crossed over and had a fire started when Larry came in with all the horses. Larry eased himself out of the saddle and found a fallen tree to sit on as Ronnie removed the packs and saddles from all the horses. "Damn Ronnie, you do make a real nice horse wrangler, I may just like to keep you around. I hope you can cook them rabbits as well as you can take care of a string of horses".

"No worry Larry, you will get your turn one of these days I have a feeling". Ronnie had to wake Larry up when the rabbits were finished cooking, he had been able to get his bedroll laid out before taking a nap.

The next day with breakfast over and cleaned up they started the ride to Jackson. Riding over a hill, the town came into view. Jackson had some mining going on so as they rode into the town the hammer mills were working away. They found the trail that would take them over the mountains to Genoa. Carson City is twenty of thirty miles to the north, they should get over the mountain late tonight if Larry can handle the saddle time. Ronnie had picked up lumber from Genoa a few years before. They came out of the mountains along the Carson River. Turning north following the wagon road they could see the lights in Genoa. Ronnie hoped to find a hotel and livery in town. Larry needed a good rest in a bed along with some good food. They did find a hotel, so Larry went and got rooms and Ronnie went to take care of the horses and see if they could secure their supplies at the livery. The livery doors were closed. After a bit one of the double doors opened and a man stepped out asking if he could be of help.

"Need to stable five horses for the night".

"Ok. I am Will Jasper, come on in and we will get them stabled for tonight". Will the owner, helped Ronnie with un-saddling of the horses.

"Will, do you have a secure location for all of the gear"?

"Yes, I do. This place is locked up tight every night. The storeroom has a lock and I have the only key".

"Great, we can just unload everything in there to save time". Ronnie walked over to each horse and removed the saddle along with bedrolls and rifles. "How much per horse"? Ronnie asked.

"One dollar that includes grain". Ronnie gave him a ten-dollar gold piece".

"We will settle up in the morning".

"Thanks" Will said as Ronnie walked out with two rifles heading for the hotel. Reaching the hotel, he found they did have a restaurant. Walking in, he found Larry sitting with a cup of coffee and talking to a pretty girl sitting at his table.

"Ronnie this is Rebecca Jensen. She has just arrived in the west after over a year of traveling all the way from Denmark, she just got this job working at the hotel and restaurant".

"Great to meet you Rebecca, I hope you find what you were looking for". After shaking Ronnie's hand, she got up and asked if he wanted coffee.

"Yes, I would". Turning she said I will be back with your coffee and take your order. "Well Larry, did she tell what the special was"?

"No". Rebecca came back with the coffee and told them that the special was so they both ordered the special, steak and potatoes, hard to hurt that food. They worked on their coffee waiting on their meal to come.

Larry asked Rebecca why are you in Genoa when Carson City should offer a better chance for jobs. "Well, I got lucky with this job, I had a job in Carson City, but some men came into the restaurant I was working in and caused me a lot of problems. There were the father and three of his sons, they look like outlaws to me, so I packed and got a ride down to Genoa".

Larry asked, "do you know any of their names by chance"?

"Yes, I do, the father is Jessie Wilson, his sons are Homer, Sandy, and Raymond. Homer I think is the boss the others seem to listen to him".

"Thanks Rebecca that is a big help, do you know when they arrived in Carson City"?

"About two days ago".

"Larry did you get us a room yet"?

"Yes". We both have a view of the street on the second floor, rooms two and four. I have dropped off my rifle and bedroll in room two.

"Well Larry, what is your plan to deal with this new gang"?

Ronnie, "I think we are in a good spot to get them locked up within a day or two. I know that we should have some help coming in the next few days from the Boss".

"We should have a telegram waiting for me in the morning or I will send one telling my boss we are in position, waiting on further instructions. Here comes the food, let's work on it and then hit the bed for tonight".

This is another great picture showing the stream flowing and the mountains in the background. How many times I have come around a corner only to find a picture waiting to be taken. (Photo by Robin Travis).

PICTURE WAITING TO BE TAKEN

CHAPTER 9 **RIDE TO CARSON CITY**

Homer rode over to Raymond. "We will ride until we find a campground and we will spend the night". They found a good spot down the road five miles. Homer rode in to check if they had water and some grass for the horses. "This camp site has been used many times, it even has a rock fire ring ready to use, Raymond you get the fire going and I will take care of the horses, check in my saddle bags, I have some cooked meat and biscuits for dinner. Get the coffee on first thing". Raymond got the fire started and placed one of their cooking grates on the rocks at the edge of the fire pit, then he walked down to the stream to fill their two small coffee pots. With the water boiling, Raymond added some coffee to each pot. After a bit he pulled them back from the fire and lifted the lids and dropped some cold water to settle the grounds. "Coffee is ready Homer and I have some meat and biscuits set out".

Raymond asked Homer, "are we going to rob another bank when we get into Sacramento or move on south"?

"Yes, we will hit another bank then make a run to Carson City so we can spend some of the cash we have now. Raymond you can now have some women and drinking money".

"I have never been with any women".

"Well, you will get your chance when we hit Carson City, Homer said".

"Raymond, we should catch up to Pa and Sandy late tomorrow just outside of Sacramento. They are going to make camp along the river just off the wagon road. Raymond, go down and water the horses before we call it a night". After leading the horses down to the river, he came back and moved the picket pins over to better grass for the night.

Cold meat and a biscuit washed down with warm water from their canteens was breakfast. They were off heading south to meet with their father and brother. Raymond was thinking, why had his father and brothers not ever mentioned Simon or Ellis? His father Jessie never even looked back at Simon when he was shot during the bank robbery, Ellis he could understand because he had just ridden off and never said a thing, except that he was not going to rob anyone the night before he rode off in the morning, I should have gone with him, Raymond was thinking. "Homer is going to kill me I think". As the day passed the sun got hotter and hotter every mile they rode. At mid-day Homer found a spot with some shade and water so he eased off the wagon road to let the horses graze for a bit and get them a drink. After an hour they were back on the road, some wagon traffic was starting to come by from the direction of Sacramento. The sun was sinking when Homer said, "let's start looking for Pa and Sandy, they should be along this road soon I can see a bridge over the river just ahead".

Just before dark they found the camp and rode in and unsaddled their horses and went to the fire.

"Well pa, did things go ok on the ride down"?

"Yes, we made it just fine".

"Pa, you and I will ride into town in the morning, we will each ride in alone and find the law office and bank locations". "Pa, you watch one bank, and I will check out another one, see if the law walks or rides around checking on their town. We will meet back here and figure which bank we want to hit tomorrow, we will hit the bank just as it opens for business. Raymond and Sandy, I want you to steal four horses. You bring them back here tomorrow. Sandy you will take our horses south of town about five miles and I want you to keep hidden along the river. We will ride hard to you, then change horses and turn the stolen horses lose they will just return back to the owners, it would not be a good idea to be caught riding any stolen horses. This should get us a jump on the law".

The next day Jessie and Homer rode into town to check out two of the banks in Sacramento. Homer wanted to find two that were smaller and the furthest from the sheriff's office. After riding through the main part of Sacramento, Jessie and Homer both found a bank that looked like it could be handled by two men. Sitting around the fire later they talked over the two banks and settled on the smaller bank called the Cattleman's Bank on the south side of town. It was also the furthest from the sheriff's office that was in the center of town. Raymond and Sandy had picked up four horses so each would have a fresh horse waiting just south of town.

"Raymond, you will hold the horses during the robbery".

"No, I won't do that Homer". Have Sandy hold the horses, I will take the horses south to our meeting place".

"Sandy are you good with that"?

"Yes",

"Raymond you just keep riding south about five or six miles and you have your horse ready so when we get there you can help us get our saddles changed faster and be on the trail to Carson City and spend some of this money we have".

The Wilson Gang was ready and waiting between two buildings watching for the bank president to unlock the front doors. "As he walked down the wooden walkway leading to the bank Homer and Jessie waited until he turned his back to them. With the key in the lock, he could see two men coming up behind him by the reflection in the window. He started to make a quick getaway, but Homer had his gun in his back, so he finished unlocking and was forced into the bank. Jessie pulled the man back to the safe ordering him to unlock it. He missed the combination two times but finally got it opened. Jessie dropped him by smashing the pistol on the back of his head.

Sandy could see the robbery in progress through the windows. When he could see Homer and his pa move to the front of the bank, Sandy walked the horses over to the bank's front doors to be ready when his father and brother came out the door. The bank president regained consciousness. Getting to his feet, he staggered around the counter grabbing his pistol. He fired thought the glass window in the bank's front door at the robbers. Homer returned fire and hit him two times in the chest killing him. The gang turned their horses between two buildings, rode south out of town at a hard gallop, knowing they had fresh horses just a few miles south.

Homer had the money bags on his horse as they rode south keeping his horse at a gallop for about two miles before dropping back to a slow trot. Jessie rode up beside him,

"Homer we need to give these horses a break, let them walk for a mile or so".

"Look Pa we need distance from Sacramento, or we will be looking out of a jail cell".

"OK. If we kill these horses, we will also be looking out of the jail cell".

Homer pulled his horse back to a walk for about a half hour to allow the horses to recover, he knew that his father was right, Homer kept going from a fast trot to a slow trot trying to cover ground but not kill these horses before reaching the exchange. Raymond was waiting with their horses. With a fast exchange they were back on the road. They found a feeder stream in late afternoon. They rode upstream to cover their tracks until they could find some cover to make camp. Homer told Raymond to "get a fire going and start cooking some food", "Sandy, you pull the saddles, get them a small drink and get them on the grass". "Put the hobbles on all of the horses then give them all a rubdown with dry grass".

Homer said, "Pa, I need to walk out to the trail and check for any other traffic heading east".

"Go ahead I will come along, Homer". Walking out to the point that overlooked the trail they sat down to go over what they would do next". "Pa, we are going to just ride over to Carson City, we can be there in three days or less if we push the horses". There is a small mining town ahead and we should be able to get they're by late this afternoon, we all need to get a hotel room and a good meal". With the horses in a livery stable, they can have good hay and some grain to help them recover from the hard riding we have put them through. They will be ready to climb the mountains tomorrow heading for Carson City.

"Homer, we are going to need to keep an eye on Sandy. He wants some whisky and a woman; he is going to cause us a lot of trouble. I think he will also have a big mouth when he gets drinking".

"Pa, did you see Raymond when I had to shoot the bank president, he is about as soft as Ellis".

"Yes, I did, he is soft. We are going to have to do something with him. Sandy is going to be a problem with any women we come close to, he has a problem I think".

The sun was just getting low when the Wilsons rode into Placerville. "Pa, you take Sandy and Raymond with you and get us four rooms at the hotel. I will get the horses taken care of for the night. We will meet at the restaurant just down the street on the left in a half hour, bring the room keys. After we eat, I want a drink. This will give us a chance to keep an eye on Sandy". All four men reached the restaurant. After their food was ordered the waitress came back with the coffee pot and cups. When she walked up to the table Sandy reached out and ran his hand up her leg. She jumped back spilling the pot of coffee all over Sandy and the table. Homer yelled at him, and Jessie told him to keep his hands on the table. Raymond had picked up the coffee pot and took it over to the waitress and apologized to her and told her he would pick up the food when it was ready.

Sandy looked at his father and brothers saying, "she is just a waitress, and we will give her a big tip".

Homer was really mad, "Sandy, are you trying to get us tossed in jail for messing with this girl in the only restaurant in town, I will tell you this if we get in trouble, the law will place us at the bank robbery and we will all hang, do you hear me"? With the meal finished Raymond took the money to the girl for their meals and left a very large tip saying, how sorry he is, and it will never happen again.

Homer said, "we are going to the hotel and get an early start in the morning". In the morning they went to get breakfast at the same restaurant and there was only the owner cooking and serving. Homer sent Raymond over to the stable to get the livery man to get their horses saddled and ready to go. After eating they found the horses tied outside of the double doors waiting, the boarding fee was paid when they left the horses yesterday.

Two hard days ride they were in Carson City with hotel rooms for three days. Homer had given one hundred dollars to his father and each of his brothers. They found a restaurant to eat after getting the horses stabled and each a hotel room.

Homer told Sandy to keep his hands to himself, we don't want any law problems. Walking in they were greeted by a young lady who said,

"I am Rebecca find a seat and I will bring you your coffee". She picked up a fresh pot to deliver to the table, the cups were on the table. When she reached the table one of the men brushed her leg. With the food order in she decided to deliver the food on the other side of the table. Two trips back she had the food delivered with no problem.

When she went back to pick up the plates, she had learned that the problem one was called Sandy, it matched his hair. As she reached for his plate, he ran his hand up her leg. The one called Homer told him to cut it out and leave the girl alone, go down to the saloon and pay for a girl. After Raymond paid and left a very large tip, then the four headed down to get a drink. After two drinks Sandy went upstairs with a girl.

Homer said that he was going to get some sleep. "Are you two coming or staying for a while"?

"We are coming to the hotel too". Sandy was feeling good after having his first time with a woman. As he walked out of the saloon, he could see the lights going out at the restaurant, thinking to himself, I feel like a second go at a woman and Rebecca is going to be my next.

Waiting in a shadow for Rebecca to come out he was feeling really alive, he had money to spend for the first time in his life and just may have a woman for the second time in one day. Rebecca stepped out onto the boardwalk, turning to go to the boarding house. Sandy was standing not two feet from her.

Sandy said, "I have money and I want you to go to my hotel room and we will have some fun". Rebecca looked at him and she could see one of the town's Sheriff's. Randal Beets was walking their way.

She called out to him saying would you walk me home. Randal walked her way and Sandy turned and walked off the other way.

Randal asked was that man giving you trouble.

"I don't know, but he was a problem today and I was kind of scared, so thanks". Randal walked her to the boarding house and left her at the door. Rebecca thanked Randal and closed the door.

The Wilsons all eat breakfast again at the restaurant but only the cook was serving. "OK. Look we need to have some fun but don't cause any problems, why don't we go over to the saloon and play some cards and relax for the day". Sandy said, "I will join you a bit later". Sandy had seen a gunsmith's sign when they rode into town, he wanted to purchase a two-shot derringer to keep in his shirt pocket. Ten dollars later he walked out with his new secret weapon. After playing cards for most of the morning, Raymond asked Homer if he could have some of the money. He wanted to go back home; this is not the way I want to live my life. Look, "just give me another one hundred dollars and I will be out of your hair I am of no use to you".

"Ok". Take this and get away from us, you are too soft, you are just like Ellis, don't ever try to come back, you don't have any place with this family".

Raymond picked up the money and walked back to the hotel and picked up his bed roll and slicker in one hand, then reached for his rifle, walked to the livery and headed back home. He would go see Sheriff Buford and give himself up. Anything would be better than a life as a robber and murderer.

Later in the day Sandy figured he would make another try for Rebecca, he knew she would do anything for money, and he had some to spend. Just after noon Sandy opened the door to the restaurant and seeing Rebecca, he found a seat. Rebecca delivered his coffee and took his order. When returning with his food he looked around and the room was empty, Rebecca placed the food on the table as far away from Sandy as she could. Looking at Rebecca he said, "How much do you want to spend the night with me? I will pay you well; I will be waiting when you get off tonight. Figure out how much it will cost me"? Sandy finished his meal and left a large tip on the table; Rebecca went into the kitchen and told the owner Clyde Schmidt she had to leave town. "The man who was just in here eating is going to try to rape me tonight. I need to get out of town".

Clyde told her to go to Genoa where his friend would put her to work, it is the only restaurant there.

"Clyde, I have a friend that needs a job, her name is Betty Taylor I will have her work for me starting tonight if that is ok".

"Great, have her come in any time".

CHAPTER 10 **THE TAKE DOWN**

Larry and Ronnie were back at the restaurant early to eat and get a description of the men who caused Rebecca all of the trouble in Carson City. After placing their order, Rebecca had their hot coffee on the table,

US Deputy McPherson asked her to sit down and tell them the whole story.

"OK, I think the four are all family, Jessie Wilson is the father, but Homer is the leader, Raymond is kind of polite and he is the only nice one of the four. Sandy was my problem, he was trying to get his hand up my dress any time I got close, he also was outside when I got off work one night". "What do they look like, and do they have any type of scars or other way of identifying them"? "Sandy is easy to spot he has light brown hair and it is shoulder length, he is the only one with a light brown hat with a snakeskin hat band. Jessie is hawk faced with a crooked nose and dark brown hair", Homer is a bit on the heavy side. He is about six feet tall; the others are shorter. Homer also has a small hidden pistol under his coat I saw it one time. "Raymond also has dark brown hair, and it is shoulder length like Sandy".

"What about their horses, Larry asked"?

"Three are brown and look about the same but Homer rides a black with one white stocking on the right front. Larry, I don't know much about horses, but these four are larger than most I see around town, all four are real pretty to look at".

*

Sheriff Duward Buford had been on the road for a few days. After returning he found out the Wilsons did indeed return and steal four of the best horses in the area. He now had a problem because the stolen horses were as fast or faster than Sheriff Buford's horse Pete. When Duward returned to find the horses missing, livery owner Wilber Jeffries was really hot about having four of his best horses stolen.

"They have three bays and one black with a white stocking on his right front", Wilber offered. Durward asked Wilber if he would check Pete's shoes and pick out a second horse for a packhorse with packsaddle and panniers. "I will need to be on the road in two hours". Durward made a quick stop at the store for supplies, asking for them to be ready in one hour so he could get on the road.

Back in his office he pulled one Greener and one of his new Winchester 66 45-90 express rifles, this rifle had a long range with stopping power. Reaching under the desk he pulled two boxes of ammunition for both weapons. "Alan you are in charge until I get back, this chase could take over a month. I will send updates from every town with a telegraph". Durward walked back down to the stable to check on the progress. Wilber was just pulling two of his new horses that had not been stolen. Wilber figured with better horses the Sheriff had under him the better chance he would get the four that had been stolen back.

"Sheriff, I want you to take the best so you can really cover ground, trade them out with Pete as you see fit, either of the two will carry the pack saddle so ride hard and kill those damn Wilsons. Shoot Jessie twice just for me, he owes me money but just put two of those 45-90 rounds into him".

"Wilber, I will try to bring them back in if possible but if they shoot at me, I will follow your directions as best as I can. How are the shoes on Pete"?

"They are just fine".

"Help me get this pack saddle on this big boy and you can load up and get on the road. I am going to pick up some clothes at the house and I will come back and pick up the horses then load my supplies at the general store". After picking up the horses he rode over to the general store to pick up the supplies he had ordered. Jake Tim's had everything setting on the counter ready to be packed. "Jake how much money did they get from you"?

"I only had about one hundred in the drawer but that hurts.

"Bill the hundred to the city and help me get this stuff into the panniers". Duward stepped up, tying the lead rope to his saddle horn and headed to Sacramento to check with US Marshal Johnson. He was leading two extra horses, one with a saddle and the other with panniers with supplies.

Today would be a short day due to the late start but he was making great time by cantering and trotting to save the horses. Duward was also changing between two horses to keep them fresh, the pack horse was not loaded very heavy, so he was doing fine, Duward rode until dark and made a cold camp to save time. The campsite had water and grass for the three horses. After they were taking care of, he built a small fire to just make coffee. He had some cold meat and biscuits. After he finished, he watered the horses one more time then rolled up and went to sleep for the night.

With some light showing in the east, he stirred the fire and put the coffee on. Taking each horse to water, he started saddling Wolf, "I like that name, we are on the hunt, the packhorse was ready for the day's ride". Duward downed two biscuits and some meat leftover from yesterday. Two cups of coffee down, he dumped the rest on the fire and kicking dirt over the coals, he stepped up on Wolf and headed south to Sacramento.

Reaching Sacramento, he rode to midtown to find US Marshal Johnson, finding the office across from the largest bank in town. Walking up, he was greeted by a Deputy Marshal asking what he could do for him. "I am looking for Marshal Johnson, is he in"?

"Yes, but he is getting ready to ride out after four bank robbers so make it quick". The Deputy took Duward back to Johnson's office. The door was open, so he introduced himself to Marshal Johnson. "How can I help you Sheriff"?

"I am after four bank robbers. They robbed the bank in Chico. I am Sheriff Duward Buford from Chico".

"Well, we may well be after the same four", Johnson said. "Duward, let's go get something to eat and we can talk over what to do".

"Ok. I have my horses out front, we can ride over to the restaurant I will meet you out front. "When Duward got to his horses

Marshal Johnson was coming around the corner of the building. I will follow you. We will just ride down the street a block or two".

Reaching the restaurant, both men tied the horses to the hitch rail. Stepping up to the door Johnson open it and walked in, the owner greeted them and told them to grab a seat. Bringing coffee to the table, she asked if they wanted the special of the day. Both took the special and turned the conversation to the bank robbery in Chico. Duward gave the information about the robbery and the two stores, later including the killing of Simon Wilson.

"You know they were local farmers with a bad habit of not paying their bills, they rode in town late in the day and pulled iron and started taking money".

Marshal Johnson asked if anyone was killed or hurt at the stores or bank.

"No, they did come back and steal four real good horses from the livery, my two deputies rode to two ranches that had some racing stock and I rode over to another town to check on another horse ranch. They rode back to Chico and stole the four horses during the night, they headed south toward Sacramento, so here I am".

With the meal on the table, they started to do some damage to it. After eating Marshal Johnson said, "Why don't you ride with me? I have my pack horse ready also with an extra mount, my deputy's loading my long guns and greener as we eat".

"Ok, Let's ride back and pick up my horses and head south".

US Marshal Johnson turned and started to tell the Sheriff about the robbery of a small cattleman's bank in the south part of town. "They killed the bank president before riding hard south. I figured when robbers ride that hard, they must have extra horses stashed about six to ten miles so we will about kill our horses in the chase. They only have about five or six hours on us, so we will just keep a nice trot, if I know them, they will try to push their horses even with the lead. I think that they will ride over to Carson City to spend their money, or I should say other people's money. Duward the funny thing is that they never even tried to cover their tracks or direction they are going, we are going to take a chance and head directly to Carson City. Larry McPherson is one of my deputies who used to ride for the Pony Express, he showed me the fastest route over the mountains to Carson City. Using this trail, we will make up some time, closing the gap".

My Deputy McPherson is also heading to Carson City with Ronnie Campbell who Larry McPherson deputized to assist with arresting this Wilson Gang. "Duward, how are your horses holding up to this fast pace"?

"They are all doing just fine. We should be able to push into the mountains by dark", Marshal Johnson said.

"That will allow us to be in Carson City late afternoon tomorrow".

"How are we going to find your two deputies when we get into town so we can lay out a plan to take down the Wilsons"?

"If we find a restaurant with a pretty girl, we will find Larry. No, we will go to the telegraph office, he will check in for any messages as soon as he gets into Carson City".

"This looks like a good spot to camp. Duward, why don't you start building a fire and I will start stripping the horses", "Ok by me"? Duward gathered wood for the fire and got it going in a stone fire ring that had been used for years. Marshal Johnson had the horses watered allowing them to only take in a small amount, then putting them on some grass, Marshal Johnson would bring them back for a long drink after they fix dinner. Using some dry grass, he gave all the horses a little rubdown as they were eating.

Marshal asked, "Duward are you a good cook or are we going to starve"?

"No, I can keep us from starving". After Duward cooked the last of the fresh meat with onions, he opened two cans of beans dumping them in with the beef. With the beef and beans hot, Duward pulled out four biscuits to sop up the juice with. "Grab a plate, we are ready to try out my favorite trail meal, the beans will probably work on you tomorrow, but it should fill you up for now".

"Dang Duward, this is good for body and soul, those biscuits were also good, I need to have you tell me how to make this chow". After two pots of coffee both men were ready for bed.

Duward had made extra so breakfast was a repeat of supper. Cooking pans cleaned, horses loaded, they started down off the mountains hoping to get into Carson City before the telegraph office closed for the day. Riding into town with a few minutes to spare before the telegraph office's closing time, they found the telegraph office and checked for new telegrams. Larry had sent one only an hour before, Marshal Johnson asked for the location Larry had given him to deliver any new messages.

Chip Miles, the operator, said that Larry was going to eat at the restaurant just across the street and he has a room at the hotel two doors down on the left.

"Thanks Chip. Come on Duward, we will see if this restaurant has a pretty girl working tonight". With the horses tied to the hitch rail, Duward and Johnson walked in to take a look see.

"You are correct", Duward commented, "I see a pretty girl".

"Well, that is my Deputy talking to the girl with Ronnie just watching. Marshal called out, "look what we have here. Are you two lost? Larry and Ronnie, I want to introduce you to Duward Buford, he is the Sheriff from Chico, this gang robbed one of his banks. Have you been in town long"?

"No, we just got in and were just asking Betty here if she knew of one old man and his three kids". Betty turned, telling them to have a seat.

She would have coffee on the table in a second. "Do you both want our special or I can also get you steak potatoes and a slice of peach pie"?

"We will take steak and potatoes for us both".

"Great, it will be right out Betty said".

"Boss, she just told me that the men we are looking for ate here the last two mornings but there are only three men. She also said that the one called Sandy was causing her a lot of problems when she delivered their food. This is the same story we heard from a girl named Rebecca down in Genoa that we talked to earlier".

"You know that I am a friend of Rebecca and she asked me to take her job because of this man Sandy".

Rebecca said that Sandy was waiting outside when she got off work, then asked her to go with him to his room for a little fun. She told us that she got away when one of the local law men, Randal Beets, was making his rounds.

Ronnie said, "I think he will show up again later tonight to try again to get Betty alone and rape her".

Betty said she also heard that the three men have been hanging out at the Silver Palace just down the street. There should be four men not three. Who is missing and why?

Betty added that all three seem to have a lot of money because they leave me a dollar to pay for a twenty-cent meal". Betty delivered the food, and the four lawmen went to work on their steak like they had missed some meals.

"Larry, how is your shoulder? It has only been a week after being shot".

"Well boss, it was a bit of trouble up to yesterday. The pain is about gone, and I have good motion, I am still a bit tired late in the day, but I am ok".

Ronnie said that Larry had a real good nurse named Doris. Her nursing seemed to have helped Larry recover but she seemed very sad when we rode north. "I just could not figure that one out, but you know Larry and pretty women".

Marshal Johnson asked Larry, "what got that shooting started anyway"?

"Well, Ronnie and I were walking into a saloon for a drink, Ronnie walked to the bar, and I stopped just inside of the door. Ronnie was ordering us a drink at the bar as he turned. He saw a man pushing back from a poker table pulling iron on me, I saw him, so I moved behind a wood post and drew and gave him a 44 in the chest.

"Ronnie, when seeing him draw on me he got two rounds into him kind of fast. After we got things calmed down, I checked him only to find out he was wanted, it was Willis Beal's. I figured that he was checking out the local bank, so we moved the money and set up his brother Dan Beale. They were going to try to rob two banks at the same time the next morning. Ronnie and the local law, Jake Sanders, took care of the one bank while Ronnie took care of the two men trying to rob it".

"I had the mayor with me to stop the other bank robbery, when the shooting started the Mayor, I think kind of made a mess of his drawers, ran off to hide. I got a bullet into one of the men but when I was moving to a better spot I got hit in the chest. Tray Davis got wind of the robbery and he saved my life, he got another round into the man I hit, then the other robber had me under his gun. I was down in the open, Tray put three quick rounds into him, end of story. All is well. You know, boss, this Tray only two weeks earlier was riding with a gang that was going to kill Ronnie and all of his family. He met a girl and changed his mind and rode away and went back to be with his now wife".

Marshal Johnson said, "are we ready to make this gang one man short, we will split up and kind of melt into the shadows. When this Sandy comes to try to take Betty, we will kind of change his mind about trying to rape anyone ever again. In the morning we will do about the same thing to the other three. From what Betty says, Homer is going to be the problem. He may want to shoot it out rather than being taken alive. Larry you are going to be the safety for all of us. Ronnie and Duward why don't you two take care of Jessie and Homer. From what we have heard Raymond may just lay down without a fight, Jessie we have no idea so be ready. Sheriff Buford, why don't you go and sit in front of the hotel and make sure Jessie and Homer don't come out and mess up the takedown". "OK" he said.

"Larry, I want you to stay in the restaurant until just before closing, everyone put your badges in your pocket. We are going to go out and find a nice place to take a rest on one of the benches just down the street. Larry, when you leave, I want you to go left, to the end of the building and find some cover so you can also keep watch. I hope that Sandy is watching you so when you come out the door, he will feel free to make his move". "Larry, you stay put for another half hour and enjoy your coffee along with Betty's charming company".

*

Jessie and Homer headed to the hotel. They were talking about Sandy, "Pa you know that he is going to still be drunk in the morning, he will spend all night with one or more of the girls at the Silver Palace".

"Homer I will meet you in the restaurant around seven."

"Ok with me Pa".

Sandy decided to have one more drink before going over to wait outside of the restaurant to pick up Betty and take her to his room. It was just getting dark when he walked out of the saloon heading for the ambush of Betty. As Sandy walked across the street, he watched the last customer turn left and head down the street going out of sight between two buildings.

Sandy reached up to touch his new toy laying in his left front shirt pocket, after seeing the derringer in the gun shop, he just had to have it, this was going to save his life, no one will know it is there. Sandy was thinking tonight must be a bad night for drunks after having to walk around the second one setting on a bench on the boardwalk. Two more doors down are the restaurant he found a sheltered place in a doorway to wait for Betty.

*

US Marshal Johnson eased up after Sandy walked around his feet that were taking up most of the walkway. With Sandy about ready to step up on the boardwalk, he stepped down to the dirt street and followed. Larry had removed his hat and peeked around the corner of the building. With the dark background Sandy could not see him. Ronnie was in the shadow of two buildings across the street waiting for Marshal Johnson to make his move. Ronnie had seen Sandy reach and touch his left front shirt pocket two times as he was watching him, thinking he must have a backup gun in his pocket. US Marshal Johnson was only twenty feet from Sandy when he heard him, Sandy had just reached for the third time when Johnson told him to raise his hands. With just slight movement Sandy's hand went under his coat, Ronnie drew and fired two times hitting him in his chest just under his arm. Sandy went to his knees and then flat on his face.

US Marshal Johnson asked "why did you shoot him Ronnie? He had not even moved, Ronnie turned him over with his foot, seeing his hand was filled with a two shot 44 caliber derringer.

"I could see him playing with the front of his shirt he had his back turned to you, I figured that he had a hideout gun.

"Thanks for saving my life Ronnie, he had me cold".

Larry said, "Boss you didn't see him playing with his shirt pocket"?

"No, with his back to me I never did see what he was doing". Betty came out after the shooting, Randal Beets was coming down the street, Marshal Johnson hollered to him telling it is US Marshal business but come on over and keep your gun locked down if you do not want to get shot.

Randal Beets came over to confront the US Marshals, saying. "This is my town you can't just come in and not let me know what you are going to do". He was about to finish when he was looking at a US Marshal's 44.

"Mister Sheriff if you don't want to be locked in your jail just shut up, we tell any local official what they can do or not do. Go get the undertaker and haul this piece of shit away now".

Marshal Johnson commented "nice job Ronnie".

Betty leaned in to tell the Marshals could you ease up a bit on Randal, he is a nice guy.

"Who is going to walk me home"?

Ronnie, Sheriff Buford and Marshal Johnson all looked at Larry- we will meet for a drink at the Silver Palace after Miss Taylor is delivered safely to her room.

One drink down when Larry wandered in and sat down asking, "Where is my drink"?

US Marshal Johnson opened the conversation with thanks again to Ronnie for coming to help, "I think we will do the same takedown in the morning, what do you think"?

Larry told Marshal Johnson and Ronnie that he had told Randal Beets to go behind the two buildings, by the restaurant so the owners do not open up and walk into a gunfight. Marshal Johnson looked up saying, "see you guys in the morning around six to get set up".

All the law dogs met on the porch of the hotel with a new day starting, "Sheriff Buford, will you go over to the livery and gather up all of your stolen horses and other equipment and supplies locked up in a storeroom, then move their horses into the large corral so the men can't get them in a hurry? After you get an idea of just what equipment and supplies, they have, come over and join us for breakfast".

"I can do that; I will be along in a little while".

*

Jessie asked Homer if he heard Sandy come in last night.

"No, but he will probably meet us around seven in the restaurant, he will want to see if he can get a hand up another girls dress". Both men went back into their rooms to wash up and be out of the door in fifteen minutes to be ready to eat at seven when the restaurant opened. "Walking from the hotel was a short walk, damn there are a lot of drunks in this town I can see two about to fall off the benches at seven in the morning". Jessie and Homer got about twenty feet past the first drunk when they heard, "raise your hands you are under arrest". Homer spun as he drew to face the law behind him, Jessie got a look at a man step out from between the next building. Jessie's 44 just cleared leather when he felt a bullet hit him in the right arm and lodge in his chest, his finger was on the trigger, but he could not seem to make it fire. He could see the smoke from the man's pistol in front of him, the last thing he felt was Larry's 44 hitting him dead center. Homer was also hit twice in his left arm and chest. Seeing smoke from the man's gun he was facing, he pulled the trigger and felt the recoil, then all went blank.

Randal peeked around the corner asking if all was clear.

"Yes", said Marshal Johnson. "Larry, you check their pockets for cash, Marshal said that he found just under one hundred dollars in Sandy's pockets last night".

"Larry you and Ronnie go up to check the rooms. Hold on, I just found a key. I will check the other one's pockets. Good, another key".

We need to go up to check their rooms Ronnie and see what we find. "I hope they have most of the cash, boss I don't think they had any time to spend much of the money".

In Homer's room they found the saddle bags full of money, it looked like it was untouched. Ronnie said, "I think the banks are going to be really happy".

"Ronnie let's gather this stuff up and go get breakfast, bedrolls, rifles". Off they went to eat, dumping all the stuff on the floor of the restaurant. Betty had coffee on the table when Sheriff Buford came in and sat down joining the others.

"Just in time I see".

"Sheriff what did you find, I seem to be one short of the stolen horses, but I gained a packhorse".

"Well, I am one man short of a full gang". Larry said, "From the papers I found on the dead men, it looks like Raymond, the next to the youngest son is missing.

Buford said, "The youngest son Ellis, rode off the day they started robbing".

"What are we going to do with our lost son of Jessie Wilson"?

Marshal Johnson told the Sheriff, "I think that will be your problem". US Marshal Johnson offered up a plan. "Larry, You, Sheriff Buford and I will take the horses back to Sacramento. Then Larry and

Sheriff Buford will take the cash stolen in Chico and the horses back to the owners. Ronnie, keep the badge if you want, you will be an unpaid Marshal. That is if you think you can stay out of trouble, why don't you go home and check on your pregnant wife and your ranch? Thanks for the help Ronnie". Ronnie put the badge back in his pocket thinking this could be handy.

"Marshal Johnson, I have one more stop before I head home, I need to go by the land office, then I will head east to the ranch".

The three law dogs were leading the stolen horses and with thousands of dollars in their saddle bags, they were keeping a close watch for any trouble. They sent three members of the Wilson Gang to hell and had another one on the run so to speak.

After deciding to leave Jake Sanders as the Manteca sheriff, US Marshal Johnson gave him some solid advice as how to run his town and if he slacked off, he would have US Deputy McPherson come back and lock him up and put him on trial. Jake Sanders did not want anything to do with Larry McPherson. But Doris Watson would like to have a lot more to do with Larry, they had become quite close as she doctored him to be in fine health.

This picture could well be the water supply for Ronnie Campbell's gold mine. (Photo by Robin Travis).

EAGLE FALLS

CHAPTER 11 **TROUBLES AT SIMPSON PASS**

Ronnie picked up Diamond and Dandy at the livery and made a quick stop at the general store to pick up a few supplies to get him home. He rode by the old Pony Express office. It had been shut down for a year or so, man I sure had a fun time for a year. Riding up and looping the rains over the hitching post, he walked into the store to resupply. Gathering up his food items then placing them on the counter, the owner asked Ronnie if he knew what the shooting was about this morning.

"No didn't pay much attention to that kind of stuff". The owner said someone told him that one of the old Pony Express riders was part of the shootout". "Could have been, I am just passing through heading east. Has anyone mentioned about any problems on the trail east"?

"Yes, I did hear of a robbery and shooting at some store east a few days ride, I think it was Brown's or something like that".

"Do you know if anyone was killed",

"No, I think the owner was wounded and lost a fair amount of money".

"That will be seven dollars and fifty cents the total for your supplies". Ronnie took two trips out to finish loading. With everything tied down, Ronnie turned east heading back to the ranch. Diamond and Dandy seemed to know that they are heading home, Diamond wanted to run but Ronnie felt that he may need horses that were as fresh as possible if he needed to run from or run down some outlaws before he got home. At the pace he was riding he would make Buckland Station by midafternoon. He planned on staying overnight. Ronnie wanted to catch up on the latest news before crossing the Carson River and continuing his ride home to the ranch. Riding in, Ronnie found an empty corral, so he unpacked and turned Dandy and Diamond out for the night, he checked the water and forked in some hay. With his rifle and saddle bags, he went in to get a room and some food that he would not have to cook himself, he would get enough of that over the next few days. After eating, Ronnie found Mr. Buckland and asked him if he had any word on the robbery of Mr. Brown's store?

"No, the only thing I heard was from one of the stagecoach drivers when he came through".

"Did he say how many robbers there were or give a description of any of their horses?

"No, they just told me about a robbery, but the horses were all bays with no markings that he could see".

Early the next morning Ronnie loaded all his gear and crossed the river and headed home, he would need to keep a close watch of riders coming from the east, they could be a problem. Many of the old Pony Express stations were starting to fall apart due to lack of care, but they still had water and that was a big help. Ronnie had just topped Simpson Pass. It was getting late, so he decided to make camp for the night. Having ridden this trail many times, he decided to turn off the trail to the south and camp under the rock outcropping it was just a short ride. Very few people knew of this jumble of rocks just off the trail offered a good wind break with enough feed for the horses, but it had no water.

Ronnie was figuring that the robbers may be just about ready to cross his path this evening. He was going to make a nice fire that can be seen from the trail inviting any passing riders to come and visit. He had Diamond and Dandy hidden from view behind the second rock outcropping, Ronnie would move them from the area to below the rocks after dark. Ronnie built his fire about ten feet in front of the rock face allowing the heat to be reflected by the rocks. After cooking his dinner, he was enjoying the last of the coffee. The pack saddle and panniers were stacked off to the side by the rock face. Ronnie had taken some dry grass and filled out his bedroll, then covered it with a blanket with his saddle at the end. This would look like someone sleeping if he had any unwanted company during the night.

Ronnie was ready to get some sleep, he had pulled Diamond and Dandy back into the rocks close to where he was going to sleep so they could feed until morning. Ronnie had his second blanket to keep the chill off, and he had just dozed off when Diamond blew and stomped a front foot, Ronnie looked over at Diamond and Dandy, both were looking past him. The spot he was sleeping was above the fire ring and bed roll on a ledge behind the rock face, he had great cover if needed. Looking over the rocks to the north, the moon was up enough to give him a little light. He eased a round into the chamber of his Henry and removed the leather strap holding his pistol in its holster. Ronnie rolled to a knee when he could just make out some movement coming from the north.

Ronnie knew no one could see him because the rock wall behind him was higher so in this light he had the advantage even with three men that were easing into his campsite.

He heard one of the men say, "pull your rifles and when I shoot fire into the bedroll, we will take all of his supplies, we should have taken more when we robbed that store east of here". "Ok, get ready, Fire". Three rifles opened up, each firing one round into the bedroll, Ronnie opened up with his Henry delivering two rounds to each of the men, only one got turned around before hitting the ground dead.

"Well, I guess I found the robbers or should say they found me". Ronnie walked around the boulders and gathering up their horses, moving them back to join Diamond and Dandy on their own picket lines. After going through their pockets, he found some money but not much, taking the holsters and pistols, he walked back to the campfire and placed the weapons on the blanket to check out in the morning.

Walking back to his bedroll, he crawled in and greeted the sun as it started to get light. Looking over at the horses, they were just eating. Rolling up his bedroll with three new holes in it he walked back to his camp, Ronnie made another attempt to find out just who these three were. Looking over the holsters and saddle bags he found some gold and about one thousand dollars in cash, extra pistols and other traveling supplies. Ronnie walked back and saddled Diamond, leading him back into camp. He pulled his rope off his saddle, put a loop over one of the dead men. Stepping into the saddle, he dragged each one down into a low spot for their final resting spot.

Riding back into camp, Diamond turned his head, ears forward looking back to the north to the trail, Ronnie pulled his head around to get a hand over his nose to keep him from nickering. Easing his Henry from the boot he levered a round into the chamber. Ronnie eased off the right side of Diamond so he would have him between him and his visitor. With the rifle laying over his saddle, he could see the horse and rider get clear from the brush. Ronnie called out to the rider, "Tony what are you doing over here"?

"Well Ronnie, I had ridden to Jim's store and found him with a bullet hole in his arm and had been relieved of about two hundred dollars and a few supplies. These three were about a day ahead of me when I got there so I just picked up some basic road supplies and started after them. So, it looks like you found them, or they found you.

"They found me about eleven last night, I just finished dragging them down into a gulley to let them rot".

"I had figured to catch them in a camp last night, but they just kept riding, I figured to catch them today".

"Well, Tony you did".

"I am getting ready to get some breakfast cooked. Do you want some"?

"Sure do, jerky has lost its appeal".

I have enough water for coffee and a small drink for the horses. We can water the horses at Sand Springs, but they will not like it, but they will get some down, we can let them drink again at Westgate or Cold Springs. I found over a thousand dollars in the one saddle bag, some pocket change in the others that amounts to under thirty-five dollars. I have no idea who any of these men are. They do not have any identification on them and nothing on the gun belts.

"Tony, did Jim Brown hear any names"?

"No, he said they just walked in, shot him in the arm, and took his money and walked out then they rode out heading west. So, we meet here, and we will just ride home".

Ronnie asked, "Tony do you know the way home"?

"I think we can just take the bridles off the horses and Teddy and Diamond will get us back to the ranch".

*

Maggie and Abby were eating breakfast as the conversation started to turn to their men, "Maggie we should ride down to Jim Brown's store and check on him, then ride west to meet Tony and Ronnie. What do you think"?

"Great idea, Maggie start packing, and I will get my two gildings saddled and a pack horse ready to go for our stuff". Andy Sams was working in the blacksmith shop when Abby came out and asked him if he could get her two blacks ready to ride along with a packhorse, we want to get on the trail as soon as we can.

"Ok" Andy along with Black Dove's two sons walked out to the corral to get Abby's two gildings, the two young Paiute boys had been learning English from Andy for months how. Andy put a halter on one of her horses and the older boy had the second one.

"Now get the horse with the Splash down his face". Splash had been stolen but recovered by Ronnie and Abby coming home from Salt Lake City after racing their horses Buster and Lightning.

With the help from the two boys, Andy had the horses ready with rifles in the scabbard's bedrolls and slickers behind the saddles. "Come on boys, let's get some food loaded on the packhorse along with a small tent just in case the weather got bad". Ammunition for the rifles and pistols in the saddlebags, all they needed was the clothes that Abby and Maggie wanted to take. Both girls came out to the horses with their personal stuff, Andy loaded Maggie's on one side of the packhorse and Abby's on the other. Andy just finished with tying down the packs when the boys came back with four canteens filled with fresh water. Andy looped two of the canteen straps over the packsaddle and one on each of the other two horses. "You are ready to ride girls".

"Thanks Andy. We will be gone for over a week if not two, keep an eye out and have Tee and White Bird patrol the ranch. Thanks again". The two girls started out to meet their men.

"Abby, we need to take it easy on this trip with you being over three months along. We don't want any problems with the baby".

"Maggie, that is why I wanted to use my two horses. They have a real soft trot so I should be just fine even with a slow canter, these long-legged horses can cover ground".

"I sure hope Jim is doing better. Tony wanted me to head home when he started after the three men. As you know, Abby, I stayed for two days to help him get back on his feet. Let's hope he is doing ok; we will find out tomorrow late. Why don't we stay overnight to help with some of his work, Jim sure has been a good friend to all of us over the years we have known him. I think the best thing he has done was giving the furniture and other supplies to Little John and Jane, what a loss by losing both Sam and Beth Applegate".

"Abby, these two horses can sure cover ground, I think Teddy and Diamond would be pushed to match the ground we have covered. Is there a small spring just up ahead on the right", Abby said, "yes, this is it"?

"Dark comes fast in these mountains", Maggie replied. "There is just enough light to get the three horses to water for a short drink".

"Maggie if we both help, we can lift the panniers off of Splash without unloading them". With packs on the ground and each horse unsaddled, they walked them back to the spring for a final drink for the night. Picket pin in the ground with plenty of rope for the horses to eat, the girls dropped their bedrolls and crawled in for the night with some cold meat, dry biscuit and warm water from their canteens.

With the sun showing light in the east, the girls headed out to do their morning business. Returning to camp, cold meat and some bread chased with water from the canteen, it was time to saddle up and get on the trail. Splash was loaded first with the panniers with the supplies, then the blacks were saddled, bedrolls tied behind their saddles. The girls stepped up and rode west. With a few hours down the trail they stopped at another spring back in a draw that is used by wild horses most of the time, small break to let the horses graze then back on the road. Just as the sun was getting overhead, they rode into the store.

Jim heard the horses coming so he came out to see who was about to arrive, Jim had the Shotgun by the door but seeing the girls he left it there and walked out to greet them.

"Jim you are looking great" Maggie said.

"Well with nurses like you how could I not get better"?

"Jim, Maggie and I are going to head toward Carson City to meet Ronnie and Tony coming home. We have been worried about you, we planned to stay here to help you for one or two days before we ride out, so let us know what needs to be done".

"If you are serious, I had a wagon load of supplies delivered just two days ago, I am working through it, but some help would be great".

"Show us the way".

"The supplies are on the back by the porch so follow me and we can get started. Stop. I bet neither of you have had any lunch so sit down and I will have my cook get you some lunch". Jim came in and sat with the girls and ate his lunch with them.

As they ate, Jim asked "do you think Tony caught up with those three"?

"Oh, ya he will catch them. Teddy can make some long miles. I have a feeling that the three are buzzard food by now. What do you think Abby"?

"I have a feeling that Ronnie is coming home from Carson City and three of them may just meet Ronnie on the trail and that could be un-healthy for them".

Two days later Abby and Maggie were heading toward Carson City. They would pick up the old Pony Express Trail late today and would spend the night at a stage relay station that had been used by the Pony Express. Reaching it late, they were able to use the corrals and feed and water their horses. They would sleep out in the barn, but they got to eat a meal with the relay station manager and his wife. Out in the barn, the girls were trying to figure out just how far they would need to ride to meet their men, Abby and Maggie figured that they could meet them late tomorrow afternoon. Thanking the station manager for helping with the packhorse, they were on the trail by seven thirty in the morning, riding along the same trail that Ronnie had ridden many times before.

Late in the day Abby started to see a dust cloud ahead about two miles.

"Maggie, we need to get off the road and find a spot we can defend. There has to be over six riders coming our way". Turning off the road they rode back into the brush and trees, "Maggie hold my horse, I am going out and brush out our tracks I don't want to let them know we are back here". Breaking off some sagebrush she walked out to try and eliminate the tracks the best she could leading from the road, Abby had seen Ronnie do it, so she did have an idea of the process. The two girls pulled their rifles and levered a round into the chamber.

Ronnie asked Tony, "did you see something on the left side of the road, why don't we slow down to a walk and pull your rifle and get ready, we may have someone waiting for us about a mile ahead on the left. We need to space out some, you drop back with three extra horse lengths, and I will keep an eye out for any movement". As Ronnie rode closer, he kept looking for tracks to show him how many people he was looking to have to deal with. He pulled his badge out and pinned it on his shirt just to identify himself as a law man.

As Ronnie reached the spot, he had seen the movement he heard,

"About time you get here".

Abby, what are you doing this far from home? Maggie you are both in trouble". The girls rode out from the cover easing the hammer down slow on their Henry rifles. Abby and Maggie moved the lever back until the cartridge came out of the chamber, watching the bolt slide home on the empty chamber, they opened the loading tube and dropped in the round and re-locked the tube in place. Sliding the rifles back into the scabbards, they greeted their men, saying, "we just could not wait any longer, so we rode down and helped Jim Brown for a day and a half then headed your way".

Abby asked, "Well who killed the three outlaws"?

"Ronnie got them just before I was able to catch up to them. The funny thing is they had no identification on any of them. They did have some fair horses as you can see". Abby for the first time saw the badge, she asked,

"Ronnie, what are you wearing the badge for"?

"I am an official US Deputy Marshal, working for US Marshal Johnson out of Sacramento".

"Ok Mr. Deputy US Marshal". Can we go home? We have a long ride ahead of us". Ronnie asked Tony, "Are you in any hurry now we have someone to keep us warm at night and cook, life is good returning to the Ruby's".

Two days later the two couples reached Jim Brown's Store to check on how he was doing and return the money that had been stolen from him by the three men Ronnie killed back at Simpson Pass. Jim walked out to greet them with a shotgun that he leaned against the door jamb before greeting his friends.

"Girls, you collected some excess horses and men, come on in and we can get some dinner and tell me about your little trip west".

Ronnie said, "I have your money from the robbery. I have never counted this money so this is a good time to do so. Do you know how much was stolen in the robbery"?

I lost over two hundred-dollars, but I am not sure of the exact amount".

"Jim, I think your money made some extra cash during my ride to deliver six bullets to three men. I found some gold and over two thousand dollars and these three horses with all the tack. Getting shot in the arm was somewhat beneficial to your bank account".

"I can't take this extra money".

"Jim, take the money and horses they are also yours".

"Ronnie I can't take all of that money and horses; it is just not right".

"No Jim, you keep it, and this is some repayment for the help you gave Maggie and Sean. Along with so many others who just got dropped onto your door and you have always helped support them".

Jim Brown said to Ronnie, "will you tell me about the trip over to see the rider who left before the gun fight with the Jarvis Baster Gang or should I say what was left of them after your first meeting".

"US Marshal McPherson and I followed him back to Manteca and his name was Tray Davis, I had intended to kill him or be friends with him. When Larry and I rode into town we were deciding either to get a drink or food, we settled on food. As we walked into the restaurant, who was sitting at a table and talking to the waitress? No one but Mr. Tray Davis big as life. He remembered Larry so he got up and came over to the table to talk. When Larry dropped his US Marshal Badge onto the table, this kid about died without even a bullet".

When Larry asked him about the raid, he came clean and told us about meeting his new girl or should I say going to be new wife, Tray had just asked her to marry him. Bridget came over to meet us. That is when Larry introduced Tray Davis to Ronnie Campbell, that was the second time Tray about died without a bullet. Bridget was the reason that Tray was not riding with the gang when we killed them all. "Now get this Jim, Tray was getting ready to go back to his new ranch with his new bride when some men started to rob two banks at one time. I and the local law had one bank covered and Larry and the town mayor had the other bank covered. When the shooting started the mayor ran, leaving Larry in a bad spot. Tray came driving around the corner heading to the general store, took one look and pulled back into the alley and came back to the street throwing led. Larry was hit in the shoulder and was under the second robber's gun when Tray tagged him with three bullets and added two more to the first robber Larry had hit".

"Tray is a real good friend, and we think he and Bridget will be coming over to trade some horses in a few months".

Then Jim asked Ronnie, "Why don't you take the horses, can't you use them"?

"No, they are all good horses, but they are gilded, making them of little use for my ranch".

Tony asked Jim. "Can't you trade these fresh horses with people who are traveling east or west"? "Yes, I can Jim said". "They will be of great value to me so thanks. Dinner is served and I am buying. Are you going to stay tonight"?

"No, we are heading back to the ranch. We can make a campsite in about 4 hours so we will eat and head that way". After dinner, the crew were walking out to tighten up the cinches, Jim came out with a bag of candy, asking them to give it to the Indian kids. You guys can also test some to see if they are fit for the kids.

Back at the ranch after a fast trip home from Jim Brown's Store, Ronnie and Tony had started looking into trading some bulls with Juan and Juanita in California. "Tony, how many of our young bulls do you think we need to exchange to keep the blood line clean? Do we want to include Little John if we move some of our stock over to the California Ranch"?

"Yes, we should ask him before making any solid plans".

"Tony, we can ride over and talk to Little John next week, we can stay over and be back in two days using the trail White Bird and Tee found. I am sure that he and Jane will want to improve their herd by having some new men for the cows to warm up to. I think we had better stay close to home for a few days. We would not want to have any of the warm reception we have been getting from our wives to end too soon".

"I am willing to go along with that idea Ronnie".

The next morning both men were smiling during breakfast. Abby asked, "what are you two going to do for the next few days"?

Ronnie said that he was going to head out to inspect the mine but should be back late today.

Tony said, "I am going to check on the cattle to see how many young bulls we have in the high country, I will be taking White Bird and Tee".

Ronnie suggested that they move about twenty cows over the pass with one older bull and one of the young ones. Abby and Maggie asked why would you do that?

"Remember girls we talked about filing on some range over by the hot springs, well I filed on all of that range when I was in Carson City before I came home. This is the starting of the Indian owned ranch in the Ruby Mountains. We will need to keep the land title until some things change, but in time this land will be the White Bird and Tee ranch headquarters".

Tony asked, "When do we tell White Bird and Tee about this new ranch for their families"?

"I think after you get the cattle over there and settled would be a good time, what do you think Tony"?

"Great idea, I will see if they understand what this means for them in the future". "Ronnie, remember back when Andy was in the forge and the Indians came to see White Bird and Tee".

"Yes, I do, Andy figured he was going to be scalped. Those Indians were others from their family, they were asking about living and working on the ranch. They came back while we were gone talking to Tee and White Bird. This could be the correct time for making some changes in the Indian's way of life".

Early the next day Tony gathered Tee and White Bird. "We need to move some cattle over the mountain today, do you have time to do this"? Tee and White Bird nodded, then rode into the hills with Tony, by late morning they had the twenty head of cows along with a couple of young bulls and one of the oldest bulls on the ranch bunched and ready to drive. Tony was on his horse Teddy. He was leading the cattle up the narrow trail with Tee and White Bird pushing them from behind, by midafternoon they had reached the hot springs area. Tony, White Bird and Tee pushed the cattle across on to the island area by the much-used campsite. This island will hold the cattle for a week with good grass and water. They then will expand their range as the food is eaten away. Returning to the ranch, Tee and White Bird were trying to figure why move cows to an area that they could not keep watch over them. Tony asked Tee and White Bird to come with him to the kitchen to talk. Maggie fixed some sweet hot tea for their guests.

Tony pulled out a map and placed it on the table so it would show the little river running the same way as it does on the ranch. Tony showed them where they gathered the cattle and the location where they left the cattle. With his finger he ran it around the boundaries of the Campbell Ranch and saying, "Ronnie's Ranch, do you understand"? They said that they did understand that was Ronnie's Ranch. Then he did the same to the other side of the ranch, then saying that is your ranch with the cows. "Both looked at Tony saying, "you say Tee's Ranch and White Bird's Ranch"? "Yes. That is now your ranch, and you need to take care of the cows like you do on Ronnie's Ranch".

Then Tony used his fingers to trace Ronnie's Ranch and then pointing to himself, then doing the same and saying Tee's and White Birds Ranch and pointing to them. Owning land, to an Indian, was hard for them to understand but he thinks that they did. Then Tony told them to come see him in the morning to talk some more.

This covered wagon picture would fit perfictly into the 1863 time period. (Photo by Robin Travis).

TEAMWORK TWO BY TWO

CHAPTER 12 **BULLS ON THE TRAIL**

Ronnie was up with the first light to start a trip over to the gold mine and check on things, he knew that things would be running smooth, but he liked to keep a close watch on all the operations. Riding into the mine site he could tell a lot of progress had been done and he found a log dining hall built over by the bend of the river, he was sure Rose was the leader on that project. Rose and Marty came out with a cup of hot coffee to greet Ronnie as he started to step down. Ronnie asked, "when did this show up"?

Rose said "I figured the crew needed a place to eat out of the weather, so this is it, we just finished it a week ago. Come take a look. We even have a covered area to cook, when the weather starts to turn cold, we will close in this end to make it a real kitchen".

Ronnie asked if they had started to build their log cabin on the bench just off the river.

Marty said that it was started with two levels of logs up and a solid foundation.

"Great, can you show me what you have finished after lunch"?

"Sure, we would love to do that. This dining area can be pulled by a team of horses so we can move it later if needed to a new location".

Ronnie asked Rose and Marty if they needed anything for their new house.

"Yes, we will need to take a few days away from work so we can go to Mr. Brown's store to purchase the items we need", Rose said.

Sean walked up from the mine to talk to Ronnie at the cook shed. "How is the mining going while I have been gone"?

"Great, we have recovered quite a large amount of gold and we need to get it back to the ranch. I have about 60 pounds of gold in leather bags ready to ship to the bank, when do you want to move this gold to a safer location"?

Ronnie said, "I am just starting to make plans to take some of our little bulls over to the California ranch soon. We could also transport the gold at the same time".

"How soon Sean asked"?

"I am thinking about two weeks from now, how much more gold do you think you can mine by that time"?

"We should be able to recover and stamp out another 10 lbs. by then I think".

"Did Andy get the steel door finished so we can close off the entrance to the mine"?

"Yes, we installed it last week".

"Ok, shut down the mining operation in one week and bring everyone back to the ranch".

Rose came over saying, "Ronnie and Sean, here is some fresh coffee, dinner will be ready in about thirty minutes, I have elk steaks with fried potatoes.

"Rose and Marty, you can come to the ranch if you want or stay and work on your house, it is your choice to make".

Ronnie asked, "Sean how are the Jenkins brothers doing"?

"Ronnie, I am seeing them change every day, the big change came after the gunfight, and you gave them the horses and their own guns. I think they now are starting to feel like they are becoming men doing men's work".

"That is good to hear" Ronnie said.

"Sean, I will talk to everyone at dinner time about a plan I have".

"Marty and Rose, is dinner ready? If so, we have some time before dinner is served so we can walk up and see your start on your new house, I think the location is the best one on the ranch. Abby and I are so happy that you are using it for your home, it is special to both of us. We camped for a week there just after we were married".

When they reached the start of the log home Ronnie pulled out an envelope and handed it to Rose and Marty. "What is this"? they asked.

"You are now the owner of two hundred acres of this valley, one hundred acres on each side of the stream running up to the top of the ridge on each side. It has been recorded in Carson City and I signed it this morning". Rose started to cry, and Marty came over and gave Ronnie a handshake and he was also fighting back tears.

"Ronnie this is the best thing that has ever happened to me or Marty in our whole life. We can never repay you for this land and life you have allowed us to have during our time on your ranch", Rose said.

"Rose you and Marty are special, I am so happy you two came into the life of this ranch and chose to stay. I see the men heading to the new eating area, so we better get back and join them".

After dinner was served, Ronnie told everyone about Rose and Marty's new home and land. After everyone had finished eating, Ronnie talked about his plan to shut down the mine for a month so each of you can take some time off, to either go to Salt Lake City or Carson City for a visit. Those who would like to go on to Sacramento they can go with us to deliver some bulls to Juan and Juanita, we will also be bringing back some other bulls to restock this ranch.

Randy and the Jenkins Brothers asked if they could go all the way to Sacramento to help with the trip. "Glad to have you come along Ronnie said.",

Back at the ranch a few days later breakfast was in progress with information going back and forth when the transfer of the bulls came up.

Ronnie asked, "Tony how many little guys do we have to take over to California"?

"We can take a look after we finish eating, I have moved down twelve of the best for you to take a look at. I see Andy has the two wagons finished with stock pens ready to load the bulls we want to take with us over the hill". Tony said, "Randy has pulled the cook wagon over to get it stocked and ready for the trip, we will repack all of the axels on each wagon. Did you see the hay packing box for the alfalfa hay? Andy made a box that he can pack the hay into and then wire it together with two wires. This allows him to stack the hay and it will not fall apart, he has enough bails for the trip. That is what Andy is calling them. He came up with the idea and made enough so we won't need to depend on having grass along the trail to feed our stock, this will save us hours every day".

"Andy also has some boxes for grain and two tanks for hauling water, so we can carry enough hay for the trip and water for cooking and our livestock. The hay and water tanks are mounted on Abby's wagon".

With the last sip of coffee Ronnie stood up and said, "Good news Tony, let's go and check on how many bulls we can get into each of the wagons". Andy hitched a team to one of the stock wagons and backed it up to a loading ramp at the end of the cattle holding pin. Ronnie and Tony rode into the pen and started to separate five of the bulls and move them to the end of the pen with the loading ramp. With a bit of pressure from behind, the five were loaded one at a time up the loading ramp in the wagon with the racks on the sides. Ronnie suggested that they toss some hay into the wagon bed and see if the bulls have enough room to lay down without any problems.

After about one hour Andy walked by, and all the five bulls were laying down. Andy went to get Ronnie to have him take a look. With Ronnie along, Tony went back to take a look to see if they could get one or two more and still have room in the portable pen.

Ronnie told Andy, "I think one more is about all we will get in each wagon; this is going to be a long trip for those little guys. Tony let's go push one more bull into the wagon pen just to make sure they all can fit. If they all have some room, we can take all twelve that we have in the pens now". Ronnie and Tony separated the single bull and pushed him up the ramp and into the wagon. They came back after two hours and all were just laying down resting, six is going to work without any problems. "Andy, can you drop the ramp down and we will see if they come out on their own after a while". Later in the day, the six were back with the others in the large pen, Ronnie could see them as he walked out to the blacksmith shop to talk to Andy.

*

Randy, Marty and Rose were drinking coffee back at the mine site's eating area, Rose asked, "Randy what are you going to do"? Rose knew that Marty and Randy had been friends for some years and had worked on the same ranches for all those years.

"Rose, I have been thinking about trying to find me a lady like you and settle down. I can see that Marty and you are enjoying life and have started to build a home. I want the same for myself". "Randy, are you going to go with Ronnie and crew to Sacramento"?

"I am thinking about doing just that, not too many women around this part of the country, I may just fine someone on the trip".

Rose said, "Randy, you know that if you want you can come back and build a place by us if you would like to do that. There is plenty of room".

"Thanks Rose, I will think on that, it would be nice to settle down, grow a garden, and live a quiet life".

"Randy, will you tell Ronnie that we kept one team here so we could skid the logs so we can finish our home? I am sure he is ok with that, but I forgot to ask him".

"Rose and Marty, I am heading to the ranch headquarters to see when they are heading west to California".

*

That evening Randy rode into the ranch yard. Seeing Ronnie sitting on the front porch, he rode over to give the apology to Ronnie from Rose and Marty. Stepping down, looping the reins over the hitching post, he was greeted by Ronnie, "are you going to make the trip with us Randy"?

"Yes, I think I would like to offer my help. Ronnie, it would be nice to see a big town just to look around, adding that Rose felt bad about keeping one of the teams at the mine site without asking you first. Rose and Marty needed the team to pull logs down to finish the cabin".

"No problem Randy, I figured that was what they were doing. I see that she did keep the two horses that were only green broke so I think she will be doing some training as she works them".

With the mine shut down things were hopping around the ranch, wagons were being checked over, harnesses repaired, wheels checked. All the draft horses that were going to make the trip needed to have new shoes. Andy had just taken care of all the saddle horses, so they were ready to head west.

Randy had been working at the mine so after breakfast he went out behind the house to check on the orchard he and Rose had planted, he also went to check on the dugout he had built into the side of the hill behind the ranch house. Opening up the door, he could see that everything was just as he had left it. Randy went back and walked his horse back to the dugout, removed his rifle, placing it on the wooden pegs by the door. Unsaddling his horse and placing the saddle on the rack under his rifle, bedroll unrolled, he was home. Walking his horse around the corner to the corral he had made during the time he had lived at the ranch headquarters, all he needed now was to bring up some hay for his horse. He had never figured to own a horse like this one. Ronnie had given him the horse after the shootout with the gang. His rifle was about new, and the new cartridge pistol was another first.

Randy gathered up some wood so he could start a fire in the stove to get rid of some moisture out of the room from being closed up for a long time. When he walked out of the dugout, he was met by some of the kids that had helped him make the storage area and his living area, they were all happy to see him. Two of the boys were Andy's and Black Dove's. They started to ask him questions and told Randy that they have been helping Andy. Randy could see that more Indians were at the camp and many more kids running around. The kids and Randy walked over to the forge to talk to Andy to see if he needed any help to get ready for the long trip, all but the two kids of Andy's went back to doing other things.

Andy asked, "Randy how are things going"?

"Andy, can you use my help with any of your work? I see that you have been feeding the two boys, they are growing".

"Yes, Randy I would like some help removing some of the wagon wheels so I can inspect them. I would have asked Jingles, but he is too busy with the horses".

"Great Andy, point me to the first one you want".

"We can start on Abby's wagon first it is also the closest to the shop. The axel jack is under the back of the wagon so get it and when you are ready, I will help block up the axel". Randy found the jack and had the wheel up off the ground when Andy came by to help finish setting the blocks. Randy had the pin out of the axel bolt and had just removed the nut and slid the wheel off the axel shaft when something hit the wagon, knocking it off the blocks. The wheel was hit by the wagon, knocking down Randy.

Randy was under the wagon with the wheel pinning his arm, he knew it was broken but just not how bad. Andy was the first to reach him, getting the jack back under the wagon to lift it up off from the wheel that had Randy's arm pinned. Andy was lifting the wagon when Ronnie got their along with Sean. Ronnie lifted up the wheel and Sean pulled Randy out to a safe place. With the wagon back on blocks, Ronnie asked what happened. Billy Jenkins said, "I was leading one of the draft horses when he was attacked by some bees, he was stung a few times. In trying to get away he ran into the wagon knocking it off the blocks I am so sorry Randy got hurt".

Randy's arm was sure broken but no bones were sticking out of the skin. Andy came over to take a look, "Maggie, and Abby had also come over to look". No one knew how to set a broken arm. Turning to one of his Indian sons, Andy told them to go get Black Dove and bring her here now. Black Dove and Tee's wife came to check out the broken arm. After talking some, they told Andy to have Randy come with them, they would fix it.

Randy was not too sure about going to the Indian camp to have his arm fixed by Indians, but what was his choice.

Andy said, "I will go over with you, they won't scalp you or anything like that". Black Dove sent her sons to gather some willows from along the stream bank, Andy had him come into the lodge, "I will need your help to fix the arm Said Black Dove".

Randy, my wife thinks you will be ok after one moon". With Randy sitting on the floor, Tee's wife, Black Feather, came back with a cup for Randy to drink, Andy told him it will help with the pain.

The boys came back with the willow sticks and dropped them on the floor for Black Dove to use to hold his arm in place as it is healing.

Black Dove said, "Andy, you hold Randy's arm behind the elbow, and I will pull his hand forward to get the bones to go back together. Randy this is going to hurt so get ready". Black Dove pulled as Andy held his arm in place, she twisted his forearm a little and felt the bones slide back in place. Randy had sweat dripping when they finished. Black Dove cut the sticks to the correct length to fit his forearm. White Feather pulled a wet rabbit skin from some hot water and twisted it to remove most of the water. The two Indian women wrapped the skin around his arm then placed the willow sticks around his arm over the rabbit skin. With the sticks in place, the women wrapped the sticks with leather strips to hold everything in place. Another young Indian woman came into the lodge, handing a cup to White Feather, she then offered Randy this cup of the strong pain killer to drink. So, he drank the mixture of God only knows what, he was thinking. Randy had never seen this other Indian before, but she looked right into his eyes when she came in, the pain was going away. Andy helped him up and as they were leaving the lodge. Randy thanked the two Indian women hoping they understood him.

Ronnie met them as they were about back to the forging area. "Well, Randy it looks like you are going to live, but I do think you will need to stay around the ranch until your arm is healed". "Yah, I think that is going to be the best that I stay here at the ranch. I need to do some trimming on some of the fruit trees in the orchard anyway". Andy was working on the wheel but could hear the conversation with Ronnie and Randy.

Andy said, "Randy it looks like we are going to be the only ranch hands left on the ranch in a few days. Why don't you eat with me and Black

Dove some of the time, that way you won't have to cook your own food with all the cooks away on their trip to Sacramento to deliver the young bulls".

Randy had his arm tied up, but he was still able to work with using one hand, he did a lot of holding things in place as they were being worked on in the ranch yard. He found that the dugout was just as comfortable as before, the stove had taken most of the moisture out of the room.

After another two days the wagons were loaded, everything set for the long ride over to the Sacramento Rancho. Ronnie gave the "wagons ho", and the wagon train was started west. Billy Jenkins was driving one of the bull wagons and Jack Jenkins was driving the cook/supply wagon, loaded with the hay and water, this wagon was Abby's. Sean had the lead bull wagon following behind Ronnie, Abby, Tony and Maggie. Only Andy Sams and Randy were at the ranch headquarters, Rose and Marty were staying at the mine to watch and finish their cabin.

Randy was up when the wagon train headed west, it was just first light. Andy came out also to watch them get started, he was ready for a slow day after the past week of getting the wagons and horses ready to travel. "Randy, have you had breakfast yet?

"No, I was just getting ready to give it a try". "Come with me and you can eat at my lodge, it may be a bit crowded, but you won't need to do the cooking". When they entered, the light was dim but as his eyes adjusted to the low light, he could see Black Dove and her two boys and another woman he had seen help fix his arm.

Andy said, "You know my wife Black Dove and this is her younger sister Morning. Her husband was killed a few months ago and she came to live with us in the village, she has her own lodge, but we eat with each other sometimes". Randy was greeted by a smile and Morning pointing to a place for him to eat, sitting beside Black Dove's two young boys. They were some of his helpers when building the cave, he used for his home before going to help Sean get the mine in operation.

This wagon wheel could tell us so many stories about how hard the life was for the families in the west around the 1863 time period. Is this wheel waiting to be repaired but they never found the time?

(Photo by Robin Travis).

Forgotten wheel.

CHAPTER 13 **WILSON BOYS MAKE GOOD**

Raymond Wilson came up in the conversation during the first night's campfire, Larry was thinking out loud about Raymond and what had happened to him. "I think he is like his brother Ellis that the outlaw life was not to his taste. The only thing we have him on is stealing the horse he is riding and holding the horses on two bank robberies, what do you think boss"?

US Marshal Johnson said, "As we all know many people get put into situations that they have little control over, Ellis Wilson was sure what he wanted in life, but it looks like Raymond allowed his father to lead him into a bad place. Sheriff Buford what do you think"? Marshal Johnson asked.

"My guess is that the horse will be at the livery stable when I get back to Chico and Raymond Wilson will be on the farm waiting to be arrested, that is what I think replied Sheriff Buford"? A few days later the three rode into Sacramento early in the morning. US Marshal Johnson rode to his office to start making reports, Deputy Marshal McPherson and Sheriff Buford stopped at a restaurant to eat then rode on north to find a camping spot for the night. Larry decided to ride late, and they would make camp at the site of the shoot-out with the Barton Gang. The next few days were without any issues or mishaps along the way. On the third day out of Sacramento they rode into Chico just after dark. Buford led the way to the livery stable in Chico, it is owned by Wilber Jeffries. "Wilber, get up, you have some horses to take care of".

"Sheriff, good to see you back, we were wondering if Jessie Wilson had killed you, no such luck for Chico".

"Wilber this is U S Marshal McPherson".

"Nice to meet you Marshal he said", "Sheriff you need to look at this, two days ago I found one of my horses that was stolen tied up to the hitch rail when I opened up the doors in the morning".

"Well Wilber, you need to take a look at what we have, because we have all of the other stolen horses, plus one new gilding. Will you stable all of the horses, and we will be back in the morning to fill you in what happened on our recovery effort".

Larry pulled his saddle and put it on the rack and unpacked his packhorse. After forking some hay for the two horses and giving them a good rubdown, he walked over to the hotel with his war bag and two rifles. Larry was greeted by the night desk clerk. After signing the register Larry asked him to put the bag of money in the safe for the night. With receipt and key in hand he climbed the stairs to his room. Opening the door, he tossed his saddle bags onto the bed then rested his two rifles against the wall by the door. Now it's time for dinner and a good stiff drink. He had passed a diner coming from the stable so turning left two doors down on the left he walked in to be greeted by a fine-looking lady. "Have a seat, do you want coffee"? Getting a yes, she gave Larry a smile and walked off to get his drink.

"Hi, you are new to Chico and the badge says you are the law, my name is Sally Wilder. We have steak with baked potatoes with fresh carrots and peach pie".

"That will work for me. Bring it on, I am hungry". Buford walked in just as Larry had ordered. He said to Sally,

"Get me the same whatever it is". Sally smiled and went to get the orders.

"Well Sheriff what do you think now? I was not surprised by finding the horse at the stable, now the question is what do I or we do about Raymond Wilson"?

Sheriff said, "Ronnie, in the morning after we deliver the money back to the bank, do you want to ride out to the Wilson ranch to see what is going on there?"

Larry said, "Sheriff Buford, I would like to go out and visit Gary Gee first. Do you know him"? "Yes, I do, when do you want to head that way"?

"Why don't we meet here and eat in the morning so we can get on the road after breakfast".

At first light Larry was washed. Picking up his two rifles and saddlebags he walked over to the livery stable to talk to Wilber and check on his two horses. The stable doors were open, so Wilber's day had started. As he entered, Larry could see Wilber brushing a horse at the back of the stable. Larry walked in to find his horse Steal, being brushed down by Wilber. "How does he look after weeks of hard riding"?

"Well, Larry, he is ok, but I did find he needs new shoes before you travel too many miles".

"Can you shoe him and have Rob ready in about one hour"?

"Sure, Larry that will be no problem".

As he walked out of the stable, he could see Sheriff Duward Buford entering the restaurant, so he walked over to join him. Walking in, Larry could see Sally was working so he walked over asking".

"What is ready to eat"?

"We have plenty of eggs, ham, potatoes and fresh baked bread".

"Sheriff, is that ok with you"? With a nod Larry ordered for both of them. "Sheriff how far out to the Wilson ranch"?

"It's only a few miles before Garry Gee's horse ranch".

"Are they on the same road?"

"Yes, they are".

"Can we circle around the Wilson place"?

"Yes, we can".

"Sheriff, after talking to Gary I want to spend some time looking over the Wilson Farm to see if Raymond is trying to work the farm or just hanging out doing nothing".

Sheriff Buford guided them around the Wilson Farm and was riding up the road leading to the Gee Ranch. As they entered the house, Gary came walking out of the barn.

"Dang Larry, you stop by with someone different every time. Buford, how are you doing? Did you catch up with Jessie and the boys"?

"Yes, I did". "Is Ellis working for you now"?

"Yes. he is working part time for me. I sold him a draft horse so he could start working the farm, he is sure he can make a living with some hard work. Buford, you need to know that his brother Raymond came back last week, Ellis rode in with him to drop off the horse he stole from Wilber. He figured that you would be along to arrest him any day, so he is working with Ellis until what he said is, (until I go to jail). Ellis is working on Saturday and Sunday to pay for the horse, that deal works for me because the horse he wanted is a small draft horse that I could not sell anyway. I made a good deal for him; I think he will make it now that his piece of crap father is gone. Is Homer alive"?

"No Gary", Homer, Jessie and Simon are all dead, they were a very short-lived gang". Homer, Jessie and Sandy were the three bad ones in the Wilson family, "I had no use for them three". "Larry what happened to Sarah Gary asked"?

"Gary she is doing great. I helped her hire some good ranch hands and get her started. I am going to stop by on my way back to Sacramento".

Deputy Marshal McPherson, "You better not stay too long, or you may never make it back to the big city"?

After a little ride Sheriff Buford eased up to a tree line bordering on the Wilson Farm, they could see Ellis plowing with his new draft horse. There was another man walking behind busting up clods as Ellis turned the dirt with the plow, birds were having a feast with all the worms that had been exposed. After a little while they rode out into the field, Ellis and who they thought was Raymond stopped work and were waiting for them. Raymond walked over to Sheriff Buford saying, "I am ready to go with you if you want, I can't turn back the time, but I can live with whatever is the correct way to handle this problem of mine".

Ronnie asked, "Raymond, what did you learn from your ride with your father and brothers"?

"My first lesson was they were bad people; my father was no good and Homer is a lazy killer. If I had not left them when I did, they would have killed me, I will tell you this Homer did not want to split any of the money with our dad, he was going to keep it all. I that my father would not have been alive after another few weeks. Homer was going to kill both of us".

"Working the farm is work but it is honest work. Ellis had the right idea". US Deputy Marshal McPherson asked Sheriff Buford if he would like to ride back to town to talk over the extent of Raymond's problems with the law are going to amount to.

"Raymond don't leave the area, I want you to ride in tomorrow and talk with us, we will be able to see where you stand with the town and the law, Sheriff Buford said".

Later that day Sheriff Buford and Marshal McPherson were sitting in the county prosecutor's office, going over the case dealing with Raymond Wilson. The Prosecutor, Jeb Dolan, asked Larry did you ever see Raymond rob any bank?

"No".

"Did he have any bank money on him?

"No".

"Did he have a stolen horse with him when you talked to him?

"No".

"Did Wilber see him with any of his stolen horses?

"No".

"Did any witness see Raymond at any of the robberies?

"No". "Larry said", "Mr. Dolan, from your point of view Raymond could not be charged with any crime, is that your position"?

"Yes, Larry I cannot see any real evidence connecting Raymond with any crime, I am not saying that he was not involved but I have no evidence linking him to any crime. Larry, look at this, I think we need to bring him into my office when he comes to town, and we will scare the holy crap out of him. I am sure that after our talk we will have two more honest citizens in Chico".

Larry asked Sheriff Buford if he was good with this outcome.

"As Sheriff of Chico I see that the horses are returned plus one additional so Wilber should be happy, the money is in the bank, the two stores got back their money so I can live with the outcome".

The next day the two Wilson boys rode into town and tied off in front of the Sheriff's office, Ellis was riding the draft horse bareback and Raymond was riding Ellis's horse. Buford and McPherson met them at the door. "Boys, we need you to come with us over to the prosecutor's office to go over your little trip of robbing and stealing". Larry knocked at the door and ushered in the two boys. "Boys, this is Mr. Jeb Dolan, the county prosecutor, and he has a few words for you Raymond.

"I know that you stole a horse, helped rob two or more banks plus two stores. You know that this could land you in jail for years". Raymond was about as low as he could get, he knew he was going to jail for years if not life because of his decision of riding with his crazy father and brother's. "You only have one chance to get out of this. That chance is what US Deputy Marshal McPherson has to say about the evidence he will put forward as charges against you. Raymond, He has the final say".

Marshal McPherson told Raymond to stand and put his hands behind his back, Larry pulled out some hand cuffs and snapped them in place.

Well. "Raymond how do they feel"? Larry told the two boys to stand, and they would go over to the jail to have a talk. Sheriff Buford was trying to keep a straight face as they walked over to the jail. Buford walked around and sat in his chair as Larry told the two brothers to take a seat. Raymond had his head down and had started to cry, the full effect had hit him, he knew his life was over, he would never be able to have a normal life. Why, had he ridden with his father and brothers, the first day Simon had been killed, damn his father.

Ronnie said, "Well. Sheriff Buford, do you think we have made a point with Mr. Raymond Wilson"?

"Yes, let's all go over and get some lunch boys".

"Standup Raymond, let me remove the iron, we still need to talk some, are you ready to eat instead of going to jail"?

Raymond said, "I am not going to jail"?

"No. We are going to eat if that is ok with you".

Raymond and Ellis were both jumping around with joy. Sally greeted them when they walked into the restaurant saying to take any seat.

"Do you all want coffee"? They all said "yes". With coffee delivered, Sally asked if they knew what they wanted to order, Larry told the boys to order whatever they wanted.

After their food order was placed, Larry asked Raymond if he had any idea of how lucky he is not to be sitting in jail waiting on a trial. "Sheriff Buford and you, Marshal McPherson, I do know how lucky I am, but I don't know of any way I can repay you for helping to get the prosecutor, Mr. Dolan, not to bring me to trial".

Larry said, "Raymond you are one of the people who have a chance to either go right or wrong, this is the time that will define you for the rest of your life". "You need to make the best of your second chance".

Ellis turned to Raymond and said, "we need to get back to the farm so we can get a crop in the ground, I have started plowing, now we need to finish that and start planting". They thanked Larry and Sheriff Buford on the way out of the door, Ellis jumped up on the draft horse and Raymond stepped up on Ellis's horse and out of town they rode.

With hot coffee on the table, Sheriff Buford asked Larry when he was heading back to Sacramento.

"Well, I will load up in the morning and head south to a ranch to check on a young lady I helped get started after her husband was killed".

Sheriff said, "Thanks for all of the help I will be in the office if you want some get on the road coffee".

"Sheriff you are great to work with",

"Thanks, it looks like a bad beginning is going to be a good finish, see you in the morning".

Back at the livery stable Larry asked Wilber to check over both horses and could he have them ready early in the morning, Larry paid the bill and gave him an extra five dollars. Larry decided to walk over and have a drink and play some cards to kill the afternoon. Pushing the batwing doors open he walked into the low light saloon and stepped to the left as was his practice to allow his eyes to adjust. There were two tables with poker games going on and two men with tied down guns were leaning on the bar looking Larry over. Both men were looking at Larry as he walked in. Heading to the bar he ordered a shot of rye.

Before he walked into the bar, he had removed the hammer loop on his guns and had re-settled them, any lawman who liked to live wanted his guns to be ready to go into action. Looking down the bar he could see both men had their heads down so he could not get a good look, but with past dealings with wanted men that was a typical action. Larry chatted up the bartender for a bit as he enjoyed his drink, out of the corner of his eye he got a look at the one at the end of the bar. Oh yes, these two or at least the one was wanted for murder, but he ran with a man who was also wanted. The one Larry could see was John Blevins. He had four or five men in a gang, John always had one of the gang with him. The bartender had his back to the men when Larry lifted his glass to take a sip, when his mouth was covered, he asked the bartender if his shotgun was on this end of the bar and is it loaded.

"Yes, it is". The doors opened and the two men turned to look, in the mirror Larry could see it was Jake Tim's, the general store owner, entering the saloon. Larry stepped around the bar and pulled the shotgun from under the counter, the bartender dropped to the floor. Seeing the movement, the two men started their draw but with the sound of the two hammers being cocked both stood looking into the double barrel 10 gauge.

Larry said, "don't touch those guns. I am US Deputy Marshal McPherson; you are under arrest. John, I am surprised to see you this far north, ease those gun belts off and put both hands on the top of the bar. Mr. Tim's, would you gather up the gun belts and put them on the table over here? I will need to keep an eye on Mr. Blevins and his friend. Thanks, have the barkeep get you a drink".

"John, now I need you to get on the floor and don't move, whoever you are put both hands behind your back and lean into the bar, please don't move, these shotguns have a very light trigger, and we don't want a bad cleanup project today". With the handcuffs on this man, Larry walked him over to a chair by the wall. With the chair pulled out to allow the man to lean back into the wall, Larry went back over to John Blevins to cuff him. Larry pulled off his boots to find a derringer along with a knife. "Well do you have any other items I might like to look at"? With a shake of his head Larry kicked him in the ribs.

"OK, I have a pocket pistol in my vest".

Cuffed and unarmed, Larry marched the two over to Sheriff Buford's jail. Larry called out to the jail to see if Sheriff Buford was in, the door opened and seeing two men being held with a shotgun he moved back and pulled his pistol to help cover them.

"Sheriff, do you have any of your deputies in the jail"?

Yes, Bill the jailer is back cleaning out the cells".

Buford called for Bill to come up front.

Larry asked Bill to go with him back to one of the cells. "I am going to have these two stripped, I also want you to go through their pockets to make sure they don't have anything to cause harm to anyone".

After checking each man and getting each one into a different cell, Larry rejoined Sheriff Buford to go over the wanted posters to see just what we are dealing with these two. When Larry came back out, he lowered the two hammers on the 10-gauge saying, "I need to get this back to the barkeep". "After going over the wanted posters both men had a reward of over one thousand dollars for murder and cattle rustling, it also looks like they typically run with at least two or three more men. Larry had pulled both saddle bags from both horses.

"Bill, will you deliver the horses to Wilber at the livery and let him know that I would stop by in the morning, but he didn't need to have my horses ready early if at all tomorrow.

With three wanted posters Buford and McPherson went to check the other two saloons in town. As they passed the first one Larry walked in and returned the shotgun and said thanks to the barkeep. "I don't know your name', "

Pete Smallwood is my name". Mr. Tim's was still at the bar, so he thanked him also for the help, the card game never missed a beat, so Larry ordered drinks all around. He walked down to the other saloons to check if any of the other gang members were in town. Finding none, Larry suggested that they go back and have a rye to polish off a good day.

Buford asked Larry. "How do you want to handle these two men I have in my jail".

"I am going to send a telegram to my boss and inform him of the two arrests and let him make the decision, he may want me to bring them back to Sacramento or send a wagon with a holding cell. We should know in the morning".

The daylight was fading so Larry headed to the telegraph office to contact US Marshal Johnson to get his orders. With the wire out he walked back down to the restaurant for some supper then he would try another drink then bed. Walking back into the saloon, Larry walked up to the bar. Pete Smallwood walked over with the bottle of rye and two glasses. "Larry, I am going to have a drink with you, thanks for handling that arrest without killing one or both of those men, shooting is not good for business".

"That's my job". Now for a hot bath and a close shave, Larry headed for his room for a good night's rest.

In the morning Larry walked over to the telegraph office to retrieve the message from Marshal Johnson. Buford came running out of the jail and headed for Larry and the telegraph office. They escaped last night. "Bill was overpowered just after midnight. He was locked in a cell until I got in this morning". The tracks lead north out of town.

"Buford, I don't think they would keep going north, this gang was planning to rob the bank in town is my best guess. How far does the wagon road go north out by Gary Gee's horse ranch? I have a feeling that John Blevins will ride north until daylight and then head east to pick up that road.

"What do you think"?

"That could well be their plan".

"Sheriff why don't we ride over to just north of Gary Gee's ranch and set up a greeting for them, do you have anyone in that area who could offer up some help with rifles"?

"Why don't we ride over to visit the almost jail bird and his smarter brother Ellis, they may just want to offer some help".

"Let's head over to the stable to get loaded up, I have enough food for a few days so we can find a good camping location and keep under cover". Later they rode into the Wilson farm. The two boys were working, Ellis was plowing with his draft horse and Raymond had a small drag busting up the dirt following behind the plow. Ellis was the first to see them when he made the turn at the end of the field, he unhooked the plow and jumped aboard and trotted over to meet Larry and Buford. Raymond drove his horse over to meet them also. Larry said, "Well boys how is it going? Looks like you are on a mission to get this ground ready to plant".

"Yes", Ellis said, "We need to make this place into a real farm". "What can we do for you"?

"Sheriff Buford and I need some help for a few days Larry said.".

Ellis and Raymond both said what can we do to help you Deputy McPherson?

"We have a problem, I arrested two men yesterday and they broke jail last night. We think they are going to circle around from the north and pick up the old trail over by Gary Gee's place, do either of you know a good place to keep out of sight along that trail and be able to watch for them coming down from the north"?

Ellis said, "yes. I do and it has some water close by with plenty of cover. I have spent many nights camping there, just to get away from my father".

"Can both of you be ready soon"?

"Yes Raymond said, "we can leave now if you want. We only need to gather up some guns and food".

"You won't need any food; we have plenty for a few days".

With Ellis leading, they headed east about five miles to cross the road. Ellis turned north for about one mile then back east into the trees. They reached a small stream just off the road. Ellis rode back north until they came to a hill and the stream turned back east, this is the spot. Larry asked Raymond to unsaddle the horses and get them on a picket line after taking them to water. Larry, Sheriff Buford, and Ellis climbed the hill to look to see if the trail could be covered. Reaching the top, they had a good mile of the road visible from the top.

Ellis said, we can go down to the bench, from there no one can see you because of the trees behind us.

Sheriff Buford said that he would start watching and send someone up later to relieve him in four hours. Larry and Ellis walked back to camp to find the horses all taken care of and a fire started in the much-used fire pit.

"Ok, boys. We need to take a look at your guns and how much ammunition you have for them". Both had guns that were in good shape along with two boxes of shells, so they should be ok. "Now do either of you have any problem shooting at some bad men and they may well be shooting back at you"?

Raymond and Ellis both told Larry that they would be ok. We just could not rob someone or kill them for no good reason. But these men are wanted killers so no. We will not have any problem pulling the trigger if we need to'. "Raise your right hands so I can make both of you a Deputy Marshals. Raymond and Ellis looked at each other and started to laugh, thinking about just a few days ago Raymond was about ready to go to jail. Life is good east of Chico.

Rotating every four hours, the day and night went awfully slow. During that time Larry set up a position for each of the men, he, with the help of the draft horse and Ellis, pulled some logs into position for them to shoot from behind for safety. On the second day Ellis was on watch when he could see some riders coming from the north. With the signal, everyone ran to their positions behind the logs, Larry was just off the road on the east side. Larry told everyone when he told the gang to drop their weapons, be ready to start shooting if anyone starts to pull iron. "Each one has a person to shoot at first starting from the left side. I would take the first rider on the left side and will take any other of the five who tried to escape. Larry ordered everyone to do as he said, "keep firing until everyone was down on the ground and not moving, don't take any chances these men are all killers".

I hope that whoever built this stone cabin had a team and a stone float to carry the rocks to this building site. The builder was a master, look at how the rocks fit into each other. (Photo by Robin Travis).

STONE HOUSE

CHAPTER 14 THE JAIL BREAK

John Blevins was sitting in jail really mad at being taken by some damn US Deputy Marshal. He was planning on how he would kill him real slow. His riding partner had also been caught flat footed without a chance to get a shot off. John asked Scotty. "When do you expect the boys to show up tonight, they should be in town by now. They should figure out we are in jail by now, keep an ear open. "It was getting late; they could hear the jailer snoring. John felt a little draft then heard a thud. The jailer was out, and the keys were being taken off the wall, the outside door opened and in came two of his gang.

"John are you ready to ride? We picked up your horses from the stable with no one knowing. On the way out they picked up their pistols, but their rifles were not in the rack and none of the keys would open the rifle rack, so they went out without a long gun. "Let's head north about twenty miles and hole up for a few days". Just as the sun was starting to show some light in the east John found a good spot to make camp. "Scotty you and Mexican Joe go find us some meat, that damn Marshal took our saddle bags with my food and extra gun and all of my ammunition". Steve Holt got the fire going and unsaddled the horses, getting them on some grass and watered.

"John, we need to give these horses some rest or we are not going to get back to Sacramento".

John heard a shot. 'It looks like we got some meat for dinner. Steve, get some water on for coffee and get ready to start cooking some supper". (By luck Scotty and Mexican Joe had found the two bed rolls with the saddles or John and Scotty would be sleeping without any ground cover or blankets). Mexican Joe had killed a nice doe, so steaks were being cooked for breakfast. John told Steve to saddle up and ride north. "There should be a trading post or town within ten miles or so, we need some supplies to cover us until we get back to Sacramento, get about five days' worth".

John was getting madder each hour about getting thrown in jail, the worst part was they should have been robbing the bank instead of sitting around a fire without many supplies and no money. That damn

Marshal had all of his operating money that was about two thousand dollars give or take some. Now he had no money, no food and not close enough to any town to rob it, he sure could not try the bank in Chico. He would be spotted as soon as they rode into town.

Steve got back just before dark with some supplies. "There was a trading post up the road a bit".

"What took you so long? It is just up the road".

Steve pulled out a bottle of whisky, handing it to Mexican Joe. "I did stay and have a few drinks before heading back. I also kinda found a girl who was willing so that took a bit of time, but I can say no one has been looking for us this far up country".

John told, "Steve, cook up some more of that deer meat and add a couple cans of corn", I am getting hungry. Ok Men. We are going to be a bit tight for money until we can hit another bank".

Steve said, "Why don't we relieve the trading post of some money just before we head south, that should be no problem, there was only one man running the place".

"Great idea, Steve, you and Mexican Joe can ride up and bring us back some operating money while we get ready to head south tomorrow". With the deer meat finished with breakfast the next day, Steve and Mexican Joe rode out north to gather up some road money. Steve walked in. The owner said, "do you need a drink? you are a little early for my sporting girl, she is still sleeping, I see you brought a friend". Steve pulled his pistol and pointed to the money drawer telling him to empty it into a sack. Mexican Joe walked around the bar and made the man lay down. After tying him, they walked out and stepped up and headed south.

John was ready to ride out when they returned, Steve handed him the sack so he could count the money. "Well, we now have all of seventy-five dollars, better than nothing". John said, "We need to keep a close watch ahead and behind us, that Sheriff may just get a posse out to try and run us down". Mexican Joe said they need some fast horses. "These horses are rested. I think anyone can catch us if they try". After riding about four hours, they stopped to let the horses eat a bit and get some water, "we won't take time to make coffee, I want to get forty or fifty miles today". "The sun was up, and the temperature was nice for a ride, after the short rest John was in the lead with Scotty on his right and Mexican Joe on his left as they rode into the early afternoon. John was dozing when he "heard drop your guns, you are under arrest".

*

John was the first to come awake and pulled his gun looking for a target, the other three were just a bit behind him. Larry had his Henry aimed at the rider on the far left and as John pulled his pistol Larry dropped the hammer, the 44 slug reached his target just as his pistol cleared leather. Scotty was falling off his horse when John was hit in the chest by another 44, the bullet lodged in his spine. The last thing he could see was the smoke from the trees beside the road. Mexican Joe had spurred his horse at the first rifle report, Ellis missed his first shot when his rider's horse jumped forward in a dead run. Ellis levered the second round into his rifle and found his target. Pulling the trigger, he felt the rifle slam his shoulder, he heard the thud when the bullet hit his target. Larry lined up the second shot on the rider running forward. He heard Ellis's rifle and the sound of the bullet hitting flesh. Larry pulled the trigger, and his round also found the target, the man was on the ground with his horse still running to the south. Sheriff Duford and Raymond had also done their job, the last horse was walking to the side of the road munching on some grass as the rider lay with two bullet holes in his chest. With the smoke starting to clear, Larry called out to the men, "are all of you ok".

With a reply, "we are ok", he felt better, job done with no one hurt or killed.

"Raymond, catch up your horse and go down the road and pick up the one that bolted when the shooting started. Sheriff and Ellis how about we get these piles of shit loaded. I see Raymond has the other horse. Ellis, you and Raymond load up these two. We will start to camp and load up so we can head to town and get this little gun fight in the books". When the two young men came into camp leading the four horses with their past owners tied over the saddles, and with everything packed and loaded, Larry said, "let's go find the undertaker before they start to stink too bad". An hour later the two Wilson Boys rode into town with US Deputy Marshal, badges pinned to their shirts. Everyone came out to see the parade of horses with dead men over their saddles. Raymond and Ellis had never been respected in any way before today and they liked it. Mr. Tim's came out of the general store to take a look. Larry told the crowd, "without the help of the two Wilson men, these outlaws would have escaped and may never been found, Raymond and Ellis stood up to bullets flying everywhere and they stood their ground and helped kill this gang of outlaws".

Ellis and Raymond both did not say a word. Larry asked them if they could take the dead men over to the undertaker and stable the horses and then come back to the Sheriff's office to do some paperwork. When they were leading the four horses over to the undertakers, they looked at each other and said, "can you believe what has happened in just two days"? With the tasks done, they both walked into the Sheriff's office and asked what they needed to do now. Larry and Sheriff Buford had talked over the events that were to come so Larry told the two men to grab some paper and write up what happened from the time we asked you to help us with this gang. An hour later they handed Larry the report and handed over the badges to Larry.

Larry said. "Give me a bit to read over your reports". After finishing one he handed it to Buford to read with both read and signed. Larry said, "thanks, you both did a fine job". "Now we have a problem with what to do with the reward money and horses along with all of the guns. Sheriff Buford and I are not allowed to collect any rewards or keep any personal property, so it looks like you two now own everything belonging to the four dead men. Their horses are also now yours to do as you want, keep them or sell them. Sheriff Buford, hand them the title to the horses. Now we have another problem that both of you will need to go with me to take care of. Come along, we need to go over to the bank and talk to the bank president about your account". Raymond and Ellis were in a fog, they could not even think about what was going on. Reaching the bank, Larry walked in and asked for the president and showed his badge. The teller walked back to check, he came back and told them to go on back to the second office on the left. Larry walked in and introduced the two Wilson Boys, "Yes I know them. Their dad and brother robbed this bank just a few weeks ago", said the bank president.

"Well, we know all about that and neither of these boys were involved, that is directly from the Chico Prosecutor, Jeb Doland. Now what is owed on the Wilson Farm"?

"I think it is six hundred dollars but let me look, yes, it is six hundred dollars".

Larry told the bank president that "now you need to sign over the title to their ranch and here is the six hundred dollars, we will wait for the new clear title. These men now, also, need to have the account changed over from Jessie to Ellis and Raymond's name".

The bank president said Jessie only had a two-dollar balance in his account.

Larry said, "that will change in a few minutes". The bank president returned with the new bank book. "Now I want you to count this money and deposit it in their account". After counting the bag of money, the bank president came up with two thousand six hundred dollars, "boys, now hand over the bank book and have him record this new amount. One more thing, or I should say, we need you to do another task, but this will take weeks to get finished. The Wilsons will also need all the reward money applied to this bank account when the Sheriff brings over the drafts from the telegraph office. Now Mr. Bank President you need to shake the hands of the two largest account holders in town, am I correct? The rewards will amount to over five thousand dollars".

The bank president was at a loss to do anything but shake their hand and said, "please feel free to come in and talk to me if you have any questions dealing with your account".

When they reached the street Ellis and Raymond asked just what happened, Larry said you are probably the two men in town with the largest bank account.

"Larry is this real? We have never ever had a dollar at one time".

"Look, if you go slow and don't spend money on things that don't count you are set for a long time. If you have any problems go out and talk to Gary Gee, he will help you with any decisions. Now I am going to get ready to ride south after I send another telegram reporting the results of the day, catch a night sleep, then I am gone. Remember you are now one of the most important people in Chico, go slow and work hard. Stop by and talk to Sheriff Buford and offer to help him if he needs any extra support, you two did a real good job. How did it feel riding into town with those badges on"?

"Shit, we felt like kings. Ma would have been proud".

"Be sure to stop by the livery and pick up the four horses or sell them, they are your problem now".

Ellis and Raymond walked over to the general store and placed a large order then, Ellis asked Mr. Tim's if he had any panniers, saying they would need two later to carry home the order. Entering the livery, they found Wilber checking out the four horses. Raymond told Wilber to take his pick of the four horses. Wilber, I feel really bad about taking your horse even though my father forced me into riding with them. This is a way of setting things straight. Wilber said, "Raymond we are good, people make mistakes and I think you have learned what is right, but I would like to purchase any of these horses you want to sell".

Ellis asked Wilber if he had any pack saddles for sale and a wagon.

"Yes, I do".

"How about this, we need two light draft horses to pull the wagon with harness for the team. You take the three horses you want and forget the pack saddle. We pay you two hundred dollars for the wagon and another hundred for the team".

Wilber said, "I think I am getting the better of this deal, I just traded for a good wagon with a team just a few days ago. But if you two men are ok with the deal I am".

"Done" Ellis said. Wilber had the wagon ready to go in just over thirty minutes, Raymond led out the horse that was left and tied it to the wagon. Ellis stepped up and drove their new wagon over to the general store to pick up the waiting order. Ellis asked Mr. Tim's if he could supply the seed for timothy hay. Gary Gee said he would purchase all they could grow. "Sure, I can have it in about one week if that will work".

"Yes, we will be back in town around that time", answered Ellis".

Raymond had the supplies loaded by the time Ellis finished talking to Mr. Tim's. Ellis stepped up onto the wagon seat and grabbed the lines and clicked up the team and headed home so they can get the last of the plowing finished.

Raymond said, "we can get a lot more done with this team to get the clods broken up". Wagon unloaded; dinner cooked. Over coffee they talked about that now we can have a normal life.

Back at the Wilson Farm both Ellis and Raymond were fixing breakfast by six in the morning so they can get the fields ready for planting. Ellis had Stanley harnessed, Raymond had the new team ready, and they were both in the field by seven thirty. Work around the farm went from early morning to about dark with an hour for the horses to eat and rest mid-day.

Ellis told Raymond, "we will need to ask around about a hay cutter, we will need one when the hay is ready to cut so we have about three months. We can ask Mr. Tim's and Wilber; they may know about one in the area".

The week went by so fast the brothers about forgot they needed to go into town and pick up the grass seed and check on any used mowing machines around the area and we also need a rake to gather the hay into rows so we can load it onto the wagon. "Raymond", Ellis said, "I think we also should look at growing some peaches and apples, they would sell for a good price, no one has any in this area that I know about".

When we get to town, we can talk to Mr. Tim's about what we need to get started".

This picture is pure joy, load testing all fours just a few days after joining this world. This is one reason that everyone should spend some time on a ranch to get a better idea of the true-life cycle. (Photo by Robin Travis).

CALF IN THE AIR

CHAPTER 15 BULLS TO CALIFORNIA

After receiving the message from Ronnie Campbell that they were taking twelve bulls to California to trade, Little John and Jane decided to build a pen on their wagon to take six of their young bulls to California along with the Campbell's. Their team was hitched to the wagon along with two of their saddle horses tied to the back of the wagon. One horse had a Henry Rifle and a saddle bag with some extra supplies, the second was going to be their pack horse with bedrolls and cooking supplies along with plenty of ammunition, plus a 10 gage Shotgun with plenty of double 00 buck shot. During the time, the two Indians had come to work they both had learned to talk some English and Jane and Little John had picked up the Paiute language enough to get along. Little John had explained that they would be gone a long time and keep the cattle and horses safe.

Elk Man and Running Deer had taken over the movement of the cattle and horses to keep them on good grass and protect them. Little John and Jane felt the ranch was in good hands with their two Indian workers. Little John never knew if he would have two helpers or five or six, the Indians just seem to come to stay and then they are gone. Jane had moved some of her cooking supplies to a cold room Little John had built into the side of a low hill, when the Indians needed any food stuff, they could get it there.

Ronnie's two Indians, White Bird and Tee, along with Elk Man and Running Deer had built up a nice size horse herd, they traded among the tribes around the area. The jockey Ronnie had working with him on the horses had some real fast horses about ready to race, Buster and Lightning were still the large part of the racing stable Jingles was working with. Little John and Ronnie could never figure out the location of the horses the Indians had but they felt it must be on the back side of the Ruby's. Ronnie told Little John that he had filed on the hot springs area on the back side of Ronnie's ranch and would in time turn it over to White Bird and Tee to establish their own Indian owned cattle ranch.

"Jane are you ready? We should be out to the road by the time they get there". After the final walk through and closing the door, she came out with her Henry and a box of ammunition. Little John gave her a hand up to the wagon seat. "I think we will really like the cushions Abby and I made; they are like the ones they were given in California on their last visit". Elk Man and Running Deer rode along with them for a short time, then turning, they rode into the hills to do Indian things. After a short ride Little John and Jane came to the road. The dust had just started to settle. With a wave, Ronnie started the wagons heading south to meet the road leading west.

Ronnie and Abby were setting a nice pace due to the wagons not being loaded very heavy. "Abby, are you wanting to go into Mr. Brown's store, or do we just send the supply wagon"?

"I don't have any need to go unless Tony and Maggie want to go, let's ride ahead and check with them". After riding ahead about one mile they found Tony and Maggie sitting under a tree talking. "Hi. We wanted to know if you two wanted to ride on into Mr. Brown's store or just send in the supply wagon"? Ronnie said. "The only reason I have is to check to see if there have been problems between here and Carson City, Maggie and I think we would like to go on in and also inform him that we will all be gone for an extended time. We need to ride back and talk to Little John and Jane to see if they need anything or see if they want to ride into the store with us".

"Hi, you two", Ronnie said. "Do you want to ride to Jim Brown's store with us? We need to purchase the supplies for the trip".

Little John said, "we have enough until Carson City, but if you are getting enough for the whole trip just order extra and we will pay our part if that would be ok".

"Sure, we can do that", Ronnie said.

"You are correct Tony", said Ronnie. "We should all go, we can leave mid-day tomorrow and spend the night there, get the supplies ordered and paid for. We can also send a telegram to Juan telling him we have eighteen bulls to trade, that way he can be ready when we get there". After lunch, the following day the four rode on ahead to Mr. Brown's store, light was about gone when they rode in and tied up to the hitch rail at the store. Jim came out to see who had arrived with his

10-gauge Shotgun. After seeing who it was, the gun went back inside the door, and he invited his longtime friends in.

Jim said, "we have supper ready if you all want to eat".

"We will sure take you up on that, will you join us so we can talk about what is going on along the trail heading to Carson City and beyond"?

Jim's cook had the food on the table with a fresh pot of coffee and a hint of having fresh pie. With the food served, the talk went to what is going on to the west heading to Carson City. Jim informed them about the stage had been robbed twice in the last month "one guard was wounded but he will recover, the telegram from the Carson City Sheriff said he thinks it is two different gangs. Both robberies were between Cold Springs and Carson City".

"How many men at each robbery"? Did the Sheriff say anything about how they pulled them off"?

"Ronnie, he said, both had five men all mounted but no distinguishing marks on the men or their horses. They were all bays from what he said". As the plates were removed a pie found its way to the center of the table with some clean plates.

"Now Jim, this is living. We should start to see some fruit from our trees we planted this year or at least next year", Abby said.

"Abby, you need to keep me in mind when you start to get any kind of fruit, I would like to have some to sell".

"We can do that, Jim".

"Ronnie and Tony, I want to thank you over again for recovering the stolen money that was a large hit to me".

"You are very welcome," they both said.

Abby and Maggie went over with Mr. Brown to start to get the supplies rounded up. An hour later they finished to find the men had moved their travel bags into the two rooms Mr. Brown had for travelers. After a great night sleep, breakfast finished, telegram sent and supplies set out to be picked up, the four saddled up and headed west to join up with the rest of the crew. They would need to wait for the supply wagon to catch up the next day. Then the little wagon train would head west to Carson City.

Back at the little wagon train, Jack Jenkins had made the turn heading to the store to pick up the supplies that the boss had ordered. Jack had driven late and had found one of the camping locations he was told to use, taking care of the horses first, he unrolled his bedroll and unwrapped some cold meet and some biscuits for dinner. Reaching into the wagon, he pulled out his most prized possession-the Henry rifle Ronnie gave him after the big gun fight. With pistol and rifle at his side, he drifted off to sleep only to be greeted by the first light showing over the hills to the east.

Horses hitched, bedroll stored, the dew wiped from his Henry and a rub from his oiled cleaning rag he was ready for the day. The sun was easing over the mountains to the east when he was munching on another cold biscuit with what was left of the meat. This was the first time he had been put in charge of anything, he hoped he would do ok. Ronnie had been allowing Billy and Jack to start working alone at times. This was a big thing in his young life, he remembered lying about his and Billy's age trying to get the job on the wagon train to bring back lumber from Genoa.

Reaching the store late, he pulled up beside the front door, setting the brake and tying off the reins to hold the horses. Mr. Brown came to the door with his Shotgun in hand saying, "you must be Jack to pick up the supplies,

"Yes sir, I am".

"Ok, Let's get these supplies loaded". Jack had helped Marty and Randy do some cooking and he was also helping Rose at the mining camp so he had an idea of how the supplies should be stacked so they could be ready for use without hunting and moving everything to get to some flour. It took about one hour to get loaded; Jack thanked Mr. Brown and stepped up to the driver's seat. Jim came back out with some food for Jack.

"Sir I can't pay for that but thanks.

"No, you just take it, Abby and Maggie already paid for this. Be safe" Jim said.

Jack drove late again because during the time it took to load the wagon his team had been watered and was given some grain and hay. Dark was full on when he stopped, Jack could just about see the road for the past hour, so it was way past time to make camp for the day. He was used to un-harnessing horses in the dark, he and his brother were given that job when they first got hired. Horses taken care of first, cold camp so he had no fire, testing some of the meat and bread Mr. Brown gave him, dinner finished. Pulling out his bedroll and the Henry, Jack was sound asleep in minutes, with first light he stored his bedroll and hitched up and was rolling in short order.

Late that day he reached the wagon train, when he topped the hill and could see the other wagons, he knew he had accomplished his first solo job and felt good. Ronnie greeted him and asked about his trip alone, Jack told him that he was worried, but he had no problem. Ronnie asked to look at the supplies to see how well he had stored the goods; it is important to check to see how much detail Jack took in his work. Jack opened up the cook station to show what he had done and started to show Ronnie how he placed each item so the things they needed every day were in the storage racks in front and the bags of beans, flour, rice were all in order. "Thanks, Jack, looks good". As Ronnie started to walk away, Jack told him that Mr. Brown gave him some food and he told Mr. Brown he couldn't pay but he made him take the food saying it had been paid for, was that, ok? "Yes, Jack it had been paid for".

*

Randy with his broken arm was of little use to Andy at the workshop and forge, Andy seemed to never run out of work. Randy had been asked to eat lunch with Andy, so he left the orchard where he had been trimming some of the trees to open up the center to allow better access for the bees to pollinate the blossoms. He had seen the Indian Girl Morning watching as he worked in the orchard. Reaching the forge.

Andy said, "let's go get some food. Black Dove was outside of a different lodge". When they reached the different lodge, Randy was waved in by Black Dove. Upon entering he could see Morning by the cook fire. Dipping a bowl into the big iron kettle, she handed Randy his food and a hand carved wooden spoon.

Randy could see when he walked in, he was going to be alone with Morning. Morning set in front of Randy as he was eating his food. When he finished the bowl, she took it and sat it down beside the cook fire. Turning back to Randy she reached behind her neck and pulled her deer skin dress over her head. When she was naked, she reached out and took his hand and placed it on her breast, Randy felt her nipple harden. Morning stood up and helped Randy with his clothes and they found plenty of soft skins to keep the chill off as they spent the rest of the day getting to know each other.

Morning had started the fire and returning to Randy to help him with his clothes "we will go to Black Dove lodge to eat", she said. Andy and Black Dove greeted them when they came back into the lodge. They both gave Randy a big smile. Andy and Randy came in to eat about dark. During supper Andy asked Randy if he knew that Morning had told him she would like to become his wife. "Randy, that is how it is done around this tribe, women pick their husbands and you have been chosen, so what do you have to say"?

"Andy, I think I have just become a married man". Andy spoke in Paiute to the two women saying, he would like to be your husband Morning.

Later Andy said Morning, has her own lodge. That is the one you had lunch with her in. So, you can move in with her, she has no children, but you can work on that over time. She said she would also move to your lodge in the hill if you wanted her to but would rather live with her people. "Andy, tell her we can live in her lodge to see how that works". Randy went over to his cave and removed his personal things and moved into the Indian Village with his new wife, he found out later that her husband had been killed in a fight with another tribe to the east a five-day ride. The raiding party were going to steal some horses and got into a fight that cost her husband his life along with another, but they killed three before coming home. This was over six months ago. That is why Morning is ready to take a new husband.

*

With everything ready to head out west, Ronnie had Jack take the lead at a faster pace, telling him to keep going for about four hours then find a spot to eat lunch and rest and feed the horses. By the time we reach you the food needs to be ready. Before leaving this morning, he had beans soaking in water for dinner, they would need some time to cook. Jack knew he was in for a new experience being the new cook, he was hoping he would not kill anyone on this trip. Later in the morning he found the spot Ronnie had told him about. After getting the horses taken care of, he got the fire going with two iron kettles over the fire, one cooking some stew and the second one starting to cook the beans. Pulling out the flour, he mixed up some dough for biscuits to go in the Dutch oven. He would put the Dutch oven in the coals and using a shovel he added coals to the lid to bake the biscuits.

Jack was pulling the Dutch oven out of the coals when Ronnie and crew arrived. Billy started feeding the horses and getting them water, that was his job along with driving one of the bull wagons. Biscuits were out of the oven, stew was ready, Jack told everyone, "Food is on. come and get it". Abby and Maggie grabbed a plate to see how Jack's first meal turned out. The biscuits were good but just a bit overcooked, the stew was very good. They told Jack that he did a good job, they knew he figured out that the biscuits were a bit brown on the bottom. After everyone had a plate, he got some food and went over to sit down with Billy. Billy said, "good meal, you did a very good job".

With the wagons back on the road, Jack finished getting everything back in place and hitching up the team. He was an hour behind the wagons. Jack set out at a slow trot; his team could keep this pace for three hours without much of a problem. He would catch up with the wagons and keep going for another three to get to the next rest location. Jack passed Billy who was at the end of the wagon train. When he was about a mile ahead, he found Ronnie, Abby, Maggie and Tony waiting for him to give him the location he is to set up for dinner. With his orders, Jack clicked up the team and trotted on ahead.

Ronnie and Tony stayed and talked about how they wanted to handle the two gangs that were waiting up the road some place. "Tony, I think we need to each take turns riding way ahead to check out the road, if I go now, I can ride twenty miles ahead and I will only need to ride back ten to meet at our overnight site. You can do the same tomorrow. That way we will have eyes on any activity in the area, I don't want to get caught short".

*

Ronnie cantered ahead. He slowed just enough to inform the girls what he was doing, Jack was surprised when Ronnie waved as he passed him and rode out of sight. What Ronnie found out when riding for the Pony Express was watch for dust ahead and to each side of the wagon road. After about fifteen miles he found some grass for Diamond and some shade for him to relax a bit, Ronnie used his hat to give Diamond some water to last him until he reached the spring about five miles ahead. Reaching the area close to the spring, he pulled his Henry and removed the leather strap holding his pistol in place, Diamond knew the drill-he walked slowly ahead, ears searching for any sound. Ronnie eased back on the reins to stop. Hearing nothing and Diamond was relaxed, Ronnie walked Diamond into the draw to the water hole. Giving Diamond a little drink, Ronnie stepped down using his left hand to refill his canteen. Still holding his cocked Henry in his right hand, he went back and hooked the canteen strap over the saddle horn. Taking his reins and tying a knot so Diamond would not step on them while he was eating, Ronnie walked around the draw to check on what or who had been using this water hole. He found what he did not want to see-fresh tracks of five shod horses leading out of the draw to the water hole. With additional searching he found that they had entered the draw from the road on the west side, but tracks were both coming and going so they must have a camped deeper into the hills. When they reach this location, he will have Tony take a look, the Paiutes White Bird and Tee have been working with Tony for a long time so he may be able to determine how long since the horses were here.

Jack gave the wagon train a little time to get ahead of him before starting to the next location for the night camp, Ronnie should be waiting but he knew the location so he could get set up without him being there. Just under an hour, Jack passed the wagon train heading to the overnight campsite. Later in the day he reached the location. Ronnie was not there so he got the fire going and beans cooking. Jack caught some movement on the hill beside the spring, it was a deer coming to water. Jack eased his new rifle out of the boot and lined up the sights and let her bang. The deer dropped in its tracks. Jack walked over and dressed it out and skinned off the hide. With the hide on the ground, he cut up the deer, placing the meat on the skin to keep it clean and cool. Jack knew that Marty and Randy had smoked some meat at one time. Checking, he found the poles and tarp they had used. He started a small fire inside of the tarp with the meat hanging from the steel wires on his little teepee smoker.

Ronnie came in with his gun ready. He had heard the shot from a few miles up the road. Seeing things were ok, he stepped down. Smelling the smoke, he walked over to take a look. "Looks like you killed a deer, steaks for dinner tonight I see".

"Yes, that is my plan Jack said". "Ronnie, that deer just walked down the side of that hill, so I let some air out of him. Sorry about not having coffee ready but I will get it on now, I had to get the meat set so it would not spoil". Abby and Maggie came into the campsite at a slow lope, Jack went to unsaddle and get their horses taken care of with water and hay from the wagon, not much grass for them to graze on close to their campsite.

When Jack got back to the cook wagon, the girls had the meat cut up into nice size steaks. Having been floured and with salt and pepper they were ready to drop into the large cast iron frying pan. Jack pulled out the Dutch oven and opened two cans of peaches, dumping them in. He grabbed some flour, mixed up a crust pouring it on top of the peaches. Jack took a shovel and removed some of the coals and set the Dutch oven on them, then added some additional coals to the top lid to brown the top crust.

All the wagons were pulled into a good defensive position, teams taken care of with their water and feed. Having the water and hay has turned into a great idea, Andy Sam's vision turned out to be a very practical method of traveling in the west. Dinner was served with the deer steaks, fried potatoes and peach cobbler for dessert with plenty of coffee. After everyone had finished, Ronnie came over to talk about finding the tracks of five shod horses at a spring further west, saying we need to all keep watch, rifles ready at all times.

Ronnie asked Jane if she could handle the wagon?

"Sure, I can".

"Little John, I would like you mounted so we can cover more ground if needed, I don't know if we will be attacked or not, but we don't want to be caught napping. Abby and Maggie, I need you to relieve Billy on the wagon, Billy, I want you to ride with Jack as his protection. From now on we will have two out riders, one ahead and one behind, what do you think about that plan? Tony, do we want to take turns, or would it be better for you to lead only because of your tracking ability"?

"Why don't we wait until tomorrow and we can look at those tracks you found", answered Tony.

Breakfast was venison and fried potatoes. They were loaded, and on the road in under an hour. Jack and Billy cleaned up and packed up and were only a half hour behind. "Billy what do you think about being attacked"? We have been in that one gunfight so I think it would be a major problem for anyone who tried a shootout with this bunch. You have seen the girls shoot, they are better than we are, I think Ronnie and Tony will find the gang and set up an ambush and wipe them out. Do you go along with that"?

"Yes, I do Jack. We need to get on the road, we should catch them in about an hour". The two brothers were on the road heading for the location for the noon break.

"Tony let's ride on ahead, I want to show you the tracks at the spring, Jack will noon there so we can ride on ahead after we check the tracks". Jack and Billy reached the spring, they could tell that Ronnie and Tony had been there and the tracks led back out onto the road heading west.

This is a killer picture. The sagebrush draws you into the trees and with a final taste of an outstanding rock formation framed in the sky. (Photo by Robin Travis).

FRAMED IN THE SKY

CHAPTER 16 **THE RICHARDS GANG**

Vergil Richards and his four men were sitting around a campfire talking about what they wanted to do over the next few days, Vergil felt that robbing another stagecoach would bring down some US Marshals or even the Military from Fort Churchill. Wally Spits said, "why don't we just set up for a few days and see if some freight wagons come along, they will be an easy target, all five of us can shoot the ears off any freight outfit". Kelly Fisk is the long gun expert with a wanted poster reading fifteen hundred dead or alive before joining up with Vergil and Wally, Wally only had a thousand dollars reward dead or alive.

*

Kelly's last job had been to kill two guards on a mining payroll in California. He had his two friends with him at that job, Zip Epperson and Doc Charles. Zip and Doc were heading in to pick up the payroll after Kelly shot the two guards. They got close, that is when a US Deputy Marshal came riding in throwing led, he did hit Zip in the arm. The only reason they got away was the Deputy had to take care of the two wounded payroll guards.

Vergil was riding hard with Wally Spits. Just two jumps behind they had a posse of about ten men hot on their tail, the bank they just robbed must have some of their money in it and they all wanted it back. Vergil and Wally were on fresh horses so how close the posse got depended on the quality of the Sheriff's chosen men. Most horses were not of the quality that Vergil and Wally were mounted on. Vergil pushed hard for a mile then slowed down a bit, they had about two miles of open ground before hitting some hills. Vergil look back to see they had some serious horses on their tail, clicking back up to a canter, he would see if they had staying power in their horses. After another mile, the posse was gaining. That is not good he was thinking. "Wally, we need to find a spot to try and turn them boys around". With another mile it was evident that the posse had good horses, the gap had closed again. "See that gulley ahead? We will set up and kill one or two and see if they still want to chase us". Wally walked their horses down the gulley some and tied them off to some brush, Vergil was just reaching the top of the lip when Wally came up to join him, they both had Henry rifles, so they had to wait until the posse came within one hundred yards. Vergil opened up with six shots, hoping they would think they had a Spencer rifle and needed to reload, six shots fired with no effect. Vergil had just lowered his head when a round came over his head, then the heavy boom. Easing his head over the top, they could see a large billow of smoke still hanging in the air. "Holy shit, they have a 50 Caliber Sharps. Wally, we are going to get our heads blown off with that big gun".

From the tree line behind them Vergil and Wally heard a heavy boom, they looked at the posse and one rider flew off his horse when that round hit him in the chest. They watched and the posse turned around with one man over his saddle. Wally gathered their horses and stepped up to see who saved their asses on this day in California. When they reached the tree line three riders came riding out to meet them, Kelly said, "how did you like what my 50 Caliber Sharps did to them boys? I have one of the new side mounted scopes. I can reach out five hundred yards. I sometimes think it makes some men weak in the knees when they hear that big boom. I am Kelly Fisk; these are my close friends Zip Epperson and Doc Charles".

"We are Vergil Richards and Wally Spits. It is a real pleasure to meet you".

Vergil said "Wally and I are kind of heading to Nevada. It is a bit too un-healthy around here, how about you three? Do you want to join up and help relieve some money from some pilgrims that just have way too much money"?

"Sounds like a good deal. Who is going to be the leader? Vergil asked.

Kelly said, "The leader is who has the most money, how about that".

"What have you got Kelly"?

"Well, we are about out of money. What have you got Vergil"?

"Well, I got the bank money you helped save and another thousand in my saddle bags, by default I am now the leader".

"Kelly, we will split the bank money with you because we would be dead by now".

"The Richards gang was now open for business".

*

Vergil said, "we will hole up for three days, but I want you, Kelly and Doc, to ride east. Take some food and plan to stay overnight so you can check out what is coming our way". Vergil had his camp in the hills just east of the Dry Creek Pony Express Station, this was a hard place to find and easy to defend. Early the next day Kelly and Doc headed out to scout the trail, Kelly and Doc both had a good set of field glasses they picked up from a couple of military officers they had killed a few years back. Kelly and Doc pushed hard a better part of the day. Finding a watering hole, they stopped for a few hours then rode on into the night. They worked their way up a game trail that they hoped would lead them up to the ridge line that would overlook some miles of road. Taking turns, they waited until dark then they dropped back over the backside to where their horses were. Eating a cold dinner, they were about ready to turn in for the night.

"Doc", asked Kelly "do you think we should take a peek over the ridge to see if we can spot any campfires"?

"Good idea", so they climbed up to the top of the ridge and settled in to have a look. Way off to the east they could see a spot of light. "Someone is camping about five miles from us. We need to get back up here at daylight".

With the sun peeking over the hills to the east, both men had their field glasses aimed at where they had seen the fire. "Yes, Yes, Yes, I can see three wagons, no, four wagons. We just hit the jackpot, let's get back and report to Vergil".

*

Ronnie had been looking to the west when he spotted a flash of light, "Tony did you see the flash of light on that ridge line about five miles on the right"?

"Yes, I did, but I thought I was seeing things".

"No, we have someone looking us over, let's grab some meat to eat on the way to check that out to see what or who was looking at us". They saddled up and rode forward to the west. "Let's start looking for tracks, we have passed the ridge line we should find some tracks soon Ronnie said."

"Look, Ronnie two riders came in yesterday and these tracks are only an hour old if that.

Let's ride up and check out the spot they glassed us from yesterday". The trail was easy to follow. Riding up to where they had tied off their horses, Ronnie and Tony walked up to the ridge line.

"Ronnie, this would be a great ambush location to cover the trail, we can go on west now to check on the tracks left by the horses, they must have a camp close".

"The tracks show these are big horses like Diamond, we need to go back and get us some food and make a plan for the next overnight campsite". Riding back, they passed Jack and Billy heading to the noon location, they waved and rode on to meet the other wagons. Reaching them, they stopped to talk. Ronnie asked Sean to set up the camp for a possible gun fight the next morning. "Find a safe place for the horses, we will be back later tonight".

When they caught up with Jack and Billy, they were starting to set up camp, Ronnie asked Jack to pack them some road food. We will be back late tonight; we need to do some scouting ahead. "After dinner I want you two to add wood and make a big fire. I want it to be seen for miles". Saddle bags with food and an empty road ahead, the outlaws two horses were not hard to track. About an hour down the road, they moved off the road to let a stagecoach pass. They kept their horses turned away, so the shotgun rider felt no kind of threat with the dust settling. They rode on following the tracks of the two men. Just as the sun was getting low Ronnie found what he had been looking for, he remembered this spring that was just off the road. When they rode to the spring, they found that the two men had also used it to water their horses. "Tony look at this setup, see the ridge to the northwest it is about four hundred yards from here, there is plenty of grass in the draw leading north to feed the stock and they would be out of the way if we get into a gunfight".

"Ronnie what are you thinking about that ridge being four hundred yards away"?

"Tony, I think we have a long-range shooter with a 50 Caliber Sharps, you remember the spot they chose to glass our camp"?

"Yes, who would go to that much trouble when they could have seen us from a lower spot, one of the two is an ambush shooter and is probably really good at what he has chosen to do for a living. We can use that to our advantage, he will never think we may lay a trap for him when he moves into a killing position. I plan to be in the area, he will get a real surprise about the time he is getting ready to make a shot. It is getting late, so we just as well stay here tonight". Horses put up and cold meat and bread chased with water from the spring, life could hardly be better.

Breakfast was the repeat of dinner last night. Saddled up and guns checked, they headed back to the wagons to get the ambush planned. They found the cook wagon with the two Jenkins Brothers getting a meal ready. The coffee was done, and hot food was being cooked when the wagons arrived, Billy jumped up and went to help, telling Sean he would take care of the stock. Billy came over to help unhitch the teams and take them to water and bring them hay. Abby had started to unhitch when Billy got there to take over. "I can get the team taken care of Abby, you go over and join the others". Little John and Jane came in to get some food. After everyone had food Jack and Billy got their food and found a seat.

After eating, Ronnie informed everyone that he and Tony had found that someone had been watching them early yesterday morning. "We think we will be attacked tomorrow morning early; we need to push a bit so we can get into a good position before dark tonight. Tony and I have the start of a plan so we will be ready by the time we get into camp; I think they have a long-range shooter who is supposed to be the reason we will let them have everything we have. I plan to be in position higher on a ridge. We think the shooter will set up on the lower part of the ridge to cover the wagons with a 50 Caliber Sharps. I plan to take him out just after sunup in the morning before he can take a shot. When you hear my shot empty the saddles, no one is to walk away".

"Ok, we need to get on the road. Billy, you and Jack catch up but stay behind Jane. We can all help with dinner if needed, I don't want you two out alone Sean said.", The wagon train had made good time and they were at the spring with two or three hours to spare, all the stock were fed and watered. Ronnie had the Jenkins Brothers gather water from the spring to replace what had been used by the bulls and all the horses at those dry camps along the way.

Working with Sean, Ronnie and Tony moved the wagons into a good location to be able to fire from behind each of the wagons. The cook wagon was positioned in the center facing west. With extra rifles set out with ammunition beside each rifle, everyone had at least two Henrys ready to spit some led. After refilling all the canteens and water storage on the wagon, dinner was ready. Maggie, Abby and Jane had taken over cooking duties for the night. Ronnie had just come back from scouting the suspected shooter's position, he had been lucky a mustang trail led up the back side of the ridge then turned up following the ridge line. Ronnie had looked over the ridge below where he was planning to set up his little surprise. Getting a plate, he went to Abby's wagon seat to eat and use his field glasses to look for dust coming from the west. It was getting dark when he spotted a large plume of dust heading their way. Climbing down, he went over to tell everyone what he had seen. "Look, Tony and I may be wrong but if we are right, we are now ready, we need to keep the fire very high. I want them to see all of us drinking coffee and sitting around the fire without a worry in the world. I want them to think we are a bunch of pilgrims heading west with no idea of any danger".

*

Vergil and his gang were about five miles out when it started to get dark, Kelly had seen the ridge before the spring, telling Vergil that he would ease up there just before light in the morning.

"I should be able to have a shot from under five hundred yards, that is well in my range". Vergil had laid out the plan to ride in during breakfast to offer to allow them a horse each, but they had to leave all the guns. He was planning after this haul, to be able to head north into Oregon and start a small ranch with the money, he had planned to get from all the wagons and horses sold, then he would kill all of his little helpers.

Vergil told everyone to spread out and walk your horses. We don't want to make any extra noise; sound travels further at night. Kelly, we will cold camp just a bit further. You ride into the desert and don't make any noise. I will expect you to be in position by first light, you can watch them to see if they expect any problems. If they are just eating and feeding the horses wait until I am within one hundred yards of the camp, you kill one of the men then we will come in to make them an offer to save their lives".

Before light was showing Kelly was working his way up the backside of the ridge to get ready to kill some people. He was in his element, he lived to see bodies flip over backwards when hit with this big 50 Caliber bullet. He wanted to start singing he was so happy. He could see the top of the ridge now and looked up and down to find the perfect spot to take his shots from. Just down the ridge he could see a flat spot that was the perfect location, he eased down and used his foot to flatten out the low grass and a few little rocks. Kelly had a blanket to lay down so he would not get dirt on his shirt and pants, but mostly he wanted to keep his prize rifle clean. With six shells laid out on the blanket he was ready. It was getting light enough to see through his scope now. Easing up the rifle he could see the men sitting on wagon tongues eating. This is nice, look at those women, they are going to be a nice distraction for a short time. Kelly was ready to go down there and strap one on right now.

*

Ronnie had reached the ridge just after midnight so not to disturb his shooter. Just before light he had heard the man move into position. Ronnie had a stick to help support his rifle when he was ready. Using his field glasses, he could see his target facing a little away from him. Turning back to the west he could see the others riding, he counted four men with rifles pulled and ready to shoot. That showed that they were ready to kill everyone. Ronnie could see the riders clear the ridge line and were walking to the camp, he could see Tony walk out to the first wagon when they reached about one hundred yards. The leader told Tony that he was going to be killed within a minute or so if they didn't lay down their guns. "You don't want to get into a gun fight with all of your women in your campsite do you. They could get shot or killed". Vergil could see all three were just walking over to a wagon like he was not even around, he walked his horse another few steps closer, but the man just stood by the wagon.

*

On the ridge Kelly was just lifting his rifle to his shoulder. The scope came into view, there we go as the cross hairs settled on the man out by the first wagon taking a deep breath and letting it out, his finger pulled the set trigger now to blow this man to hell and gone. Kelly had moved his finger out and had just reached the one that made the gun go boom. As he felt the second trigger, he heard a click as he turned, the 44 bullet found his left side of his chest taking his heart and lungs with the bullet lodging in his upper right arm before he could hear the sound or see the smoke, Kelly never did pull the trigger.

*

At the sound of Ronnie taking out the sniper out upon the ridge, Tony pulled his Henry from the wagon. It was cocked and ready to fire. Tony snapped the rifle to his shoulder. As the sights lined up, he pulled the trigger. He could see the dirt puff from the bullet's impact with the leader's chest. Vergil had raised his rifle to line up on Tony. He had started to pull the trigger; he was just a second too late. Tony's 44 bullet hit Vergil dead center in his chest, the bullet driving a hole through his heart and lodging in his spine. Vergil had just started to squeeze the trigger on his rifle when he saw the smoke billow from the man he was shooting at, he felt the impact, forcing his shot to go high. He was losing his sight and felt the start of his falling to the ground. During his short trip to the ground Abby and Maggie had also assisted in helping him off his horse, Abby's round took him just under his chin as he was falling, Maggie's bullet just missed him and hit Wally dead center in the chest, so her bullet didn't go to waste. The Jenkins brothers both hit their targets with their first and second shots killing Doc Charles and Zip Epperson. Little John and Jane were shooting from the back of their wagon, they both got off three rounds, but the smoke was so thick neither knew if they hit anything. Sean only got one shot off, he thinks he got his shot into the leader but was not sure, Sean is a much better miner than he is a shooter. Ronnie had the big 50 ready to fire by the time the shooting was over, all of about six seconds for around twenty bullets to be sent out of their guns. The only one who got a round off was Vergil, so only one gun would need to be cleaned from the Richards Gang of five.

With the smoke clearing, everyone walked into the center making sure they were all ok. Head count made, Billy and Jack walked out to gather the four horses. They could see Ronnie leading a horse with a man over the saddle. Abby and Maggie went to make a fresh pot of coffee. They could use some quiet time. Sean walked out to check on the horses to make sure they were ok. Ronnie stopped the horse and pushed the dead man off and stepped up to go and bring back Diamond from up the canyon. Returning, he found the coffee ready. Tony and the Jenkins Brothers had pulled all the saddle bags and checked the pockets of the dead men. In the saddle bags he had found letters and other information so they could identify each of the men, Ronnie sent Jack to go and get an empty flower sack to store the personal items so they could give them to the Carson City Sheriff.

Ronnie had just picked up his coffee and was sitting on a wagon tongue beside Abby when Jack Jenkins said, "I bet those men got the biggest surprise they never got to see". That broke the tension, and everyone laughed. Ronnie said, "I don't know of any other three women who would have been able to meet a threat like this and stand their ground, then just shoot the shit out of a gang of killers, all of you are one tough bunch, I am glad to be riding with you. Ok, Girls, how did you three all start throwing lead so quick"? They all stood up and pulled their dresses around the barrel of their Henrys, you could not see that they even were armed. "We had out rifles with us at the campfire, so we just needed to get behind some cover and we were ready to start shooting and we did just that. We have a short ride to lunch due to this little delay, Tony why don't we go drag that trash back into the canyon and leave them".

"Good idea let's go. I will get Teddy and join you". Everyone else started to bring in their horses so they could get on the road.

Little John and Jane had their team hitched with their packhorse and the extra saddle horse tied to the back of the wagon. Ronnie and Tony had finished with dragging the dead men back into the canyon when all the wagons were ready to head west heading to Carson City.

Ronnie had told Jack to lead out and drive for three hours to find a place to do a short rest for the horses, Jack went ahead at a stiff trot so he would have time to get some food ready, Billy was back on the wagon and both Abby and Maggie were back on their saddle horses riding with their men leading the way west. Ronnie had everyone do a quick cleaning of their rifles and he and Tony cleaned the five rifles the gang left behind. Ronnie was keeping the big 50 Caliber Sharps it was under his left leg with his Henry under his right leg. Ronnie had wanted to pick up a Sharps for a long time, during the chase and killing of the Baster Gang he felt he could have killed Jarvis and Sid Davis two times during the chase. With the range of over five hundred yards, you have a lot of options when chasing outlaws.

Ronnie and Tony had been seeing tracks of the gang in the road. Ronnie said, "Let's pick up the pace, I want to follow these tracks and find their hideout and make sure we don't have any extra members hanging around". Remembering what Mr. Brown had said, there were two gangs working between his store and Carson City. Into a lope they went, Tony was watching for the tracks to find the spot where they turned off the road. After another two miles Tony called a stop, they are heading northeast. Five miles off the road they eased up to the back side of a low rise, walking their horses forward and stopping every few steps so they would not be high lined by the sky. This rise dropped into a draw with some cottonwood trees and a small pond. Ronnie pulled out his field glasses and took a long look. Not seeing anything, they rode into the Richards gang's hide out.

Finding very little of value they just piled everything up and lit it on fire, they waited for the fire to burn out then dumped some water on the ashes to make sure. Dropping the iron skillet by the fire ring, they rode back out to the road leading to Carson City. Reaching the road, they could see the wagons had passed so they kicked up to a canter and reached the wagons in a short time. Ronnie rode up beside Little John and Jane to inform them about the gang's camp and it was also destroyed. Jane asked Ronnie, "why do you think just five men would try to get us to give up everything"?

"Jane, most people along this road are from back east, they are used to having the law protect them from bad people. In the west we cannot allow anyone to intimidate us, that is why Little John started teaching you about guns as soon as you met him. I see that you got in your licks today also".

"Yes, I did, I must have become a western girl".

"Damn right you are".

Reaching a lunch rest area for the horses, they left them hitched and ready but fed them in place and had water for all. After an hour they were on the road. During the afternoon Ronnie was thinking that we need to let those bulls out and run a bit, they had been stuck in the wagon pens for the whole trip. After talking to Tony and Little John, they figured they could let them out overnight and reload them in the morning. Finding a good location to stop for the night they pulled the wagons close together with the rear gate facing just inside the front wheel on the next wagon. They had used some rope to fill in the gaps to keep the little bulls inside of the circled wagons. Ronnie said, "Let's get the ramp down and see if they will come out on their own". With the opening in the back and the ramp in place it took only seconds before the bulls were sliding down the ramp running around bucking. With all the bulls on the ground it was a wild few hours before they all calmed down. In the morning, with the pens cleaned and with fresh hay, the little guys wanted to be back inside to eat. All loaded and breakfast finished, the wagon train headed west. Jack was back on cook and cleanup duty, so he was about an hour behind with he was rolling along at a stiff trot.

A few days later they reached Carson City only to find they had a ready market for some of the bulls. Some of the local ranches had found out about the wagon with young bulls so they had some of the local bulls to trade and sell. Ronnie and Little John did make some trades with some extra cash to seal the deal. Restocked, they headed for the Sierras with new supplies after a trip to the Sheriff's office to go over the details of the shootout with the Richards Gang. The Sheriff had pulled all the wanted posters and found out that this bunch were some bad men, three had over one thousand dollars with Kelly, who had a fifteen hundred and the final prize was Vergil Richards who had two thousand dollars. Tony and Ronnie were just thinking that is a pile of money, now what should they do? Ronnie told the Sheriff to hold the money until they came back in a few weeks, he was ok with that.

Ronnie walked back in and told the Sheriff just put the money in one of his ranch accounts at the Bank of Carson City. "Tony, we will figure it out before we get back, I hate to temp a Sheriff with that kind of money, I think we need to get on the road to catch up with the wagons". The wagons were making good time they, should be in the mountains by tomorrow and another few days we will be at the rancho drinking strong coffee.

Ronnie had camped just short of the rancho after a no event trip from Carson City. Ronnie wanted to get into the rancho about nine or ten so Juan would be able to get his ranch work started. He knew no work would get done for a day or two, it would take that long to just get the news talked about. Ronnie, Abby, Maggie and Tony rode into the rancho's front gate at a slow lope. Reaching the hitch rail, they got attacked by the kids followed by Juanita and Juan. Ranch hands picked up the horses but not before Little Juan and Hector were on Diamond and Teddy riding to the stable.

   Two half brothers ready for another adventure, Diamond is on the far side and my horse Dandy is on this side. Dandy and Diamond both were Pony Express Horses and had carried the mail many times. My favorite ride on Dandy was at one or two in the morning pitch black at a gallop over Simpson Pass.

This picture was taken by Ron Bell, at this re-write diamond is passed and Dandy is retired. I spent time with him yesterday, what a horse.

CHAPTER 17 **SARAH'S HORSE RANCH**

With Chico behind him, Deputy Marshal McPherson was thinking about Sarah and her horse ranch, well more about Sarah than the horses, it had been a long time since he had been able to see how her cattle and horse ranch were doing. Larry had helped her get past her husband's death at the hands of the Barton gang, she had to kill one herself and Larry had directed the reward money her way to get her a new start.

Juan, Ronnie Campbell's partner, had directed some great help to her ranch just before he had to help deliver some mining equipment to Ronnie's ranch in the Ruby Mountains in Nevada. Larry should have to make one overnight stop before reaching the ranch. Rob and Steal were making great time so far today after a short rest around mid-day. Larry started to think he could push a bit harder and make it to Sarah's ranch just after dark. Both Rob and Steal were two horses he had kept after helping to kill the better part of the Barton Gang, at the time it seemed like the right thing to do. His horse was ok but was a bit slow walking so these two were larger with longer legs and both can walk. The first thing an outlaw wanted in a horse is fast, able to run a long time and willing to walk like they wanted to get someplace, both had that.

The sun had set by the time Larry rode into the ranch yard, Larry could see a lamp on in the kitchen, so he stepped down and walked to the porch, he was greeted by a double barrel shotgun being held by a very pretty woman. "Sarah don't shoot, I come in peace".

"Larry, it is you, get in here now". Shotgun set by the door, door locked, and Sarah jumped into Larry's arms saying dinner is ready but right now I want you. Up the stairs they went and much later they come back down to eat dinner.

Larry reached out but found no one beside him. Stretching and swinging his legs over the bed he could smell some good stuff. Washing up and pulling a clean shirt out of his kit, he found his way down to the kitchen to find Sarah with hot coffee ready, food about ready to eat and a very happy face. Larry walked over and gave her a better than a friends type of kiss. Smiling up at him she said, "we will work on that later, I am hungry". Breakfast finished, they returned to work on becoming close friends again, later Larry asked her how is your ranch doing, "I am selling some trained horses and have three that need to go back to Gary Gee per our agreement".

"But I have been missing some cattle on the back range, I know it is not any of my men, they just don't have time to be away from the normal ranch duties".

"Are all of the men Juan sent you still working"?

"Yes. They are all on the ranch and I have one other who is also a relative of my original crew". So, it looks like we need a meeting to talk this over with all the crew and find out if any of them have seen anything out of place.

"How many have you lost and over what period of time"?

Sarah told him, "Francisco is the new one, but he is also a cousin of Julio Garza. Sonya is doing the cooking for all of us most of the time, Jose and Victor are both doing great so I know it has to be someone else stealing the cattle".

"Julio and I will ride back to take a look in the morning. It would be good to reconnect with the crew today if that is ok with you, Miss Sarah".

Larry, "I will be able to show you my horse operation today. You may like what you see at the horse barn,"

"I already like what I see so far but I just may need to keep looking a little bit more today". Sarah was already working delivering just what US Deputy Marshal McPherson had in mind, in fact his mind was about ready to explode.

Washed and dressed again, they went out to saddle up and ride over to the horse training stable with its new training corral. Sarah had this large training corrals built with one small square starting pen and two connected round pens, "Sarah, you have been working, this is the best layout I have seen. Why the small square pen"?

"That is when I am starting a young horse. They cannot get any speed in this short space, so it is less likely to get hurt, along with me not getting as many hard knocks. The stables have been expanded some so now I can keep twelve horses in training at all times, Larry, let me show you the three I am going to deliver to Gary Gee soon". Walking into the barn, Larry found everything in order and clean, the first three stalls on the left had direct access to the large corral or arena. Sarah opened a stall door, the little bay walked up to get a neck rub. "Gary didn't tell us that all of the mares were going to foal, from what I see the Morgan Stud is the father of all three".

"I was surprised when Julio told me to check all of the mares, he thought that they all were pregnant and after checking, he was correct. I had not taken time to really check them over, we just had had too much work that needed to be done when Julio and his crew arrived. I think I will take them to Chico in three months so they can grow some. All three are halter broke and have been handled by all of my crew, you can inspect all of their feet, with no problem they think that is nothing to get excited about".

"I am hoping that the others drop fillies so I can keep them".

"Sarah, I don't think Gary is expecting any of these foals".

Sarah said, "I shook my hand on that so I will deliver them unless he tells me otherwise". Sarah saw Julio riding up to the barn, so they walked out to greet him.

"Larry, good to see you. How long are you staying"?

Larry said for a little while, we will see, but at least one week. "Julio, do you have time to ride back into the hills with me to see if we can find any reason Sarah is missing some cattle"?

"Sure, we can go any time Mr. Larry,"

"Julio I would like to ride that way now if it is ok with you".

"Let's go, all of the men are working on jobs that will take them a day or two".

"Sarah, can you put us some travel food? We may be out overnight".

"Julio, go and get your rifle and bedroll, I will get some food. Meet me at the house when you get back". Larry and Sarah headed up to the kitchen to pick up Larry's bedroll and his rifle, food was packed in his saddle bags behind the saddle, rifle in the scabbard when Julio rode up saying he was ready. Sarah gave him a very nice sendoff kiss, Larry stepped up and they headed out to the mountains on the back side of the ranch. When they rode past the waterfall, Larry remembered some nice afternoons with Sarah playing in the water and under the shade of the large oaks.

Larry was asking Julio about when he started missing the cattle and the location of the herd at that time, Julio was telling Larry about the first few cows he thought were missing were in a small valley about one mile ahead. This country was all broken canyons with little flat sections with either a dry wash or a small stream running down to the lower valleys. They reached the area Julio thought some young cows went missing. They rode along the edges looking for any kind of trail leading further back into the mountains.

Larry found many deer trails leading out of the valley but so far none of them looked like any cattle or horses had been ridden on them. Larry came to a lone tree at the head of the valley. He stopped for a bit to look around, there was two deer trails, one on each side of the tree. He stepped off his horse Steal, to take a better look behind the tree. Behind the tree the two trails came back together making only one. About one hundred yards up he found the first hoof print of a horse heading up into the mountains. Off to one side he found some cattle tracks and another horseshoe prints. Walking back to Steal, he stepped up and called Julio to come join him.

"Julio has any of your men been back into the mountains from here"?

"No, senor, when we gathered the cattle, they were in the lower part of the valley".

"I have found some tracks leading back into the mountains. We need to take a look and see where this trail leads. We may find some of

Sarah's lost cattle". Larry was in the lead taking his time, each time they came to the top of a hill Larry would get down and find a tree or bush to break his silhouette from anyone looking in his direction.

This went on for hours. They had found another trail joining the one they were riding on that had cattle tracks also, cattle and horse tracks were showing signs of more recent passing. Larry told Julio to pull his rifle after Larry had pulled his and levered a fresh round into the chamber, both men and rifles were prepared to defend themselves if needed. The trail was a bit wider now and was making a slow decent around a hill that looked like it was dropping into a valley Larry could see once in a while. Larry found a flat spot under a tree and asked Julio how good are you with that rifle, "I can shoot pretty good Mr. Larry".

"Ok, raise your right hand and say what I say, you are being made a US Deputy Marshal as of now".

"Now this is just what I want you to do. I think we will find a small ranch in this valley we are riding into. You need to stay back about fifty yards and watch my back; you look at everything except the person I may be talking to. If anyone pulls any rifle or pistol, shoot them, can you do that? This may be no problem, but we need to be ready, when we ride in, I want you to stop, if there is some good cover you can watch from there. Ok, Deputy Julio lets go and see if we can find some cattle rustlers". Larry rounded the hill and rode into some oaks at the head of the canyon and just down the valley they could see a cabin with some corrals.

Larry rode in at a slow walk, keeping the barn between them and the house. It was early afternoon so whoever was working this ranch should be around the barn or corrals at this time of day. As Larry came around the backside of the barn, he could see a man on horseback moving some cows in a pen. Julio stopped at the corner of the barn so he could cover Larry as he rode over to talk to the man on horseback. When Larry reached the cattle pen, the man looked up and started to reach for his pistol. Larry raised his Henry and told him he was a US Deputy Marshal and drop the gun.

"Who is in the house"?

"I am alone" he said.

"You know if anyone surprises me you will be dead. Julio go over and check the house, leave your rifle with your horse and pull your pistol. Make sure you check every room, even the cold room or cellar. With the house cleared, Larry called Julio over to look at the brands on the cattle, Julio rode into the cattle pen to take a look. The ones he could see had Sarah's brand on them. Larry asked, "what is your name"?

"Willey Stewart".

"Now Mr. Stewart what have you got to say about these cattle with brands from over the mountain"?

"I needed meat a few months ago so I went out to find a deer and I ended up in the valley with some cattle, so I drove one home for meat. Then I decided that I could just take a few to get my ranch going and now you are here to either put me in jail or hang me".

"I had twenty head and a bull until a gang of outlaws came in and took over my place for about a year. They killed all my cows except two and my bull. That damned Barton Gang left me some time ago and I have not seen them for months now. I hope they rot in hell".

"Why did you think it is ok to steal cattle to replace the ones the Barton Gang killed? Did you go to the Sheriff in Sacramento"?

"No, I didn't think about that, I just figured no one would miss a few head of cattle so I just stole them".

"Ok, Mr. Stewart how much money do you have, and do you own this ranch and how many acres do you own"?

"I have only one hundred and fifty dollars in a can in the house, yes I do own the ranch and it is one thousand acres free and clear".

"Mr. Stewart, you do know I can take you to jail or even shoot you or hang you right now".

"Yes, I do."

"Go in the house and put some coffee on, we will follow. Do you have anything to cook for dinner"?

"Yes",

"Then go ahead and get started cooking, we are spending the night. Julio, would you put up the horses then come in and we will see how good of a cook he is, if he can cook, we may not shoot him".

Wally could cook. He must have had some of Sarah's beef because dinner was good. Over coffee Larry laid out a plan to keep Mr. Stewart from going to jail of even getting shot. "Mr. Stewart this is just what you are going to do, get out your deed to your ranch and sign over fifty percent to Sarah James. From now until you repay her for the cattle you stole, she will hold this deed to your ranch, I am making out a bill of sale for the twenty heifers you stole not counting the one you have, or we have eaten. Will this work for you? This way I won't need to shoot you and drive these cows back over the mountain".

"Yes, this is better than I deserve".

"Sarah will expect you to ride over to her ranch in the spring to let her know how many live births you have and, in the fall, to tell her what the head count is on the cattle. Also, she will need to know how many bulls you have, and, in the future, you will need to exchange bulls with her. In the morning you fix breakfast and then we are heading home".

Early in the morning Larry opened one eye to check to see if smoke was coming from the cook stove, Julio had been up feeding the horses and taking them to water. Larry decided to crawl out of bed and face the world. Rolling up his bedroll, he walked to the saddle rack his saddle had been on when he went to bed only to find it on his horses back, ready to ride after breakfast. This Julio is a good riding partner, he does the work and I get to sleep late.

With the bill of sale in Wally's pocket and the signed deed in his, Julio and Larry rode back around the mountain heading back to Sarah James's ranch to see if she is ok with Larry not killing Mr. Stewart over twenty head of cattle, she did become half owner of another one-thousand-acre ranch, she may like the deal. He may just explain the details of the arrangement in a more tender moment late tonight.

Riding in late, Julio just kept riding after reaching the ranch headquarters heading home to his wife and kids. Larry put up Steal back in a stall beside Rob and walked up to the house to see how Sarah was doing, hoping she had some dinner ready. Larry walked into the kitchen to see the large wash tub with hot water waiting for him with clean towels and a bar of soap, Larry had just got his clothes off and settled kind of in the water when Sarah walked in with wet hair and a smile. "Larry, I came to see if you needed any help, then pulled up a kitchen chair to watch the fun, small tub, large man. Later Sarah, asked Larry, "what did you find if anything?

"Well, you may not like the outcome I left the twenty head at the ranch we found them at".

"Why would you do that"?

"This man Mr. Stewart was also a victim of the Barton Gang but yes, he did steal your cattle, so I either had to hang the man or shoot him or put him in jail".

"Mr. US Deputy Marshal, just what did you do? Do I need to smell your gun or check your rope to find out"?

"No, I just had him sign over half of his thousand-acre ranch to you and I made him out a bill of sale for the twenty head of /S branded heifers. He will come over in the spring to report to you how your investment in his ranch is doing".

"Larry that is a long-winded explanation telling me I am ok with moving twenty head over some mountains and I get half of a ranch and I keep my cows".

"Yes, that about says it all.

Do you want to do this over to see if it gets better"?

"Yes, I do and sure hope everything gets better Mr. Deputy Marshal McPherson".

Over the next few days Larry worked with all of her ranch hands to get them able to protect Sarah in any emergency, even Sonya joined in learning how to fire and load both pistols and rifles, he had four extra Henrys that he had picked up along the way to bring his version of justice everywhere he travels. In each barn he stashed a rifle with a box of ammunition, each of the two ranch houses had extra ammunition and

Larry got Sonya and Sarah ready to get into the cold room or cellar to protect themselves and the children. At the end of the week, Sarah was not wanting Larry to ride off chasing the bad guys. The last night they were laying close when Sarah offered Larry half of her two or should say two- and one-half ranches, he said that if he quit being a US Deputy Marshal this would be the first place he would come.

"Sarah, let me think on this for a bit, let's talk in three or four months".

Sarah said, "We are going to have the best going away party ever just you and me".

Party over and the sun coming up over the mountains, Larry was loaded. He was riding Steal and Rob got to be the packhorse today. Sarah came out and gave him a kiss.

"See you in a few months",

"Yes, you will, I need to take care of a few things, but I will be back". Riding out of the ranch yard he felt like he was doing the wrong thing, this just may be his final run of catching bad men. It is sure nice to have a bed partner and friend all in one. Riding into the US Marshals office in Sacramento he was met by Marshal Johnson.

"Come on back. We need to talk over your last few trips".

Johnson and Larry talked all afternoon and went to dinner to finish going over all the details of Larry being shot and his recovery. Larry told the story about going to Manteca and meeting Tray Davis and getting that settled about the raid on Ronnie Campbell's ranch, along with the details of getting shot at in the saloon only to figure out about the bank robbery planned for the next day. I had the mayor and Ronnie had the almost useless Sheriff Jake Sanders, Sanders stood fast and helped some, but the mayor, when the first shot was fired, he ran like a little girl, and I am quite sure he had a problem that needed to be cleaned up. That Tray Davis saved my bacon by killing the second robber and finishing off the one I had shot.

So, I decided to list him for all of the reward money, horses and other personal property, they also had some money so he also got that for helping, Ronnie would not take any of the money or other stuff, so

Tray became the owner. The ranch that was owned by Jarvis Baster needed an owner, so Tray now is the owner raising horses and some cattle. "Well, Larry, it sounds like Tray came away with a new future and some cash. I think that was a good outcome".

"Now, what about that Wilson Gang"?

"Boss you know that one of the brothers walked off and went to work for Gary Gee part time along with starting to rebuild the family farm. When they were ready to rob the Carson City bank, one of the other sons rode off before the robbery. When Sheriff Buford and I returned the money to the bank in Chico, the horse he had stolen was returned and he was working with his brother on the farm waiting for me to come and arrest him. So, Sheriff Buford and I had him ride in to turn himself over to the Sheriff. Both boys came, Ellis was riding his draft horse bareback with Raymond riding Ellis's old saddle horse. Old Buford and I scared the holy shit out of that kid, had him about to wet his draws you could say, I laid out how he could spend most of his life behind bars but in the end, I felt that that kid will never cause any more trouble. So, Old Buford and I took him and his brother over to the café to get a steak to celebrate his good luck".

"Now get this, after getting that settled, I was going over to the saloon to get a drink, who do I find but John Blevins, he is one man we have been chasing for a long, long time boss. So, I got a gun on him and his riding partner, managed to get them in jail but they were rescued by others of the gang. Instead of chasing them Old Buford and I rode out and enlisted the help of the Wilson Boys. Ellis knew of a great spot to ambush the gang, we figured that they had come to rob the bank and would head south so we with the help of the Wilson Brothers, punched their tickets to hell. Sheriff Buford and I can't take any rewards so for the help, those brothers are now set up so they can farm without having any money worries".

"On my way back, I spent a week with Sarah teaching her ranch crew how to defend themselves, I also found out that she was missing cattle, so Julio and I followed the cattle trail and found the twenty head on a small ranch. This owner named Wally Stewart had also been held captive by James Barton Gang for months prior to them killing Sarah's husband. He lost all his cattle then went off to the shady side and transferred some cattle to his ranch, for his misdeeds I had him sign over half of his ranch to Sarah James to cover her loss of twenty head of heifers. I made him out a bill of sale for the cattle naming Sarah's brand so he would be legal owner. So, Sarah lost twenty head of cattle, but she still owns them and is now part owner of his ranch and he does not go to jail, and everyone is happy. Yes, Boss they are. I forgot Wally Stewart can repay Sarah and get the deed back or he will just work with Sarah as an extension of her ranch. I think Wally is happy to have someone to report to, he is just not a solid leader. Sarah will help him become a better rancher Larry said".

Moving cattle with your horse is a bonding that many men never get to experience. A good horse with cow sense was one of the most important part of a cowboy's life on the range. (Photo by Robin Travis).

MOVING CATTLE HORSE AND RIDER

CHAPTER 18 **VISIT TO THE RANCHO**

"Boss, what now do you have for me to do"?

"I would like you to ride down to the Morales Rancho, Ronnie and crew are about there by now. I got a telegram from Ronnie telling me that he had a minor gunfight with five men whose leader was Vergil Richards. He also gave us some help, Ronnie killed Kelly Fisk. Kelly was a man who liked to shoot people from close to a half mile away, three others also made a one-way trip to hell. Larry said, "you do know that Ronnie Campbell is an un-paid US Deputy Marshal, I had him keep his badge just for problems like he ran into in Nevada".

"Good idea, have him keep it, Ronnie is a real asset to the US Marshal Service".

Larry and Johnson parted ways with directions to head south in the morning. Rob and Steal were in the livery close by, so he walked over to talk to the owner. Walking in, Larry found both horses standing with Pete Scrubs working on Steal's feet. "Mr. Scrubs did you find a problem"?

"Yes, I was waiting for you, these two big boys need shoes if you plan on any long rides any time soon".

"Pete, go ahead and shoe them both. I need to rent a horse for a couple of days. I will be riding south about forty miles tomorrow. I have some people coming in from Nevada so you can take your time with the shoeing".

"Great," Pete, told him," "I will have your stuff loaded by six. I'll give you the buckskin, you have used him before, he is a fast walker".

"Ok, In the morning take your time. I will be along around nine I have some paperwork to finish at the Marshals office".

Paperwork done; Larry was on the road right at nine. If he pushed, he could be at the rancho before dark. The sun was low as he rode into the rancho yard, Juan came out to greet him and one of his hands took the buckskin to the barn to be cared for.

"Larry, what are you doing down this way"?

"I got word that Ronnie and crew were coming in over the next few days, so I came to check on them being attacked by a gang over east of Carson City". Juan invited Larry into the hacienda to be greeted by Juanita.

"Welcome to our home. It has been a few months since we have seen you. Can I get some refreshment"?

"That would be great if it's not too much trouble"?

"I spoke to my stable man and your bedroll will be in the same bedroom you used last time". "Thanks Juan, how is the ranch doing? Everything looks great. You have made many changes just in the ranch yard, I am sure many other changes have also been accomplished while I have been gone".

Juanita came in with the drinks and joined them. "How is your mother and father if I may ask"?

Juanita told Larry about her father passing just a month ago, but her mother is doing fine. "You will see her at dinner. I think she is getting stronger after the passing of Don Jose, she spent so much time caring for him".

"I am sorry to hear that. I know it was a hard time, Little Juan and Hector probably helped you to keep the sadness away. They were both on the buckskin by the time your stable man had reached the barn. They have sure grown".

"Juan when do you expect Ronnie and crew"?

"My guess late tomorrow or early the next day, I would like to stay until they get here if it is ok". "Larry, you can stay as long as you want, give back that Marshal's badge and come to live and help with the ranch".

"That is not a bad idea Juan, but if I do that it will be a bit north to a horse ranch".

"Oh, you mean Sarah James would get first choice of your services".

"Yes, we have talked a bit about that subject. Is there anything I can help you with during my stay"?

"Yes, my men have told me that we have some cattle missing back by the river, you remember that Harding and Stanton had the ranch that borders our rancho. I think we have another owner who is gathering some of my calves after they are born, I found two mother cows looking for their calves yesterday. We roped the mother cows so we could check if the hair on their udders was rolled up from a calf nursing. Both mothers had a calf nursing, but we could not find the calf, we need to talk to your men who look after those cows".

"Sometimes they will remember a special marking of a calf with the mother's, some vaqueros will have a name for each cow that he takes care of, we will see in the morning". After an early breakfast Larry and Juan went out to the cook shack to talk with his men about the missing calves out by the river. Juan talked to the men asking if they remembered any special markings on any of the missing calves. Gomez said that he could identify both of those calves, but the best way is to just drive the two mother cows over into to the rancher's cattle. The mother will find her calf in a short time. "Great Idea, I am sure the new owner will not like it too much, but I have the badge so let's go cut out the two cows and move them next door".

There was a gate just a short way from the river, the vaquero Gomez, Juan and Larry cut out the two cows and moved them into the other ranch, the two mother cows were bawling and walking toward the other herd. Two riders came up telling them to get off their property or they would remove them laying over the saddle. Larry pulled his pistol and eased back his coat so they could see his Marshal's badge, the mouth of the two started to say something when Larry cocked the hammer with that 44-pistol pointing right between his eyes. "Now boys, unbuckle them guns and drop the two rifles on the ground real slow, just to let you know I do like to shoot people".

The cows were still four hundred yards from the other herd. Two little calves came running out to start nursing on their mothers. Larry told the non-mouth to ride back to the headquarters and bring back the owner. If he is armed when he gets close, I will kill him instead of hanging him. "Do you understand exactly what I said, and I will shoot him". Juan asked Gomez to ease out and keep the two cows from joining the other herd. Juan and Larry rode over to look at the brand on the two calves, both had been doctored and not a very good job of it.

Larry could see about five men riding their way, the mouth said you will not like this greeting, Larry asked Juan if he had a rifle with him, "No".

"Ok, take this Henry and I will use my Greener double barrel shotgun, it sometimes has additional influence at times like this". Larry rode over to the mouth and placed the business end of the greener just under his chin and cocked both hammers. "How do you like this big mouth with no guns"? About fifty yards out the five riders came to a stop. Larry told the owner to ride forward, and he had better not have a gun. Larry could see him unbuckle and hand his pistol to one of the other men. As the owner rode up to Larry, he eased the Greener 12 gauge and pointed it at the ranch owner, "who are you"?

"I own this ranch; I am Murdock Holms".

"I am US Deputy Marshal Larry McPherson; I want to know how these two calves have doctored brands and are in with your herd".

Murdock said, "I have no idea but if they are with my cows, they are mine".

"Mr. Holms how long have you been ranching"?

"I just purchased this ranch only a few months ago".

"So, you are dumb as a post then, this ranch must develop cattle thieves, the last two owners are dead from trying to steal cattle from their neighbors. Now you show up and develop the same habit. Step down Mr. Holms. You are under arrest for cattle rustling and altering brands". Larry told the mouth to ride back to the other men and take them back to the ranch and be ready for a full inspection of their herd in the morning.

"If any of you have any wanted posters on you it would be best to find another ranch to work on, this one may cause you to be arrested also, Remember, if anyone pulls a gun I will start shooting and not stop until I feel the threat is reduced to no one with a gun still standing. Mr.

Holms turn around, we will be getting to know each other better. Juan, we may just move these two back to your property, Gomez how many calves do you think have gone missing"?

"I think not too many so far but these two sure were stolen and the brand changed".

"Now the question is going to be is Mr. Dumb Ass the blame or is someone else trying to do a takeover of your ranch"? Mr. Holms you better start talking to me and fill in the gaps, who and how did you get involved with this ranch"?

"Where did you come from? You sure don't look like you have been on a horse very much, and with you not even knowing that another cow will not nurse a calf other than hers. These two would have died within a few days, so who wants you hung or shot? Who told you to ride out to meet me with a gun when I told the other hand to make sure you came un-armed, or you would get shot? Someone has a poor vision of you as a ranch owner".

"It was my foreman", he said. "Only a coward would ride out to meet with a US Marshal without a gun".

"Did you hire this foreman"?

"No". He came with the ranch. I was a banker in Kansas City and made a lot of money, I started to look for a ranch out west. One of my clients told me of this ranch".

"Who is this client"?

"He was the manager of a gambling establishment in Sacramento owned by two men, a Mr. Stanton and Mr. Harding. They have retired so he is the owner now, his name is Fargo Quinlan".

By the time they got the cows back into Juan's herd it was getting late in the day, Gomez had joined some of the other vaqueros heading for the ranch's bunkhouse. Juan, Mr. Holms and Larry rode into the ranch yard to see that Ronnie and ranch crew had arrived. Larry led Mr. Holms up to the porch, telling him to just sit and do not talk. Larry and Juan went inside to join the crowd. After a bit Larry asked Ronnie to join him on the porch.

"Ronnie, I have arrested Mr. Holms for cattle rustling and doctoring brands, but this kind of stinks of Harding and Stanton".

Ronnie asked, "how could that be I killed both of them".

"Mr. Holms invested a lot of money in their old ranch that was being run by their old manager. Mr. Holms has no knowledge of cattle or ranching, his foreman advised him to come out to meet me with a gun when he was informed, he could get shot if he had one. Bad advice I would say wouldn't you Ronnie? Ronnie here is the kicker, Juan had two calves stolen and rebranded, we drove the two mother cows over to Mr. Holms herd and the two calves came running out to eat. Mr. Holms did not know that one cow will not nurse another's calf".

"Mr. Holms" Larry asked, "Who would own the ranch if you were not alive? I hope you have a next of kin".

"No, the ranch would go back to the last owner that worked for Mr. Stanton and Mr. Harding". "How much money do you have invested in this ranch"?

"   Fifty thousand cash", Mr. Holms said.

"Stand up Mr. Holms". Larry removed his hand cuffs then asked him if he has any money on him?

"Yes, I have about a thousand dollars".

Ronnie, "I am going to go and get Juan, we need to talk". With Juan joining them, Larry asked if he could loan Mr. Holms "a horse to ride into Sacramento and keep for a few days".

"Yes, I will get one saddled for him". Look, Mr. Holms, you are about to be killed by your own men, I want you to ride into town and find a hotel. In the morning you need to go over to the Marshal's office and give Marshal Johnson this note and be sure you don't talk to anyone other than him, stay in your room and don't go to any saloon, eat at the hotel's restaurant, and keep in your room until one of us comes and gets you, it may be a few days. Here is your horse, remember stay out of sight and a good place to stay would be the River Front Hotel. Keep riding till you get to the river. The hotel will be on your left, and they have a stable and restaurant on site. Don't leave the hotel until we come and get you".

"Ok, I will stay and not go any place, Thanks Larry".

Larry and Ronnie were talking about what was going on with the staging of those two calves, no one except Mr. Holms could be that dumb not to figure out he was being set up to get shot. We need to get up to Sacramento and look into the gambling establishment, that building must develop crooks. We should go join the gang inside so we can get caught up on all the latest news, so we will be ready to ride out in the early morning.

Juan asked Ronnie, what did they find out about the two rebranded calves that we found on our neighbor's ranch?

"Juan, Larry and I are going to ride into Sacramento in the morning, we sent Mr. Holms to get a room at the River Front Hotel to keep him safe. We think he was being set up to be killed, he has very little knowledge of cattle ranching, it is our guess that he was about ready to be cheated out of his investment money, by the old business partner of the two crooks Harding and Stanton".

Larry and Ronnie reached the US Marshal's office before noon and were able to meet Marshal Johnson for lunch to go over the problem with Mr. Holms and his ranch. During lunch Larry went over the problems as he saw them, I had the ranch owner come up to Sacramento to keep him safe. I felt after I arrested him that the ranch foreman was trying to get him into a gun fight so he could be killed. "Boss, this is what I think we need to do, we need to check the title for the ranch to see who is listed as the owner and see if someone else is listed on that title. My guess is that the new owner of the gambling house that Stanton and Harding used to own may also be listed on that title. Boss, can you get another Marshal to go over to the River Front Hotel to interview Mr. Holms about how he came to be the owner of this ranch. He was a banker from Kansas City".

At the county clerk's office Larry and Ronnie found the deed did have another name listed as a partner. The name was Fargo Quinlan, Larry asked for the title and business license for the gambling house that was owned by Stanton and Harding a few years ago. "It is now called

Fargo's Card House. Guess who is also the owner? Fargo Quinlan was listed as the owner. Ronnie let's go back to the office and check on wanted posters to see if you can find one for the foreman and the other two wranglers you got a look at".

One name that came up was a Quinlan Fargo-wanted for murder, rape, cattle and horse theft. This is a nice guy with a listing for reward of twelve hundred dead or alive. We will have the deputy that is going over to interview Mr. Holms to show him it is in his best interest to help us and stay hidden. We need to check to see if our Mr. Fargo has any others with wanted posters that have been riding with him. Look Ronnie, on the bottom of the wanted poster there are three others listed as co-robbers of a bank in Utah, Goddard Cummings, Mike Vincent and White Diggs. "After going through the wanted posters they found two of the other three, Mike Vincent and White Diggs both were wanted for robbery and murder with a thousand dollars each dead or alive".

"Two stolen calves sure is turning into a larger outlaw ring than we could have thought of Ronnie you know what I think. We'd better be ready for some gun play when we try to arrest the whole crew at the ranch let alone the card house. I like to shoot bad man anyway so let them resist". Marshal Johnson walked in to see what they had found out.

"Well, boys what did you find"?

"Plenty, we know right now that there are at least three killers with a thousand or more dead or alive wanted posters".

US Marshal Johnson asked how Ronnie liked having the Deputy badge with him all of the time.

"I felt better when I had to kill that gang on the way up to the rancho, I would have still done the same thing, but this badge made the action legal".

"You just keep it; you do know that being a non-paid Marshal you can collect rewards and property".

"Great, Marshal, I didn't know that".

Larry said, "Boss, I think we need to ride out to the Fargo's Card House and arrest the whole bunch and sort it out in a few days. What do you think"?

"Let me get my horse and we will do just that; I will stop by the City Marshal's office and have them bring their portable lockup wagon since we don't know how many men we will be arresting". "Great Ronnie and I will start easing that way, thanks for lunch boss".

"Ronnie, I think I see that you have a shotgun",

"Yes, it is my 10 gauge Greener".

"Good, when we go in, I want you to cover the gambling area as Johnson and I go in to gather up Mr. Quinlan Fargo".

Marshal Johnson rode up with them just under a mile from the card house.

"Do you two have a plan"?

"Yes, we do, Ronnie is going to cover the gambling area with his 10 gauge Greener, you and I will go back into the office area and collect Mr. Fargo".

"Ok".

Reaching the front door, the three walked in. Ronnie had the shotgun alongside his leg and was a step behind Larry and Johnson. Ronnie stopped at the door as Larry and Johnson walked to the bar. Larry asked for a drink. When the bartender walked over with two glasses and a bottle Larry eased his pistol over the counter asking him if he had a shotgun behind the bar.

He said, "Yes I do, one at each end of the bar".

Larry said, you walk down to the other end and pull it out with the barrel pointed down and bring it to me. Now with both shotguns in his possession Larry asked him if there is anyone who could be a problem in this room, "Yes, this first table playing cards are two-gun slicks and they are fast". Larry looked at Ronnie and pointed to the table and showed him two fingers. Larry walked over toward the table. When one of the two looked up to see the marshal badge, Larry told the room that they were all under arrest so don't move. The one looking at Larry pulled iron and Larry shot him dead center. As Larry re-cocking his pistol the second gun slick was just coming up when Ronnie took a step to the left so he could not hit one of the other men. The gun slick was greeted by a load of double 00 buckshot rendering him out of commission. His gun rested on the table as he fell to the floor.

Marshal Johnson had one of the shotguns pointed at the door of the owner's office. With the first shot, Johnson kicked in the door and found Mr. Fargo sitting with a pile of money on his desk.

"Stand up Mr. Fargo and keep your hands on the desk". Ronnie had joined him to put the cuffs on Mr. Fargo.

"Well, Marshal Johnson this is our second trip to this office for about the same problem", offered Ronnie.

Larry was talking to the barkeep and getting a lot of information on the goings on with Mr. Fargo and this card room.

Larry said, "Boss you need to get Mr. Fargo to open the safe. It may be interesting information for the district attorneys to look at".

"Larry, do you see any other problems in this room, if not let's send them home".

Larry looked at Ronnie, "I just don't know what this badge does to some people, they just seem to feel impelled to try to draw their pistols, such a poor choice".

With the safe opened and Mr. Fargo loaded in the police wagon and the two dead men loaded, the police wagon started back to town to introduce Mr. Fargo to his new home. Larry, Ronnie and Marshal Johnson were going over the books and titles of many ranches around the local area.

"Boss, Ronnie and I are going back to the rancho for the night, we will need the police wagon tomorrow about noon to receive some new jail birds. We are going to arrest the whole ranch crew at the ranch that Mr. Holms purchased. I will have Juan check the brands on the cattle on the Holms Ranch after we remove the gang members that are now living there. If all goes well, we will see you day after tomorrow about noon".

Marshal Johnson said. "Thanks, see you two then".

Reaching the rancho about dark, they rode directly to the stable and were met by one of the stable hands to take care of their horses. Ronnie and Larry pulled their guns that had been fired so they could clean them so they would be ready in the morning. The black powder had one major problem; it would corrode the barrels if not cleaned soon after being fired. Abby came out onto the porch to greet them saying, "dinner is ready so clean up and over dinner you can give us the story".

Little John and Jane were back from visiting two other ranches close to this rancho, they had traded bulls with two different ranches and had their new bulls in a holding pen waiting until Ronnie and Tony were ready to head back to Nevada. Abby and Maggie told them they need to take a couple of days to visit one of the hotels in Sacramento that had the large copper tub in the room and gave them directions. This can be your honeymoon, take a few days, we still have some things to finish before we head back.

Juan said, "I will get out one of our buggies for you to use, you can drive into Sacramento tomorrow and stay two or three nights.

Juan asked, "Larry how did your trip go today"?

Larry told them a quick version of the day's events, leaving out the two men they had killed by just saying we hauled back three from the card house. In the morning we are going to arrest the ranch hands over at the Holms ranch, we found out a lot about what is and has been going on with many other ranches in the area. The two calves were a set up so the new owner would get into a gun fight with us to cover him being killed by his own ranch hands. He is not the only name on the title. We should start to get to the bottom of the problem tomorrow or at least we hope to. "With the leader in jail we now can work on the other outlaws involved with whatever is going on at this ranch".

Larry and Ronnie were about to ride out to confront the ranch foreman and ranch hands, Little John and Jane were loading up to drive to Sacramento for a few days honeymoon at one of the great hotels.

They talked for a bit then Little John slapped the reins to the horse's rumps, and they were off at a stiff trot. Ronnie and Juan had both stayed at the hotel and enjoyed the copper tub for a few days. Now Little John and Jane can see if it still holds the magic.

"Ronnie, how do you think we need to start this little problem of arresting seven people with only you and me? The odds are a bit on their side don't you think? We can scout around some to see if we can find a good location that we can cover most of the house and barn from. The house is backed up to a hill so we may just want to ease up the backside and check it out".

"Larry you may not know but I have a 50 Caliber Sharp's so I can cover some long-range shots if needed".

When did you get that"?

"The man Kelly I shot coming over was using it when I shot him. He had set up to kill some of us at five hundred yards".

Reaching the backside of the hill, they found a good location with some large rocks to be able to shoot from behind. Ronnie pulled out the 50 Caliber Sharp's rifle then, reaching into his saddlebags and pulled out a box of shells for the big 50. Larry asked Ronnie how far you think we are from the barn. The back of the house is about one hundred yards, one fifty to the front of the house, three hundred to the front of the barn and the back side around three fifty give or take a few yards. I can cover every bit of those ranch buildings and even out to the back corrals, Ronnie informed Larry about his new gun and its shooting distance.

Smoke is coming out of the house so they must be cooking breakfast, there has been four ranch hands go into the side door of the house.

"Ronnie, I am going to ride down to that tree about one hundred yards from that side door and call out the house. They cannot get behind me from that location and you have the yard covered, we also can see the side door and the bunk house. I will ride down and see if they all want to surrender like nice outlaws". Larry rode around the hill and came up to the back side of the big oak tree, taking Rob back further into the trees to keep him safe. He returned to the tree and called to the house saying that he was a Deputy US Marshal and for everyone to come out with their hands raised. He received an answer quicker than he had expected, a bullet hit the side of the tree he was behind taking a chunk of bark with it. Larry called out, "Goddard Cummings are you in there? You had better come on out or we will send a large chunk of led into the kitchen".

Larry gave Ronnie the sign to send in a round to let them know that he really was packing a large gun. Ronnie pulled the set trigger aiming at the roof over the kitchen easing his finger back to the hair trigger and gave a little pressure and the big 50 bucked and with a very loud noise and cloud of smoke the round was on its way, it would take about a second and one half for the bullet to reach the kitchen. A very loud noise came from the kitchen, the bullet went right through a cast iron frying pan and into the fire box of the stove sending a shower of sparks flying in every direction. All the men ran for the front door and headed to the barn. Wolf the cook and Jordan the housekeeper headed down the stairs to the cellar for protection, they both were shaking from the bullet coming through the ceiling in the kitchen. Wolf had just placed the cast iron skillet on the stove and walked to the pantry when all hell broke loose, all the men crashed through the door leaving them alone in the hallway by the stairs.

Goddard was in the barn with a large beam in front of him and feeling safe, Ronnie had seen him stop just inside of the door. Ronnie aimed at the large wood beam and sent the round on its way, hitting the wood beam about six inches below Goddard's chin. The bullet took out about half of the beam and sent splinters in all directions, imbedding some in Goddard's face. Goddard reached around the beam and fired his Henry rifle at Ronnie at the top of the hill, Goddard had figured he would have a good ten seconds for the Sharps to be ready to fire. Ronnie had a round in the chamber in four seconds and had the set trigger pulled and was ready to pull the second trigger just as Goddard opened fire. The second round Goddard had fired was met by the big fifty entering his chest blowing his heart apart and removing six inches of his backbone before striking Mike Vincent in the upper leg. Whitey Diggs saw the damage the big gun had done. He decided to surrender, calling the other ranch hands together and walking out of the barn with their hands over their heads. Larry had kept one of the two shotguns from the card house, so he pulled it and called for Ronnie to come down and help cuff some very scared men.

Whitey asked, "Larry what was that? A cannon"?

"No just a nice long-range rifle".

As Ronnie came around the hill to the main road, the Sacramento Sheriff's office jail wagon was just turning into the drive. Ronnie led them into the ranch yard to receive the prisoners. When Ronnie came up, Larry said I need to talk to some of these ranch hands. Larry led one back into the barn, Goddard lying dead did have a profound effect on the first ranch hands next decision. "Marshal, I am only a cowboy and only Whitey out there is an outlaw. Goddard and Mike Vincent, who is bleeding there on the floor, are outlaws. The other two and me were working for the other ranch foreman when Goddard just walked in and killed him then turned to us three to ask if we had any problems. We knew we would be dead if we opened our mouth, so we have just been doing what we were told to do".

Larry asked, "Who branded the two calves."

"Me and Little Billy did it with a gun pointed at us by Whitey".

"Who are you and the other ranch hands"?

"I am Stuart Bronson; the others are Little Billy and Chester Kellogg".

"Ok, Mr. Bronson you go get the other two hands and gather up all these three men's horses and other items they have in the barn. Billy and Chester come and give me a hand. Larry walked over to Mike Vincent to see how bad his wound was only to find him dead, over half of his upper leg was gone. That bullet must be the size of a small plate when it hit his leg after going through Goddard Cummings. "Well, that will save hanging him". The ranch hands came back with the horses Stuart Bronson asked Larry, "what do we do now"?

"If I, was you, I think I would make sure there is no other stolen cattle and wait to see what Mr. Holms is going to do with this ranch, I have a feeling that he wants to raise cattle and you boys just may have a long-term job. Have any of you ever been a foreman on a ranch before"?

Stuart Bronson said that he worked as foreman on two small ranches, Little Billy worked for me, Chester Kellogg is just a new hire.

"Ok. Stuart you are the boss for now, load those dead men into the jail wagon so we can get these gents to Sacramento to be buried".

"Whitey you get into the jail wagon with your friends, Stuart, tie them horses to the back of the wagon, I don't want them coming untied and run off".

Ronnie and Larry rode back to the rancho. now their marshal business was done, Larry needed to gather up his war bag and head back to Sacramento. After Larry headed north, Ronnie wanted to check up on the progress of the bull trades was going, Little John had traded with other local ranchers and he and Jane were he hoped having a great time in Sacramento. Ronnie decided to ride back up to Sacramento tomorrow to check out a horseracing track that had just been built south of town.

As he rode back into the rancho, Little Juan and Hector were flying off the porch. When Ronnie got to the hitch rail, "can we ride Diamond to the stable"? Ronnie stepped down and tossed the two up on the saddle telling them to just ride him over to the stable. Little Juan had the reins and was trying to get Diamond to run but he was walking along like an old plow horse with the two boys doing their best to get him moving faster. Reaching the sitting room, everyone was talking about what was going on in their lives, come to find out all the young women were pregnant but due a month or so apart.

Ronnie was asked to give them the story about what went on over at the ranch next door, "Well, I kind of retired a couple of outlaws and Larry is hauling them to Sacramento as we speak, the new owner had been set up to be killed. Those two calves were the bate trying to get Mr. Holms to pull a gun on us so the ranch hands could kill him, the man we arrested yesterday we think is the boss and had a deed with his name on the ranch as half owner. We also found some other deeds with the same problem. US Marshal Johnson and Larry are going to get to the bottom of what was going on with about five different ranches.

"Abby, do you feel like riding into Sacramento to look at a racetrack, we may want to stay there and send a telegram to Jingles to bring over Buster and Lighting. I want to look at purchasing a small ranch over here so I can raise racehorses".

"Ronnie, do you think Jingles could handle all of the horses we have"?

"No, I am thinking we may need to go hire some help to go back to the ranch and help him bring all of the racing stock over here. Tony what do you think about having the two Jenkins brothers come back to help Jingles but I hate to take them away from the mining operation, they are a big help to Sean".

"Ronnie, why don't I send two of my vaqueros to go along to help with the horses on the trip back to the rancho"? Juan said.

"Juan that just may be the best idea. We will think on that for the next couple of days".

Early in the morning, Ronnie and Abby started their ride north to take a look at the racetrack and hope to talk to the owner or owners. When they got there the track was far from complete, they had no stands or decent stables for the horses to be stabled during every race. As they rode around, Ronnie rode out onto the track to see how if felt. Turning to Abby, "this is a great track, it is better than Jim Baxter's track in Salt Lake City". They were walking back to the buildings when they could see someone working on one of the buildings, they rode over and introduced themselves to the man. Ronnie asked him who is the owner.

"Well, I suppose I am why"?

"I am Ronnie Campbell and my wife Abby. We want to bring a few racehorses over and do some racing".

"I need to tell you I had a partner who was going to put up the money and I was going to run the operation, but the money man got shot at Fargo's Card House so no money".

"What part of this do you own"?

"I own it all, the investor was going to start putting money into building the stables, grandstands everything else you don't see".

"Did you have a contract with your dead partner"?

"No, we were getting ready to go to a lawyer to have the papers drawn up".

Do you have any experience in operating a racetrack?

"Yes, I ran two different tracks in England until about a year ago, I wanted to see the west so here I am".

"   If you have been in England, do you know a jockey named Jingles"?

"Yes, Jingles Abernathy, he is a good steady rider".

"Jingles works for me riding and training my racehorses over in Nevada". What is your name anyway"?

"Sir Walter Pennington the Third at your service Mr. Campbell".

"Mr. Pennington, how much of a partner do you want or how much of the racetrack do you want to retain as your interest in the track.

"I own the land and have invested about ten thousand so far building the track and the utility buildings. I think it is going to cost about sixty thousand to finish the grandstands and stables. Then it would take another one hundred thousand dollars to cover the betting operation".

"Mr. Pennington the third, that is a lot of money".

"Yes, it is, I would like to retain a twenty five percent ownership if I could".

"Ok. Mr. Pennington what do you bring to the table that does not take money"?

"Well, I know how to run and set up every part of the business. The betting bank is the critical component to any racing operation, the layout is also critical, so the racehorse owners are kept happy, feed and stable operations. All I need is the money".

"Mr. Pennington, Abby and I will check back tomorrow afternoon to talk some more. Something you need to know, if Abby and I become partners we will be involved in every dollar you want to spend, and we will write all of the checks".

"That's ok with me Ronnie".

Ronnie and Abby rode into Sacramento to talk to one of their bankers and get a recommendation for a lawyer. Entering the Sacramento National Bank, they were greeted by a clerk. Ronnie asked to see Wilhelm Gooten, tell him Ronnie Campbell asked to see him. Mr. Gooten came out of his office telling him and Abby to come back to his office. The clerk was told to make a fresh pot of coffee and bring it back when ready.

"Ronnie and Abby what do I owe this visit"?

"Two things we need, one we need to check on our bank balance and we will need you to weigh out some additional gold from the mine for deposit. The second is do you know a good lawyer close to the bank so we could talk to him today"?

The banker called out to one of the clerks, he came back to the door and peeked in.

"Jimmy, go get Lawyer Durst Langston now, have him come over to the bank now if possible".

Ronnie had Wilhelm and his head cashier start weighing out the gold while they wait for the lawyer to come over if he had time. Abby looked up when the door opened and in came the teller and another man with a briefcase, Abby figured that must be the lawyer. Wilhelm told him to use the other office so he could talk to Mr. And Mrs. Campbell from Nevada. Ronnie and Abby with Durst Langston following went into the empty office, Ronnie told Mr. Langston to take the desk seat and they took the two chairs in front.

"Mr. and Mrs. Campbell, I am Durst Langston. What can I do for you? The clerk said you were in a big hurry".

"We wanted to know do you have any experience with contracts involving buildings and property, we are talking to a man who is building a racetrack south of town. His investor was shot at a card house east of town, so he is going to need a lot of money to finish the building and get the operation started. Is this something you know anything about? If so, tell us about your experience with this type of projects".

"I am handling many out of town and in some cases out of country investors in many of the existing ranchos around the area. I just put together a group of investors to purchase a gold mine east of Sacramento".

"Please tell us how you think an investment like this should be established".

"How much money does the owner have invested as of now."

"He has ten thousand dollars spent so far, but we will need to see his books to make sure it is his money, and he did spend that amount up to now".

"Mr. Langston, can you ride out to the property and talk to Sir Walter Pennington and investigate his information like who he is banking with and does he owe any other money on that property".

"I think I have time today to ride out to the racetrack if I hurry".

"Thanks, we will see you tomorrow at your office. Yes, it is just two doors down on the same side as the bank".

Mr. Langston walked out of the doors and Ronnie and Abby walked back into Wilhelm Gooten office to see what the count was.

"Mr. and Mrs. Campbell with the gold we just weighed up, your new total in your account is now four hundred thousand and fifty-eight dollars. I made the adjustments to your bank account".

"Abby let's go get a hotel room and find a nice restaurant for dinner".

"That sounds great for me". Over dinner they talked about what are the benefits to doing this and is there any reason not to do it. At the end they decided if all checked out, they would do this deal, one thing is we may not need to purchase a ranch to keep our horses at if we develop this racetrack. We will put into the contract that we will have a ranch house on the property close to the stables.

After breakfast they walked over to the Marshal's office. Finding no problems with Mr. Pennington, Ronnie and Abby walked over to Mr. Langston's office to see if he had found out any negative information on Sir Walter Pennington the third, they could see through the open door that Mr. Langston was in, and he was motioning them to come into his office.

"Take a seat, do you want some coffee"?

"Yes, we would both like a cup", Langston got up and came back with two cups for them and returned to get a cup for himself.

"I was able to find out from Mr. Pennington that he banked at the Cattlemen's Bank just down the street. Checking this morning with the bank president about his account, it is all in order. The president indicated that he did have a decent amount still in his account".

"I also checked at the lumber and hardware. Mr. Pennington is also current with his bills for lumber and other building supplies".

"Mr. Langston, Abby and I checked with the Marshal's office, and he had no problems with them, in fact they had no idea who he was but did remember a shooting at the card house a few weeks ago. Mr. Langston, can you draft a contract for us to look over before going to re-visit Mr. Pennington at the racetrack"?

"I may have been forward, but I told my law clerk to write up a contract last night knowing that you have to do some other things rather than waiting for me to get a contract ready. Ronnie, I have not read it yet, but I will read the first page then give it to you, we can see if my instructions reflect in the draft contract". Langston finished the first page and handed it over as he started on the second, Abby was reading following Ronnie.

Ronnie said we will need to have the wording about us building a house on the property for us to live in when we are in Sacramento during the racing season.

"I can write that as an appendage to the contract, that will only take a few minutes". Later, with contract in hand, Ronnie and Abby stepped onto their horses and rode back down to the racetrack to have Mr. Pennington look at the partnership agreement. After a short ride they found Mr. Pennington working on the same building as yesterday.

"Mr. Pennington, we have a contract for you to look at, we met with Mr. Langston, and he drew up this agreement, see if it covers your concerns and wants".

"So, you really think you want to get involved with a racetrack, and do you really have the money to cover this large investment"? "You two are quite young".

"You read it and if you like it the money is no problem, you do know Abby and I will be in total charge and will write every check during the build and startup to the fully operational racetrack". Every decision you make, we will do it together. If you agree to that you can read and sign. We will have a racetrack up and running very soon". Mr. Pennington spent about an hour looking the paperwork over. He came back out from his small office in the shed and handed the contract to Ronnie saying, "I have signed it and when do we get started"?

"Get your horse and ride back into the bank and we will also introduce you to Mr. Langston". Ronnie rode directly to Mr. Langston's office where he and Abby signed it having Mr. Langston as a witness.

Mr. Langston followed the new partners over to the bank to visit the bank president Mr. Wilhelm Gooten. Wilhelm walked out to greet them and invited the four back to his office so they could discuss their business in private. Ronnie told Wilhelm that Mr. Langston had drawn up partnership papers between Abby and I and joining Mr. Pennington to develop a racetrack south of town so we need a company bank account set up.

"I want two hundred thousand transferred into that account with Abby and me as signers. Then I want a construction account setup with a starting balance of fifty thousand dollars. I want you to keep track of this account and transfer twenty-five thousand from our joint account when the construction account drops below fifteen thousand.

Abby and I will also keep track of the expenses as we move forward. I also want a safe deposit box set up for us today".

"Ok, Mr. Pennington, Abby and I will be back in a few days, you need to get three contractors to bid on the grandstands and stables and they will have a performance contract so they either do a good and fast job or they will not be paid. Mr. Langston, we need a performance contract drawn up so when Mr. Pennington gets the bids, he can also show each contractor just what he is getting into before he starts to build".

"I will bring it out tomorrow for Mr. Pennington's approval if that is ok".

"Abby, we have a new partner".

Shaking hands, they said that this should be a great adventure.

"Yes, I am ready, I will also have you a timeline for construction when you get back".

Ronnie and Abby mounted and started the short ride back to the rancho to tell everyone about their new project and finish picking the new bulls that will be heading back to the Campbell Ranch in Nevada.

Later at the ranch Ronnie asked Juan and Tony to walk out to the barn so they could talk. "Abby and I just made a deal with a man in Sacramento to build a horseracing track, I have been wanting to raise racing horses for a long time".

"Ronnie, what about the mine and ranch"?

"Tony, you and Juan are part owners of the ranch, so Tony, the only change is that you will make all of the decisions regarding the operations of the Nevada Ranch. We can exchange telegraph messages one a month or sooner if needed, I have a contract for Sean on how I want the mine to operate, Sean will be the operations manager for the mine. He will make all decisions about the mining operations".

Juan, can I send two of your Vaqueros back to the ranch to help Jingles bring the racing stock back to the rancho until I get the stables built in Sacramento"?

"Sure, Ronnie that will be fine. I am sure they will enjoy the trip to see some new country. They also can get away from you for a month, they sure will like that".

They returned to the house to see if Abby had informed the girls of the new venture into the horse racing business. Walking in, Ronnie could tell that the news had been delivered. Ronnie asked for everyone to join him and Abby in the large sitting room.

"What do you all think"?

Juanita was the first to say that it will be great to have them living so close and until their new home was built, she expected them to stay at the rancho. Juan gave that a strong second. As they were talking, Tony said that he was thinking about taking three or four additional chestnut mares back with him to expand his Palomino horse operation.

"Tony, when do you want to start back to Nevada"?

"Day after tomorrow. That should give Little John and Jane time to get back and we will have finished selecting the bulls that will make the trip back to the ranch".

Just before noon Little John and Jane came driving into the courtyard to be greeted by Little Juan and Hector asking if they can ride the buggy horse to the barn. With the travel bags unloaded from the back of the buggy, Little John tossed the two boys onto the back of the horse. He could see the stable ranch hand waiting at the door for the two boys. Walking in, they found the whole gang in the sitting room talking. Come on in, we have some new things to talk about. By the time Little John and Jane were caught up, lunch was ready. Ronnie and Little John were talking about the racetrack and horses. Little John asked Ronnie if he could send two colts back with him to give a try on the track in a year when they get started. Ronnie remembered the big mare he picked up after killing the last of the Spike Martin Gang. Tee and White Bird had stolen the gang's horses. Tee showed me one good looking mare and she is big, close to seventeen hands. She foaled soon after that, the foal was a colt, and he is looking great. I rode that mare, and she is fast. I would like to have you take her and the colt with your racing stock. I would like to see just how fast she is on a racetrack.

"Well, I think that is a great idea, it is a done deal".

The trip east preparations took another day to get everything loaded and bulls sorted, they were loaded the night before heading out to get them accustomed to their new traveling arrangements. Early the next day all were ready to head southeast with the three wagons loaded with eighteen bulls to be the new breeding stock for the two ranches. Abby and Maggie talked for a long time. It is going to be hard to adjust to a new life with her friend. Ronnie and Tony had talked late into the night going over everything that could come up, Tony had become a man working with his brother Juan and Ronnie developing the ranch in the Ruby Mountains.

Ronnie had given Tony the big 50 Caliber Sharps rifle; this will be your long-range protection if someone has evil intent.

"I want you to go out with Rose hunting a few times when you get back to the ranch, she is the best shot I know of with a Sharps".

"Ronnie, I will go hunting with Rose to see what pointers she can give me".

Tony stepped up and rode over to join Maggie. Turning out of the gate, the trip was underway. Tony could feel the big gun under his left leg, under his right leg was his Henry rifle that Ronnie had given him on the first cattle drive he had gone on when Ronnie had started his ranch with his brother Juan. Tony had never been totally in charge before, this was new. Looking around, he could feel the new pressure to keep everyone safe and make it home without losing anyone.

Talking to his horse Teddy, Maggie asked him who he was talking to.

"My horse, I guess. Maggie, I just figured out that Ronnie had a lot of responsibility, I had just supported him. This is different, I hope I am up to the moment".

CHAPTER 19 **RONNIE'S NEW ADVENTURE**

Ronnie and Abby had waited for three days before going back to the racetrack to see how Mr. Pennington was coming along with finding contractors. Ronnie and Abby rode into Sacramento to talk with Deputy McPherson and Marshal Johnson to see how the case was coming along with the bad boys at the old Stanton and Harding card house. Riding to the hitch rail at the Marshal's office, Larry was walking out with Marshal Johnson. "We were just about to come in to look you two up. How is the case going for the Holms ranch"?

"Let's go to lunch and we will fill you in on what we know as of now".

Lunch ordered; Larry told them that Mr. Holms sure was a target along with what we think now is three other ranches in the general area.

"Do you have enough evidence on that Fargo guy".

"The prosecutor thinks with the testimony from the one you didn't shoot we have a great case. Now the second thing is the banker going to keep the ranch or sell it? If you two are around this afternoon, Mr. Holms is coming in to make a statement, we should know at that time".

"Can we go out and burn down that card house Marshal"? The prosecutor found out an interesting twist to the ownership of that card house. Mr. Holms had in his contract that if anything happened to Mr. Fargo he would become the new owner, Fargo never figured he would ever live past last week.

"Larry, does Holms know about that twist"?

"I don't think he has ever figured that out with all of his other problems".

"Abby, do you want to stay over tonight just to see how that works out"?

"Yes, that could be interesting".

"Why are you so interested in that ranch"?

"Well, I think we need to fill you in on our last few days. Abby and I now own controlling interest in the new horseracing track just south of town, we signed the contract just a few days ago. Abby and I have talked about if Mr. Holms has lost his idea of being a ranch owner, we may just want to buy him out. I think he has little or no knowledge of the value of this ranch, with Fargo going to kill him the money he put in was way under its value so we may just make him an offer he may like".

"Abby, we have time to go down and check on the contractors and get back in time to sit in on the meeting with Holms. Let's get out of here, we need to make a fast trip". Mr. Pennington was in his office when they rode in. He came to the door to see who was coming to the racetrack.

"Hi, you two, I have some bids for you to look at. Partner, what do you think about the offers we have so far? I think one is a good one, he is not the lowest bid, but I rode over to two of his projects and they look like he does great work".

"When can he get started after we sign a contract"?

"He has just finished a large project, so he has the men to start Monday of next week".

"How much down does he want? How would he like to work this payment schedule for his work"?

"He wanted me to transfer ten thousand to get the project started and will work that down to three thousand then we transfer another ten thousand. This is just for the grandstand, he thinks we are a little high on our overall cost projections, he thinks the grandstand should only cost about twenty-three thousand. We had figured sixty thousand for both grandstands and the horse barns. He thinks we should only figure around fifty thousand for the total not the sixty thousand".

"Who is this contractor"?

"Mr. Thomas Sutter, his office is in Sacramento just down from the Marshal's office.

"Great, we will stop by on our way back to town. Great work, I am happy with your ability to find a contractor in such a short time".

"Abby, we have a meeting to get to in town, see you later Walter".

Back at the Marshal's office Ronnie pinned on his badge so he would not look out of place and be asked could they help him. Ronnie had met most of the deputies in the office, so he and Abby walked back to Marshal Johnson's office, Mr. Holms had just arrived, and Larry and the Marshal were walking down the hall to a conference room. Ronnie and Abby followed them in and found a seat, Marshal Johnson started the interview by asking Murdock Holms how did he come to get involved with Fargo Quinlan?

"Fargo has a relative in Kansas City who was one of my clients at the bank. We got talking about how I wanted to own a ranch, a week or so later he came back in and told me he had found just what I was looking for and could get in at a great price".

"I came out to the Fargo's Card House, and we made a deal for the ranch".

"Do you know that what you paid was very low for that size of a ranch"?

"No. I had no idea of what a ranch should cost, I had the money that he was asking for the ranch, so I signed the deed and gave him the money. When I got to the ranch the foreman Goddard Cummings started telling me about the neighbor steeling some of my cattle and he wanted us to go and bring them back even if he had to shoot someone.

I was really mad, so I felt that was the thing to do at the time".

"Just so you know I have Mr. Fargo in lockup, Goddard Cummings is dead, Mike Vincent is also dead, Whitey Diggs is the only one of the outlaws alive. He has made a statement to the prosecutor that will get Mr. Fargo hanged for sure. So, I have one other thing to inform you about, the contract you signed listed you as title holder of the card house if anything happened to Mr. Fargo Quinlan. Mr. Quinlan will not live past next week, what do you want to do with the ranch and the card house Mr. Holms"?

"I don't think I will make a rancher so I may sell that and keep the card house. I know a bit about gambling and being a banker, I know how to handle money".

Ronnie spoke up telling Mr. Holms that he would give him his investment back in gold if he would sell.

"You have fifty thousand in gold"?

"If you want to sell, I will have the gold in your hands in less than one hour".

"I sure will sell for that amount".

"You finish you interview with Marshal Johnson; Abby and I will be back real soon".

"Ronnie and Abby walked over to the Wells Fargo bank and had the safe deposit box opened and the gold ready to go within twenty minutes. Gold weight receipt in hand they were back at the Marshal's office walking into the meeting to present Mr. Holms his gold. Marshal Johnson had the deed from the safe at the card house, so he laid it on the table. Mr. Holms signed and Ronnie signed. "Mr. Holms this is a weight receipt for this bag of gold, it reads fifty thousand dollars' worth of gold".

"Thanks" Ronnie said.

"No Thank you Mr. Holms said".

"Abby, how are you going to like living next door to Juanita and Juan"?

"Great, I think we are now set. I don't want to get involved in any more business deals". Ronnie just smiled. Ronnie un-pinned his Deputy Marshal badge and was handing it to Marshal Johnson.

"No. You just keep it. You never know when you may just need it". Ronnie and Abby walked out to their horses. Mounting, Abby turned to Ronnie, "what project do we start on first? Let's ride back down to the ranch, we need to get it settled and see what we need to do to make it our home. What about the house at the track"?

"It will just be our home during the racing season, and we will have the racing offices located there".

Reaching the ranch, Ronnie found Stewart Bronson riding back into the ranch yard with Little Billy and Chester Kellogg. Stewart looked up to see Ronnie and Abby riding into the yard. "Hi, good to see you again, did you see Mr. Holms and when is he going to be back"?

"Well, he will never be back because we just purchased the ranch from him, so we are the new owners.

"Meet Abby, she is the real boss".

The three ranch hands said hello. "If you need anything just let us know.

"Thanks men we will have a meeting at breakfast in the morning".

"Abby, we should take a look at the house to get an idea of what condition it is in, we don't even know if we have a cook or any other help". Walking up to the house they walked in to find a clean well set up house. They could hear someone in the kitchen, so they walked in to see who they hoped was the cook.

Reaching the kitchen, Ronnie walked in to find two people, one was a young lady was sitting at the table and an older man was filling her cup with some coffee. Both turned to see Ronnie and Abby walking in, the man asked if he could help them.

"We are the new owners of this ranch, and we are Ronnie and Abby Campbell and could we have a cup of coffee also".

The man grabbed a cup and the lady started to get up when Abby asked her to sit down so they could all get to know each other. The man said, "my name is Wolf Stinson, and this is your housekeeper Miss Jordan Langdon, pleased to meet both of you". Over coffee they found out that the ranch was about out of supplies and both workers were happy with the killing of Goddard Cummings. Jordan told Abby that Mr. Cummings was trying to force himself on her and she had been ready to find a job at another ranch.

"Jordan, could you go with Abby to do a walkthrough of the ranch house to see what we will need, and I will talk with Wolf about kitchen supplies? Wolf will you make a list to supplies we need and why don't you show me the cold room to see how it is set up". Abby and Jordan re-made the bed in the large bedroom and cleaned out the junk Goddard had left in the closet. Abby found a pair of saddlebags resting in the back corner of the closet. Abby picked it up to take down to Ronnie after they had finished the walk through of the ranch house. Ronnie was surprised when Wolf led him to a cellar carved out of solid rock. When they walked down the stairs Ronnie could feel the change of temperature from the first floor, this cellar was about the same size as the house. With the house on top of a bit of a hill, on the north side was a thick double set of doors leading to the back of the house. These doors could allow a wagon to be backed into this large room.

Meeting back in the kitchen and a fresh round of coffee Ronnie and Abby knew they had really good household staff. "Jordan and Wolf where do you live."

"I have a cot in the small room off the door leading down to the cellar, replied Jordan.

"Ok. We need to go and take a look to see what that room looks like. Reaching the room, Abby found a cot with little else.

"Jordan, you move your things into the bedroom just off the dining room until we find a better living arrangement".

"Wolf where are you living now"?

"I live in the bunkhouse, Mrs. Campbell, with the ranch hands".

"Call me Abby both of you please".

Wolf suggested to Abby it is getting on toward dinner time, do you want some beef stew and biscuits?

"Yes. If it is ready, we can all eat at the kitchen table".

"Jordan, we can get the table set if you want to".

"Sure, but we were not allowed to eat with Goddard and crew".

"New owners now, we will all eat together, Abby I am going out to get the crew so set three extra plates". Ronnie walked into the bunkhouse to tell the crew to get washed up and join them in the kitchen-stew is ready.

In the kitchen, the large table was set, and the ranch crew and owners all seated, Ronnie said "pass the food and let's eat". After everyone had their food, the conversation turned to the ranch and how Ronnie and Abby ended up as the owners. Ronnie told about the plot to kill Mr. Holms and take back the ownership of the ranch, but Fargo Quinlan made a major mistake by having Mr. Holms listed on the deed as the owner if he was to be killed. Well, Fargo did die before getting Mr. Holms killed so Mr. Holms ended up owning the gambling house and this ranch. So, I made Mr. Holms an offer and he wanted the gold instead of the ranch. "So here we are".

Wolf said, "Ronnie, you know Jordan and I about had a heart attack when you fired that bullet into the kitchen hitting the cast iron skillet. Jordan had just finished serving the food and had walked back into the hallway by the pantry and I had just placed the skillet on the stove. We were both in the hallway when all the men ran out of the doorway heading outside to the barn. We opened the door to the cellar and stayed there until things quieted down. Later Stewart filled us in on what happened.

"Stewart, do you think we made an impression on Goddard's gang with that shot"?

"Yes, I sure do, and you damn well made an impression on me and the ranch crew".

Ronnie asked, "Stewart did you find a tally book on the cattle and horses on the ranch"?

"No, I have looked all over the bunk house but could find no book".

Back in the kitchen Wolf made a fresh pot of coffee and Ronnie walked over to refresh his cup. Coffee in hand, he picked up the saddlebags and walked out onto the back porch. Ronnie dumped the saddle bags onto a table. Extra pistol and two boxes of ammunition, other junk and a tally book, that is just what we need, let's hope it is up to date with brand records for all of the cattle on the ranch. With a quick glance at the book, if it is correct, they now own another six hundred head of cattle and around fifty horses and two mules. With all the ranch hands at the table working on the biscuits and stew, Ronnie was telling Stewart and crew about the tally book that he found, he asked him to get the head count for the horses and cattle and not to forget the two mules.

"Ronnie, I think the cattle count is down from what is on the ground now, last week Goddard pushed about fifty or sixty head to the northeast section of the ranch and told us to stay away from them".

"Stewart, we will ride out in the morning to check on the brands of those other cattle, it is a good chance they are stolen".

"Ronnie, I am going to have Little Billy and Chester ride out to the river and get a head count on our cattle and horses while we check the other cattle".

"Jordan, are you set in your room"?

"Abby thanks. I will enjoy the extra room and be able to hang my clothes up for a change". After dinner, Ronnie and Abby found two rocking chairs on the west porch with the sun going down, they started going over the last few days.

"Abby what do you think about Mr. Pennington? If he keeps ahead of the construction of the building, we should be about ready for racing in six months, what do you think"?

"Yes, you are right on target".

"I am waiting to see what Jingles has to say about our new partner. We have a very tight rein on him so his success is totally up to him, Abby we are going to start attending events in Sacramento so our name can get around to all of the money people.

"Are we going to become the upper crust "Mr. Ronnie Campbell"? "On our next trip to Sacramento we need to talk to a contractor to build a small house with two living quarters for Wolf and Jordan". "Good idea that should not take very long to have built".

After breakfast Ronnie and Stewart saddled up and started out to the northeast section of the ranch, Ronnie surprised Stewart with loading up two long guns, one his Henry and the other his 45-90 Winchester. When Ronnie and Stewart rode out of a stream bed back up on to the flats, Ronnie could see three men riding out by the cattle. Turning to Stewart, "keep behind me and get your pistol ready for action", "I don't like the looks of these three men". Ronnie had also pulled his Henry rifle, resting it over his legs behind the saddle horn. As they rode up, the three men turned their horses to face Ronnie. Reaching about thirty feet, one of the men asked Ronnie what he was doing riding on his property.

"Mister what makes you think this property is yours"? "Well Goddard runs this place, and these are my cattle".

"Do you have a bill of sale for these cattle Ronnie asked."?

"No, I don't. Goddard has it but it is not any of your business".

"You two ease those horses back beside the mouth, I may just think you are trying to get an angle on me. My name is Ronnie Campbell I own this ranch, and the boys just put Goddard under the ground with some lead still in him. My advice is for all of you to ease those colts out with your two fingers and drop them on the ground, then we can have a nice conversation about who is the owners of these cows". Ronnie, saw the eyes tighten just before the mouth started for his gun. Ronnie palmed his 44 and fired just as the mouth cleared leather and placed one round dead center in his chest. The other two were also making their draw as Ronnie thumbed the hammer and fired two very quick shots into each of the other two. Stewart's horse had started bucking, and by the time the shooting was over he was still working on getting his horse under control. Ronnie had three men on the ground without any of them getting a round off, Ronnie was thinking why if they are that slow why try, they must have wanted posters on them, so they would rather get killed in a gunfight, but they sure didn't want to hang. "We will see".

"Stewart, you need to work on that horse, he will get you killed".

Stewart said, "I never figured to ever get into a gun fight, you just never know when one is delivered to you without even trying".

"Go and gather up those horses, we need to load up these dead fellers". As Stewart was chasing horses Ronnie walked Diamond among the cattle, he only found two different brand and it did look like about forty head. Stewart came back looking a bit sick, first time at a gun fight, you get used to it over time Ronnie told him. "Go through their pockets I will look into their saddle bags". Stewart had a hard time with the first dead man but got through it and he found thirty dollars in folding money.

"Stewart, pull their gun belts and hang them over their saddle horns". When he finished, Stewart had one hundred dollars and some change, three pocketknives along with three large hunting knives.

"What do I do with this money and knives"?

"Split it up with the other ranch hands, they will not need it anymore.

The dead men loaded, Ronnie and Stewart rode back into the ranch headquarters to check in with Abby and see if she wanted to ride into Sacramento to make the report. Stewart was surprised to see a US Deputy Marshal's badge on Ronnie after the shooting and asked him about it.

"Yes, I am a Deputy Marshal just for things like we ran into today". The other two hands showed up just after Ronnie and Stewart arrived.

"What happened with these three men", they asked. Stewart told them the one started to draw and the other two followed and by the time I got my horse under control the three men were dead on the ground.

Ronnie turned to the men, "Can any of you shoot off your horses"? All replied we have never tried. Now let me look at your guns".

"Boys, go and clean your guns, do any of you have a long gun"?

"No", they all said.

"Ok, pull a long gun and Scabbards from each of those horses and the pistols. Use them and keep your snake killing guns for a spare. I will be back after checking with Abby to see if she wants to ride into town with me and deliver the three dead men". They would not talk much, and it is a long ride. As Ronnie was starting to go to the house Stewart asked if it was ok to ride out and bring the stolen cattle into the holding pen close to the barn. "Good idea, after lunch you can do that but sort them by brand and use the two pens to hold them in overnight".

Ronnie grabbed some lunch and was going to make the ride alone; Abby was going over to Juan and Juanita's to tell them that they were now neighbors. "Say hi for me". Stepping up on Diamond with three horses following head to tail, Ronnie started the two-hour ride to town. Marshal Johnson was walking back from lunch when he found Ronnie tying up hitch rail at the Marshal's Office.

"Ronnie, you are getting way too good at finding bad guys. I am going to need to hire you full time, you are making Larry look bad".

"Marshal, we need to check to see if these three have wanted posters on them, they were way too slow but were not going to give up their guns, all three drew on me when I asked them to drop their guns".

"Also, I have what I think is stolen cattle on my ranch, they are being driven into holding pens by the barn today. Do you have any ranchers who have lost some cows? It looked like twenty cows from two different ranches".

"Larry is out checking on some cattle as we speak, he should be back in another hour. We have time to check on the wanted posters before Larry gets back, we may find that some killers are out of business". As they walked into the office, the Marshal told two of his men to go out and check the three dead men for any identifying marks and report back to him. Then take the dead men to the undertaker but bring back the three horses and saddlebags. "Ronnie, you know by not being a real paid Marshal you collect all of the reward, you piled up a lot of money on your trip to town from Nevada and now I will bet all are wanted just by what you said about them not wanting to get rid of their guns".

I found that the ranch I purchased from Mr. Holms is in very good condition; we are in process of counting the cattle and horses on the ranch and I have two mules. One of the Marshals that Marshal Johnson sent to check came back to his office to report his findings. They all were wanted, two had a thousand dollars and the other has fifteen hundred. They were wanted for murder, rape, three bank holdups and one mail train. "Thanks, the horses should be back soon, the dead men are being delivered to the undertaker now by my men, you took care of the hard part".

Larry walked in just after the other Marshal walked out.

"Yes, Boss. Two ranches with about twenty head each lost, two or three days ago, I will get tracking in the morning if that is ok".

"No, you need to ride back to Ronnie's new ranch in the morning".

"Boss I need to get on the trail of those cattle, the owners are some pissed". Ronnie just removed the three who stole them, and he has the 40 head of cattle gathered at his ranch".

"Larry why don't you ride back tonight with me and stay over, we will help drive them home tomorrow if that will work for you".

"Great, Ronnie let's get on the road".

We need to wait for the three horses. As they were talking, the horses were brought back so they could start riding to the new ranch.

"Larry if we hurry, we can be at the ranch by dinner time". Larry was riding Rob with an extra horse on a lead rope and Rob wanted to run so Ronnie had two of the outlaws' horses on lead ropes, but he gave Diamond his head. Both horses were covering ground with three others working hard trying to keep up. After about two miles they started to ease back on the reins, bringing both horses back to a stiff trot. "With the horses catching their breath, they were back to a nice canter". What seemed like a short ride, they rode into the ranch that Ronnie and Larry had just killed two men and delivered another to the jail in Sacramento just a few days ago. The ranch hands were just heading for the main house for dinner when they rode up, side by each sliding to a stop. Dropping the reins, they both stepped down. Little

Billy and Chester Kellogg came over and offered to help take care of all five of the horses,

"Ronnie, can we put them all in the small corral"?

"Yes, that will be just fine". Walking into the dining room, Ronnie surprised Abby by being home so soon, Larry was surprised by a pretty-young lady by the name of Jordan.

"Jordan, this is US Deputy Marshal Larry McPherson".

"I am pleased to meet you Larry".

"I am Jordan, their housekeeper".

With all of the ranch crew at the table, dinner was served. Ronnie was telling about talking to Marshal Johnson about the forty head of cattle, Larry had been out investigating two ranches that had twenty head or so stolen just a few days ago.

"Men, we will assist Larry in driving the cattle back to their owners tomorrow".

Abby and Ronnie were sitting in the rockers enjoying the evening with a light breeze blowing out of the northwest, this feels like a sea breeze. It may be coming from the Sacramento River and mixing with the ocean breeze from San Francisco Bay. Whatever it is, it feels great. Larry came around the corner of the house with Jordan to join them.

"Jordan, did you show Larry around? The last time he was hiding behind that big tree beside the road coming in while I had to keep him safe from Goddard and his friends".

"Ronnie, this is a great ranch from what I see, I don't think that Holms guy even had any idea of what a nice place this is". Jordan told them that Mr. Holms was afraid of Goddard and the other two men he brought with him, I heard Goddard yell at him to just shut up and he would not get killed.

"Well Jordan, Mr. Holms is the owner of a card house and Abby and I own this place; we are the winner don't you think"?

"Yes. I sure do Mr. Campbell".

"Jordan, just call me Ronnie".

In the morning after breakfast all hands were ready to ride and push the cattle north to their home ranches. "Men I think we will just bunch them all and we can deliver all to one ranch then they can separate them on their own time". Heading the herd down the ranch entrance, one old cow with a nice set of horns took the lead and started marching out ahead of the rest of the herd. Ronnie called out. "We have a leader so just keep the pressure on, she will take them home". Five hours later, with Larry just ahead of the cows that he was leading, they rode under the arch naming the ranch, Larry rode ahead to meet some cowboys heading his way. The ranch owner was in the lead when they met.

"I have your cattle and your neighbor's. Can we deliver them to you and you two sort them out"? "That will be just fine". Larry rode back to Ronnie and turned over the forty head to the ranch owner, with a wave and a short thanks Ronnie and crew headed back to the ranch.

"Larry, are you riding back to the ranch or going to Sacramento"?

"I think I will ride back with you, my interview with Jordan was way too short last night Ronnie".

Dinner was still hot when they returned, Wolf and Jordan had the table set waiting for them. The men put up the horses after a rubdown and some extra grain. With all of the horses in the pen, Ronnie and crew stormed the kitchen. They were all ready to eat anything that would slow down. "Abby, we returned the cattle to one of the owners, they can figure it out between themselves who get what cattle". Jordan and Wolf had fixed a plate earlier, so they served the ranch crew and Larry.

Larry said, "Thanks, men you all did a great job today, as you can see how much damage to a ranch just the loss of a few head of cattle can be".

"Ronnie, and all of you men, when I interviewed both ranchers, this loss would make the difference of them being able to pay the bank note this year".

Wolf came out with two hot apple pies. "Does anyone want any of this"? After dinner Larry asked Jordan if she would like to take a walk?

If a foal could show expression this one would be saying look at me, I can do it mom. This picture just brings me joy. (Photo by Robin Travis).

FOAL ON THE MOVE

CHAPTER 20 **BULLS HEADING HOME**

Tony was leading the wagons by about two miles keeping watch for any problems, the wagons had made it to Carson City without any interruptions. Tony had a feeling that things were about to take a turn, he had never been in total charge having to try to keep everyone safe. Ronnie had always been the leader; this was causing him some worry the farther into Nevada they moved. Tony remembered that Mr. Brown said that there were two gangs working east of Carson City, one had been eliminated by Ronnie and the crew on the way to California. In Carson City he had talked to the Sheriff and found out that two stagecoaches had been robbed just one week ago. Tony asked if they had ridden after the gang. He also said that he could not get enough men to form a posse.

The two vaqueros were well armed, and both could help protect the wagons with the bulls. As he was thinking about the problem, he could see a stagecoach heading west so he rode off to the side of the road to let them pass. As the coach reached him, they slowed down and stopped. Tony rode over to talk to the driver.

"I am Lines Thornton. I have been shot in the arm but am still able to drive the team. The Shotgun rider is in the coach with a shoulder wound, can you help us in any way"?

"My wagons are just ahead, and we can doctor your wounds".

"That would be great if you can, Stumpy Barns needs help".

"I will ride on ahead. You come along slow, by the time you get to my wagons we will be ready". Tony turned and galloped back to his wagons to get set up to help the stagecoach driver and guard.

By the time the stage arrived, Jane and Maggie had everything ready. Billy had some wood planks in the cook wagon-he used them to make a table. When the stage came in, they moved Stumpy to the table so the girls could work on him. Little John brought over a heated kettle with hot water to help clean the gunshot wound. After getting Stumpys shirt off, they could see the bullet had gone in the front and out the back, but it did not look like any bone had been hit. Jane told Abby, "we need to check the shirt to make sure no pieces of the shirt were inside of the wound", Jane had helped her father a few times on her time with the wagon train. Her father had had her help with anyone that had been shot. Looking at the shirt she could see that part of fabric was missing. Jane leaned down to tell Stumpy she was going to have to probe the wound to make sure it was clean. Jane pulled out a cleaning rod for a pistol. Taking it to the boiling water, she cleaned it with some soap, then placed it into the fire to kill any germs. This is what her father had always done before probing for cloth or any leather pieces. Jane gave him a piece of leather telling him to bite on it because this is going to hurt, but I just do not have any choice. Jane ran the cleaning rod into the wound in his chest and as she pushed it out his back, she had a piece of cloth on the steel rod. Stumpy had passed out so she worked fast, adding carbolic acid into the front hole and did the same to the hole coming out of his back. Maggie gave her the sewing kit with a threaded needle, Maggie used some pure alcohol to kill any germs on the thread. Closing the wound is important so each hole was sewn shut.

"Jane, I am going to get some pain medicine that Andy's wife, Black Dove, gave me. I have had some soaking in warm water while you were sewing him up".

"Maggie how do I use it"?

"Just put some under both front and back then just apply your bandages, Jane".

"It is ok to move him back to inside of the stagecoach. Lines come over and I will take a look at your bullet hole". Lines Barns was not happy to be forced to remove his shirt in front of women, but they did get it done.

Jane said, "Lines, it looks like I can just stitch you up and I will put on some carbolic acid along with a bandage and you will be sore but will be ok". With his washed arm, eight stitches and a clean bandage, Mr. Barns was ready for his shirt. Jane told Mr. Barns to get Stumpy to a doctor as fast as he could drive this stagecoach. I did my best and good luck.

Jack and Billy had taken care of the four horses on the coach, giving them feed and water while they were waiting. Tony had talked to

Lines about the attempted holdup. Lines told him that they had picked a bad spot to make the robbery attempt due to a downhill stretch of road. I just pushed the horses into a hard run, Stumpy shot one of the gang and I think he hit another with the second barrel. One of the gang got a bullet into him just after he made his second shot.

"How many men were in the gang"?

"There were four that I got eyes on. The only thing I can say about the horses is they are big; all were bays without any markings that I could see".

Lines got back up to his seat and gathered his lines, clicked the horses forward. Billy and Jack turned the horses loose and stood back as the coach went past.

"Good luck Lines they called". Tony gathered everyone together to tell them he had a spot to camp just up the road. We will make an early overnight stop.

Tony dropped back to talk to Jane and Little John.

"Jane, we never knew you were so talented".

"Tony, my father, was a good home remedy doctor. He had done some doctoring in the war before being sent home with a bullet wound of his own".

"Well, I am sure Stumpy, and Lines will be glad you were able to help them. Little John and Jane, do you think it would be ok if I asked you to drive your wagon so I could have another armed and mounted rider for protection"?

"No problem I am glad to drive and will still have my rifle ready by my seat".

"Thanks, we can talk some more after dinner if it is ok". Jack pulled the cook wagon into position and the others drove in close so they can have a better protected camp. Tony also suggested that they give the bulls a chance to run around some, so they were all turned loose for overnight. The results were the same as on the trip west, those little guys ran and bucked butted heads then found a spot to lay down and rest.

Tony asked Little John to ride ahead as the scout today, "I want to back track those robbers. I may get a chance to give them something to think about with that big 50 Caliber Sharps rifle Ronnie gave me to help protect all of us". Little John felt a bit better when he moved out to be the scout when Jaime Roman rode with him. Jaime is one of Juan's vaqueros, his brother Hector is also along to help bring back Ronnie's racehorses to his ranch in California.

Jaime was not a very talkative man, but his eyes were active and Little John was glad to have him along for support. Tony found the tracks and some blood beside the trail as it looks like the gang had been waiting for a long time. Tony had been working with Tee and White Bird learning to track, he had come a long way in becoming an exceptionally good tracker. He could see that the horses had been waiting for hours due to the amount of grass that had been eaten and then the horses started on the low brush. After the failed attempt at the stage, they had stayed to doctor the wounded man, he had lost a lot of blood. Walking with Teddy following, Tony was tracking the four outlaws from the location of the would-be holdup their horse's tracks were leading back into the hills. Stepping up, he still could read the tracks without any trouble. After an hour the tracks started to look fresh, he had gained on the gang and would need to keep a close watch for an ambush.

Tony had been following the tracks further back into the mountains and it looked like there may be a small valley with some water, the dry wash was damp now and when he started it was dry- Tony needed to find a game trail to get some elevation so he could see what was ahead. Both sets of tracks were in this wash and many other days of riding. Easing up into a little cut he found what he needed a small trail with deer and wild horse tracks leading around the hill. Teddy was a good mountain horse, so the narrow trail was no problem. Tony was seeing that the valley was opening up some as he gained some elevation on the hill. Ground tying Teddy, Tony walked ahead with his Henry rifle. He had been correct-there is a valley with some cottonwood trees and willows along the middle of the valley floor telling him there is a stream.

Reaching a tree, Tony pulled out his field glasses to take a look. He figured with outlaws being lazy they should be close to the start of this valley. After a few minutes he could see some smoke by the willows under one of the cottonwood trees about five hundred yards from his location. Tony eased back to Teddy, he pulled the 50 Caliber Sharps from the scabbard and walked back to his spot behind the small pine tree, he needed to see if these men were the ones that tried to rob the stage. Easing the big gun over a low limb for support, Tony was able to get a steady rest so he could use the telescopic sight to try to find the two wounded men. Two men were walking around camp tending to the horses and other things, then one man walked over to what looked like a blanket and a saddle. He took a canteen and lifted the blanket so Tony could see a man laying with his head on the saddle. From behind a tree came another man with his arm in a sling. Tony could see blood on it. Now Tony had a problem-do I shoot without giving them a warning? Tony figured that they were trying to kill the stage driver and guard so why should he allow them to try and kill his wife and friends.

He eased the lever down to open the breach so he could load that very large cartage, then closing the breach and slowly centered the cross hairs to one of the men that was not wounded, if he was going to shoot someone it had to be one that was not hurt. That would only leave one of the gang without any wound after Tony pulled the trigger, I want to kill this one and hope to get a second shot at the other man that was not hurt. Easing back the set trigger and letting out a long breath, he eased pressure on the trigger, Tony didn't know when the rifle went off until he felt it slam his shoulder. Lowering the lever, the spent round came out and Tony slid in the second round. Closing the breach, he looked for the next target. He could see the one he shot at was down and the other man was hiding behind a small tree. Tony centered the cross hairs on the tree and sent the second round at the hiding man, the man behind the tree could see the smoke and was about to move when the bullet cut the tree in half and blew a hole in his chest you could put your fist into. Tony walked back to Teddy and slid the big gun into the scabbard. Teddy had to work at getting turned around on the narrow trail so they could ride back to the wagons.

Reaching the road, he could see that the wagons were ahead of him so he touched Teddy up into a canter, he would catch them within the hour. Tony felt bad about killing the two men without warning but as he rode up beside the wagons and could see Maggie, he was glad he had taken the leadership role Ronnie had entrusted him with. They would find a spot for lunch and Tony would inform the crew that the threat was eliminated for the present. During lunch Tony cleaned the big gun and gave Ronnie thanks for sending it with him. Tony told the crew about killing the two men who had tried to rob the stage and leaving the two wounded men to figure out how to get back to Carson City. With lunch finished, Tony told Jack to lead out and find them an overnight camping spot. As he was leaving, Hector rode out with him for protection or just so he would not be alone on the road.

*

Randy eased out of the warm buffalo robe finding Morning beside the fire making his breakfast. He walked out to the trees and relieved himself. Returning, Morning handed him a bowl of food, He sat down by the fire enjoying the heat. As he ate, Morning was showing him things and giving the Paiute name for them, and Randy would reply in English. His arm was starting to be able to move without hurting, he was thinking it may be well sooner than one moon.

Andy was just getting the fire started in the forge when Randy walked up.

"Andy what are you going to work on today?

"I am going to need horseshoes for all of the stock when they get back to the ranch. The two work horses Rose and Marty have are also about due so I have a lot of work to finish within the next week. I have a feeling that Tony and crew should be showing soon".

"Randy, do you think you could drive the light wagon and team"?

"Yes, I can".

"I need to get into Mr. Brown's store to pick up a load of steel for making horseshoes. I can send Will and Core with you to harness the team and help along the road".

Randy asked, "Who is Will and Core anyway"?

"I named Black Dove's two boys the other day. Will is the younger one, he is always willing to help but does not quite know enough, now Core, he is the older boy, and he is also willing and he most of the time is correct, so he is Core.

"Andy, I can leave now if you want, we need to go over to my lodge to see what Black Dove needs and get the two boys started getting the wagon ready to roll".

"Andy, are those two boys big enough to harness the team"?

"Stand back and watch them".

Black Dove met them at the door. Andy told her what they needed, she called the two boys over and Andy told them what they needed. Morning came over and Andy told her that Randy was going to be away for a few days. She followed them into the lodge. As the men drank some coffee Black Dove gathered some things placing them in a deer skin bag. Andy told her to let the boys take their bows so they could hunt rabbits to eat during the trip.

Coffee finished, Randy and Andy started back to the forge to get the wagon ready. As they came close, they could see that the boys had the team ready and hitched to the wagon. Andy told them to go back and get their things they wanted to take with them. Randy went to the gun room and picked out a Henry and a box of ammunition. Going to the pantry he picked out some canned meat and other things for them to eat along the road to town. Calling it a town is a bit over the top, but there were three other businesses around Mr. Brown's store now. With his supplies loaded behind the wagon seat he was ready for Will and Core to load their things. With everything loaded, Randy rolled a tarp over the supplies. Morning came over to Randy and handed him a bag and she gave him a real nice going away kiss.

Tossing the bag to Will, he stepped up and slapped the reins on the rumps of the two horses and the trip was started. With this light wagon he clicked the team up to an extended trot and he would be able to keep this pace for hours. The two boys were trying not to show they were excited to go on this supply run for steel for Andy. With a short stop at noon, Randy found out what was in the bag. The two boys pulled it out and Randy found a large stash of jerky Morning had made from the Elk that Rose had killed. Rose was a great hunter and rifle shot, every few weeks she rides in and drops off some fresh meat. Reaching one of the overnight camping spots, Will and Core jumped down from the wagon and started unhooking the trace chains. Will could just reach the hook on the back of the harness but made it, Core had finished with his side then released the wagon tongue from the front of the team. Gathering the lines, he drove the horses around to the back of the wagon. Sam Applegate had Andy forge a set of harness hooks on each wagon, so the boys removed the harnesses and hooked them on the wagon.

Randy had gathered some wood and had a small fire going when the two boys returned after getting both horses watered and on some grass. Will and Core grabbed their bows and faded into the brush, Randy gathered a pot of water to make coffee and set up the steel cooking kit that Andy had forged. Randy was just going to the wagon to collect some of the canned food to warm up when the two boys came back into camp with two rabbits cleaned and ready to cook. He grabbed some salt and pepper and the rotisserie shaft to cook the rabbits over the fire. Core took the shaft from Randy and attached the rabbits to it and mounted it to the two vertical posts so they could turn the rabbits as they cooked. Randy was thinking it is time to just relax and enjoy watching his dinner being cooked.

The sun was about down when Core pulled the two rabbits from the fire. Randy was about going nuts listening to the sizzle every time some grease dripped onto the hot coals. Randy had pulled three plates from the food box. Core cut the one rabbit in half and gave Randy the whole one to eat. He watched the two boys pull apart the rabbit and started to eat. Randy laid down his knife and fork and started to pull apart his rabbit to match them. It tastes better that way he found out. Core and Will went back out to check on the two horses and took them to water. Randy rolled out his bedroll, but the two boys went out to sleep with the horses.

Randy had only eaten half of the rabbit, so the two boys finished it for breakfast. He ate some jerky with two cold biscuits washed down with a cup of warmed up coffee. Will and Core had the two horses ready, and their bedrolls stored. Randy helped them hitch up to the wagon. They had an early start and would make great time today. They may even make it to the store by late afternoon, he was remembering when the road was just a trail full of rocks. Randy figured that the one rock would never be removed, it was the one that saved Tony from being shot by Bob Stanton and his friend Joe Harding. With another short noon break, they did make it to Jim Brown's Store by late afternoon, Randy was greeted by Mr. Brown with the shotgun, but seeing Randy, he put it back inside of the door. Come on in. We still have some food left so you may as well eat. Randy stepped up but the two Indian boys waited by the wagon. Randy went out and had to ease them into the store, they had never seen so many things. "Mr. Brown, neither of these boys have ever tried to eat with a spoon or fork so this could get interesting. We will give her a try and see what happens.

Jim and Randy had the steel loaded and ready to make the trip back to the ranch just after the sun was up, Will and Core had steak and potatoes for breakfast and that went well, as they were leaving Mr. Brown gave them each a bag of candy.

"Thanks, Mr. Brown for everything. Hope to see you soon".

"Randy, do you have any idea when Ronnie and crew will be back?

"Andy and I were talking just a few days ago about that. We think within the next few days is our guess".

Randy had just started back to the ranch when he heard,

"Randy what are you doing here"?

Tony and Maggie were riding in at a canter, he stopped the wagon. Stepping down he walked over to talk to his bosses.

"Where is Ronnie"?

"Long story we can get into that later".

"What have you got on the seat"?

That is Will and Core, that is their new names. Andy said that he named them that because Will is a willing worker and Core is slower, but does thing correct. So that is what we have, Andy felt I needed some help with the team, so he sent them with me. I have to tell you they are every day good help".

"Why don't you get started and we will catch up, you should meet the wagons at the noon stop at the junction".

"Maggie those two boys can't be over ten and twelve what do you think Randy"?

"I think you are correct on that one Maggie. Tony Said. Randy: I need to get a telegram sent to Ronnie so he can relay the information to Carson City so they can watch out for two wounded men with two extra horses". The telegram sent.

Tony told Mr. Brown that Ronnie was opening a horseracing track south of Sacramento and had purchased a small ranch bordering Juan's family rancho.

"Mr. Brown what is the new building that has just started"?

"I found a blacksmith so I am setting him up so he can help keep travelers around, so they spend more money".

"Great Idea, we need to get on the road to the ranch".

Randy did meet the other wagons at the junction as Tony told him. Just as he parked the wagon, Tony and Maggie rode in to join the crew for lunch. Jack was eating his lunch when the wagons started, Randy stayed around to help him clean up and would travel with him to help with the cooking as much as a one arm man can help.

"Randy, I see you have the two boys of Andy and Black Dove".

"Yes, I sure do Jack".

"Andy thought that I needed some help with the horses and cooking, so he sent his two sons to help. I got to tell you, wait until tonight and watch those two get the horses un-hitched and taken care of, harnesses on the rack and the first night out they killed two rabbits and cooked them". "Those two boys are as I told Tony, full time help. Jack you will find out when we reach the ranch, but I have married an Indian girl and moved in to join Andy in the Indian camp".

With the cleanup finished, Jack started after the slower wagon train and Randy gathered the reins of the team with the steel and the two Indian boys. In just over an hour, they passed them and moved on to get set up for the noon stop. Tony had told Jack to make the meal something quick so they could just rest the horses and then get back on the road. Jack pulled into one of the many campgrounds along the road to the ranch, Will and Core started watering the horses and getting them grain with some alfalfa, they had watched Billy and Jack use the supplies that were on the front of the cook wagon. Jack had some beans ready, so he added some canned beef to a large frying pan to heat with onions and mild peppers. In another pan he was frying up tortillas and stacking them on a plate. As he finished frying thirty, the crew started to arrive. He and the two Indian boys started hauling feed to the horses along with water. Will was just about too short on one end when it came to hauling water, Jack told Randy that with a couple of burritos he may grow enough to haul that big water pail.

Tony had never watched either of the two sons of Andy Sams before but was impressed, they did not talk much but it was for sure those two were smart and liked to work. Maggie walked up and sat on the wagon tongue with Tony, "they sure are a big help aren't they. Randy said that he had married one of the new Indian girls and was living in the Indian camp. He looks happy so I guess that will work for him, Andy seems to be happy with the move into Black Dove's lodge. Both of those two boys are learning to forge steel, Core is a bit older, and I have seen him pounding the hot metal. We may need to talk to Andy and see if they need to be paid for their work".

Randy said that on this trip after Andy's steel he just about has to do nothing, they do most of the work.

Back on the road with the wagons after the fast rest stop, Tony told Jack to stay with the wagons, he thinks they can make the ranch late tonight, so get another meal about like this one ready before you start to catch up with us. We may just allow the horses to eat at the same time we do. If we are close, we will push on to the ranch tonight. Randy and Jack prepared the food and packed it away for later and started after the wagons. Tony pulled into a rest stop with a stream flowing over the road. He waved Jack on past them and told him to pull up just far enough to allow all of the teams to water, then get the food out and heated. We will only rest about an hour. Jack and Randy watered their team side by side then moved ahead to allow the others to water.

Jack pulled out the food and the two Indian boys had the fire going, Randy assembled the cook rack and Jack was frying tortillas, the beans and meat was warming over the fire. Tortilla's stack was getting lower, and everyone was eating. With one hour rest the wagon train was on the road to the Campbell ranch, they would get in well after dark. Little John and Jane had pulled into their road an hour back so they should be home by now. Tony and Maggie waved and rode ahead at a gallop. They should be home in just over one hour it they kept up a good trot and canter.

As Tony and Maggie rode into the ranch yard at a trot they were met by White Bird and Tee.

"We take horses all is ok", Tee told them.

"Tony, can you believe that we are home, and we have our own bed"?

"Yes, I have been thinking about that for the last few days".

"Start a fire and do what you want, I am taking a bath just as soon as the water is heated".

"I will heat the water and start the fire in the fireplace, and I just may join you in the tub, to see if anything is wrong with my little red head.

"Promises, promises but no follow through" was her last words before closing the door.

Andy heard the wagons come in so he went to the barn and lit all the lanterns, hanging some on the corrals so the men could see to unhitch the teams. Tony came out to talk with Andy, he was relaxed and well washed to a large part because of Maggie, she likes to clean. The first wagons started to arrive; Randy was driving the light wagon with the steel, so he parked it beside the forge shop out of the way. Will and Core had the team unhooked and harnesses removed and hanging on the holder on the wagon. Andy pointed to the boys to put those two horses in the two stalls at the end of the forge. With the team watered and fed, Andy sent his two sons to his lodge to see their mother, he was sure they had a few stories to tell her about the trip.

Jack was next with the supply wagon, so he pulled over by the side door leading to the cold room and kitchen. Billy had his team settled into the large corral by the barn, they would need the teams in the morning to move the wagons around and unload the little bulls. Tony directed the men to just leave them in the pens for the night and they would release them tomorrow. After the horses were taken care of, Billy and Jack went to the bunkhouse to get some sleep. Tony returned to a warm bed with a hot wife. Randy made his way over to his wife's lodge only to be greeted by a very naked wife with ideas. Life is good in the Ruby's.

This picture is one of many reasons I like black and white photos. The contrast just pops out at you in this picture. I feel the movement of my horse as I explore the hidden valleys in and around these mountains.

Riding looking between the ears of a horse, in this picture it makes me want to stop and go and enjoy exploring many days and nights. (Photo by Robin Travis).

HIDDEN VALLEYS IN THE MOUNTAINS

CHAPTER 21 **BECOMING KNOWN**

US Deputy Marshal McPherson had received the telegram from Tony asking him to tell Ronnie that he had just taken care of the other gang east of Carson City. Tony had killed two of the gang and left two wounded men to find their way back to a doctor. Thanks for the big 50 Caliber Sharps, it sure can reach out a long way, over six hundred yards. Larry was thinking that Tony may become another bad ass like Ronnie Campbell. Not a bad thing.

Ronnie and Abby were having coffee when the baby came up. "Ronnie, we need a nice buggy to drive. I have made my last ride on a horse until after we have this baby".

"That sounds right to me, I will ride into town today and check if we have any telegrams from Tony and I will come home with a nice carriage so we can ride in comfort to the racetrack and into town when needed. Abby, I want a matched team, what do you think"?

Yes, I do, but do you want grays or blacks, Ronnie"?

"I will check out what is available that I can take delivery today so we may not have the best choice. But we can get another team later that will meet our requirements. I think I will leave Diamond home today and take one of the horses we seem to acquire from time to time, I can use him for a trade".

In under an hour Ronnie was riding one of the dead outlaw's horse with a strange saddle heading into Sacramento to talk to the Marshal's and check on a telegram from Tony. "After that is finished, he was going to the wagon shop to check on a nice carriage and a matched pair of horses. Tony had purchased some wagons from a shop up by the river, his name was I think Tom Chancy. Those wagons were well made so that is a starting place. Ronnie found Larry in the office when he walked in.

"Ronnie, what are you doing in town? I was just getting ready to ride down to see you, I got a telegram from Tony. All is well with him. Here, take a look for yourself".

"Damn, Larry, he is getting a little mean streak in him. A year ago, he would have ridden into that camp and got shot at the best. He just found them, made sure they were the men he was hunting and punched their ticket with that big 50 Caliber Sharps. He is from good stock. Juan is a lot like you Ronnie, well kind of like you but he was too nice I think".

"Larry, did you send a wire to Carson City to inform them that the stage should operate without any problems for now"?

"Yes, I did. What else are you in town for? I see you don't have Diamond with you, any reason"? Yes, I am going to purchase a carriage for Abby, she told me today she is not riding a horse until the after the baby is born".

"Where are you going to look"?

"Larry, you remember the wagon maker that we purchased the wagons from. He did incredibly good work".

"I have some time Ronnie, so let's ride over and see just what he has ready to roll".

"Ronnie, I will go get Rob from the stable. I will join you out front". Ronnie was waiting in front of the office when Larry rode out front to meet him, they reined their horses around and headed north from the Marshal's office. Reaching the river, they headed to the wagon yard, as Ronnie and Larry rode in they were met in front by the owner, Mr. Tom Chancy.

"Larry, I remember you, who is this"?

"This is Ronnie Campbell",

"Son, you can have anything we have at a great price. The service of killing those two crooks is a blessing. Ronnie what are you looking for"?

"I want a real nice carriage so I can travel from my new ranch to the race track I am building with a Mr. Pennington".

"Ronnie, I have three real nice models in the storage shed, you may like one of them. They all have very plush leather interiors, plush is the word, I think. Can you wait for just a minute while I get one of my men to pull them out of storage and into the yard so you can take a good look at them"? Mr. Chancy returned and asked Ronnie and Larry to follow him to the wagon shop to check them out.

"Ronnie, are you going to drive the rig or have a driver"?

"To tell you the truth I had not thought about that, but it could be both depending on what we were doing".

"Ronnie let me show you one that I think may fit your situation, if you look at the third one it is only set up to have a driver, but this first one would allow you to have a driver or drive yourself if you wanted. I like the side curtains that can be dropped down if needed with bad weather. It has a station for a driver but also has a slide so you can drive from the enclosed cabin for protection.

"Mr. Chancy, I like this one but what about a matched team to pull this carriage"?

"I do have a green broke team of sorrels, they are one year apart and are brother and sister, the gilding is four and the filly is three years old. The gilding is a stable leader his sister needs some miles to get her settled. "Tom let's hitch them up and we will go for a ride to see how they handle". Ronnie and Larry eased out of the wagon shop onto the main waterfront street. With the Sacramento River on their right, they headed downtown. Ronnie was up front, and Larry was in the cabin. After a bit of high stepping the two sorrels calmed down, Ronnie handed the lines back to Larry to see how that worked out driving the team.

"Ronnie, I think you could stay dry with the curtains down. Here, take the reins back, I want to ride in luxury for a change. You need to tell Marshal Johnson this is the way I deserve to travel".

Back at the wagon yard, Mr. Chancy was waiting to see how the drive progressed. "Ronnie, how did the team drive? I watched you as you made the turn and headed toward downtown. It looked to me that the team was acting up a bit, how long did it take to get them to settle down"?

"They are a bit green, but they came around by the time we got downtown, Tom, these two sure look nice. Well, Abby wanted grays, I wanted blacks and you have sorrels how it that going to work? Get me a cost for the total package".

"I will see if I can get Larry out of the leather seat. I think he likes the way this carriage rides". "Ronnie, I need four hundred for the carriage, then I would like three hundred for the tack and horses, total of seven hundred for everything".

"Ok. Mr. Chancy, I need a solid one hundred for my gilding and saddle can you do that"?

"Done deal, Ronnie, I can live with that for your horse and saddle".

"Good, I didn't want to take him home, I have way too many extra horses at the ranch".

"Think on this Ronnie, I will take all of your extra horses if I can get them for sixty dollars a head, twenty for saddles if they are in good shape. I am getting men dropping by about every day to purchase a decent horse so any extra you have will help me". Ronnie pulled a bank draft out and filled in six hundred made out to Chancy Wagon Works. "Larry, tie Rob to the back and I will deliver you to your office, one more ride in luxury".

"Ronnie, I think it would be a fine time to go and pick up Marshal Johnson and give him a ride to a nice restaurant for an early dinner, and you might as well pay a little more money, that shouldn't hurt too bad".

"Done, sit back and enjoy, this rig sure does draw some looks. Dang Larry, you may even pick up a dinner guest before we get to the restaurant, that lady's sure looking at you". At the Marshals office Larry jumped out and gathered the boss up and delivered him to the upper-class delivery service.

With the carriage parked at a nice restaurant, many of the people were trying to figure out who the carriage belonged to. Ronnie eased into the driver's seat and the two Marshals took the plush seats in the back,

"Boss I think this is how I should pursue the bad men, I could be more rested that way, boss what do you think"? Marshal Johnson gave Larry a hard look but no answer. Reaching the office, Ronnie said we will see you two again soon.

"Gentlemen, I got to get home in time to give Abby a little ride to see if she can do without her match grays". The two new horses made the trip at an extended trot and made it a short trip to the ranch, Abby was on the porch when he drove in.

"Mr. Campbell you did it, I see no grays or blacks either".

"Best they had, and they match the color of the carriage". Giving Abby a hand, she joined him in the front seat. Ronnie clicked up the team and down the road to Juan and Juanita's rancho to give them a ride. Juan was on the porch when he drove in and stopped beside the hitching post.

"Juan, get Juanita and we will give you a ride in my new carriage, Abby has not figured out yet if she likes it or not".

Juanita and Juan loaded into the back seat and off they went for a short ride. Returning to the rancho Juan said to come in and eat dinner with us, it will be ready. Tying the team off to the hitching post, they went inside to enjoy a dinner and talk over the events of the past few days. Larry relayed the telegram information to Juan, "your younger brother has stepped up to be a solid leader. I always knew he could handle being the decision maker. He got tested on the way home, a stage was shot up some but got past the robbery attempt, but the driver and guard were wounded. Jane and Maggie patched up the two, getting them back on their way, Tony hunted the robbers down and killed the two flat out and left the two who were wounded to find their way back to some place to get doctored. By doing this he could have saved many lives of our friends. Tony is now the leader of the Nevada Ranch I am so proud of him. I remember when I gave him the first good rifle".

Yes, "and you gave me the brand-new Henry the same day". I don't know if you have been told yet, but Abby and I now own the ranch next door, Mr. Holms decided he would make a better gambling house owner".

"Great, Ronnie, I may now be able to keep some of my calves this season and I sure like your new carriage".

"Thanks. We needed it because besides the ranch we are building a horseracing track. Abby is not going to ride horse anymore, so if I am to get any help with the racetrack, I had to get a better mode of transportation". Reaching the ranch, it was dark when they drove in. Stewart came out of the bunkhouse along with Little Billy to take care of the horses and new carriage.

"Ronnie, the boys and I will put the carriage in the barn tonight and we will get some lumber tomorrow and start building an enclosed carriage room so we can keep the dust off your new rig. We will also build two new stalls inside of the barn beside Diamond and Dandy for the two new carriage horses, that way they will be close at hand when needed.

"Good idea, Stewart we will meet after breakfast in the morning. Thanks men".

After breakfast Ronnie and Stewart retired to his office and were joined by Abby so they could go over the ranch operations and see what the new foreman had on his mind.

"Stewart, what ideas do you have to improve this ranch in the short term and the overall vision as you see it"?

"Mr. Campbell, I think we need to move many of the older horses to the sale yard or we are close enough to Sacramento to sell them from the ranch. I know we are short two or three new bulls because we have over forty cows per bull, now that caused us to have a low calf count this year".

"Ok, Stewart we can move the extra horses to Sacramento to Tom Chancy's wagon yard, he will take all of our extra horses. When we get rid of some of the older stock, do we have any three or four-year olds to train for replacements?

"Yes, there are about ten in a pasture you have not had time to look over. It is on the other side of the river. There is a crossing of sorts, but we will need to swim the horses to get a look at the stock, I plan on keeping two finished horses for each man and sell the others".

"Long term I would like to make a major change in the way we operate the ranch, if we fenced off the ranch in holding pens or grazing plots then we could rotate the cattle from one location to another all year. This would save feed costs and help keep our eyes on them, we would be able to find any that are sick or injured. I would like to fence a center lane forty feet wide running from the barn to the river with gates at every fenced grazing area. If we had that the three of us hands could handle moving the cattle, doctoring, and it would make it awfully hard to steal any of your stock".

"Stewart, figure out how much this would cost me to implement that plan".

"Another thing, Ronnie we need to grow our own alfalfa, this could also save us money every winter by not having to purchase tons of hay to keep the weight on our cattle".

"When we ride out to look at the horses across the river we can take a look at this idea, we have a small waterfall on our north corner of your ranch, the south side of your ranch that joins your friends ranch is three feet lower".

"I get it, you want to dig a ditch to irrigate both ranches from north of the waterfall".

"Yes, Juan and your ranch can both irrigate alfalfa fields with water coming from your ranch". "Stewart, my blacksmith in Nevada, is doing that now on two small alfalfa fields. If the two of you join in this you could only need to purchase one set of harvesting equipment, I saw a new cutter in Sacramento last month when I was in town.

"Ronnie, the last thing we need to do is, I would like to hire two young hands so we can train them from the start".

"Ok, just do it".

"What do you think Abby"?

"Mr. Boss Ronnie, I would get started on Stewart's plans now, but start the cross fencing as soon as we can get the wire and posts, having that center isle will save so much time in moving the cattle".

"Great job Stewart Abby said", "Ronnie that new house needs to have a foreman's quarters included".

"Ronnie and Abby, if it is ok, I will take the men along with the wagon into town to drop off the horses to Mr. Tom Chancy at his wagon yard". "That way we can pick up some fence posts and a load of wire when we come back to the ranch".

"Stewart, Abby and I will open up a credit line with the hardware store so you can just pick up what you need as you go along. Abby and I will need the carriage ready to go into town when you get back to the barn, have the boys get the team hitched up and ready to go, say in a half an hour. Thanks Stewart".

Ronnie and Abby stopped to get the account set up and moved on to the construction site to see how the project was moving forward. Reaching the office building, Ronnie could see some men talking to Mr. Pennington and it looked like he was being threatened. "Abby, you take the reins, and I will step out and you drive around behind the building until we see what is going on". Ronnie stepped down and pulling his Henry out with his left hand, his hammer loupe was off from his pistol. "Men may I be of some help? You seem to have problem with Mr. Pennington". The leader turned to Ronnie, telling him to move along, this was not any of his business, the other two moved sideways to flank Ronnie on each side.

The leader reached out to put his finger into Ronnie's chest and at that moment he was greeted with the receiver of the Henry just over his nose, sending him flying onto his back out cold. The man on Ronnie's right started to reach for his arm only to be greeted by the butt of the Henry delivered to his midsection causing him to join his friend on the ground trying to gather his breath. The third one was not even a bit smarter; he was pulling his pistol when Ronnie pulled his colt and shot him in the shoulder, with his gun only just clearing his holster it fell into the dirt just before its owner joined it. Abby drove around the building to see the finished results just as the last man was falling backwards landing with a thud. Ronnie had gathered the weapons by the time the so-called boss was just waking up from a short rest.

The boss man started to speak when Ronnie put his finger to his lips telling him to shut his mouth. Turning to Abby, "would you drive into town and get the marshal? Mr. Pennington are you all right? They didn't do you any harm did they"?

"No, I am ok, these three came up telling me that they were buying me out and were taking over this racetrack. As of now I don't think they got very far with that idea".

"Do you know who their boss is and what is behind their idea"?

"No, this is the first I have ever seen any of the three". The leader was trying to talk again so Ronnie walked over and asked him if he could just sit there and not talk, if he couldn't do that, he would just shoot him, Ronnie put a foot on his chest and pushed him back until he was lying flat on his back looking up into the dark hole of Ronnie's 44 pistol.

"Mr. Pennington can you get me some clean rags so I can plug up the two holes in this guy's shoulder"? He was still laying on his back bleeding from the bullet holes going all the way out the back. Mr. Pennington delivered the rags to Ronnie. "Give me a hand with this guy. We need to lift him so I can stuff the rags into the two holes". As Ronnie was pushing the rags into the holes he started to return to the real world, his first words were, "you shot me".

"Yes, I did. Who are you anyway"?

"Bubba Dawson".

"You drew way too slow to carry a gun, you may just get yourself killed some day, I decided that with this being our first meeting I would let you live, but there will not be a second chance. When you get those holes fixed you will find a new location to live and work, because if I ever see you the second time, I will kill you without any talking. Do you understand"?

"I need a doctor; I am going to die".

"You just may do that, but you will need to wait until the US Marshals have a look at you, by the way you need to learn to be more respectful to others".

"Now let's see who we have here laying on the ground. Mr. Pennington, would you go into the storeroom and get me some rope"? "I feel the need to tie these two up so I can have a little quiet time with them". With the one man who seemed to have it figured out that the less he said the better off he was going to be. Now being tied up, he just relaxed to see what was going to happen next. "You with the broken nose, you first walk into the office and take a seat". Ronnie tied his hands behind his back and his feet to the chair. "Now what is your name"?

"None of your". then the pistol barrel made a slight thud on his head.

"Now would you like to start over, your name please"?

"Horace Taylor, he said".

"Now was that so hard? Who do you work for and why do you want to take Mr. Pennington's racetrack away from him"?

Horace found his voice. "You don't have any idea how many people my boss has killed while getting what he wants".

"That so. I killed five outlaws just last week and another five the week before that, so I am supposed to be scared of your boss? Who is your boss and why does he want this racetrack"?

Horace started to say I don't, "slap" right on his broken nose. "Carl Abernathy, he owns three of the gambling houses in Sacramento and is working on plans to put Mr. Holms out of business soon".

Abby returned with US Marshal Larry McPherson and the County Sheriff Mark Underhill riding along side of her as she pulled up to the field office for the racetrack.

"Ronnie, I would like to have you meet Mr. Mark Underwood, he is the county Sheriff".

"Great to meet you, do you know any of these three lost souls"?

"Well, I see you have been introduced to Horace Taylor, we have talked a few times over some card sharks cheating some miners that were gambling at their tables. We have not had enough evidence to press charges, but the district attorney is really close to opening a case naming Mr. Carl Abernathy as the defendant".

"Sheriff, how strong is your sensitive nature"?

"Not so much Ronnie. Horace, we need to have you lay out the whole scheme for Larry and the Sheriff".

"I am not going".

Crunch as Ronnie kind of rapped him on the broken nose again.

"Look Horace, you are not going to be working for Mr. Abernathy anyway so just tell us all you know. Remember rule one is if I see you ever again, I will shoot you on site, so no pressure just tell the Sheriff the whole story".

Bubba Dawson spoke again, "I need to see a doctor bad". Larry looked over to Bubba and told him to shut up or he would shoot him in the other shoulder.

"Bubba come to think about it I think I have a wanted poster on you dead or alive that amounts to eight hundred dollars, you can pick the way you want the poster retired".

Horace decided it was in his best interest to talk, as they say he was moving on to another project and would not feel bad to be gone from Sacramento. He was better suited for the east coast; they speak a bit differently than they do in the west. Horace had been in the business of causing people to change their mind about many different things over the years, he had never looked into the eyes of a man who would pull the trigger without thinking it for one second. Boston was looking like a nice place to visit, in fact a place to retire.

Larry asked "Ronnie, what do you want me to do with this calf you have tied up over here? Do you think we need to brand it and cut it nuts off so he will change his ways"?

The first words out of the last of the three so called enforcers was, "I have friends in other places and need to visit them as soon as I can get on my horse".

"You Mr. I don't know, do you have anything in Sacramento"?

"No, I will re-stock on supplies down the road on my way to Nevada".

"Mr., I don't know. One piece of advice don't slowdown in Nevada. I have another ranch over there and I have Paiute Indians working for me and they really like to hunt down my enemies".

"Ronnie, we now kind of have an idea of the scope of this Mr. Carl Abernethy so I think we can release Mr. I don't know to ride anyplace he wants, give him the empty gun back and his horse, with a warning don't load that gun until you are way down the road".

Larry said, "Bubba, you are going with me back to the jail and I will have a doctor visit you after we get you settled into your new room".

"Ronnie, what about Mr. Horace with the broken nose? You have told him if you see him anyplace, he will be shot. I think we can let him ride out of here and not ever see him either or he is also dead. Is that correct"?

"Yes. Larry, you can let him go, he will ride south and never come back to Sacramento". Is that correct Horace"?

"Yes. I will not go back to Sacramento".

"Mount up and ride".

"Larry and Sheriff Mark Underhill, thanks for hauling that piece of shit to jail for us. Mr. Pennington, why don't you join us for a short ride into Sacramento for an early dinner and a drink, you look like you need one".

Sheriff Mark Underhill said, "I will lock up Bubba and will join you.

Ronnie said, "Mr. Pennington you and Abby ride in the back, I will be your driver". During dinner Mr. Pennington asked Abby does Ronnie handle everything like that little problem like we had today.

"Yes, that is very typical Mr. Pennington but as you can see things get settled fast".

"Ronnie, do you think we will have any more problems with Carl Abernathy"?

"I plan to have a up close and personal talk with him tomorrow. Do you want to go along"?

"No, I am just fine with the way you have with words and actions. If I can change the subject a bit, I have two contractors coming in to start work on our buildings in the morning around nine".

Reaching the racetrack office, Mr. Pennington turned to Ronnie and Abby saying if you had not become my partner, I would have never been able to stand up to men like that.

"Thanks Partner".

Abby joined Ronnie in the driver's seat saying, "you do have a way with words and actions my fine husband. I sure like this carriage, it sure drives nice, and I am so rested you may just need to join me in my bath when we get home".

"Just join you, is that all you can offer"? With the carriage put up and the two new sorrels in their stalls, Ronnie started to the house when Stewart and crew rode in with the wagon full of supplies and no extra horses. Stewart pulled up beside Ronnie asking how his day went?

"We had a bit of action at the racetrack, but all ended well, and you"?

"Here is the cash for the horses. Mr. Chancy said thanks".

"Thanks men, see you in the morning. I have a job to take care of, so I need to go". Ronnie walked into the kitchen to inform Wolf that the crew had just returned from Sacramento and should be in to eat soon, "Miss. Jordan, how was your day"?

"Fine", she said, "Wolf and I got a lot done today".

Ronnie walked back to the extra-large bedroom they shared in the new house, this was the only ranch that they knew of that had a new boiler that heated water and Abby had the old small bathtub removed and a new extra-large copper tub installed just a few days ago. When Ronnie entered the room, he found Abby up to her neck in hot water.

Ronnie was only a few minutes until he joined her so she could get every bit of dirt off him. He was sure it would take quite a long time because he was very dirty and would need plenty of attention. Abby had become particularly good at taking her time with him to make sure everything was cleaned to her approval. All was quiet when they went to the kitchen to get some cold meat and bread for their dinner, they had had other things going on when the others had eaten.

CHAPTER 22 **INDIAN RANCH**

Tony was up with the first light to start unloading the calves and getting them into one of the box canyons to allow them time to get used to the new area. Coffee was on as he entered the kitchen as the men came alive. They all made their way to the coffee pot to get the day started. With Ronnie and Abby out of the house, Maggie had started to look at how she could make this her home instead of feeling like a guest. Breakfast was a fun time with most of the crew at the table at one time, Randy told everyone about moving into the Indian camp and marrying Morning, Andy's wife's younger sister Morning is her name. The Indians were a large part of the ranch's day to day operations, they handled about all the cattle movement around the ranch and a good part of the starting of all foals. Jingles found out that he and the two vaqueros Jaime Roman and his brother Hector would be heading back to California with the racehorses within the week, this would be a new chapter in Jingles short time in America.

Tony went to see Andy to see how Tee and White Bird were dealing with the ranch idea. Andy was forging a horseshoe when they walked up. Andy handed it to Core, the oldest Indian boy. Core just went about finishing what Andy had started.

"Tony how can I help you"?

"Well. I am trying to figure out if Tee and White Bird understand that they are the owners of the ranch over the mountain".

"Tony, they have been over to my lodge many times during the time you have been gone, I think they are getting the idea of it being their ranch because they have Gray Eagle and Raven spending most of their time over on that side of the mountain taking care of the cattle".

"Andy, you know now that Ronnie and Abby are going to stay in California, they want to racehorses and are building a racetrack just south of Sacramento. They also are the new owner of a nice size ranch about an hour south of the racetrack, that is why Jaime and Hector are working with Jingles with getting the horses ready to move over to the new ranch".

"Andy, is there anything you need or want"?

"You seem happy those two boys are sure becoming extremely helpful. Let me know when it is time, I need to start paying them for their work. From what Randy told me they took care of him when he took them to Mr. Brown's Store, I was watching them work, they are already worth paying, so you let me know when".

"Thanks Tony, I will do that when it gets time".

"Ronnie told me he wanted to build a barn and other storage building on the Indian Ranch". "Would you help me figure out what they need or want"? "I think when Randy's arm is working, we will go over with Tee and White Bird to build them a log storage shed and barn so it will look like a real ranch, we are also going to need to work out a wagon road south around the Ruby Mountains to meet up with the main wagon road coming from the east. We will also need a light wagon and team so they can get their supplies for the man working on the ranch".

"Go talk to Little John and Jane, they have been training some work horses. We need to talk Mr. Brown; he may have a wagon we can buy for that ranch".

Tony used the shortcut over the mountains to reach Little John and Jane's ranch in four hours instead of the normal one and half days by the road due to it following the stream. Riding into the ranch yard he found Little John and his two Indian ranch hands working with some young horses in the large pen. Jane was coming out of the house as he rode up to the arena, Little John handed off the colt to Elk Man so he could go visit Tony.

"Tony, how are you? Is everything ok at the ranch"?

"We are fine, but I wanted to know if you have a light team about ready to sell, we moved some cattle over to the property Ronnie filed on for the Indians. Andy and Randy are going to go over and build a barn and some storage sheds. I am going to Mr. Brown's Store to see if he has a wagon that he would sell".

"I do have two teams about ready to be sold, I have both in the barn harnessed, we were going to work them after we finished with handling these colts".

Little John asked the two Indians to put the colts up and bring out one of the wagon teams. Tony come in and have a cup of coffee and some lunch. Running Deer and Elk Man will have them ready right after we eat. Elk Man was walking by so Jane gave him a sign telling him to eat first then get the horses ready. Tony had seen her telling the two Indians to eat and then get the horses.

"I see that you are learning some sign language.

"Yes. I am also learning to speak their language". How did your bulls make the trip"?

"All of ours did fine. We held them in the box canyon for a few days before turning them out with the herd. We kept them in close for about the same time, Running Deer and Elk Man moved them back with our cattle yesterday. Ronnie was glad that you traded with other ranches, that way we have bulls to trade in three to four years".

Tony said, "I guess lunch is over, I hear the first team is getting hitched to the wagon now". They all walked out to see how easy the team was able to be hitched. Both horses were standing as the wagon tongue was hooked by Elk Man then Running Deer walked around and hooked up the trace chains on both horses.

"Little John, you told me that they are only green broke, they may be just a bit better than that, let's go and take a ride to see how they act with the wagon".

"You want to drive Tony"?

"No, you can do better than I could. Let's take some edge off these two". Little John kicked them up to a gallop with the wagon bouncing around and making a dust cloud down the road.

"Now Tony, let's see if they will come back to a walk". Little John eased back on the lines and telling the team easy, easy, they started to slow and when he got them at a walk, he released the lines to see if they would stay walking after they had a good run.

"Little John, figure me a price and we don't need to look at the other team". Back at the kitchen table Jane and Tony were talking about the price for the two horses".

"Jane, it looks like we are going to talk money".

"Yes, Little John does not like that part, he wants to do the training and then I smile and charge a higher price than he would".

"Jane, what do you think you need for the team"?

Tony, I would be happy with three hundred dollars, what do you think about that number"?

"Can you deliver them to Mr. Brown's Store for that price"?

"Yes, we can".

"I think Mr. Brown has a light wagon for sale. I also need to get a set of harnesses made for these horses; Mr. Brown told me that the blacksmith he set up also can repair leather so I am going to check to see if he can make the new harnesses. I will be back in two days after I check on getting everything I need. "Ok Jane that is a good price. I will be glad to pay the three hundred dollars any day, that is a nice team. If it is ok, I will pay you when I come back from town".

With a deal set, Tony needed to purchase the wagon and check on the harnesses and on getting the team shod. Mr. Brown met him at the front door then put back the double barrel shotgun, he is making sure that he knows who is coming into his store.

"Mr. Brown, is that wagon I saw on the way back to the ranch for sale'? "Yes, it is, I had the blacksmith check it over and make any repairs need so it is ready to roll".

"How much do you want"?

"Two hundred will get you the wagon, another hundred you can have the set of harnesses. The owner came in with a wagon pulled by two worn out horses that had pulled the wagon as far as they were going to go. I traded two saddles and saddle bags with enough supplies to reach Carson City. So, I have the wagon with the harnesses ready to go. Tony, make it two hundred and fifty dollars and we will call it a deal".

"Mr. Brown, will you weigh out your money and another three hundred for Little John and Jane? I just purchased a team for that wagon. Also take out enough to shoe the two new horses, how much gold is left in the bag"?

"You still have just under five hundred dollars".

"Ok. keep that on account for the Indian Ranch Ronnie has set up on the back side of our ranch, Tee and White Bird are going to run the ranch with our help, they have some cattle for a start. This wagon is going to be for the ranch, Little John and Jane will deliver the team in a few days. Set out the basic supplies when the Indians come to pick up the wagon, tell them to come in for supplies whenever they need them. Let me know when you start to run low on the gold, and I will send you some more to keep ahead of their needs".

Tony rode back into the ranch yard at the Applegate ranch to deliver Jane her money in gold, it is much better than paper money.

"Hi Tony, we figured you would be coming by today, want to sit and try out some bear sign? They were fresh this morning".

"Sure, would like that, I have your money, I hope gold is ok".

"I had Mr. Brown weigh the gold out for you, he did have a wagon so whenever you can deliver the two horses, he is ready for them. Jane, hot coffee and bear sign, life would be hard to get any better. "Little John how do you stay so thin with Jane cooking"?

"Tony, she feeds you better than me".

"Thanks for the snack and a good team, I need to get home".

The next morning back at the ranch Tony, Tee, and White Bird were walking over to the forge to go over everything he had setup for the new ranch.

"Andy, you help me out if I have trouble explaining about getting the wagon and building the barn and storage sheds. Tee and White Bird you will need to go over to your ranch and start making a wagon road leading from your ranch all the way to Mr. Brown's store. You have a wagon with horses and food waiting for you at the store, so you need a road to your ranch at the hot spring". Andy talked to them for a long time as they only nodded their heads, Tony was hoping they understood, Randy had come over to listen after Andy finished. He asked if it would be ok if he rode with Tee and White Bird to the store and back to help them.

"Great idea Randy, we can leave in the morning to ride over the mountain. I will take a pack horse to carry the two-man buck saw to remove the trees that are in the way".

"Andy, I would like to take your two sons along, they are great help, and it would be a good adventure for them".

"Thanks Randy, they are still talking about their last trip with you". The five rode out at first light following the trail over the mountain to the hot springs ranch headquarters. As they came over the ridge Gray Eagle met them and led the way down the mountain to their camp, the cows were still feeding on the island. White Bird told Gray Eagle and Raven what they were doing, and Randy thought they understood. Randy started down the mountain making sure a wagon could drive through. Not far down the mountain Randy found a problem with three trees that had to be cut down to allow a wagon to pass. Pulling out the two man saw, Tee came over to help, Randy set the saw just above the ground so the wagon could pass over the stump. An hour later the three trees were laying down and the men moved on down the mountain, Randy felt that they had been lucky by only having three more trees that had to be removed to get to the base of the mountain as it met the desert. Gray Eagle took the lead, he and Raven had come this way many times hunting antelope and when they stole the extra horses on the last of the Baster Gang. Gray Eagle and Raven found a wash leading further into the desert, after a mile they turned back south to follow the base of the mountain. They would need to go around the eastern end to meet the road coming from the east.

Going was slow at times because of having to climb out of dry washes and move some boulders along the way but they made it to the spring that Gray Eagle and Raven had camped at many times to make camp for the night. Randy figured it would be a short day tomorrow getting to Mr. Brown's Store to pick up the supplies and the wagon along with the team of horses. Will and Core were helping with getting the horses taken to the spring for water, when each horse came back Randy helped them to set the picket pin deep so the horses could not get away during the night. After dinner, the two Indian boys went back out to take each horse to water for the night. With the sunup and breakfast finished they headed southwest to meet up with the road. A few hours later they rode into Mr. Brown's Store. Randy introduced the Indians, and they loaded the supplies.

Tee asked Mr. Brown about how to pay for the supplies. Mr. Brown told him that Tony had already paid for everything and when he needed more supplies they were to just come back and get what they needed.

When Tee was outside, he found Randy and told him that he had some money and could pay for the supplies, Randy explained to him that he could keep his money until after they get the ranch in operation.

Tee said he will talk to Tony and pay him if he let me. Horses hitched and supplies loaded, they were ready to start back to the new ranch headquarters. Mr. Brown came out and gave the two boys some candy, they both took a piece and passed the bag around to everyone, Gray Eagle and Raven had never tasted candy before. Randy and Gray Eagle led the way with Tee and White Bird driving the wagon heading back to the first Indian Ranch in Nevada. Life is great in the Ruby's.

The trip was slow because when they found a bad spot for the wagon, they either filled it in or shoveled out the steep banks along some of the dry washes. Making the turn to head up the mountain, Raven found tracks of four riders heading up the canyon to their new ranch headquarters, Randy pulled his Henry, Tee and White Bird gathered their horses and had Raven drive the wagon. Randy told Will and Core to stay with the wagon. Tee and White Bird both had Henry rifles, Tee told Raven to go on ahead and when he gets close go around and get ahead of the four men and wait for them to come up and talk to them.

Tee was leading when they reached the camping spot that is going to be the new ranch headquarters. They found the four men with a fire going and one of the young bulls had been roped and pulled to the fire either to be killed to eat or have the brand changed. Randy rode up to thirty yards from the fire and called out to the men, Tee and White Bird had eased into the trees and were just easing into the clearing when

Randy told the men to drop their guns and raise their hands. The one on the horse told Randy to be on his way, this was not any of his business.

"Gents, this rifle is dead center on you on the horse so don't think about going for your pistol". As they were thinking about what to do, Raven sent an arrow at the feet of the three men standing on the ground. Tee and White Bird levered a round into the chamber of their Henrys. Randy could feel the breathing stop at that sound. "One more time, drop your guns and step back with your hands in the air".

The one on the horse said, "kill them" and started to draw, as his hand went to his pistol an arrow entered his chest just under his arm killing him before he left the saddle. Randy shifted his rifle to the left and pulled the trigger, taking his target dead center in the chest. Tee and White Bird both hit their men, but one had dropped down and was hit high in the chest taking off part of his lung. Randy rode over to check on the would-be cattle thieves. Finding the one still breathing, he took his guns away and asked him what were you four thinking?

He said that they had been told of some cattle in the mountains, so they figured to steal them. "Didn't you see the arrow brand"?

"Yes, I told the boss that this was not a good idea with them cows branded but he was not to have his mind changed".

"Do any of you have wanted posters on you"?

"Yes. But the funny thing is I am the only one that is not wanted, the other three were proud of the poster so you can check their saddle bags, you will find the posters". That was his last words.

"Tee, have the men go through their pockets to see if they have any money, White Bird, why don't we pull the saddlebags and check them out to see if they had anything worth keeping". Raven was just pulling into the clearing. He stopped to see if Randy wanted the two boys to come any further. He asked for Raven to stay there until the men had been moved into the trees. Gray Eagle stepped up on the dead man's horse. When the calf had been released, he pushed the bull calf across the river to join the others. Then Gray Eagle roped the feet of each of the dead men and using their horse he dragged them deep into the woods far away from their camp. After all four men were pulled away Raven drove on up to the fire. The saddle bags had over two thousand dollars and the men had another one hundred fifty in pocket money.

"Well, Tee and White Bird, you men will have some reward money for this bunch".

"Randy, how do we get reward money"?

"I will have Tony send in the paper on the three men and after some time the money will be sent to Mr. Brown's Store because he has a telegraph, and you can pick it up there".

Gray Eagle and Raven dragged the bodies a long way down the mountain. They knew of a deep cut in the rocks, so they just pushed them off the cliff and they were done with that. Raven rode over the mountain the next day. They found out from Tony they also were to keep the horses and saddles, even the rifles and pistols.

Tee asked about Randy getting part of the money and a horse.

Tony told Tee that Randy had told him to give everything to the new Indian Ranch, he said that he already had a horse and was doing great. Gray Eagle spent the next few days making shelters for the horses and a shelter for the supplies.

Andy and Randy figured that he was well enough to start working on the new barn and storage building on the Indian Ranch. Maggie had ridden out to the mine site with Tony to visit with her father and catch up on Rose and Marty, they reached the mine just as lunch was about to be set on the table. Rose and Marty greeted everyone and went back to work, Sean came in and sat down with Maggie, talk about the trip with the bulls was the main subject. Billy and Jack were happy to see them. Her father was also telling her how much the two brothers have learned and are becoming great help. After all were fed, Tony and Sean went over the mine operations and checking on how the gold vein was holding up.

Sean said that it was not quite as good as it was in the beginning, but they were still making good gold every day.

"Sean, I am going to ride into the telegraph office next week. Anything you want to let Ronnie know"?

"Why don't you tell him that the vein is pinching down a bit and the gold is down about ten percent, the best I can figure without a gold scale".

"Rose and Marty, I am going to make a run to Mr. Brown's Store. Can you get me an order ready to take with me"?

"Tony this should take care of our needs for a month".

Tony said, "Maggie we need to head back soon". She got up and climbed on her horse, said goodbye to her father, and they rode back to the ranch. Over dinner they were talking. 'When is the baby due Tony asked"? "I am about four months; Abby is a month or two ahead of me".

"Do you want to take a stage over to be with Abby and stay until after our baby is born"?

"I don't know but I will think about it. Rose could help me; she would like that I think. We need to keep this in mind, so we don't wait too long to make that decision".

Over at the Indian Ranch with Randy running the building crew and Andy felling trees the barn was moving along fine, Randy was surprised with how fast the Indians learned to use the tools needed to notch the logs and level them. Randy had made a solid rock foundation that came above the ground by one foot so the bottom logs would not rot over a long time. With the first round of logs set in place for the foundation, each log had been planed flat making good contact so the interlocking notches would hold it all together. By the end of the day, they had three rounds high, Andy had one of the larger team of horses that had come from Gary Gee in Chico California. Randy was watching Andy as he worked the team, he told Andy his team can really pull, Andy just smiled and skidded in four more logs before dark, so the building team had a good start on the fourth round.

After a quick breakfast, the crew started to notch the logs Andy had hauled in last night. The light team that Tony had purchased from Little John was being used to roll the notched logs on the ground up on top of the last level. By the time Randy would get a log up to the next level, Andy had the next one skidded into his work area. Randy wanted a solid set of double doors for this barn so as Andy would skid a log in to the staging area, he was looking for logs that were very straight and didn't have any twist. Finding two trees, he had them cut into twenty-foot length and after the bark was removed Randy gathering up the wedges, he would use to make the heavy boards for the door, he started placing them in the top side of the tree. It is important to follow the grain with the placement of each wedge, with the wedges placed every five feet. Two men started driving them into the tree. After the wedges were driven in about two inches the log started to crack. Now with the crack started, Raven and Gray Eagle could see what they were doing. When the wood gave way, they had a one-inch plank for the siding for the barn. Randy came along with a two bladed ax and cut the small strips of wood holding the plank and tree together, after cutting them the plank was ready to start making the door. This process was repeated until they had the planks for the doors ready to put in place on the frame.

After a long day, the barn was ready to put the roof on starting in the morning. Tony had done a good job with the long nails to anchor the logs when the doors were cut and some windows for ventilation. Randy had the roof figured by having the front of the barn high and the back low so he could get storage for hay and other feed stores that need to be kept dry. One week working on the Indian Ranch they had the barn ready and two other log cabins ready to start being used. Andy and Randy were taking bets as to when Gray Eagle and Raven would move into the cabin with the cook stove and two bunks built into the cabin walls. Andy had the pack horses loaded and he and Randy was riding home. As they started up the trail, Tee and White Bird joined them. Andy rode until he was just inside the tree line. He stopped and turned to look back, speaking as much to himself as anyone. "That was one week of hard work but look at what we finished". Turning up the trail and over the mountain to home, Andy, along with Randy, were ready to get re-acquainted with their wives. Reaching the yard, they went to work taking care of the tools and putting them away and horses fed and watered, they walked over to the Indian village and home.

Tony had been out checking on his horses to make sure they were all ok. When he reached the herd, he found he had three new foals during the time he had been away. Maggie will want to ride out to see this, so he headed back to the ranch to saddle her a horse. Reaching the ranch, Tee and White Bird rode out to meet him, they wanted to talk about something, he was sure. They all rode to the corrals and stepped down and walked to the fence. Tee and White Bird came over to meet him. "Tony, we want to know if we can still work on this ranch or do, we need to go over the mountain".

Yes, I want you to still work here, but the other ranch is going to take years to have enough cows to make a living for you and your people. I want you all to stay. I like having your village so close.

"Ok. We want to stay; everyone wants to stay Tee and White Bird said".

"Look, The Indian Ranch is for your long-time place to live and help your people.

Maggie and Tony rode out to look at the new foals, they rode slowly through the horses, talking to the new babies so not to scare them. "I will bring the new mothers with their babies back to the ranch so they can get started being handled".

"Maggie, do you think you are going to be happy living on the ranch this far away from anything"? "Yes, Tony I am and will be, but I want to make some changes to the house".

CHAPTER 23 **RACETRACK CHALANGE**

Ronnie was up early to check with his foreman about the fencing, he had been thinking about the barbed wire along the center isle that would run from the barn area to the river. Ronnie decided to use cedar post with cedar planking, this would protect the cattle and horses as they were being driven from one pasture to the other. The wire would be fine in the holding area or separation of the different grazing pastures. Stewart thought that was a great idea saying he was trying to save some money.

"Stewart, ride up to the lumber company and place the order for the cedar, but you can start now on the outside fencing. I want a large gate out by the river joining Juan's ranch next door, the cross fencing should wait until we see how many pastures, we will need to graze our cattle".

"Ronnie, I think if we separate the grazing land into one hundred and fifty acres this should hold our herd for four weeks then move them into another pasture. You have just over twenty-five hundred acres so that would give us twelve pastures to amount to eighteen hundred acres in fenced pastures out of the twenty-five hundred, that will leave plenty for the horses. They stay most of the time over the river".

Ronnie saddled up Diamond to ride up to the racetrack to check on how things are going with the two building projects, he was thinking also about going to see Mr. Carl Abernathy to see if his lust for the racetrack had diminished any after his men had their minds changed during their last meeting. Mr. Pennington was standing in the racetrack looking back at the grandstand as it was being built. The stables were also being worked on at the same time. Ronnie had the north south alignment changed to east west to allow the cool breeze to flow though the stable each afternoon, that seems to be the direction about every day.

"Mr. Pennington, how are things going? You are getting a lot done every time I show up, I see no one is causing any problems today".

"Yes, I have not seen anyone hanging around or even talked to anyone except the contractors". "Great, how is the money holding out"?

"I think we are under budget as of now but it's way too early to make a solid statement on that subject". Ronnie figured it was time to stop by the mayor's office and see what kind of a leader he is and talk about the racetrack and what it could do for the city of Sacramento over the long term. Reaching downtown he rides up to the city hall building. Tying Diamond to the hitch rail, he walks in to find the mayor's office. Reaching the front desk, he asked to see the mayor. The young lady asked him if he had an appointment to see him. Ronnie said no I just dropped in to see if he would see me today.

"I am Ronnie Campbell; my partner and I are building the new horseracing track just south of town".

"Let me ask. Mr. Stout will see you for a minute". "Thanks".

Entering, he was greeted by. "I am William Stout the Mayor, and you are"?

"I am Ronnie Campbell".

"I have heard your name before, I think it was dealing with the two crooks, Mr. Stanton and Mr. Harding, a year or so ago am I correct"?

"Yes mayor, that was me".

"Mr. Stout, I am building a horse racing track just south of town and figured that may have some interest to your office because of the amount of people that will be coming to race their horses every year".

"Ronnie that does bring up some ideas, the city would like to see if we could become in a small way involved with this project. The city would like some additional income and for that you could also gain some advantage by being favorable say operating advantages like lower taxes and zoning in the future".

"Mayor I want you to know that I had some men from one of the gambling establishments come by to pressure my partner, one I shot and is in jail now, another one decided that he wanted to live so he informed me of who wanted me to be removed. The smart one just got on his horse and rode to some other location past Nevada. If I see any of them, I will shoot any of them on sight".

"I also want you to know I am going to have a loving talk to the man who sent the three men, we will come to some agreement as to him staying out of my business or he may need a change of cities".

"Ronnie, do you have a wife"?

"Yes, I do, we have a small ranch just south of town. We are raising racehorses and are grazing a few hundred head of cattle at the present time".

"Great, I would like to invite you and your wife to a party Saturday evening. It will be at our residence. Can you come"?

"We would love to. This will be our first time we have had a chance to get to know some of the local business owners and political leaders around Sacramento".

Returning to the ranch late in the afternoon, he found the men with the wagon loaded to the top dropping cedar posts every ten feet, Stewart had used lime as the marking agent. When riding down to check on the men he eased over to look at the markings, they were in a straight line leading out of sight heading to the river.

"Men, how are thing going"?

"Great", they all replied.

"Stewart, this is progress, we are started, I think this is going to be the best way we can control the grass".

"I found a man who can dig the irrigation ditch, he has two other men working with him. They have some giant draft horses that pull a dump tool that digs out the dirt and they drive ahead and dump it to make a higher bank. They will be coming next Monday I hired the two new men we talked about today, they will be moved in this afternoon so they can start tomorrow".

"Stewart grab your horse so we can ride out to look over the path of the ditch and the ground that we will grow the alfalfa on. Let's ride over to talk to Juan about the alfalfa, I have not talked to him about any of what we are going to do over on this ranch". Juan met them as they rode in.

"Juan, I want you to meet my foreman Willey Stewart". We would like to show you a project we are going to start on Monday.

"Sure, let's go. I will grab a horse". Juan rode out of the barn on the horse that he had traded the two Indian ponies for after his cutting horse was killed the day he and Ronnie met".

You must like that horse Juan. You could own any horse you wanted".

"Ronnie said, this horse is not the same as the one the Indians killed but overall, he is a better horse". "Juan, Stewart came up with an idea and I like it, we are going to grow our own alfalfa for winter feed to save money over the years. You know I have a small water fall just inside of my property line on the north".

"I have seen it but what does that have to do with growing the alfalfa"?

"This is what, that falls is about two feet high so we are going to dig a ditch with some gates to block the water when we don't want any, so we can flood irrigate the alfalfa all summer. We should get four cuttings many five each summer. The other thing you may also think about we are dividing the ranch into separate pastures about one hundred and fifty acres so we can rotate the cattle each month all year so this should save labor when trying to doctor cattle, you won't need to ride all over the ranch to find them". When they reached the river, they rode up to the fence line separating the properties.

"Stewart, tell Juan about how we can grow the hay together. I am leaving one hundred acres bordering your ranch and if you fence off that area, we can remove this fence and run the irrigation ditch beside the river and end it on your property. With water gates we can both use the same ditch to water, then we also can get only one hay cutting machine and one stacking machine so both ranches save money".

"Mr. Stewart, can you explain this to my foreman and you two make it work"?

"I think it is a great idea, Mr. Stewart and be sure to visit the house when you have time, my wife and I would like to have you visit".

"Thanks Juan, great to meet you".

Ronnie and Stewart opened the gate and rode onto their property as Juan started back to the ranch house.

"Ronnie this ground looks level but I will bet is not level enough to do an even flood irrigation so we may need to plow it and then drag it level".

"Stewart, we can get a survey team out and mark the elevation change on it after it is plowed. Go tomorrow and see if you can find someone to come and get both fields plowed so we can get the alfalfa seeded in a few weeks". The first job the next day was to mark out the field that was going to be plowed. Little Billy and Chester Kellogg started marking out the hundred-acre field. The two new hands were making fence post holes and setting posts, the twelve-pound post mall was getting old after a few hours. They needed a job, so this was the new life until the fence was finished. Stewart rode back to the lumber yard for a load of cedar planks to start building the three-board fence. On his way back he stopped by the man that was going to dig the irrigation ditch to see if he knew anyone who could plow the two hundred acres. He was in luck; he did know someone that had a two bottom plow pulled by three big draft horses. Stewart stopped by the house that he had been told to visit to talk about the plowing of the fields, an exceptionally large man came out of a shed to meet him.

"Mister, are you the man who can do some plowing"?

"Yes, I am the one. Do you have a field that needs turning over"?

"Yes, I have two hundred acres and don't have time to do it myself, can you do the job"?

"Yes, I can start tomorrow if you like, we just finished a field yesterday".

"I will need stalls for my team with wood flooring, I have a load of cedar will this work"?

"That is fine, how far to your ranch"?

"We are about five miles to the south".

"I will bring my wagon to live in during the time I am plowing for you is that ok"?

"Yes, I will be waiting for you in the morning".

The next morning Ronnie could hear a wagon turning into the ranch yard. Stewart told him that a man would be showing up with a wagon with a little house on it and a wheeled two bottom plow being pulled behind. His third horse was following along beside the wagon without any lead line on him. Ronnie and Abby walked out to give him directions to the back side of the ranch by the river. The man greeted them with "I am Mort Hansen".

"Well Mort, I am Ronnie, and this is Abby, my wife. You will find Stewart about a mile back toward the river, just follow the lime markers, the field will be on the right side and Stewart will be there to show you the fields. Do you need money now or when you finish"?

"When I finish, we can settle".

Over the past month many things were changing, the party that William Stout hosted at his home turned out to be major successes for Abby and Ronnie's joining of the community around Sacramento. They met so many people who had fast horses and with lots of money. This crowd were the men and women who made things happen in and around Sacramento, Ronnie had baited many men to see if Carl Abernathy was known to them. None seemed to have any knowledge of the gambling houses that he could tell, he was surprised by seeing US Marshal Johnson at this party, he had moved up in the social standing, being a US Marshal did foster a lot of respect in the community. Marshal Johnson never indicated that he knew Ronnie when the mayor introduced them.

The racetrack was taking shape now that the stables were finished with the grandstands close behind, the construction is coming to a close and Mr. Pennington had kept the project under budget. Ronnie was going to have a small house built for Jingles just off the west end of the stables so he could keep watch on his racehorses. Jingles had arrived a week ago with the help from Juan's ranch hands, Jingles had said that he had been almost without a job to do during the trip, the two men handled everything along the trail. The crew that worked on the stables now are starting to work on the two-bedroom house for Jingles and should be finished in another two weeks, it was a simple house to build.

Back at the ranch Ronnie was checking on his racehorses and was building some training pens out by the first cross fence. Mort Hanson had finished the plowing and would be back today to start on the leveling off the field so the water would settle at the same height in the field. Mr. Hanson had a wide blade that pulled behind his large horses to move dirt to level the field. Instead of the two horses this time he had four large draft horses pulling this leveling machine, Mort would ride on it and adjust how deep a cut he would take each pass. Mort had left his living quarters after plowing the two fields, so he stayed by the field as he worked on the leveling project. Stewart and his crew had to build water headers and make wooden gates for the water shutoff and to open so the water could flow into each specific field. The river inlet took some time, they had to damn up the water at the site of the water inlet, with that done they mixed cement and rock to make a small dam to redirect the flow into the irrigation ditch.

With the first field finished, Stewart and crew removed the upstream dam and opened the first gate to allow the water flow into the ditch. Stewart had the wooden header that blocked the water from flowing past the first gate. Mort had leveled the first divider in Ronnie's first twenty-five-acre field.

"Open the gate Little Billy". As the gate was lifted the water started to flow into the freshly planted field, the seeds had just been planted the day before. This field had a one-foot drop from the gate to the far end, Stewart hoped that they would get an even coverage of the field. It took just over an hour for the water to reach the other end. Stewart let the water run for another twenty minutes then he sent Little Billy to close the gate. Stewart hoped the water would take two or three hours to enter the ground, it took just under three hours so he felt the moisture would stay long enough to germinate the alfalfa seeds. Mort was finishing the second of the four fields on Ronnie's ranch so he would let him finish the other fields having the one foot drop that seemed to work just fine.

At the end of the second week all of Ronnie's fields were planted and had been watered, Stewart could see some green starting on the first field, so the seeds took. He hoped to be able to cut a small amount of alfalfa by fall. From what Ronnie told Stewart, the alfalfa plants should produce for seven to ten years before they would need to rotate another crop.

Ronnie had not been to the racetrack for a week, Mr. Pennington had been doing a great job with all the little details. Jingles was living in the new house and had started to get the training started on all of Ronnie's horses. Mr. Pennington did know Jingles; Jingles had ridden on the tracks in England where Pennington had been manager. Jingles came down to the ranch to look at the other horses Ronnie wanted to start training up at the track. Ronnie had made an exercise track at the ranch; it had extended into the pastures by the barn, so Ronnie had decided to only have eleven separate pastures. They should be able to make that due.

Ronnie, Abby and Jingles were having a mid-morning coffee break or talk. Hearing a horse, they got up and walked out to the gate by the porch. Mr. Pennington rode in on a sweating horse. He jumped down telling Ronnie that someone had set a fire to one of the end stalls.

Ronnie, "lucky you had the solid wood headers between the stalls, so the fire stopped with only one".

"Mr. Pennington have you had anyone come and pressure you in any way"?

"There was a man who came by to check on the cost to stable two racehorses, I told him that we were not ready to open to the public. He then told me that I would stable his horse, or he would make trouble for me, I asked him what was he talking about? He then said you won't have long to wait to see just what kind of trouble he would cause for me".

"If you could see this man at a distance, could you recognize him"?

"Yes, I could tell him any place he also has a scar on his chin about two inches long".

"Mr. Pennington, I think we are going to have a second wave of people who think we can be pushed around. I would bet that Carl Abernathy is behind this fire. Take an easy ride home and I will be up in the morning to do some checking around to see if I can smoke someone out into the open. Be ready to take a carriage ride and be gone most of the day. I will bring some lunch and drinks to hold us on our little outing".

Ronnie was at the racetrack by eight the next morning, Mr. Pennington was just riding in at the same time. Let's get into Sacramento I am going to stop at the marshal's office to see my friend Deputy McPherson, to see if he can come along with us. Marshal McPherson was in, and he joined them to do some undercover work, Ronnie drove over to the card club he figured was the business headquarters for Carl Abernathy. "He would have some muscle hanging around so how do we get to see what talent they have Larry".

"Ronnie, see the small card club a few doors down the street? I would bet that Carl is the owner of that one also, he would never allow any competition this close. I can't go in and push around their small-time muscle, but you could go cause them some type of problem and Mr. Pennington and I could see who they send to restore order. See you in a few minutes". Ronnie walked into the card club, he walked up to one of the card tables and took a seat. Ronnie told the dealer that he wanted to wager his bag of gold on one hand of draw poker, the dealer called over the floor man to see what he wanted to do. The floor man said that the table limits were only twenty-five dollars each bid, Ronnie started to raise some noise saying the place was crooked or they would take the bet. As this was going on the floor man had sent a runner to see Carl Abernathy to tell him they needed some help with a customer. Carl told two of his best men to go over and remove the man from his club any way they felt was the most convenient. The runner and the two muscle men left the club and ran down to the small card club.

As the man came out of the door, Pennington told Larry, "There he is the second one, he is the one". They reached the table where Ronnie was sitting waiting for the bad boys to come and ask him to leave. The two men came up behind Ronnie. The one pulled a gun, "you are going to leave right now mister". Ronnie stood up and picked up the gold telling them if they can't cover a thousand dollars it was not much of a gambling establishment anyway and walked out. Ronnie walked out and across the street to an alley. He stepped in and watched the two walk back to the other club. After they went in, he walked back to the parked carriage, stepped up and drove off down the street.

"Did we find the correct man"?

"Yes, the tall one is the person who came down to the racetrack".

"Lunch is on me and yes Larry it will be a big steak, Mr. Pennington, this man does like to do three things, one is eat, second is shoot bad men and the other is watch good looking women".

During lunch they talked about how to push them into making a move. "I know how to get them really pissed. We are going to have two pre-opening-event, two races at the track with the winner gets a thousand dollars cash prize for each race. Jingles told me that Buster and Lighting are as fast or faster than they have ever been. This will really get Carl mad because he wants to handle the betting. We will open the track two weeks prior to the race so the owners can get their horses used to the new track.

"Mr. Pennington can you have the betting operation ready in three weeks? We will start to advertise this week and open the track the next week".

"Ronnie, we need to charge each owner to enter the race an entry fee of one hundred dollars".

"Mister McPherson I think if we get the word out that we have forty thousand dollars in the safe to cover the betting, I think it will be just too much for Carl not to try and rob us. What do you think"?

"You very well could be correct Ronnie".

Ronnie said, "Mr. US Marshal, let's think about this. We need Mr. Pennington to go and purchase another safe for the wagering operation, it needs to be the cheapest one you can find but it needs to be impressive looking. After you purchase it, take the wagon and park it in front of the large card club, go in and have a drink or two", The new signs you had made-put them on the wagon so everyone will know this safe is being delivered to the racetrack". This safe will be placed front and center behind the ticket windows, the safe we have now will be moved to our tack room at the end of the stables. We will line that room with oak planking top to bottom, we will have a steel door made to be set behind the one we have now".

"Larry, I will drop you off and Mr. Pennington off at the track, then I will stop at the building contractor we used to build the stables".

Larry said Thanks for another great lunch to Ronnie as he stepped out of the carriage. Down the road they stopped at the contractor's office to talk about the project at the stable. Horace Woodward greeted them as they walked into his office.

"You two are my favorite people".

"You may like us even better", Ronnie added. "We have a special project that needs to be done with upmost security. This is what I want done. I want a short wall beside the safe in the office, and at the end tack room lined with two-inch oak planking and a steel security door installed behind the one that is now there".

"Ronnie, I along with my son, will do that job and no one will know about it".

"How much do you think it will cost Horace"?

"Five hundred should cover everything".

"We think alike Horace. This bag has six hundred in gold, no bill or invoice is to be connected with this project".

"No paperwork or invoice from a supplier will ever be seen Ronnie".

"Horace even your wife is not to know about what we are doing, when you finish, I would like you with your son's help, to move the real safe into that secured room".

"We will do that and thanks for the trust, Ronnie that means a lot to me".

Back at the track Ronnie said, "Mr. Pennington you will start to stable your horse in that next stall to the end so if anyone is watching, you are just saddling up to go home, you need to carry the same thing every day. I will bring you a set of saddle bags to carry the money in each day, you will need to enter the safe room and return with your saddle and saddle bags. We will place the haystack for that line of stables in front of the door on the west end, and we will add another haystack at the east end of the stalls. This will also help cover you as you open the second door. This should set the trap for Mr. Carl".

CHAPTER 24 **SETTING THE TRAP**

Abby was getting close to delivering her baby and this racetrack thing is kind of getting in the way of the baby business. With the new house finished for the cook, housekeeper and ranch foreman, Abby had someone around all the time. Jordan Langdon had informed Abby, that she had helped with delivering three other babies on her own and helped her mother who was a midwife in her hometown. Ronnie, Abby, and Jordan were going over how they were going to deal with the racetrack's first race and be able to be home when the baby comes. Abby figured that with Jordan in the house and others close, she would send a rider to get Ronnie when the time came, so no problem.

Ronnie was going out to check on the progress of the many upgrades to his new ranch. Ronnie pulled Dandy out of the stall to give him some needed exercise, Ronnie had him come along with the racehorses from his Nevada ranch to his new one. During the trip from Nevada, Jingles kept him saddled and had him with six lead lines bringing his six horses along, Dandy just came along with his nose beside Jingle's right knee, any speed you wanted to ride, Dandy was right there. Stewart, Ronnie's foreman, was making many changes and Ronnie wanted to look over the fencing and the four twenty-five-acre fields of alfalfa, this was the first time he had ventured this far out in weeks. As he rode out just past the barn, he found the aisle way blocked by a wagon hitched up with two mules, they were just standing, his two mules, every ranch needed at least two mules. Just past the wagon Ronnie could see an open gate leading into one of his new grazing pastures ahead. Ronnie could see that Stewart and his crew were moving the cattle from the first grazing pasture to one closer to the ranch headquarters. He and Dandy watched as the cattle came down the aisle way and turned into the new grazing pasture just like they planned. With the gate closed. Shorty Blevins climbed up on the wagon seat eased back on the reins to back the team of mules (My mules Ronnie's said.) enough so they could sidestep to the right and make the turn to return to the barn. After closing the gate, Ronnie asked Stewart to join him to ride out and take a look at the other fields.

"Stewart, how long did it take to move the cattle to the new pasture"?

"Only about two hours is all, I sent two men to start the gather to push them closer to the gate. I had the team hooked up and I had them driven into place to block the aisle. We opened the gate and rode down to the pasture the cattle were in. I stayed by the gate to push them this way then closed the gate and here we are job done".

"How much is the grass eaten down"?

"I moved them before it was over grazed so the grass would have a chance to recover. If we get any rain the grass will come back in a few months". They had reached the alfalfa fields and Ronnie could see that the first field was coming along great, and the others were all doing well.

"Do you think we will get a cutting this year"?

"Yes, I do think we will get the one by the looks of this first field, it has been irrigated two times so far and growing really well. You better get the hay cutting machine delivered and the stacking equipment, we are in the hay business". Looking over the fence they could see that Juan's alfalfa field was coming along but behind his by a few weeks.

With the pre-opening race getting closer, Ronnie was spending more time at the track, the racehorses would start arriving today. Ronnie and Mr. Pennington were going to have all the owners put their horses in the first stable closest to the track, they didn't want people around the safe room at the west end of the second set of stables. Ronnie and US Deputy Marshal Larry McPherson were checking in the racehorses and assigning the stalls.

"Ronnie, look what we have coming, this is one of the two employees from the card house.

"Let's put them in the last stall on the east end". Larry showed them to their stall and informed them to go up to the office and register for the race and pay the entry fee. "If you need anything just let me know and have a great race".

Ronnie had walked over to the office telling Mr. Pennington to stack all the money in the safe and leave it open for Mr. Carl's men so they could get a good look at the cash, they are just stabling their horse now and should be along soon.

"Hi, I am Duncan Sharps. I work for Carl Abernathy. We just stabled our racehorse and need to register".

"Great, I am Mr. Pennington, I run the bank for the track. I will take your money and register your horse for the first race or the second".

"We want the second race".

"Ok, this is your receipt for your money and your second race ticket", Mr. Pennington walked over and opened the safe then placed the money in the safe so Mr. Sharps could see the forty thousand just sitting in the safe with the door open. Duncan's eyes popped open of all that money and in a safe he could break open in ten minutes at most, Carl is going to really like this information. Duncan had left the stable hand with their horse, he would sleep in the adjoining tack room to keep a close watch on Carl's pride and joy, Duncan felt Carl liked the horse better than anyone including his wife.

Stage set. Now to see if the actors perform as planned, Ronnie and Larry felt the robbery would take place after the first race before any payout were made. Carl wanted to break the track's bank so he could walk in and take over the racetrack. He also planned to kill Mr. Pennington and Ronnie Campbell during the robbery. Duncan reported to Carl about the junk safe and all the money.

"Carl. I can open that safe in minutes and I want to kill those two men during the robbery. We will pull it off just after the first race, no one would expect anything like that to happen on the first race at a new track".

With Duncan gone, Mr. Pennington re-stacked the money, Ronnie and Pennington had made a stack of papers to look like the money with some hundreds covering the paper stack to look like the safe was full of money. The real count was only a thousand dollars, the real money had been transferred a little each day by saddle bags

Pennington carried every day to the stables and went into the end tack room. Each day he would add the money to the safe, then pick up his saddle and the now empty saddle bags and rode back to his house. Carl's stable hand was watching from the corner of the other stables, by the time of the big race he reported what he had seen, Mr. Pennington walks over and opens the door and gets his saddle and comes back out and saddles up and ties his saddlebags on every day is the same thing.

"Did he see you watching"?

"No, He never looked my way, I stayed hidden in the shadows".

Ronnie and Larry took the carriage to visit with Marshal Johnson about the possible robbery on race day. Ronnie thanked Marshal Johnson for allowing Deputy McPherson to work undercover for the two weeks prior to the race.

"Marshal, I don't want to have any of the Sheriff's Department in on this undercover operation, I don't know if any are taking money from Carl, so what do you think"?

"I think the Sheriff is solid, but I think we should just handle it on our own".

Ronnie, I and two other deputies' will be there without our badges showing. We will be wearing some plain working clothes so to blend in with the crowd".

Ronnie added that Mr. Pennington is in the most danger if they pull the holdup off just after the first race. I had an oak plank wall built sticking out beside the safe, when he is forced to open the safe, he has been working at getting behind this wall when the robbers look down to check on the money. I don't know of any other way to handle it. When Mr. Pennington is behind the wall, he can go through the open door to the office, then I can come in to help take down the robbers. After the first race we will get ready to open the two doors allowing in the winners to cash in their tickets, I am sure the first two or three people at each door will be the holdup men, so if you and your Deputies can come right behind them and block the door, I will come out from the office that Pennington will enter, that will give me a different angle on the robbers.

Ronnie reached the ranch to check on Abby, she was not having any fun and could hardly get around for the past two weeks. Walking in, he found Jordan helping Abby out of her chair and was heading to bed. Ronnie had been sleeping in another bedroom to allow her as much room as needed.

"When do you think girls"?

"No labor yet but we are hoping Jordan told him". Abby was not talking much. Jordan had opened all the windows in Abby's room to help cool her off the best she could. Ronnie went out to the kitchen to see if there was any food he could gather up, Wolf came in and said he would make him some dinner. As Wolf heated up some food, they finely had a chance to talk about if he was doing ok and if anything needed changed".

"No. Mr. Campbell this is the best job I have ever had, getting a nice place to live is the first time I have a bedroom without a bunch of cowboys making noise. I do like the boys but having my own place is the best I have ever had. Thanks".

After eating, he walked into Abby's room to see if she wanted to talk. With the cool breeze gently blowing over her from the window Abby felt better, Jordan had put a pillow under her feet to help relieve the swelling.

"Abby how are you doing"?

"Better now, I am laying down. This baby stuff is not so easy. Jordan has been so much help; we were lucky to have her".

"She is becoming more like family than help. Tomorrow is your big day for the track Mr. Campbell. I am sorry I can't be there to enjoy the opening with you. Ronnie, do you expect any trouble from Carl"?

"Yes. We are ready for a robbery after the first race. I will be leaving early so I won't see you in the morning, so wish me good luck tonight".

"Be safe Ronnie. We will be having our baby any day now. Good night, come in and give me a kiss before you go to bed".

When Ronnie headed to the track, he had the whole ranch crew well-armed. They were going to keep his horses safe and protect Jingles, because he was going to have his hands full trying to keep Mr. Pennington alive and well. Reaching the track, Ronnie sent his crew to the stables to be with Jingles and help with the horses if needed. Ronnie had been in the background all morning. The first race was being called in five minutes. Ronnie had seen the additional Marshals along with Larry just easing around looking like they were just some ranchers who came to see the races. Ronnie needed to make sure that only Mr. Pennington would be in the payout area behind the ticket windows after the first race. The two clerks will close the two entry doors as soon as the first race has started and exit through the office door Mr. Pennington will also use to make his escape.

At the stable Jingles was being helped by Stewart, they had become friends during the time Jingles had stayed at the ranch. The first race Lightning was going to run. This race is one mile in length. But Jingles figured that the second race, Buster was better matched by the field, Buster had that mean streak in him, if he was behind at the turn, he would find the extra to win. Now Lightning, Jingles felt at any race of one mile or longer he would just outrun the other horses.

"Stewart, give me a leg up". The first call had sounded. "Stewart, walk me out to the track. Keep him away from the other horses, he may go after them or start bucking. Hold him until I tell you to let go, we are having a walking start so I don't want him too close to the foul line". "Stewart held him until the next to last horse was close to the line". Jingles told him to let go, Jingles had just reached the tail of most of the horses when the gun went off. Lightning was moving forward at the gun and in three jumps was past most of the other horses and heading for the lead, Jingles kept him in third place until the end of the back stretch making the final turn. Jingles relaxed the reins a bit. Lightning started to ease up beside the leaders-that made three across making the turn in to the straight heading for home. The leader was a stud and didn't like to be challenged, he laid his ears back and turned his head to bite Lightning. That was all it took; the stud lost his stride and Lightning went past him and just kept going to win by two lengths.

With the winner called, Mr. Pennington walked over and unlocked the two doors. It looked like the first four men were the robbers, he found out when three of them walked behind the cage and the other one stopped and blocked the door. With a pistol pointed at Pennington, he put his hands up. The leader told him to open the safe and then step aside or he would shoot him. Pennington walked up to the safe and opened the door. The man dropped his eyes to the money, so Pennington stepped aside and around the corner of the wall and was gone. The leader took a shot at him but only hit the oak wall, the four US Marshals opened fire on the men blocking the door and one more behind the counter. Ronnie stepped around the corner of the wall and shot one of the men going after the money. The leader was on his knees pulling the money out of the safe into a large open travel bag. Hearing the shot, he started to stand up when his head met the 44-pistol coming down. The Marshals told everyone outside to give them a minute and they can cash in their winning tickets; the three dead men were pulled into the office and the leader was still out when he was cuffed sitting with his three dead partners. Mr. Pennington and his two clerks opened the doors and invited the winners to present their tickets. After the payout was finished, they started to sell the tickets for the second race. Mr. Pennington turned and told his clerks this is just another day at the new racetrack in Sacramento, get selling tickets for the next race, we only have an hour before the race is called, let's get moving men.

Ronnie and Duncan Shanks were having a little conversation about his boss, Jingles came in to see Ronnie and could see he had someone who was trying to keep his mouth shut. Duncan, after a couple of bumps on his head with Ronnie's pistol, he told them that Carl Abernathy is the boss.

Jingles jumped up saying "that son of a bitch, he is here". "Ronnie, that man is a killer, and my uncle. He is the reason I came to the United States so I could get away from him. He tried to get me to throw races so he could win more money". "He is wanted in England for murder and many other crimes he just got on a ship to beat the hangman's noose".

"Shoot that bastard when you see him". Ronnie stepped out to talk to the US Marshal Johnson after Mr. Shanks started to talk. Larry had been taking notes as Mr. Shanks blew the lid off the gangs in Sacramento. Mr. Shanks was in fact singing a death song for his boss, Mr. Abernathy. One new revelation was that Mr. Abernathy had placed a $5,000.00 reward for anyone who killed Ronnie Campbell. After being told that Ronnie Campbell and his wife Abby were partners in the racetrack and the history of Ronnie's harsh dealings with the prior owners, Mr. Harding and Mr. Stanton of the card club. His new business associate, Fargo Quinlan may also have problems with Ronnie because of the ranch Fargo sold to the banker Mr. Holms.

Larry said, "Ronnie you need to hear this".

"Let's get ready for the nest race Ronnie said".

They just had called the second race and he wanted to see how Buster did when challenged by some real fine horses. Stewart was helping Jingles get aboard and lead Buster over to the track to start the race of his life, that is what Jingles figured. He had watched many of the horses that were in this race, and all are fast. Jingles was not worried about Buster jumping the gun, so he had him close to the horse he figured to be the next best horse in the race. With the gun Buster and this Black Stud were neck and neck, past the stands these two were a length ahead of the pack. At the first turn the Black had Buster by a nose but that didn't last long, by the back stretch Buster was ahead by a nose. The rest of the field were three of more lengths behind the leaders. At the middle of the back stretch the Black had Buster by a half-length but was not able to gain anymore. At the start of the turn Buster had come back to challenge him and was again nose to nose. Both horses were running loose and fast, Jingles felt this was the fastest he had ever ridden a horse. Jingles was talking to Buster, "easy boy, we will put him away on the home stretch". "As the Black Stud and Buster were making the turn for home, the crowd could now see the two horses coming into the straight stretch running shoulder to shoulder with dirt flying from their hooves and all were on their feet cheering. No one in the Sacramento area had ever seen a race like this one. By now the pack was twenty lengths behind and they had their own race going on for third place. As the turn led the two horses into the straight stretch the Black made a move and gained a full head on Buster, Jingles felt Buster make a change in his stride, he had lengthened it and was truly flying, Buster regained the lead by a nose and then a head. At the finish line he had the Black by a half-length. Jingles knew he would never in his lifetime have a ride like this one. When he pulled up, he could hear the crowd going crazy after the turn for home. He never heard a thing but the breathing of the two horses. Walking back to the barn, the jockey who rode the Black rode over and they walked back together talking about the race. Jingles told him that he felt that was the fastest he had ever ridden on any horse in his life. The other jockey felt the same. Buster had never lost a race and only tied one race in Salt Lake City, but he had a bad start. What a shame Buster and Lightning had been gilded, they would have dropped some crazy fast horses.

When Ronnie made it back to the office, Marshal Johnson had decided to lock up Duncan but not tell anyone until they decided how to take down Carl and his outlaws at the card club. As he walked from the track, he could see the mayor and some of the men he had met at the dinner he and Abby attended at Mr. William Stout's home.

"Ronnie, when you get time next week, come by and some of us would like to talk about the future of Sacramento and your part of this future. What was the shooting about"?

"We had an attempted robbery, but we put it down within seconds and reopened for the last race. mayor have you ever seen a better race than that one"?

One of the other men spoke up and said that he never had. (It was the owner of the horse that Buster had beat.) "Hope there is no hard feelings with the loss, your horse is the best Buster has ever run with, he did tie one time in Salt Lake City, but he stumbled at the start. "Mayor, we want to have a city-wide grand opening in a couple of months, the two months will give us a chance to get people from all of the major cities. mayor and friends, I have to go and check on the business part of this event".

Ronnie checked with Mr. Pennington to see how he was doing and see if they had made any money on the first two races at the new track. The cash room was a happy place, the money had been counted and they made over twenty thousand on the two races. "If you are all ok, I am heading home to see if we have a baby tonight. I have a feeling". Reaching the house, Jordan told him that Abby's water had broken, and all was well. "You need to go find something to do. Juanita was also on the way with Juan she said. You two go talk horses and your opening of the racetrack".

Juan and Juanita drove up in their buggy, Juanita got out and Ronnie got in. "Juan why don't we ride out and look at our alfalfa fields. Have you seen them in the past few weeks"?

"No, that is a good idea, and I can tell you about the opening of the racetrack".

"Ronnie how is this fencing working? I think it will help keep weight on our cows, the reason is they have less work to get their feed, so they are laying down sooner in the day. The grass seems to recover quicker without taking it so low to the ground. I have seen how fast a small crew, say three of four men, can handle all of the cattle without any problem, when they hit the center lane, they have only one place they can go and that is into the pen with the gate open".

"Juan, you got the latest start in planting, but you should get a small cutting this year, I will get more than you, that is only because I got an earlier start, some by a full month".

"Ronnie, I do have a question, do you think we could use your ditch to water our fruit trees"?

"Juan, this is our ditch. I own a part of the ranch so the trees are part mine to make the best we can".

"My father nor I had even thought about irrigating or even growing alfalfa as a supplement feed to carry us over the winter".

"Your foreman has helped far beyond just a thank you".

"Juan, he has been a real surprise to me. When I got the ranch, I figured he just had a little more time on the ranch, so I made him the foreman".

"Lucky for both of us I think".

"Let me tell you about the attempted robbery at the racetrack today. In Sacramento there is a major crook, and he is trying to muscle into many different businesses with gambling and the track is one of his targets. Mr. Pennington had been intimidated by some men and I shot one and sent two others to a different part of the country. But he started over when we posted the two-race limited opening of the racetrack by sending his racehorse over and having him stabled. The man they left with the horse didn't know the feed end to the back end of a horse, I had Pennington set him up, we built a special room to hold the main safe for the track and purchased a cheap one to put in the office so when the spy came to register for the race, he would see the junk safe and know they could bust it open without a problem. We moved some of the big money every day over to the secure room with a pair of saddle bags. The spy never figured it out so after the first race they tried to rob the forty thousand we supposedly had in the junk safe, we had four of the US Marshals standing behind the four would be robbers and when Mr. Pennington opened the safe, he just stepped around a heavy wood wall, and I replaced him. I shot one and killed him and knocked the leader over the head, putting him out of the action. The Marshals killed the other two, so we moved the dead men and cleaned up a bit and re-opened like nothing ever happened at the betting office, just some noise".

Guys, we need to go over and take a look and see if we can get a treat. It is interesting to me when I ride back into the hills around the wild horses, they at times will challenge you, other times they are just checking you out. (Picture by Robin Travis).

HORSES COMING TO VISIT

CHAPTER 25 **PROBLEMS IN NEVADA**

When Sean and crew rode into the ranch, Tony was working with Tee on some groundwork with one of his year-old golden stud colts, teaching him to be handled and lead with the halter. This was the first groundwork without his mother being in the corral with him, it had taken over two hours of gentle pressure to get him to quit looking for his mother. Tony could see the mining crew riding into the yard, Rose had an elk tied over the back of one of the workhorses she was training. "Sean what do I owe this visit"?

"Tony, the gold vain stopped. We mined another ten feet but found nothing of value. I figured we needed to talk this over. I don't want to spend labor just to dig dirt". Rose and Marty rode over to the side of the house where the cold room was located, Maggie met them as they reached the side porch.

"Great to see you Rose, this meat will come in handy, it looks like we have some extra mouths to feed".

"Ya, Sean told us the gold vain ran out, so we all needed to come back to the ranch to figure out what we need to do".

Marty said, "let's get this meat cut up, and in the smoker, so we don't lose any, I just killed it a few hours ago and it is cool enough to last for another three or four hours, but we can have it cut up and in the smoker in short order. With the three of them working, the fire had been lit and producing smoke by the time the elk had been cut and hung. Morning, Randy's wife, came over to ask if she could have the hide to tan.

"Morning, we don't have any use for it, so it is yours", Rose replied, "and I have five or six more salted down if you want them. I will bring them to you in a few days".

"Rose, I would like any you have, I make moccasins out of the elk hide, they last longer. The hide is strong, would you like me to make you some moccasins. I think you will like them".

"Yes, I have wanted moccasins for an awfully long time. Thank you, Morning,".

"Sean, we will ride into town tomorrow morning and have the telegraph operator send a message to Ronnie and see what he would like us to do about the mine". Tony called a meeting to talk about some things that needed to be done and the major item is branding all the cows and calves.

"Tee and White Bird can you bring all of the cattle down to the alfalfa field so we can brand them? Tee you take half of the men and White Bird you take the others, and we will do a proper roundup and branding.

"Sean and I are riding into town in the morning and will tell Little John and Jane to come over and help. After we finish, we will then go over to the Applegate Ranch and brand their cattle".

"Randy and Marty would you make sure everyone has a bedroll and restock the hay, grain, and water in the supply wagon"?

"Jack, you make sure we have all the supplies we need to feed everyone out of that wagon, you get to be the cook, Billy just can't cut it, but he may be able to help".

"Neither Tony nor Ronnie had an exact count on how many head of cattle was on the ranch, they were sure it was close to four hundred head". Riding out in the morning, they took the shortcut over the mountain trail to save time, this cut off about a full day. It was Tee and White Bird who showed them this short cut, they said it had been used as far back as anyone could remember.

The mountain trail is in the Paiute history in song, the Shoshone had raided a Paiute Village stealing some horses and a young girl. The song tells about the chase and how a vision seeker saw this trail in his vision, the war party of Paiutes used this trail and were able to catch the Shoshone sleeping. They had been chased for days when the rear guard said the Paiute had lost their trail. What had happened was through the vision the Paiute was able to catch them camped for the night. "The Paiute war party came in after everyone was asleep and stole all of the horses and recovered the girl. The war party rode home on the captured Shoshone's horses, this was a big victory for the Paiute Tribe". "The Applegate Ranch house is on the site that the girl was recovered".

Reaching the Applegate Ranch, Jane invited them in to eat lunch with her and Little John. "Great to see both of you. How is everything going"? she asked.

"Things are moving along. I wanted to talk to you about joining our roundup and branding". "Tony, you know we would love to help with your branding, that should be fun. Jane and I will pack up some stuff and have Running Deer and Elk Man come over to help".

"Little John, we would like to come back here and help you with your branding if you want us to". "Jane and I were going to ask if we could get some help, but we don't have to ask do we".

"No Tony Said".

"When are you starting with your gathering of your cattle"?

"They are starting to move cattle today, but we needed to send a telegram to Ronnie, so we are going to be delayed a few days. We will be back in time to smoke some hair on them cattle with the branding iron". With lunch over, Tony and Sean started on their way to contact Ronnie. They had been talking about what they should do about the mine. Sean felt that the vein had just petered out and it must have been just a pocket of gold due to the lack of color in any of the other draws leading to the stream. Sean was telling Tony that he and Ronnie had panned further up into the hills and had not found any sign of gold.

Reaching Mr. Brown's store, or should say a developing town, the one store now has six building around all doing different types of business relating to either cattle or wagon traffic heading east and west, the stage is using it as an overnight layover. The telegraph is in a small corner of Mr. Brown's Store. This was a big boost to Jim's business, just about everyone comes into his store. Tony gave the operator the message and went over to get a bite to eat and talk to Mr. Brown.

"Mr. Brown you are starting to look like a town".

"Yes. we are starting to get some people stopping for good, and it is turning into a nice place to live. I am building another building and I will bet before it is finished someone will want it to open a store of some kind. We need a hardware store, I bet it won't be long until that will happen". "We are going to stay overnight so we will need two rooms if you have them". "

"I do so take the first two on the end".

"We need to wait until we get a return message from Ronnie in California".

In the morning they received a response from Ronnie saying:

"Sean, do you think we should mine another twenty feet to double check on the gold vain to see if it would start further into the mountain? Return message to Ronnie".

"No, we did go ten feet and no color at all". An hour later the message came in that changed things a bit.

"Sean, stop mining and close up the shaft. Do you want to come to California? The message back to Ronnie".

"No. I am going to stay close to Maggie and the baby".

"Mr. Brown, we just talked about a hardware store, do you want one"?

"Yes, I will provide the building for a five percent cost on sales".

"Mr. Brown we are now in the hardware business. Message to Ronnie".

"I need the use of two wagons. I will come to Sacramento and pickup supplies for a hardware store. The message back to Sean".

"Head this way, I will have supplies ready when you get here".

"Tony, what do you think Maggie is going to say with me doing this little venture"?

"She will be so glad to have you close it will be just great". Ronnie had been very generous with Sean with the gold he had more than enough gold to pay cash for the supplies he would need.

"Ok, Mr. Brown, I am going back to the ranch and get the wagons and head to Sacramento for my supplies, will you have the building finished by the time I return with the goods? You know I will need plenty of shelves along the walls and two sided in the middle".

"Sean it will be finished, and I may just help you stock them shelves". It was time for lunch, so they ate and had a cup of coffee. After paying, Tony and Sean walked out front and stepped up and rode off at a canter.

"Tony, I am not going to be much help with the round up and I have a problem".

"What is that Sean".

"I am going to need the Jenkins Brothers to help me with the wagons. Will that cut you too short on the branding"?

"No, we will have enough help, but Randy is now going to be the cook, hope he likes that promotion".

Two days later Sean was talking to the Jenkins Brothers about going back to Sacramento to bring back supplies for his new hardware store. Billy and Jack said we are ready anytime you want to start. Tony came over and told Sean you need to take that supply and cook wagon because of the lack of water and feed along the trail. We will do the cooking out of the two ranch's kitchens so remove the bedrolls and check with Jack about the food, feed and water, it should be ready to roll.

Billy and Jack found Sean and asked him if they should take their horses along with them on the trip.

"Yes, that would be a good idea, we are each going to drive a wagon, but the extra horses would be a good idea and we will bring an extra draft horse, you never know what could happen". At Sunrise the following day the three wagons were heading west to California, Jack led off with the supply wagon with the three extra horses following. Sean pulled three extra rifles so each of them would have plenty of fire power if they had a problem. With the two gangs killed off between the Campbell Ranch and Carson City it should be an easy trip.

*

White Bird and his men were working the high country and Tee was working the lower elevations, they had a good start on the gather. Tony was helping Andy to get the branding area ready for the cattle to show up, Tony felt the cattle would stay on the good grass in the alfalfa field so they would not need any fence. After the branding, each day Tony was going to drive them into one of the box canyons to hold until all branding was finished then drive them back up onto the mountain. Andy had a wagon load of oak wood unloaded at the branding site ready to start the fires. Tony could hear the cattle way before they started to pass the house, they were lucky that Randy had built a fence by the garden and house to hold the cattle back from eating everything green. They pushed the cattle over the stream and into the alfalfa field until they were ready to be branded. Tony figured it would take another two days to get all the cattle out of the hills. Jane headed into the house and Little John saddled up and rode out to find some branding action with the men. Little John and Jane had passed Sean on the road heading to Sacramento,

The branding was slow to start. None of the Indians had ever seen or branded any cattle before so it took some time, but after the first day things started to get some flow. Tony had figured it would take four or five days to get finished and it was a late day on day five. But they were finished and now they had a good count on the cattle. Three hundred and twenty-five is the total count, they cut all the bull calves because they had their replacements ready to turn loose with the herd. In two years, they would be the main bulls and the old bulls would be butchered to feed the Indians and the ranch hands. At dinner Tony told everyone short day tomorrow, we drive the cattle into the lower pastures and get back to the ranch we are going to have a party. Tomorrow we start the move over to the Applegate's and start over.

*

Sean and his crew were making good time with the light load, they could trot most of the day, reaching Carson City was only a few days of hard traveling. In the morning they would make the push over the Sierras, three more days they would be at Ronnie's ranch just south of Sacramento. The drive over the Sierras was pleasant and they made good time with the light load. The supply wagon had the heaviest load, so Billy set the pace during the whole trip. At dinner that night, Sean offered that we should get to Ronnie's ranch within two days.

"What do you think boys"?

Late the second day they drove into Ronnie's new ranch. Ronnie came out to see who had driven into his ranch yard. "Sean, it is so good to see you. It has been a while, come in and say hi to Abby she is due any minute". Abby was resting on the couch in the sitting room, Jordan was able to meet Sean at the same time, she had heard so much about him. After introductions, Ronnie and Sean went into the kitchen to talk. "Sean, I have everything waiting in Sacramento for you to pick up tomorrow if you like. Now, we need to go back and talk about the mine, from what you indicated, the vein just stopped and there was no more quartz in the rock".

"Yes, the boys and I dug another ten to twelve feet looking for any sign of quartz and there is not one flake in the rock".

"Sean, that gold has set us all up, so we have little to worry about for a long time if ever, don't you think".

"Yes, Ronnie. I have been able to save all of the money you paid me so I am able to pay cash or should say with gold for all of the supplies you have ordered".

"Sean, no way you are going to pay. We have already paid for the two wagon loads of supplies; you keep your gold. Sean, you could not have done a better job of getting that gold out of the mountain, you and Maggie were such an asset to what we wanted to do. I could never have gotten that gold out and into a bank, this new start for you is going to be paid by some of the gold you recovered for me and Abby. Your room is the second one on the left. Move your stuff in and we will have dinner in about two hours".

Jack and Billy were in their element with Ronnie's other ranch hands, they were telling them how they had lied about their ages when they got the job helping with the wagons full of lumber. "Ronnie is the best kind of boss we could ever have; he even gave us our horses and rifles from one of the gunfights we have been in with him. He is one bad ass".

Stewart spoke up, "well, he just shot the shit out of a gang at the new racetrack the other day and I don't think it is all over yet". Jingles told me that there is a gang that wants to take over the racetrack". Billy and Jack both said they'd better fine another racetrack or they may just end up dead. From what we have seen anyone pushes Ronnie too far will have a problem breathing very long". Stewart told them about the first time he had seen Ronnie and US Deputy Marshal McPherson. "The Marshal came in down by those trees and Larry was up on that hill behind the house. The Marshal told everyone to put their guns down. Those damn fools started shooting pistols at men with rifles, Ronnie took out part of a post with a big 50 caliber sharps rifle, wounding one man and that bullet continued on hitting the foreman and killed him".

"Those two don't mess around".

Dinner time let's go get some food, the cook is really good also.

Ronnie said, "Sean, we can drive up to the warehouse in the morning and get you loaded, we should be able to be loaded and be back for dinner tomorrow".

The two wagons were loaded with about anything anyone could ever need and had it fixed to send in orders by mail and they would send the supplies by stage or by a freighting company that goes to Salt Lake City every month. Sean and the Jenkins Brothers were loaded and ready to start the return trip in the morning. Billy and Jack had a great time with the ranch hands on Ronnie's new ranch. With first light the horses were hitched, and the crew headed back to the ranch.

Ronnie told the Jenkins Brothers that if they wanted to come back, they would have a job waiting for them.

"Sean, when you get back your give this note to Tony. Abby and I want you to keep her wagon and team to deliver your supplies. Jingles brought her two gildings with him so you keep the team and wagon so you can make deliveries, rent it by the day to Mr. Brown or he will keep it in use all of the time". Jack clicked up the team and they were heading back to Nevada to open a new hardware store.

When they reached the mountains, they cut some small logs to use as blocks to put behind the rear wheels to hold the wagons from rolling back when they stopped. They loaded them on the supply wagon so Jack could set the brake on his wagon and drop the logs behind the wheels at each rest stop for the other horses. There were only a few locations that they had to do this; Sean felt that the brakes on the wagons would hold going down if they went slow. Reaching Carson City and no more hard grades ahead and they were only one day behind the time going west to Sacramento.

With some hard days they were looking forward to being at the little town that is getting a new hardware store.

"Jack, cook up some extra food tonight so we can just hitch up and get on the road early so we can make it to town tomorrow". With a cold breakfast, the three wagons were on the road as the sun was just coming over the mountains to the east. Jack led off with the supply wagon. They were getting low on water, but they still had enough to reach Mr. Brown's store and a good supply of water. Jack was the first to drive into the cluster of buildings. As he reached Mr. Brown's store, Jim walked out and told Jack to follow him. As he turned onto a street with four buildings, he could see the new one with a sign over the front saying Hardware Store. Jack pulled his wagon up to the front and Mr. Brown motioned the others around to the back side.

Sean pulled his wagon up to the back of the building and stepped down to look at what he had to work with as to the arrangement of the shelving Mr. Brown had constructed during his trip to Sacramento for his goods for sale. Sean could see a large pile of dirt off to one side of the building. Meeting Mr. Brown inside, he was given a tour of the store. It looked like he would have plenty of room to store and display his hardware items.

"Sean come and look at this". To one side of the store, he could see a stair leading down to a cellar. Reaching the bottom, he did not need a lantern to see, Jim had built the foundation up three feet above the ground so with the windows located around the exterior walls he had plenty of light. This room will keep cool during the summer and warmer in the winter.

"I took the liberty to have a room built under the stairs for you to live in".

"This looks like we need to get my supplies on the shelves while I have some help, the Jenkins Brothers will need to take two of the wagons back to the ranch as soon as we finish emptying them". They worked late into the night stocking and re-stocking the shelfs when things didn't look like they were in the correct location. The brothers stayed over and worked until noon of the next day to help Sean finish his unloading of the wagons and getting it all on shelves. Sean took them over to Mr. Browns store to get some gold weighed out to pay Jack and Billy for a great job helping him get set up.

Mr. Brown came over for coffee after the brothers had started back to the ranch.

"Well, Sean, what do you think about your store? Is the layout going to work for you"?

"Jim, you did a great job and having a place to live is a great addition to the store and a good thing to have. This will save me from building a house for a long time".

"Jim, I would like to ask you something, do you really want to be part of the hardware store, or would you rather have me pay you for the building in gold? It is up to you. I am good either way". "Let me reheat the coffee and think about that". With the coffee hot and with no one in the store they talked about the options.

In the end Jim said he would like the gold if it would not leave him short.

"No, I am going to be just fine, Ronnie had been very generous to me with the gold I helped him mine, so I am set".

"Sean, I will give you a bill of sale for the building and the land, you never asked me how much it is going to cost you".

"Whatever it is will be fine, you have never overcharged anyone that I know, even when you could have, so just tell me what you need, and you can weigh it out in gold".

"Jim, I am going to ride up and see Maggie and Tony, their baby should be coming any day, so I won't open for a week or so. If you need anything just come in and get it, we can work out the cost later".

When they unloaded the supplies, Sean had seen a corral and shed out behind the store. Come to find out this was also on his property; the Jenkins brother must have known because they had unloaded most of the extra hay from the wagon and the watering trough was also full. Now Sean needed a saddle horse or a buggy to travel to the ranch with. Mr. Brown over the past few years had been trading for many things like horses and wagons so Sean went in to see if he had a buggy or a good saddle horse.

"Hi Jim, I need to purchase a buggy and horse or a good saddle horse so I can get up to the ranch without taking the wagon".

"The blacksmith has just what you need, the owner was killed a few months back, so he won't need it. You know I own part of the blacksmith shop, but I will have my partner make you a deal, I will walk over with you if it is ok".

"Sean, I have a question about your team and wagon, sometimes I may need a wagon to make deliveries, would you do that if you have time"?

"Yes, I will do that, but I would ask when I am gone someone would feed and water my horses". "Great, let's go see if you like anything Shorty Blevins has at his shop".

"Jim, when are you going to name this little town, you have started"?

"I have been thinking about Eureka, how does that sound"?

"Great, I can now say I am living in Eureka, it has a good sound to it".

"Shorty this is Sean, and he would like to look at the horse and buggy we got when that man got killed a few weeks back".

"Nice to meet you, Sean. We should be good friends; I need plenty of things you may have in your store".

"Come over and if I don't have it, I will order it and we should have it within a few weeks".

"This gilding is about six years old, and the buggy is in good shape, I will hitch the horse up and you can take a ride".

"Shorty, he needs to drive up to the Campbell Ranch and will be gone for a week or so, why don't you just have him take it and if he likes it, he can pay when he gets back".

"Sean, are you ok with that?

I just put new shoes on him so give him a good tryout".

"Shorty, it is early so I may just load up some supplies and head to the ranch".

"When I am gone could you throw hay to my two horses and check the water"?

"No problem, I will do that".

"Have a nice trip," I think your butt will like the leather seat and soft springs on this ride". Sean gathered up what he would need and added his two Henry rifles to the buggy, and he was on the road within an hour. Shorty was correct on the ride and this horse was making great time. As he started out from Eureka, he clicked up the horse from a walk, this horse went into a gate he had never seen-both feet on the same side moved together. He had never in his life heard or seen the likes of this, this is not a gift horse, but this horse was covering ground and seemed to not be using much energy. Sean had been trotting, if that is what you would call it, for over an hour before slowing him down to check how he was breathing. After walking for a few minutes, the horse was back at the same gate but a bit slower but still making time. He reached the famous ditch over an hour before he was expecting to be there. Easing into the ditch and riding out, he missed the rock that Tony will not let be removed and he reached the first campground way early, so he rested and fed his new horse. After an hour they were on the way again at the same ground covering trot, he could not wait to have Tony along riding when he opened this horse at his special gate.

Having this horse and buggy, the trip was much shorter. By driving late and a cold breakfast he was going to be at the ranch close to a day earlier than he had figured. Late the second day he pulled into the ranch yard at the slow trot, Maggie was on the porch with Tony when he made the turn heading to the hitch rail. Tony stood up to see who was coming in, seeing Sean he walked out to greet him. "Sean what kind of a horse is this? I never seen anything like this". Rose came over to see Sean and asked, "where did he ever find a pacer in the west"?

"What do you mean pacer"?

"That is the gate this horse has, only very few horses have that style of trot. I bet he can cover some ground; I saw some of them on the plantation years ago".

"Rose, I am trying this horse out and the buggy to see if I want to purchase it from Mr. Shorty Blevins at the forge in Eureka".

"Where is Eureka at? I don't know of any Eureka. Mr. Brown is naming the settlement that"?

"Maggie when am I going to be a grandpa"?

"Very soon, I think. Rose is going to stay until we have the new arrival".

"How did the branding go"?

"We got all of the cattle branded on the two ranches, it turned out to be a great party having everyone working together".

"Sorry we missed but I am now in the hardware business in town".

"The Jenkins Brothers told us that they helped get things into the store and ready to start selling".

"Maggie, I purchased the store from Mr. Brown instead of having him as a partner, that sometimes can cause problems".

"Dad, I agree with you, owning the store outright is always better".

"Dad, we will have dinner in a little while".

"Great I am getting hungry".

"Tony, what did Billy and Jack decide? Are they staying here or going back to California to Ronnie's other ranch"?

"Sean, I am glad they decided to ride back over to California and help Ronnie, I would not have much work for them with the mine shutting down".

"What about Rose and Marty? They were working at the mine and what will they do now to make a living."

"I talked to them the other day and they have their home on the best view around and from what Marty said they have all of the money they have been paid so far and plan to just live, grow a garden and if they need any money there is still some gold in the stream they can pan. Rose and Marty both feel that some contact with people is ok, but a full time is not what they want. When we need supplies, we will bring them to the ranch and Rose is going to keep us in meat. She also is going to help with the orchard and is going to expand it so we all will have plenty of fruit for years to come".

Sean woke up to the whole house in motion, Rose gave everyone their orders and those she didn't need were sent out of the house. Tony and Sean were sitting on the porch talking. It seemed like days, but it was just getting dark when they heard the baby cry. Andy's wife, Black Dove, came out to tell them they were the father and grandfather of a fine red headed boy. "We will come get you later", she offered and walked back into the house. Later Rose came and got them to see the new baby, Maggie had the little man in her arms and was smiling at the little boy.

"Tony come and take your new son".

Tony reached out and pulled the little boy to him and showed his granddad the prize of life. Sean kissed his daughter on the forehead and smiled as he walked out telling them to take this time alone, we can talk more later today.

For the next few days Sean spent with his daughter and Tony talking about everything that had happened from the first time Tony had seen Maggie at Mr. Brown's Store. They had been completely broke with a dead horse, Mr. Brown had given Sean a little job just to cover their food and necessities. Tony added that if Ronnie had not saved Juan from the Indians none of this could or would have happened.

"Guys, I am going back to open my store and I have a new life to start, and it is great to be so close to you and the baby. When I get back, I will just pay whatever they want for the horse and buggy, this was the easiest trip I have ever made to the ranch". When Sean was finished with his breakfast and kissing the new baby and daughter, Tony walked to the waiting buggy. Sean stepped up and they shook hands and Sean started on the road to his new life in Eureka at the hardware store.

Mining gold and silver kept the north's engine going to end the war between the states. The Pony Express kept the news and information flowing to also help this same effort. (Photo by Robin Travis).

MINING IN NEVADA

CHAPTER 26 **JINGLES HAS HIS WAY**

Ronnie and Juan were out checking on Ronnie's alfalfa crop on the ranch, they had been told their help was not needed or wanted so to stay gone for a few hours. Returning to the ranch house they were relegated to the chairs on the front porch. Juan asked about the attempted holdup at the racetrack the other day. "Juan, we had set a trap to catch some of the gang that is working at getting established in Sacramento's gambling card houses. The Marshals office and I have worked together to get them to show themselves and they did. I killed one of the men and the Marshals killed two others, the leader took a shot at Mr. Pennington after he opened the safe. I shot one as I came into the room by the safe and knocked the leader over the head with my pistol. We reopened the gambling ticket windows within minutes and things went on almost like nothing happened. My horses took both races, and the crook Carl had a horse in the race, so we took his money. In fact, it was quite funny the leader we have in custody bet over three thousand dollars".

Ronnie, Juan and Wolf eased into the kitchen and fixed themselves some dinner as the labor continued for the next four hours, just before midnight the sound of a crying baby drifted down the hall and out onto the front porch. Jordan came out sometime later telling them that they did have a baby boy. Abby wanted to see Ronnie in a bit so they could name their new son. When Abby was ready, Jordan came out to get him to see the baby and spend some time with Abby. Walking in, all he could see is the smile on Abby's face and the baby in her arms. Ronnie kissed her and picked up his son for the first time, looking at Abby, "we made this little man".

"Ronnie, can we name him after my father's name Lee and you like Ronnie for the first name, Ronnie Lee Campbell is that ok with you"?

"Abby that is a great name for our son". Ronnie walked him out to the front porch so all the ranch hands could see the baby they would watch grow up with them.

Ronnie rode into Sacramento two days after his little son was born to talk with US Marshal Johnson and hoped to see Deputy McPherson at the same time. Marshal Johnson's office was open when he came into the office, Ronnie walked back to the door and knocked before entering. "Ronnie great to see you, are you a father yet? I know it was close when we were at the racetrack". "Yes, He was born a couple of days ago and is doing fine along with his mother".

"Marshal how are we coming with the Carl Abernathy problem"?

"As far as I know Abernathy doesn't know what happened other than three men were killed but no names were released, and Duncan Sharps is not even listed in the booking log at the jail. We have been waiting on Larry to finish his inquires around town and he should be back within the hour to report on his investigation. Let me get you a cup of bad coffee but is hot and all we have".

Deputy McPherson walked into the office as they were talking about the baby and how the ranch was doing.

"Larry what do we have on Carl to date"?

"I have talked to every card club around town, and they all have been pressured to sell to him or have already sold".

"How many men does he have for protection at the main club and those close by"?

"Carl has four new hired guns at his main club and one or two at each of the other four clubs". "Marshal, it looks like to me we need to hit the main club with a large force and take them out then split up and hit the other three with at least four men with shotguns".

"You are correct Ronnie, our primary weapon will be the twelve-gauge double barrel with double 00 buckshot, we don't want to take any chances with these outlaws".

"Now when do we close in and shut down the entire operation in one quick action? Larry how many men do we have in town today that can help with this total take down of Carl Abernathy and crew"?

"Boss, with you and Ronnie we have only six Marshals, but I have talked to three of the Deputy Sheriffs and their boss. So that gives us ten men to go in and finish off Mr. Carl".

"Larry, can you gather them up and we all can meet back here in an hour? Larry don't let any of them out of your sight and only talk to them in private. When they say ok then stay with them. Start with the Sheriff and you go with him to gather his other three men. No one can know about this until we walk into the card club's door and get them under our guns". An hour later Larry came into the office with the city's elected Sheriff and three of his men armed and ready".

"As you know I am US Marshal Johnson, so this is how I want to do this, everyone raise your right hand and say what I say. Now here are four US Marshal's badges so we are under federal law. This is to protect you from any prosecutions of any kind".

"This operation is going to work like this, I have a slicker for every one of you to wear so your shotguns can be covered, it has been raining a little off and on today, so the slickers won't look out of place. Ronnie, I want you and the Sheriff's three men to ease in and order a drink. Time your entry so you can space yourselves all along the bar. Here is some money, just toss it on the bar then order your drink, the bartender will probably take one of the bills and return the change. "Ronnie, I want you to make sure the bartender does not get into the action. When you see me walk back to the offices, the guards will try to stop me. Larry, you and our other four men spread out, taking the right-side wall and the front tables. I have seen the other muscle using them to play cards so they can cover the room".

"Sheriff, cover me when you enter the club, your face is the most known of the whole crew. When you get into position, check the location of the others so we don't shoot any of us by mistake, that makes for a bad day".

The ten lawmen worked their way to the main card club. The rain had started again so the slickers would never stand out in the club. Ronnie and his three Sheriff officers entered one at a time and took up positions along the bar, Ronnie tossed his cash on the bar and ordered a rye whisky, the barkeeper took the bill and dropped the change on the bar. Ronnie thanked him and watched the other three follow along. Ronnie had the shotgun resting on top of his boot on the foot rail. Sipping his rye, he could see Marshal Johnson easing back toward the office entrance, he turned to the bar and looking to see if all the US Marshals were in position. Turning back to the office area, Marshal Johnson said.

"This is a US Marshals raid so everyone sit still, if anyone moves, they will be shot". Three men at one of the front table jumped up and started to draw, Larry downed two with the first blast from his shotgun. The third man was taken out by the Marshal behind him. The barkeeper started to reach for his shotgun, but Ronnie cocked his shotgun at the sound. The barkeep moved back and placed his hands on top of his head saying.

"I am out of this".

Ronnie told him to reach over and pull out his Shotgun with two fingers and hand it to him. As the barkeeper reached for the gun, Marshal Johnson jumped to his left as someone fired a shot at him but hit the barkeeper dead center in the chest, he dropped the shotgun and dropped to the floor. The Sheriff fired both barrels of his shotgun into the hallway and then heard a yell for help coming from that direction. A white flag on the end of a rifle came out of one of the doors in the hallway, Marshal told whoever was holding the flag to come forward with their hands up.

Ronnie, the Sheriff and Marshal Johnson had the hallway covered, the door opened a bit more and they could see someone starting out into the hallway, but the door was still covering most of the man. Marshal Johnson told the man to walk clear of the door or he was going to shoot through the door, Mr. Carl Abernathy eased into the open, Marshal Johnson told him to walk out into the room and lay down the rifle.

"Carl is there anyone else in that room or any other room in this building"?

"No. I am the only one left in this building". With the handcuffs on Carl, one of the Marshals that Ronnie didn't know took

Carl down to the jail to join his friend. Marshal Johnson said, "let's split up and go hit the other three card clubs".

"Do each the same way, everyone ready let's go". The next club was just a half block down the road. "You two Deputies go with Larry, the rest of you all go with me, we will take care of the small club two blocks to the west. Come back here when you finish and don't take any chances, shoot first but be safe".

Reaching the small clubs, Ronnie said he would go in and take care of the bartender, there should only be two guards in this place but be ready for anything. Ronnie came in slapping his hat on his leg to get rid of the water. Walking up to the bar, he dropped his money on the bar and ordered a drink. The two guards were at a table in the center of the card room close to the manager's office. Ronnie's men had made the way to the other side of the card room. Ronnie called the bartender over. When he reached Ronnie, he could see the double barrels looking at him. "What do I need to do"?

"Hand me the shotgun and come out from behind the bar and take a seat at a table". With the card room covered, Ronnie told everyone "US Marshals. Raise your hands, no one touch your guns, if you do you will be shot". The two men at the front table started to reach when they heard the cocking of the shotguns behind them. (That is a very loud sound)

Ronnie told the Marshals to collect the guns from the muscle at the front table, he asked one of the men to be his backup when he entered the back office to arrest the card room manager. Reaching the door, Ronnie knocked, and a voice told him the door is open, standing to one side of the door and his backup on the other, Ronnie turned the door handle and pushed the door open with his foot. As the door opened, he could see a man doing paperwork. He looked up and Ronnie told him "US Marshals don't move'. The man looked at Ronnie and wanted to reach for his pistol but with the double barrel shotgun looking at him he changed his mind and raised his hands. With all the card clubs emptied, managers and muscle under arrest, all of them were being walked to the county jail for booking.

US Marshal Johnson thanked everyone and collected the badges saying we will have a dinner in a few days to celebrate our good luck that no one was hurt on this cleanup of our town. "Marshal, I am going back to the ranch".

"Thanks Ronnie, we will be in touch in a few days, Larry wants you to bring the new carriage, makes him feel important. Larry wrote me an official request to supply him with one just like yours but wanted me to have a blacksmith put steel rings so he can chain his prisoners to them when transporting back to jail. I told him none lived long enough to get any value from the money we would have to spend, he will have to get along with Rob and Steal for the time being". Ronnie had driven the carriage to Sacramento instead of riding Diamond, he liked the comfort that the carriage provided on even short trips.

*

Back at the county jail, Carl Abernathy was being moved to a different cell by only one guard, as the guard was unlocking the cell, Carl smashed his head into the bars and stole his gun along with keys to let himself out of the building. Reaching the street, he stole the first horse he could find that had a rifle in the boot. Stepping up, he started south to take care of that Ronnie Campbell, he had lost everything because he would not sell the racetrack and had killed his longtime friend Duncan Sharps. Carl was pushing his horse hard, he had only one mission and that was to catch Ronnie on the road and then he would get lost in the west. Carl could see some dust ahead, he hoped it was that bastard Ronnie Campbell. As he rode closer, he could see the carriage and it had slowed to a walk. Carl was now gaining fast; he would be beside the carriage within minutes. Reaching down, he pulled the rifle, levering a round into the chamber. He could see Ronnie looking down the road at two riders coming toward him, Carl was riding at an extended trot as he passed Ronnie and shot him in the back. "Kicking his horse in the ribs he rode off at a gallop".

*

Abby heard the shot and walked out onto the front porch; the carriage was coming into the yard, but Ronnie was laying in the seat bleeding. Stewart came running out with the other ranch hands, Abby yelled for Stewart to grab a horse and get the Doctor, kill the horse if needed but get the Doctor now. Jordan and Wolf had joined Abby at the carriage, Abby told the men to get Ronnie into the house. She had been folding diapers, so she still had some in her hands. As the men pulled Ronnie from the carriage, she pushed one over the wound in his back and the other one under his shirt in the front. As they got Ronnie out of the carriage, they heard rifle shots coming from the south. Stewart rode past them at a full gallop heading to town, a new Doctor had opened an office a bit south of town about the same distance as the racetrack. Stewart dropped his horse back to a fast trot for a mile to give him some rest and then back to a canter. He would be at the Doctor's office in a short time.

They had Ronnie laying on the large kitchen table cleaning the wounds with hot soapy water, they had the bleeding stopped and packed the holes in his chest to keep his lungs from collapsing. Ronnie was not bleeding from his mouth, so it looked like the bullet missed his lungs. They heard a knock at the front door, they knew it could not be the Doctor, so Jordan went to see who was there. When she opened the door, she was looking at Jack and Billy Jenkins.

"You are back".

"How is Ronnie? We were just down the road when this man rode by and shot Ronnie in the back. We both shot him, and he is dead tied over his horse out front".

"Come in, we are working on Ronnie now, but Abby can tell you what to do with the body, I think you two need to take it into town to the US Marshal's office in Sacramento".

Jordan came back and told them to do just that.

"When you get back let us know what they had to say".

*

Stewart found the Doctor in and he was on his way to the ranch, Stewart needed to cool out his horse and get it a little water before starting back to the ranch. Stewart had just stepped up when as he looked to the north, he could see a large dust cloud heading his way. Deputy Marshal Larry McPherson was the first to reach him. Stewart what are you doing up this way, have you seen a man riding south fast.

Yes, he shot Ronnie and kept riding south.

"How is Ronnie"? he asked.

"I don't know, I rode to get the Doctor, I didn't have time to check, they were just getting him out of the carriage when I rode past at a gallop".

"Let's go, we need to catch Carl Abernathy before he can get away. Riding south to the ranch they could see three horses coming their way, so they slowed down to a walk and pulled their rifles. The Jenkins Brothers also slowed to see who was coming their way, when they got close, they could see it was Larry McPherson, so they stopped. The posse stopped and seeing the body over the horse Larry asked who is this on the horse.

Billy said, "I don't know but he shot Ronnie, so we gave him some lead, he is dead".

"Boys you just saved us a long chase; this man just escaped from jail".

Larry turned to the posse and told them to just go on home and could one of you drop this dead man at the Marshals office, and thanks for riding out with me.

"Jack and Billy let's go check on Ronnie and thanks for killing Carl, he was a very bad man". Reaching the ranch, they entered the house to find everyone waiting in the living room.

Larry asked if they had heard any news from the Doctor yet.

"Larry, the Doctor has been in the kitchen with Wolf, and Jordan, but we have not gotten any word to his condition".

"Jack and Billy, we all want to thank you for taking care of the man who shot Ronnie". All eyes moved to the door leading into the kitchen as the Doctor stepped out to inform them on Ronnie's condition".

"Abby, I think he is going to make it, he seems to be breathing better".

"Can we move him into the bedroom"?

"Yes, but we need to be very careful as we do that. Let's get two men on each side, now lift". Abby and Jordan had the bed ready as the men entered the room.

"Now down easy, Ronnie now had to fight for his own life".

With everyone out of the room, Abby placed little Ronnie on his father's bare chest, then gently placing a blanket over the two and took a seat beside the bed.

Later Abby picked up the baby to feed him, when finished he was fussing so Abby placed him back on Ronnie's chest and he quieted down and went back to sleep. Ronnie started to open his eyes then closed them for a short time, then they came open and looked down to his chest. Little Ronnie was sleeping with a blanket covering them.

Abby said, "you're back, we thought you were gone".

"No, I have been talking to an angel for a while, did you see him, Abby? How long has Little Ronnie been sleeping on my chest".

"Most of the past two weeks, this is the only place he will sleep. I feed him but he will not let me hold him, he has only wanted to be where he is right now".

"You said two weeks"?

"Yes, Ronnie, you were out for two weeks. Welcome home".

"Abby, after Carl shot me, I think I heard two other shots".

"Did he hit me more than the one shot"?

"You did hear other shots the Jenkins Brothers shot Carl to rags".

"They have become men Ronnie said".

"I need to go to sleep Abby, let Ronnie sleep on my chest, he feels so good".

The end.

Little Ronnie just may be in the saddle for the next book in the Ronnie Campbell Series.

Thanks for reading Kill Ronnie Campbell this is book three the of the Ronnie Campbell Series telling about the life as I believe it was lived in the 1860 time period. Those times were harsh with the need to make the hard decisions as they presented themselves.

Ronnie Campbell had a vision and was able to bring along people who was able to share this vision and help him move forward so he could do important projects and enhance others' lives. His vision of having an Indian Ranch bordering his would have lasting impact on the Paiute Indians in this story. Did it happen in real life? I don't know but I hope it could have been real.

The women in the three books reflect some if not many strong women who lived in that time period. Why are so many women written into stories the weak sister type of woman? I feel many the women in that time period knew what they wanted and were not afraid to do what was needed to make their life better but were looking to what kind of life their children would be exposed to growing up.

Again, thanks for reading my work, I hope you enjoyed the stories presented over my three-book series.

Book #1 THE PONY EXPRESS RIDER

Book #2 RUBY GOLD

I hope you enjoyed all three of my Books as much as I did write them. Look for my new Book.

The Cabin Under Flat Iron Point a story starting on an all-day ride in the mountains in Pennsylvania in 1953 I was just ten years old. Then the book is about who built the cabin and how did he get there, did he have a wife, so many things are waiting to be told in this story. I am writing chapter 9 and the Delaware and Seneca Indians are at war and Billy is in the middle.

Ron Bell AKA Ronnie Campbell

Keep checking in to see when the next event is going to happen:

ronbellbooks. com

www.ingramcontent.com/pod-product-compliance
Lightning Source LLC
Chambersburg PA
CBHW070208260626
47160CB00002B/488